D0387490

CITY OF FIRE

Also by Robert Ellis

The Dead Room
Access to Power

CITY OF FIRE

Robert Ellis

St. Martin's Minotaur
New York

This is a work of fiction. All of the characters, organizations, and events portrayed in this novel are either products of the author's imagination or are used fictitiously.

CITY OF FIRE. Copyright © 2007 by Robert Ellis. All rights reserved. Printed in the United States of America. No part of this book may be used or reproduced in any manner whatsoever without written permission except in the case of brief quotations embodied in critical articles or reviews. For information, address St. Martin's Press, 175 Fifth Avenue, New York, N.Y. 10010.

www.stmartins.com

Library of Congress Cataloging-in-Publication Data

Ellis, Robert.
  City of fire / Robert Ellis.—1st St. Martin's Minotaur ed.
    p. cm.
  ISBN-13: 978-0-312-36613-1
  ISBN-10: 0-312-36613-2
    1. Policewomen—California—Los Angeles—Fiction.   2. Serial murders—Fiction.
3. Los Angeles (Calif.). Police Dept—Fiction.   4. Los Angeles (Calif.)—Fiction.   I. Title.

PS3605.L469C58   2007
813'.6—dc22   2007009102
                          First Edition: June 2007

                  10 9 8 7 6 5 4 3 2 1

To Charlotte

Acknowledgments

This novel could not have been written or accurately portrayed without the help and guidance of LAPD detectives Rick Jackson and David P. Lambkin from the Robbery-Homicide Division, Cold Case Homicide Unit. The author would also like to express a great debt of thanks to Art Belanger from the pathology department at Yale University School of Medicine, and H. Donald Widdoes, a longtime friend, for his work in firearms and ballistics. Although this story may have been inspired by real events, it is a complete work of fiction, so any technical deviations, errors, or exaggerations are the author's responsibility alone.

A very special thanks must also go to my agent, Scott Miller, for making all this happen. And to my editor, Ben Sevier, for his contribution to this story. The entire experience has been wonderful. The author is also deeply grateful to John Truby for his help in polishing this story. Without John's advice and guidance, this would only be a dream.

Great help and contributions to the story were also made by Margie Becker, Michael Conway, and Meghan Sadler-Conway. And by Joe Drabyak, Barry Martin, and Mark Moskowitz. Thank you for your knowledge and experience and friendship. But also, thank you for providing the inspiration for this story and for wrestling with that massive first draft. For this the author will always be grateful.

Much thanks must also go to my friend Christopher Rising for his help with this story. Chris's contribution to chapter 50 took it over the top. Way over the top.

The author would also like to thank Linda E. Burg, Lisa Cabanel, Neil Oxman, Katy Sadler, and Jean Utley for their help and unyielding support during the writing of this novel. And Victoria Horn and Jenness Crawford for their great help and attention to detail in getting this work out.

Last but really most, the author wishes to thank Charlotte Conway, to whom this book is dedicated. Without her grace and understanding, the author wouldn't get past go.

CITY OF FIRE

1

She rolled over in bed, nudging the corner of the pillow with her cheek and burrowing in. Dreaming. Sleeping. Searching out cool spots with her legs and feet beneath the clean sheets and extra blanket.

She could hear the curtains moving somewhere in the foggy haze at the edge of her dream. Moist, chilly air filtering in through the open window from the ocean. The promise of sunshine burning the clouds away sometime tomorrow afternoon.

It was April in Los Angeles—Nikki Brant's favorite month of the year. And things were good right now. Better than they had ever been before.

She groped in the darkness for a second pillow and drew it closer, snuggling with it and pretending that she wasn't alone. She was dreaming about her secret. Her special secret. The one her doctor told her just after lunch. The one that began with a single word.

Congratulations.

Nikki didn't really hear the rest. Nothing registered after that word. She couldn't concentrate because her heart was beating so fast—everything streaming by in a joyous blur. It began the moment her doctor stepped into the examination room and flashed that smile. The moment she caught the glint in her doctor's eye.

But her doctor was only confirming it for her. Deep inside she already knew.

She stirred and cracked her eyes open, sensing that someone had entered the bedroom. It was James, home from another late night at work. She could see his figure in the darkness, the rim of light from the clock radio behind him outlining his body in neon blue. It seemed as if he was staring at her from the foot of the bed as he got out of his jacket and loosened his tie.

A dog started barking somewhere in the distance.

She guessed it might be that small, white terrier three doors down the street, but she wasn't exactly sure. Her doctor had given her something to help with the nausea, saying it wouldn't hurt but might make her feel drowsy. When the dog quieted, Nikki glanced at James's figure and lowered her head—drifting off again—her body weighted down in the ecstasy of fatigue.

They had met three years ago after being introduced by a mutual friend in graduate school at the University of Oregon. James was high-strung and hard to read at first. He was in his last year at the Lundquist College of Business. She was finishing her dissertation in art history and had already been hired by a small college in Pasadena to begin teaching the following year. At the time, it seemed as if they were from two different planets spiraling in opposite directions. But James was persistent, and after a while he began to grow on her. There was something about his smile. Something about the way he made her feel when he told one of his corny jokes and looked at her with those big brown eyes of his. Within six months they were living together. On the first anniversary of their meeting, they were married. Forget the honeymoon—they were too busy packing. They found a house in West L.A. and would be living within walking distance to the beach.

But when should she tell him her secret?

She opened her eyes again. James remained at the foot of the bed. She wondered how long she had been asleep but couldn't see the time because he was still blocking the clock radio on the dresser. After a moment, he pulled his shirt out of his trousers and began unbuttoning it.

When should she tell him?

That was the big question. She wanted the moment to be just right.

For the past ten days James had been working until dawn, only coming home to grab a few hours' sleep before showering and changing and heading back to work again. He was the chief financial officer for a small company merging with a larger one. A young man in an even younger company that no one thought would end up being a company at all. James was overseeing the audit before the deal was finalized. Even though he told her that the merger was friendly, he seemed nervous about it, even grumpy. She knew that he was trying to prove himself. That he was hoping he would still be needed when the two companies eventually came together as one.

She eased her way back to the surface.

Peeking over the blanket, she watched him toss his trousers on the chair and step out of his boxer shorts. As he peeled off his socks, he lowered his head and the clock finally came into view. It was early. Only 1:30 a.m. When he called to check in at ten, he told her that he would see her in the morning. She couldn't make out his face in the darkness, but it looked as if he was smiling. Maybe they decided to take the night off. Or just maybe the audit was finally done, and they could have their lives and marriage back again.

She wanted to say something to him but was afraid he might guess her secret by the tone of her voice. She wanted to sleep with her secret. Revel in it on her own for a night or two or even longer until she picked exactly the right time. She knew it wouldn't be easy. She also knew that James wouldn't be as happy about the news as she was. A couple of times last week she'd given him hints—tried to feel him out—but the whole thing turned into one big argument. A horrible fight that lasted longer than all the others and ended in a torturous day of *the silent treatment*. Why couldn't he understand why this was so important to her?

That stupid dog started barking again. Louder this time, and at a higher pitch.

She sensed James moving toward her in the darkness. He pulled away the second pillow and slipped beneath the covers on her side of the bed. He kissed her on the lips, deeper than she expected. Harder than she was used to. As he rubbed up against her, she realized that he wanted to make love. She smiled and sighed and kissed him back with her eyes closed, wishing she hadn't taken that damn pill.

He stroked her chin with his finger. She could smell all over his skin the scent of the soap they used at the office. It was laced with cocoa butter, reminding her of suntan lotion and days spent lazing side by side on the hot sand at the beach. On a chilly night in April, the fragrance seemed so out of place.

He rolled over her leg, finding the center. As he entered her, she wrapped her arms around him and held on as well as she could. Drifting. Sleeping. Keeping her secret locked away in her dreams. She was glad that he'd come home early tonight, glad they were together. This was the way things were supposed to be.

James and Nikki Brant together.

Funny, but she didn't remember hearing his car pull into the drive, or even the sound of the front door, which always seemed to open with a deafening creak. . . .

2

Lena Gamble dropped the crossword puzzle on the table and reached for her coffee mug. As she sipped through the steam, the piping hot brew tasted rich and strong and just about perfect. Starbucks House Blend, purchased at the Beachwood Market for three times as much money as any other brand. For Lena the additional expense was worth it—her one big gift to herself—and she brewed it by the cup every morning with a teakettle and filter paper as if a junkie doling out heroin in a red-hot spoon.

She was sitting by the pool, trying to wake up and watching the sun rise over Los Angeles. Her house was perched on top of a hill over Hollywood, east of the Cahuenga Pass and just west of Beachwood Canyon—the view magnificent from here. She could see the clouds plunging in at eye level from the ocean fifteen miles away, the Westside still shrouded in a dreary gray. To the east the marine layer had already burned off, and the Library Tower, the tallest building west of Chicago, glowed a fiery yellow-orange that seemed to vibrate in the clear blue sky.

For fifteen minutes the city had the look and feel of a postcard—the kind a tourist might send back home while on vacation in paradise. For fifteen minutes it all looked so peaceful.

This was an illusion, of course. A trick that played with the senses. Lena knew that Los Angeles was the murder capital of the country. Over the past month there had been thirty-plus murders—more than one homicide for each day of the week. But at dawn on this day, the air was almost clean, the streets appeared almost manageable, and she still had half an hour or so before she had to leave for work.

She glanced back at the house, noticed that she forgot to close the screen door on the slider, but didn't get up. Instead, she pressed her shoulders into the chair and let her eyes wander down the steps off the porch, along the stone pathway by the garden, and then up the side of the house to her bedroom window on the first floor. It wasn't a big house. Still, it was her anchor to the city. The only real thing keeping her here other than her job. She'd inherited the property from her brother, David, five years ago.

Built in 1954, the house would probably have been called a modern version of a California Craftsman back then. But every time Lena looked at the weathered cedar siding, the shutters and white trim, she couldn't help but think that it belonged on a beach at Cape Cod rather than the top of a hill in Hollywood. It was an eclectic mix of wood and glass that had somehow managed to stay nailed together after five decades of what they called seasons here. The earthquake season seemed to run off and on for twelve months out of the year. But there was also the fire season, the Santa Ana wind season, and if you were really lucky, enough rain to fill the reservoirs, marking the start of flood season.

David had bought the house because their parents were long gone, and he'd always said that if he ever made any money, he would buy a place in this world that he and his big sister could call home. But it wasn't the warmth that seemed to emanate from the house, or even the view of the city and basin, that caught David's eye. It was the land, the privacy, and finally, the garage—a two-story building that stood fifty feet away on the other side of the drive. The David Gamble Band needed a home as much as he and his sister did, and that garage looked as if it had potential. Once a down payment was made and the papers were signed, David used what money he had left to convert the building into a state-of-the-art recording studio. A photograph of his pride and joy appeared on the inside booklet of the band's third CD.

But that was all over now. The studio was dark and quiet and had been that way for the past five years. The band's third album had been their final one. And David died before they could tour and bring home any real money.

Lena took another sip of coffee, the hot caffeine lighting up her stomach but not doing much for her head. She had gone fifteen days without a break at work until yesterday, and she felt groggy after taking the day off. Besides, she didn't like thinking about her brother. She missed him and the loss was still way too painful.

Lena was alone, holding the world and the people in it at arm's length. She couldn't help the way she felt, and she couldn't do anything to change what had happened in the past. Still, she worried that she was dumping too much of her paycheck into the house. That she spent too much time trying to keep the place up. That somehow her home had become an obsession, and she was clinging to the property because she couldn't deal with her brother no longer being here. Things had been so good when he was around.

She picked up the Calendar section of the newspaper, deciding to take another stab at that crossword puzzle. It was Friday, and the puzzles were becoming more difficult with each day of the week. Lena enjoyed the challenge because it took her mind off things. And she was good at it, using a pen rather than a pencil, except on Sundays. But as she reread the last three clues, she knew that it was hopeless. The key seemed to be 51 DOWN, a ridiculously easy clue referring to a woman who'd won a million dollars in a reality series on TV. Lena didn't watch much television and only turned it on when she had to. She didn't like what the box did to her head.

She tossed the puzzle down in frustration, sifting through the paper until she found the California section. A local story on page three caught her interest. A twenty-nine-year-old woman from Santa Monica was claiming to be pregnant even though she hadn't had sex for two years. Lena started reading the article but stopped when her eyes slid across the word *Jesus*. She shook her head. This was the kind of story that seemed to make the news these days, part of the routine and fabric of the city that everyone else in the country called L.A. Lena was twenty-nine and hadn't had sex in two years either. With no one on the immediate horizon, she didn't consider her quandary a laughing matter.

Her cell phone rang. She looked at it on the table, recognized the caller on the LCD screen, and opened it. It was her partner, Hank Novak, calling at 6:00 a.m. They worked out of the Robbery-Homicide Division. Lena guessed that Novak's call had nothing to do with an immaculate conception in Santa Monica, or getting laid by Jesus.

"Hope you're rested," Novak said.

"Yeah, I'm good," she said. "What's up?"

She grabbed her pen. She could tell from the gravelly tone of her partner's usually smooth voice that he hadn't been up for long. From the sound
of the wind in the background, he was on a freeway somewhere rolling at
high speed.

"Nine thirty-eight Oak Tree Lane," he said. "West L.A. Page forty in my
fifteen-year-old *Thomas Guide*. Take Sunset out to Brooktree Road and
hang a left. Looks like it's a block past the entrance to Will Rogers State
Park. Oak Tree's off Brooktree about a quarter mile down on the right."

"Sounds like a lot of trees," she said.

"I thought so, too. The house you're looking for should be the third one
on the left. By the time you get there, it'll probably be easy enough to spot."

She was writing everything down on the masthead of *The Times*, becoming concerned because Novak was spitting his words out and seemed all
tanked up. He'd never acted this way before, but then, they were still getting used to each other.

Lena had worked out of the Hollywood Division until two months ago,
when she was promoted to the elite Homicide Special Section under a new
mentoring program established by the LAPD. She was the youngest detective at the table, one of only two women in RHD, and had been fast-
tracked up the line because there was yet another chief in town and he
wanted to change the face of the department one more time. Although she
hadn't been chosen for her sex, she knew that to some degree her gender
would always be in play as long as she remained a cop. But it was her age
that had given her the boost this time, and her promotion had been one of
many across the board. The average age of the department had slipped to
just twenty-five. Everyone knew that cops were leaving the city in droves,
headed out of the combat zone for greener pastures, and that those who
stayed had their eyes on retiring with a full pension before they left town.
The new chief understood that the institutional memory of the department
was in serious jeopardy. And he was right. Although Lena had earned praise
from her commanding officer and quickly risen as an investigator in Hollywood, her experience was limited to two years working narcotics and burglary, six months ferreting out white-collar deadbeats in bunco forgery, and
only another two and a half years at the homicide table. Investigating a

murder meant dealing with a lot more pressure. It still felt new. And Novak, due to retire sometime in the next couple of years, had been given the task of trying to bring her along as quickly as he could.

"What's the name on the mailbox?" she asked.

"Brant," he said. "Nikki Brant."

Novak fell silent, and she couldn't get a read on him. She heard the road noise vanishing in the background and guessed that he was closing the window.

"We're not alone on this one," he said after a moment. "Sanchez and Rhodes got the call to assist."

Novak was worried. She could hear it in his voice. Tito Sanchez and Stan Rhodes were another rookie-veteran team, put together a month before Lena had partnered up with Novak. Because of the heavy workload, RHD teams were budgeted out. For their lieutenant to spend two teams on one case didn't make any sense, unless—

"How many bodies are there?" she asked.

"Barrera only mentioned one."

"Was she famous?"

"Not yet, but maybe they'll make the movie."

"Then why two teams?"

"It was his idea, not mine," Novak said. "Maybe it's got something to do with the high-rent neighborhood."

She heard the phone drop on the seat, and Novak fumbling with it as he swore. She stepped into her boots, zipping them over her ankles and pulling her jeans down. Then she stood up and started pacing.

"I'm back," he said. "I'm juggling things."

"It's not the neighborhood, is it, Hank. That's not why we're doubling up."

He cleared his throat. "That's probably only part of it. We'll see what's up when we get there."

Lena's introduction to RHD had been the Teresa Lopez murder case. If she could handle what happened to Teresa Lopez, then she could deal with this. An image flashed before her eyes. A warning beacon. Her brother, David, slumped across the front seat of his car on a side street off Hollywood Boulevard. It had been so dark that night, so unexpected, that she'd thought and hoped he was only sleeping as she approached the car. . . .

Lena stepped around the pool, gazing at the house at the bottom of the steep hill. Behind the house was another pool, and she could see a middle-aged man with a hairy back and a beer gut taking an early-morning swim. In spite of his physique he seemed to be gliding, his strokes short but easy. Lena gritted her teeth, focusing on the man until the image of her brother finally dissipated.

"You're the primary on this one," she heard Novak saying.

She walked back to the table and sat down. "What are you talking about?"

"We've been partners for two months, and I think you're ready. You've got what it takes, Lena. It's time to start alternating cases. This one's yours. You got the address?"

She felt her stomach begin to churn. She was awake now.

"Got it," she said.

He repeated it for her anyway, told her to hurry, then hung up.

Lena closed her phone, eyeing the address she'd jotted down on the newspaper and committing it to memory. As she finished her coffee in quick gulps, she looked past the lip of the pool hanging over the city and the round man swimming long laps a hundred feet below. The sun had cleared the horizon, losing its color and taking on the form of a white-hot disk. She turned, glancing at the Westside long enough to see that it was still buried in the gloom.

She was the lead on this one.

She bolted up the steps, crossing the porch into the house and dumping the newspaper on the counter between the kitchen and living room. Hurrying around the counter to the stove, she traded her empty ceramic mug for a battered stainless-steel travel model, already filled with coffee for what she had anticipated would be an uneventful commute downtown.

She was the lead, which meant that she was responsible for solving the murder of someone named Nikki Brant. Lena would be held accountable for the outcome.

Was it dread following her through the house? Or was it that sinking feeling in her gut that maybe she didn't have the stuff to work a murder case at this level or any level? Homicide Specials were the cream of the crop.

She noticed her hand trembling slightly but ignored it, crossing the living room into her bedroom and the table by the window. A crime scene was just a crime scene, she told herself. Criminal investigations were a team sport. Besides, Novak was a D-3, the highest rank a detective could achieve in the department. Her name might be listed beside the victim's in the murder book, but Novak would be in charge.

She clipped her badge on her left hip beside her cell phone and handcuffs. Then she grabbed her holster and gun, a Smith & Wesson, .45-caliber semiautomatic, clamping it to her belt on the right. Getting into her blazer, she snatched her briefcase off the chair and headed for the door.

Her Honda Prelude fired up on the first try. As she sped out the drive and raced down the twisting hill, she lowered the windows and let the breeze knock against her face. After a few moments, she noticed the radio was switched to KROQ. They were playing a song by Nirvana.

"Come As You Are."

She turned the volume up, glancing at the time: 6:16 a.m. No question about it—that fifteen minutes of paradise only lasted for fifteen minutes. You could set your watch by it. But now it was all used up.

3

Lena steered into the last curve on Gower, ripping down the steep incline fast and easy like a 737 with its wheels ready to catch some ground. The road finally straightened out as she hit the Pink Castle, a landmark home that no one wanted to live in until it was converted into condos about fifteen years ago. The building had been painted a hot pink and given the nickname by locals for as long as Lena could remember.

She caught the stop sign but didn't go for the brakes. Instead, she glanced at the Monastery of the Angels on the right, then jammed her foot to the floor all the way down to the red light.

Franklin still looked clear, but so did the Hollywood Freeway.

As she waited for the light to change, she took a moment to consider her route. Oak Tree Lane couldn't be more than fifteen miles from here. But during rush hour, fifteen miles could easily translate into an hour-and-a-half drive. In Los Angeles, rush hour began at 6:30 a.m. and usually lasted until 8:30 at night. Even if she didn't get bogged down in traffic, Sunset coiled through the hills like a warped spring and was littered with signal lights. It would take her an hour just to reach the Westside.

She checked the clock on the dash and looked back at the 101. If she jumped on the freeway, the first five or six miles would be spent moving in the wrong direction toward downtown. But if she lucked out, if she reached the city and the road remained relatively clear, she could roll out the Santa Monica Freeway and cut her drive time in half.

She mulled it over, struck by a sudden feeling of déjà vu. She had been here before doing this, but when? As she sifted through her memory, the weighty feeling inched away and finally vanished, and she wondered if it wasn't just a case of the jitters.

The light turned green. Lena crossed Franklin and looped around the freeway, deciding to take a chance. When she reached the entrance ramp, she clicked through the gears and brought the car up to speed in heavy jerks. Easing into traffic, she found the left lane at a smooth 85 mph and settled in behind the wheel.

At least she wasn't driving a take-home car and could make time. While RHD cars remained unmarked, if you chipped through the paint, you would find a retired black-and-white cruiser hiding underneath. Lena had logged enough miles in uniform to know that even in their prime the cars rolled and pitched around corners. By the time they earned their makeover, the cars bobbed down the road like toy boats. Hers had been in the shop for the past three days, and it was a relief to be in her own car again, despite its age.

She grabbed the shift, gearing down as she exited onto the 110.

She was heading south, skirting the city raked in bright sunlight. After a mile, she finally reached the road west and pointed her car toward the dark clouds. The glare lifted away from the windshield and she raised the visor. As she slid into the left lane, she realized that the risk had paid off. The road appeared clear all the way to the ocean. But as she settled into her seat and reached for her coffee, that feeling of déjà vu came back. Heavier this time. Close enough to touch.

Novak said that Oak Tree Lane was off Brooktree. Why did it seem so familiar?

It dawned on her that she already knew the back end of the neighborhood. It had been four years ago. Lena was working narcotics at the time, and a two-strike loser named Rafi Miller had a pound of grade-shit junk to sell. Rafi was holding a half-price sale because his stash was so dirty that end users were dying before they hit liftoff. Word of mouth wasn't doing much for the dealer's reputation. By the time Lena and her partner tracked down

Rafi as the source and made an offer to buy him out, he was more than anxious to play *let's do da deal.*

Lena took another sip of coffee as she thought about the bust.

She could remember Rafi picking a remote location and insisting that Lena come alone. Rustic Canyon Park was set in a quiet neighborhood by the ocean and didn't amount to much more than a public swimming pool and a couple of tennis courts. She could still see Rafi's face as he climbed out of his yellow Mercedes and winked at her in the darkness. Still remember the strong smell of vinegar permeating the smack as he popped open the trunk, handed her a sample, and gave his personal guarantee that the shit was prime-time.

The south end of Brooktree Road was half a block down from the park. It had been sealed that night as a possible escape route just in case Rafi broke loose and made a run for the bank.

Lena knew the neighborhood after all.

She looked out the window at the ocean as she cruised off the 10 and up Pacific Coast Highway. The sun was gone, lost in a thick, blurry fog spitting against the windshield. Switching her wipers on, she made a right on West Channel and began working her way through the narrow streets into the hills. Within a few minutes, she spotted Rustic Canyon Park in the gloom and made a left onto Brooktree. As she glided down the hill, she caught the flares burning in the street and saw a cop standing before a small wooden bridge. She lowered her window, glancing at the stream as she reached for her badge and flashed it. When he waved her through, she idled over the bridge and down the road as if passing through a gate into the sleepy little neighborhood in the woods.

Novak had been right. She didn't need an address to spot the death house on Oak Tree Lane. Easing by a long row of black-and-whites, she glanced at the yellow crime-scene tape already stretched around the perimeter. The open spot at the curb would be left for the Scientific Investigation Division truck when it arrived. But the coroner's van was already here, backing into the drive under Novak's supervision and leaving enough space for what Lena guessed would be a temporary command post beneath the eaves of the roof. Novak spotted her and waved. Lena nodded back, then pulled forward and found a place to park three doors down the road.

Cops in uniforms were already knocking on doors and working the neighborhood for possible leads. Lena finished off her coffee, felt the buzz light up her head, then climbed out of the car into the heavy mist. Stretching her legs, she took a deep breath and exhaled slowly. The air was genuinely clean and appeared free of jet fumes and bus exhaust. The slight breeze had an earthy scent, peppered with a faint edge of eucalyptus. But even more striking was the stillness. She couldn't hear a freeway or traffic rolling up and down PCH. Other than the birds, the only sound seemed to be coming from the water spilling over the polished rocks in the stream. As she popped the trunk open and reached for her briefcase, she glanced down the block. The houses were two to three times the size of her own, some even bigger, but stood within twenty feet of the road. In typical California fashion, privacy was reserved for the backyard, the narrow lanes between the houses blocked by fences or stone walls with iron gates.

Paradise looked as if it lasted longer than fifteen minutes here. Unless, of course, you were unlucky enough to live in the house three doors down the road.

She slammed the trunk and heard a dog start barking in the house before her. As she turned away, a door opened and she glanced back. A small, white terrier on a leash was rushing toward the gate with a middle-aged man wearing a bathrobe in tow.

"Excuse me," the man called out. "I was hoping you might tell me what's happened?"

Lena slung her briefcase over her shoulder. "Have the officers stopped by?"

The man shook his head and appeared frightened. "My neighbor called and said that someone was murdered. That it might be Nikki."

"Then you know as much as I do."

It hung there, the man visibly shaken. Ordinarily, Lena would have cut the conversation short. But when she noticed the outdoor thermometer attached to the house, she glanced at her watch and stepped toward the fence. At 6:55 a.m. it was still only forty-nine degrees. She took another step forward. The dog started barking again, wagging his tail and trying to pull through the gate. The man tugged on the leash—gently, Lena noticed.

"How'd he sleep last night?" she asked.

"Not very well. He woke us up."

"What time was that?"

The man thought it over, beginning to relax. "About one-thirty. Then he started barking again around two."

"How did he do after that?"

"Slept like a baby, while me and my wife tossed and turned."

The man shot her a look and smiled. He obviously loved his dog.

"Does he bark a lot at night?" she asked.

"Only when someone leaves the gate open and the coyotes wander into the backyard. I checked this morning, but the gate was closed."

Lena noticed the SID van pulling around the corner.

"What's your dog's name?"

"Louie," the man said with pride.

"Make sure you tell the officers about Louie when they stop by."

The man nodded. She pulled a business card from her pocket, a generic card provided by the department, and filled in the blank spaces with her name and phone number. She had placed an order for preprinted cards last week. Like her cell phone, she would have to pick up the expense on her own. She passed the card over, then asked for the man's name and phone number. Shielding her notepad from the drizzle, she wrote the information down and drew a circle around the time the dog started barking last night. It was only a hunch, but odds were that the deputy coroner and pathologist would match it with the time of death.

Slipping her notepad into her blazer pocket, she thanked the man and headed down the street. But as she passed a hedgerow, her view cleared and she slowed down to take in the death house through the mist. It was an older home, probably built in the 1920s, and had the feel of a one-story gatehouse leading to something bigger hidden in the foliage. The exterior walls were a mix of smooth river rock and cedar clapboard that had been stained a dark brown. Patches of emerald green moss marred the slate roof along the seams. Behind the house she could see a grove of sycamores and two huge oak trees. The canopy overhead looked particularly thick. Even on a clear day, she doubted the place got much sun.

She stretched the crime scene tape overhead and stepped beneath it. Then a cop handed her a clipboard, and she signed in with her name and badge number. As she crossed the yard to the drive, she sensed the tension in the air. Crime scene techs were readying their equipment, absorbed in their tasks, speaking in whispers if they spoke at all. She looked for a familiar face but didn't recognize anyone. All except for the burly figure with the coffee-and-cream skin hopping off the back of the SID van. Lamar Newton flashed an uneasy smile her way, scratched his head, then sat on the rear gate and opened his camera bag. They had known each other since the bust at Rustic Canyon Park. Two cameras equipped with night-vision lenses had been mounted in the trees overhead. While Lena met with Rafi Miller, Lamar sat in the community center, documenting the event on videotape. Lena and Lamar shared a bond after that night, working well together ever since.

She stepped around the coroner's van and found Novak standing on a six-foot ladder, clipping a blue tarp to the rain spout. He seemed concerned with the view from Brooktree Road and took a sip from a can of diet Coke as he made an adjustment. If the press arrived, they would come with cameras and long lenses, maybe even lip-readers. Novak was trying to buy some privacy.

"You made good time," he said, climbing down.

His smile was forced. She caught the ragged look in his blue eyes, the gray overtaking his blond hair, his ashen skin. He looked ten years older than he did before they'd grabbed a day off. She felt her stomach begin churning again.

"You took a peek," she said.

He nodded. Novak was the first one here and had to look.

"How bad is it?"

He didn't say anything right away. Instead, he turned toward his unmarked car backed into the drive across the street. Lena followed his gaze. An identical car was parked beside it. She could see Tito Sanchez sitting in the front seat beside a man she didn't know. He looked about thirty and appeared distraught, and Lena guessed that Nikki Brant had a husband.

"Remember Teresa Lopez?" Novak asked in a low voice.

The memory registered. Her partner didn't need to say anything more.

They may still have been getting used to each other, but Hank Novak was easily the best partner Lena had ever had. At six foot one he was taller than her by three inches, but they always seemed to stand eye to eye. Their friendship had begun the moment Lieutenant Barrera introduced them and asked Novak to show Lena her desk. He seemed pleased with the partnership rather than burdened and did everything he could to make her feel comfortable as he showed her around. Novak was divorced but had three daughters, and Lena could tell that he liked women, which was important to her. Although retirement was a favorite subject, and the front seat of his car was littered with travel brochures and fishing magazines, he loved talking about his twenty-seven years as a cop. The mistakes he'd made, and what he'd learned as a result. Lena often wondered how Novak managed to survive with his humanity intact and hoped that she would be as lucky.

She pulled a fresh pair of vinyl gloves from the box she kept in her briefcase and slipped them on.

"Where's Rhodes?"

"Inside stretching tape," Novak said. "The body's in the bedroom. That's James Brant in the car with Tito. He says he got home around five-thirty after doing an all-nighter at work. When he found his wife, he dialed nine one one."

She took another look at James Brant, concerned that he might have contaminated the crime scene.

"How long was he in the house alone?"

"About half an hour. West L.A. had him in their cruiser when I pulled up. Brant says he didn't touch anything. That he never got past the bedroom doorway. He took one look and made the call."

"What about West L.A.?"

"They never entered the room. They backed out and sent the paramedics home. The case got bumped to us based on the view from the bedroom door."

The view from the bedroom door.

Lena tried not to think about it, but she knew that it was already seared into Novak's brain by the way he drained the can of Diet Coke as if it were a Bud Light and he could still drink beer. As she turned away, Stan Rhodes walked outside carrying a spent roll of crime scene tape. He looked at her with those dark eyes of his, something he hadn't done since she was promoted to RHD. They shared a history, but Lena didn't want to deal with it right now. His gaze appeared steady and even, the way it used to be, and she guessed that Rhodes was looking at the situation just as she was.

"It's clear all the way to the body," he said to her. "SID ready?"

Novak answered for Lena. "In a minute."

"I'll meet you guys in the foyer," she said.

"Sounds good," Rhodes said quietly. "But I wouldn't wander too far down the hall."

4

Lena stepped over the threshold into the death house. She might have been anxious, but she also wanted to get a feel for the way Nikki and James Brant lived before the investigation really got started. It had been her practice ever since she'd shed her uniform, particularly when entering a home with a dead body. She wanted a clean view, an unbiased first impression no matter how sketchy, before her mind was forever jaded by the sight of the victim and how they met their end.

The house was smaller than she first thought—about thirteen hundred square feet. And the layout was more open than most homes of the same period. From where she stood in the foyer, she had a partial view of the kitchen on her left and the living room through the archway. To her right was a small den and the hallway leading to the back of the house.

Nothing seemed out of place. There were no obvious signs of a struggle. Just the yellow tape Rhodes had strung across the entrances to each room and along the walls, roughing out a safe zone down the hall to the bedroom in the very back.

The murder room.

Lena looked away, sensing a chill in the air. It felt almost as cold inside as it was out. She glanced at the table and mirror opposite the front door and spotted a thermostat on the wall, wondering why the heat wasn't on. Digging into her pocket for her notepad, she wrote down the temperature, then took another look at the table. The lamp was still burning, and she noted the lack of dust, the faint scent of polish. The house had recently been cleaned. Not yesterday or even last night in order to cover something up, but sometime over the past week. Dust and the story it left behind was a tech's best friend. No one from SID would be pleased.

Lena turned to a blank page in her notepad and made a rough sketch of the floor plan. Peeking into the kitchen, she noted the stack of newspapers by the breakfast table and the dinner dishes set beside the sink. There weren't many dishes, and she figured it had been dinner for one last night.

When she moved to the archway, she noticed the lack of furniture in the living room. Pressing her body against the crime scene tape, she leaned forward for a better view. The ceiling was vaulted, the rear wall lined entirely by glass. Through the French doors she could see a flagstone terrace giving way to a sizable backyard enclosed by a fence. She looked back at the empty room, searching for personal items but not finding any. Just a TV on the floor set beside a boom box and short stack of CDs.

Lena turned to the front door, saw Lamar Newton asking Novak a question in the driveway, and crossed the foyer for a quick look at the den. The walls were lined with books, but the shelves were built-ins. The only furniture in the room was an old leather couch and a small wooden desk and chair that seemed better suited for a child. A table lamp was set on the floor. In lieu of a coffee table, fifteen oversize books were spread out on the white carpet as if someone had been studying them from the floor. A path had been cleared from where Lena stood in the foyer to the computer on the desk.

She thought it over, cataloging the inventory in her head. In spite of the address, money had been an issue for Nikki and James Brant. Their home was nearly empty. What they owned could easily fit into a van or small trailer. Yet a presence was here. Something extra Lena couldn't put her finger on.

Her eyes drifted down to the books laid out on the carpet. They were filled with works of art. Paintings, sculptures, but also buildings dating from the Renaissance to the nineteenth century. Lena recognized one of the books on architecture because she'd read it as a student at UCLA before she'd ever dreamed or even thought about being a cop.

She looked back at the shelves, scanning the titles with surprise when she didn't find a single work of fiction. At eye level every book was about business. At knee level the subject switched to art.

"We're ready, Lena," Novak said in low voice.

She turned to the door. He was entering the foyer with Rhodes. Lamar followed them in, along with Ed Gainer, an investigator from the coroner's office Lena had met several times. Their preliminary sweep would remain small.

"Let's do it," Rhodes said.

They started down the hall. They moved slowly, without words, the only sound coming from the hardwood floor creaking beneath their feet. Closet doors and a laundry room filled out the left wall. They passed a bathroom on the right, halfway down, and didn't stop until they reached the door at the end. The reason the case had been bumped up to them.

Rhodes gave her a look. She saw the deputy coroner flinch and thought she heard Lamar whisper, "Oh, shit." She gritted her teeth and peered into the room.

The curtains were drawn, the handles tapping in the breeze. It took a moment for her to realize that the walls had once been painted white. That she wasn't standing in a slaughterhouse at the edge of civilization, but in someone's home on a quiet street. She took a deep breath and exhaled. There was more blood than she had ever seen. The spatter fanned out from the middle of the room, blowing against the walls, dusting the vaulted ceiling, and splashing across the floor. Yet in the center of the room, the eye of the storm, there was a certain peace. A small body, seemingly at rest, was carefully posed beneath a clean white bedspread.

It wasn't a murder room, she thought. It was a death chamber.

Lena's eyes cut through the darkness, searching out the victim's face. When she couldn't find it, she realized that the young woman's head was wrapped in a plastic grocery bag.

"Watch the steps," Rhodes whispered under his breath.

Lena glanced down at her feet. Like the living room, the bedroom was three steps below the rest of the house. As she followed the crime scene tape, she wondered how Rhodes had managed to find a clean path to the body. The task seemed impossible, but somehow he had.

She needed a moment to collect herself. When the blue-shaded room lit up in a quick succession of white flashes, she stepped out of Lamar's way and joined Novak and Rhodes at the foot of the bed. She noticed a photo-graph set beside the clock radio on the dresser. She glanced at the picture without touching the silver frame. Nikki and James Brant were sitting in a field of grass with their arms around each other. They seemed so innocent, so happy. Lost in their dreams and ready to face a future together that didn't include this.

Lena shook it off and moved to the open window, parting the curtains and checking the floor and sill for blood. Next to the body itself, she knew the point of entry was the most likely place to find blood. She didn't see any and wondered if the open window was in play. Moving closer, she drew fresh air into her lungs and studied the backyard. The fog had become more dense, lingering beneath the roofline and settling onto the ground. Still, she could make out the faint outline of a tennis court on the other side of the fence and knew that she was looking at Rustic Canyon Park.

She turned back to Lamar, watching him cover the body in wide shots and close-ups. After burning through a roll of film, he pulled the camera away from his eye and gave her a look. The department had upgraded to digital cameras a few years back but still relied on film to record crime scenes.

"Let's pull the covers," Novak said in a low voice.

Lena stepped out of the safe zone and worked her way around the spat-ter to the far side of the bed.

"I'm going to pull the spread off first," she said. "There might be some-thing underneath."

Novak agreed. "Nice and slow," he said.

She gripped the spread with both hands and pulled it away to reveal a white blanket. Two plumes of blood had risen from the body and were ooz-ing through the fabric like lamp oil working its way through a wick toward the flame. As Lamar popped in another roll of film and documented the bloodstains, Lena pointed to Nikki Brant's neck, which had become more visible now. The plastic bag hadn't been draped over the woman's head, but was wrapped around her neck and carefully tied into a bow.

Lamar zeroed in on the knot from the other side of the bed. Lena looked back at the bag, trying to decipher the print through the spatter with the hope of identifying the grocery store. When she leaned in for a closer look, she flinched. She could see the young woman's face through the opaque plastic. Every time Lamar's camera flashed, the image became clearer and more eerie. Nikki Brant's eyes were open. And it looked as if she were staring back at Lena through the smoky plastic—as if for a split second their eyes met.

An ice-cold chill ran up Lena's spine. She took a deep breath.

Lamar lowered his camera. "Got it, Lena," he said.

She nodded, ignoring the horror and struggling to keep it buried. Gripping the blanket, she pulled it away, carefully folding it over without touching the bedspread. The small body was beginning to take shape beneath the covers now, the two bloodstains more pronounced. When she noticed an extra blanket pushed against the foot of the bed, she pointed it out to Lamar. Once the image was recorded, she gripped the top sheet with both hands and peeled the final layer away to reveal Nikki Brant's dead body.

A stillness permeated the room. No one moved or said anything for several moments as the weight of the horror nipped and pulled at them.

Dwarfed by the size of the bed, Nikki Brant looked like a child.

She was lying on her back with her legs spread open. Her hands had been placed beside her hips and, like her head, bound in plastic and tied around her wrists. Her body was soft and curvy. Her breasts small and round and tattooed with bruises. Semen stains dotted the sheet between her legs and appeared wet but smeared. But it was the two stab wounds that played with Lena's soul. The first was just below the collarbone. A through and through that looked clean but unusually wide, almost as if she had been speared. The second wound looked more jagged, the knife ripping upward through her belly. Based on the heavy amount of blood loss and the condition of the room, Lena had no doubt that the young woman was alive through most of the ordeal.

"We need to think about what we're seeing," Rhodes said in a voice that was barely audible. "Whether we're looking at things the way they really are, or the way someone wants us to think they are."

"We'll talk about that later," Novak said.

Lena took a step closer, eyeing the wounds carefully. She had seen them once before, but never in this context.

"It's called the juke," she said. "I saw it working a dope deal with South L.A."

"Gangs do it for the effect," Novak said. "They think the brutality impresses their friends."

Lena stepped away from the bed as Lamar moved in with his camera, her mind rattling through possible motives. Nothing she saw so far indicated a robbery. There wasn't anything in the house worth stealing other than Nikki Brant.

Parting the curtains, she took another look at the park beyond the fence and wondered what the view would be like on a clear day. The view from a car parked in the lot at night. This was about anger, she thought. A six-pack of anger. Somebody overdosing on rage.

When she turned back to the room, Gainer had approached the bed and was examining the body. The sheet was still partially covering the young woman's left foot, and he pulled it away, then jerked his hand up. No one said anything, eyeballing the foot and doing the math. Nikki Brant's second toe was missing. Something had been taken from the house after all.

Gainer shrugged off the horror as best he could, his face pale, his eyes rising up the body until they reached the plastic bag over the victim's head.

"I don't think we should pull this thing," he said. "Not here anyway. There might be something inside worth preserving. What do you guys think?"

"We need a picture of her face," Rhodes said. "A Polaroid to show the husband. And we're gonna need a rape kit."

"I understand," Gainer said. "But if we pull the bag at the autopsy, we'll have more control."

Novak thought it over, his eyes on Gainer. "You got any idea how fast we can get her in?"

"We're backed up two or three days, Hank. But under the circumstances, I'll bet we could bump her to the top of the list. If you want, I'll make sure it happens. We'll schedule the cut for late this afternoon."

Rhodes stepped across the safe zone to the other side of the bed. "What about slicing the bag open for the picture?"

Gainer nodded in agreement. "Seems like the way to go."

"Then let's do it," Novak said.

Gainer pulled a razor-sharp scalpel from his kit and drew the blade down the center of the bag. As he pulled the plastic away from Nikki Brant's face, everyone stepped closer.

"There's moisture," he whispered. "She was breathing when the bag went over her head. We need to get a shot of this before it dries."

Gainer leaned out of the way to give Lamar room. After a Polaroid was taken, Lamar switched back to his Nikon, the camera eating up another roll of film. As the strobe light started flashing again, Lena stared at Nikki Brant's face and tangled black hair. Even with her eyes open, her gaze just off-center and lost in a thousand-yard stare, Lena could tell that the victim had been a beautiful woman. Before last night anyway. There was a certain innocence about her. A certain something Lena couldn't really put into words.

"Did anyone talk to the husband about notifying her family?" she asked.

Novak couldn't meet her eyes right away. An awkward moment passed.

"She's an orphan," he finally said. "Other than us, he's the only one she's got."

The room fell silent, lost in the metallic rhythm of the camera's motor drive. Lena knew that Novak had hesitated because she was an orphan, too. About the same age as Nikki Brant. As she turned back to the corpse, a deep feeling of loneliness welled up inside her, mixed with an overwhelming sense of compassion.

And then the room appeared to shake.

For a split second Lena thought it might be an earthquake. She felt her chest tighten. She saw Rhodes flinch. Novak reached for the wall and Gainer dropped his scalpel.

But it wasn't an earthquake at all. It was music, blaring from the clock radio. Everyone turned toward the dresser and glared at the fucking thing.

Lena grabbed it, fumbling with the dials until she found the right switch. As the music bounced off the bloodstained walls and finally dissipated into the gloom, everyone turned back to the dead body with the severed toe and checked their watches. Their nerves.

The alarm had been set for 7:30 a.m. Time for Nikki Brant to wake up.

5

It was part of the job, but that didn't make it any easier. They needed to place the victim at the crime scene and ID the body. They needed James Brant to say that the picture of the corpse Lena held in her jacket pocket was his wife.

Brant leaned against the open car door, burying his head in his arms. Lena stood beside Novak facing Brant on the other side.

"Where's Tito going?" Brant asked in a shaky voice.

"The Red Cross is here," Lena said. "He's getting you a cup of coffee."

Brant looked up, his curly brown hair dusted with droplets of rain. Lena followed his gaze to Sanchez, strolling across the lawn toward a pickup truck parked in front of the next house. The Red Cross would provide food and drinks to the neighborhood until the street was reopened. And Sanchez would take his time bringing back the coffee. It had been a group decision. No one wanted to crowd Brant. Lena and Novak would make the identification with him on their own. Because of her easy manner, Lena would take the lead. Because of Novak's trained eye and experience, he would observe.

"I want to go in," Brant said to her. "I want to see Nikki. I need to hold her."

"We're sorry for your loss, Mr. Brant. But your house is a crime scene now. People are working. We're trying to find out what happened."

"I want to see her." Brant's voice rose from his gut as he lowered his head and stared at the pavement. He clenched his fist, then punched the inside door panel and stood up. Lena suddenly realized why the books about business were at eye level and the art books filled out the lower shelves in the study. James Brant was well over six feet tall. His wife was easily a foot shorter and by any standard would have been considered petite. The books had been placed on the shelves as a matter of convenience.

"She's all alone. I should be with her. She didn't deserve this."

"No, she didn't," Lena said. "And I agree with you that this is total bullshit."

Whether it was the tone of her voice or the words she used, Brant turned from the house and looked straight at her. His eyes sharpened and the muscles in his face and neck began to twitch. In spite of his wrinkled suit, Lena could tell that Brant was powerfully built and wired tight as a drum. He had obviously been an athlete in school, probably football or soccer, and still worked out.

"If you agree," he said, "then why can't I see her? I want to know what happened."

"We do, too, Mr. Brant. The sooner you realize that, the better off we'll all be."

He thought it over, his eyes losing their focus and turning inward again. "I've already told Tito everything I know. I came home and found her . . . like that."

"He told us. It must have been extremely difficult. We appreciate everything you've done to help."

Sanchez had already filled them in on his conversation with Brant. It had been part of the plan. While everyone else kept their distance from within the confines of the crime scene, Sanchez sat with Brant hoping to become his next best friend. James Brant was twenty-eight years old and worked as the chief bean counter at the Dreggco Corporation, a fledgling biotech company located just south of Venice Beach. Lena had been right. Money was still an issue in their lives. Brant had won the job and title because of his youth and willingness to defer most of his salary in favor of a piece of the action. The Dreggco Corporation was banking on its research. If their work panned out, everyone would reap the rewards. If things went south, Brant would leave with enough experience to move on at a higher salary. According to Tito, it sounded as if the company had hit on something and was about to be flooded with cash in a buyout scheme. Brant told Tito that he had been working all-nighters for more than a week. That the deal hinged on the numbers. Although things were good with Nikki—they had only been married for two years—it hadn't been easy. They lived on her salary, which wasn't much because she taught at a small art college on the other side of Glendale. The mortgage on their home didn't leave room for anything but the necessities.

"I loved her," he said. "Things were perfect until this."

"Perfect?" Lena asked.

He met her eyes and held them. "Perfect," he repeated. "Until now."

"Mr. Brant, I need to show you something and it isn't going to be easy."

Brant seemed to know what was coming. He reached for the top of the door with his right hand as if grabbing hold of the ropes in a boxing ring. He looked punch-drunk, as if maybe he didn't have enough left to make the last round.

"Show it to me," he said.

Lena glanced at Novak, but her partner's eyes were glued on Brant. Reaching into her pocket, she pulled out the Polaroid. It was a close-up of Nikki Brant's face poking through the rip in the grocery bag. As Lena held it out, she measured Brant's reaction. His eyes didn't hit the photo and slide off as if trying to forget a memory. Instead, they met the image of his wife's fate and appeared to crumble.

"Is this your wife, Mr. Brant?"

He rocked his head up and down, unable to speak, then started shaking. After a moment, he closed his eyes, wilted onto the front seat, and cradled his head in his arms. The cries came in deep, long stretches, followed by breathless gasps for air that ripped at Lena and jabbed at her.

She slid the Polaroid into her pocket, stepping away from the car with Novak.

"You think he's legit?" she asked.

When her partner nodded, she nodded back, feeling nauseous.

It was part of the job, but that didn't make it any easier. Showing Brant the photograph seemed both absurd and exceedingly cruel. She eyed him through the windshield and listened to him weeping. It was the sound of agony, wisping through a quiet neighborhood in the woods. The sound of someone hitting the wall without any traffic noise to dull the thud. She knew the tone and cadence from personal experience. It was the indelible sound of paradise lost.

6

The wood-plank fence stood six feet high. Lena grabbed the top, lifted her legs over the boards, and hopped down on the other side. A gravel path led through the trees toward the tennis courts and community center up the hill. She checked the ground before taking a step forward. Satisfied that she wasn't contaminating an extension of the crime scene, she headed up the path toward Rustic Canyon Park.

She still felt nauseous. She needed distance. A breath of fresh air and the chance to clear her mind, if only for five minutes. But she also wanted a look at the Brants' house from the parking lot on the hill.

The path circled around a grove of trees, passing a set of concrete steps on its way to the ocean half a mile due west. Lena veered to her left, climbing up the stairs to the community center. The pool remained closed for the season. No one was playing tennis in the drizzle. When she reached the top, she checked the lot and found it empty. But the view was pretty much what she expected. A straight shot through the trees to every backyard in the neighborhood.

She moved away from the steps, scanning the ground for debris and searching for any indication that the predator responsible for this hideous crime had been here. Spotting a trash can, she lifted the lid and peered inside. The plastic liner appeared new, the container, empty.

When she closed the lid, a squirrel shot out of the underbrush, racing across the lot toward a tree. Ten feet up the trunk, the animal stopped and turned. Lena followed its gaze over to the building and saw a coyote hiding behind the corner. As she walked back to the top step and sat down, the wild dog trotted to the bottom of the hill and silently cantered past the Brants' backyard.

Her eyes drifted over the fence.

Stray bands of sunlight were leaking into the smoky fog, igniting the moisture and causing it to glow. In spite of the spectacle, she had a bird's-eye view of the house. As she thought it over, she wondered if the doer had sat on this very step. It didn't amount to anything more than a distant feeling, but it was there as she took in the view. She could see an SID tech studying the garden below the bedroom window. He had been at it for fifteen minutes and told Lena on her way out that he hadn't found anything. She could hear the sound of power tools coming from the house as two more techs ripped up the bathroom plumbing. Because the blood evidence was limited to the bedroom and the doer hadn't left a trail, it was a safe guess that he'd cleaned up before leaving.

But the concept made her feel even more uneasy than she already was. The idea that the doer took the time to clean up instead of bolting the moment he committed the murder indicated a certain measure of confidence, even arrogance. That he clipped off the woman's second toe and took it with him pointed to the outer reaches of madness.

Someone switched on a light in the house directly before her. She looked through the window and saw the man she'd met with the white dog at his kitchen counter pouring a bowl of cereal. Next door she noticed an old man reading the paper on his sunporch. To the right of the Brants' house, an older woman was pretending to water her garden in the rain while sneaking peeks at the crime scene tech on the other side of the fence.

It was an established neighborhood in a remote location. A neighborhood that was aging.

Lena let her mind drift, trying to imagine what it must have been like before the murder. She had seen the photographs of the victim. She saw her face and body. Nikki Brant was a beautiful young woman. Although there were curtains in the bedroom, the large panes of glass in the living room had been left bare. If the doer sat here trying to make a decision, if the seed of the crime began with rape, he had a wide-open view and Nikki Brant would have been his obvious first choice.

The breeze picked up, the branches rustling overhead. She saw Stan Rhodes enter the backyard and reached inside her pocket for her can of Altoids. Popping a mint into her mouth, she watched Rhodes scan the property. His jacket was off, his sleeves rolled up to the elbow. Rhodes didn't have the bulky figure of someone who belonged to a health club and sat at a machine performing the same mind-numbing exercises over and over. Instead, his body had the smooth elegance of a long-distance runner—lean, long, and trim. His brown hair was rich and dark. He had a strong chin, a smart face, and Lena could still remember what she was thinking the day she first met him.

Bad timing.

Rhodes had been seeing the same woman for more than two years. Lena had met someone new three months before, and though it had its ups and downs and eventually blew up in her face, the relationship felt pretty good at the time.

She smiled at the memory. The bad timing.

Their attraction for each other had been immediate. When they spoke about having an affair, Rhodes told her that his relationship was on the rocks and that he had never been more willing. But as Lena thought it over, she couldn't go through with it. She didn't want to be the cause of a breakup, and mixing her job with her personal life seemed too complicated. She had just become a cop and hadn't even finished her rookie year. They hadn't seen each other or spoken since. And now that they could, it seemed as if he was deliberately ignoring her. Their desks were on the same floor, facing each other less than half a room apart. Over the past two months, she hadn't caught him looking her way even once. It seemed so forced, so rigid and absurd. She felt awkward whenever he was around, often wondering if she'd read it wrong and made a mistake. Until today, she thought. Until he'd stepped out the front door of the death house and looked at her as if everything between them was okay again.

She stood up and stretched her legs, then moved quickly down the steps, anxious to get back to the crime scene. As she climbed over the fence and hopped down on the other side, Rhodes was still in the backyard. He looked at her with those dark eyes of his and moved closer.

"Anything?" he asked.

"He could've sat in his car and picked her out," she said. "It reads like a menu."

He turned and gazed at the back of the houses. When he spotted the old man in the sunporch, Rhodes smiled and got it. His hand brushed against her shoulder, and they crossed the lawn to the house.

"We're okay, aren't we?" he said.

She met his eyes and nodded. In spite of the horror of the crime—whom it hurt and what it left behind—she hoped they could work together like this.

7

Lena's eyes snapped across the white carpet between the books laid out on the floor, following the spots leading to the desk in the study. There were two, so small and colorless that she hadn't noticed them when she'd first entered the house and taken a cursory glance at the room.

She stepped aside as a tech entered the foyer with an ultraviolet light and headed down the hall toward the bedroom. Then she dropped her notepad on the floor and slipped beneath the crime scene tape stretched across the doorway. Inching forward on her stomach, she worked her way down the carpet until she reached the first drop.

She felt her heart flutter in her chest and tried to get a grip on herself.

It was semen. And it hadn't dried in the cool, moist air.

She arched her back and leaned forward. As she studied the carpet beneath the desk, she spotted a third drop hidden in the shadows at the base of the chair. Her eyes rose to the computer and lingered there as she thought it over. When she heard someone enter the foyer, she turned and saw Novak moving toward the doorway.

"Have you seen a thermostat?" he asked. "Gainer's trying to guesstimate the time of death. They're gonna move the body."

"On the wall behind you," she said. "But the temps are in my notes. What's he saying?"

Novak knelt down and grabbed her notepad. "Between one and three. She's just beginning to harden up."

Lena took a deep breath, staring at the carpet and mulling over the implications of her discovery. The horror that it implied. She turned to Novak, back-paging his way through her notes. He was studying the diagrams she'd made of the bedroom as if the lines and measurements might provide a certain degree of order to a world that had been ripped off its axis and thrown down the hill.

"They're on the first page," she said.

He nodded, jumping ahead in the book until he found them.

"We've got a problem, Hank."

"That's one way of putting it."

He had something on his mind and wasn't listening to her. After writing the temperatures down on a blank sheet of paper, he tossed her notepad on the floor.

"Whoever did this didn't run away," she said.

Novak started to get up. "Maybe not."

"There's no maybe about it. He did what he did to Nikki Brant, and then he sat at this desk and used the computer. You ever hear of anyone hanging out to surf the Web?"

He gave her a long look. She had his attention now.

"Why are you lying on the floor?" he asked.

She pointed to the carpet without saying anything. Novak's eyes rolled off her finger and stopped on the first drop of semen. A moment passed. What the image implied had a certain amount of juice.

"Gainer doesn't think she was raped," he said. "There's no vaginal bruising. He thinks she did it with someone she knew."

It hung there. Someone she *knew*. . . .

Lena thought about the semen found on the sheet between Nikki Brant's legs. The appearance of her vagina and the lack of any visible discharge. Someone had attempted to clean her up.

"What about the autopsy?" she asked.

"We're in," Novak said. "Late this afternoon. I told Lamar to meet us there."

"We'll need the UV lights," she said. "We need to scan this room. And we'll need to pull the computer."

Novak agreed, his eyes following the drops of semen across the floor to the desk. As she turned back, Rhodes stepped into the foyer from the kitchen doorway.

"Things just got stupid," he said. "Take a look."

She slid beneath the crime scene tape, following Novak into the kitchen. The dishwasher was open. Rhodes pointed to the twelve-inch chef's knife in the upper tray. The blade was forged from a single piece of high-carbon steel and appeared sharp enough and long enough to be the murder weapon. On the counter Lena noticed six knives from the same set sheathed in a wooden block. The seventh slot remained open, waiting for the twelve-inch blade to hit the rinse cycle.

"Someone washed the dishes," Rhodes said. "But they were in a hurry and forgot to add the dinner plates."

Lena glanced at the dishes by the sink—dinner for one—then turned back to the dishwasher. The trays were only half-full, the contents clean. Peeling off her gloves, she dug into her blazer pocket for a fresh pair. Then she picked up a saucer in the upper tray and felt the heat—the faint glow well above room temperature that remained. Clearly, the sole purpose of the wash had been to sterilize the knife. She passed the saucer to Rhodes, who smiled a little as the radiant heat broke through his gloves. The knife in the upper tray was most likely the murder weapon.

"The dishwasher works on a ninety-minute cycle," he said.

Lena did the math. "Then someone turned it on around three."

She looked at her partner. He was staring at the open drawer beside the oven and appeared shaken. The drawer was filled to the brim with plastic grocery bags. No one wanted it to go this way, but there it was, dragging them into the black.

"They match the bag over his wife's head," Rhodes said. "They're from the same store. Hollywood Veggie Mart. Only it's down the hill on PCH and not in Hollywood. It's an independent. The only one in town."

Lena looked out the window. She could see Tito Sanchez getting out of the car and walking toward the house. James Brant was still sitting in the front seat, but the tears were gone and his swollen face appeared to have hardened around the edges. As Sanchez entered the foyer, Novak steered him into the kitchen.

"What's Brant saying?"

"The same thing I told you guys before. He's going around in circles. He needs to use a bathroom."

"That's what neighbors are for," Rhodes said.

Novak turned back to Sanchez. "You've spent the morning together. What's your take on the guy?"

"I can't really get a read on him. He's angry. Nervous. He's all over the place. I guess if it was my wife, I might be acting the same way."

"What about work?"

"No enemies. One big happy family."

"Then you think he's legit," Novak said.

Sanchez spotted the knife in the dishwasher and caught the vibe. The big turn.

"I didn't say that. I can't tell, Hank. It could go either way."

"What about his fingerprints?" Lena asked.

"SID already got them," Sanchez said. "They wanted to clear him. They got them while they were waiting to get into the house."

The telltale sound of wheels rolling down the hallway underlined the moment and rusted out the edge.

Lena turned with everyone else to watch the gurney pass through the foyer and out the front door. Nikki Brant's small body barely filled out half the blue bag. When Gainer popped his head in the room, Novak pulled a sheet of paper from his pocket and handed it to him.

"The temps," he said.

Gainer nodded, handing him a receipt for the body and walking out.

Then Novak joined Lena by the dishwasher for another look at that knife. As a ray of sunlight poked through the window, the blade appeared to glisten before their eyes.

"I think it's time we took advantage of our size," he said to her.

"You want to split up?"

"We'll get started on his alibi and let these guys finish up here," Novak said. "I want this knife at the autopsy, so let's get it logged in."

8

The Dreggco Corporation was located just off Main in Venice, within walking distance to the beach. As Novak pulled into the lot, Lena eyed the two-story building and guessed that it had been constructed sometime within the past three or four years. The corrugated-aluminum siding remained unblemished and appeared freshly painted a shade darker than sand. Although there were no windows on the first floor, the second story was wrapped in a band of darkened glass.

They got out of the car and walked through the drizzle toward an aqua blue awning that marked the entrance, the sign by the door too small to have read from the road.

THE DREGGCO CORPORATION
FOOD TASTES BETTER IF DREGGCO EATS IT FIRST

She saw Novak reading the slogan and turned back to the lot. From the number of cars, less than a hundred people worked here. But what struck Lena most was the lack of any visible security measures. This was Los Angeles. Hollywood might be the gutter. But if the city had a drain, Venice was it.

"Are you seeing what I am?" she asked.

"There aren't any surveillance cameras."

"And there isn't a gate or a guard or even a card-key access box."

Novak flashed a subdued smile and reached for the door. "No record of who walks in or who walks out."

"Or what time it was when they did," she said.

They stepped inside, met by a rush of warm air as they entered the lobby. A young woman dressed casually in jeans and a black V-neck sweater sat on the other side of the counter, answering phones and directing calls throughout the building. As they approached, she signaled with a raised finger to wait while she listened to someone on her headset. Lena noticed the book pack by the woman's feet. The textbooks on the counter by her mug of hot tea. The receptionist was a college student.

While they waited, Lena stepped away from the counter. The furniture was sparse, but modern and expensive. On the walls, three high-resolution photographs lit with small tungsten spotlights depicted an apple, an egg, and what looked like a grain of rice in the palm of a child's hand. There was a stairway leading to the second floor but no sign of an elevator. At the base of the steps a set of double glass doors led to a hallway that cut into the center of the building. Along the hallway were several doors, and like the building's entrance, they didn't require an ID card to pass through.

"I'm sorry," the receptionist said. "May I help you?"

Lena returned to the counter as Novak smiled at the young woman.

"No problem," he said. "We're here to meet with Milo Plashett. He's expecting us."

The receptionist's eyes rocked from Novak to Lena, then back again, her easy manner fading into one of fear as she suddenly realized who they were and why they were here. Word must have gotten out. Because Plashett wasn't a suspect—the visit more or less routine—Lena had called ahead to make sure that he would be here. Based on what Sanchez had learned from James Brant, Plashett owned the Dreggco Corporation and had hired Brant himself.

The receptionist pointed to the stairs as she pressed the first button on the telephone console. "Mr. Plashett's office is at the end of the hall."

They crossed the lobby. As they rose to the second floor, Milo Plashett met them in the foyer, shook hands, and introduced himself.

"This way," he said anxiously. "Please."

They followed him toward the rear of the building. Plashett was on the short side with a robust body, his steps meaty and determined. His scalp was tan, his dark brown hair mostly gone now. Lena figured he was about fifty. As they passed a series of doorways, she spotted a sign on the wall with James Brant's name on it and gave Novak a nudge. Plashett didn't notice that they had stopped right away. When he did, he hurried back.

"May we take a look?" Lena asked.

"Sure," Plashett said. "Under the circumstances, I'm sure he wouldn't mind."

Under the circumstances, she thought, maybe he would.

She stepped into Brant's office. The room was small and nondescript, his desk and the floor around it piled with stacks of files and loose papers. As she moved to the window, she could see a small piece of the ocean leaking out from between the buildings at the end of the street. On the sill she found a photograph of Nikki Brant, smiling at the camera. Lena recognized the building behind her as well as the fountain. The picture had been taken at the L.A. County Museum of Art on Wilshire.

Plashett cleared his throat. "There were times when I'd be walking down the hall and see him holding that picture just like you are. He was staring at it. I can't imagine what he's going through."

"He told us things were still good between them," Lena said.

"I used to joke with him about that. They'd only been married for a couple of years. Take notes, I used to say. Do your twenty and call me back." Plashett's voice trailed off into what seemed like genuine sadness.

"So as far as you know," Lena said, "he didn't fool around?"

Plashett hesitated a moment. But he wasn't considering Lena's statement. Instead, his eyes were locked on her hips.

"No," he finally said in a quieter voice. "He didn't fool around."

"Is there a problem, Mr. Plashett?"

His gaze rose to her face. "Your gun," he said. "I've never seen a woman wearing a gun like that before. It makes me think that the world has changed."

"You're right about that, Mr. Plashett. The world's changed."

He smiled at her and checked his watch. "Let's go down to my office so we can talk. I've got a class at one. I'll have to leave soon to make it."

They walked down to the end of the hall, passing what looked like a control room or an operations center. Twenty-five desks were set up in cubicles without partitions so that the employees could see each other and talk. No one in the room looked older than thirty.

"You teach?" Lena asked.

"I'm afraid so," he said. "This place is actually an extension of my work for the university. At some point we outgrew the classroom. Who knew that it would come to this?"

They entered his corner office. Plashett closed the door, offering them chairs with a sweep of the hand as he moved around his desk. Lena glanced about the room. The window on the right matched the view from Brant's office, as did the gray Formica desk. But the matching Formica counter against the rear wall seemed to be the place where Plashett did most of his work. His computer was here, and the entire surface was littered with open three-ring binders, oversize sheets of paper containing diagrams, and an array of manila file folders. But what made this office unique were the casement windows above the counter stretching across the entire wall. The large windows opened to the rear of the building and flooded the room with a soft, almost heavenly light.

Lena sat down in the far chair. Novak remained on his feet, taking in the room as he spoke.

"What is it that you do here, Mr. Plashett?"

"We've developed a new technology. Something wonderful."

"Something worth a lot of money," Lena said.

Plashett smiled. "Something that will make everybody's life better. You just won't hear about it for a couple of years. Now, why don't you tell me why you're here."

"It's just routine," Novak said. "Brant told us that he worked all night and we thought we'd stop by and check."

"He's preparing an audit for the company. Along with the report, he's working up a series of projections and business models."

"On his own?" Lena asked.

Plashett laughed. "We're small but not that small. He has two assistants. They've been putting in about twenty hours a day."

Novak pulled a notebook out of his jacket pocket, along with a pen. "Then Brant was here last night."

Plashett paused a moment, clearing his throat and wiggling in his seat. All of a sudden, the man looked uncomfortable.

"That's where it gets tricky, Detective."

"Tricky?"

"You have to understand. James is a good kid. He works long hours at a quarter of the pay he really deserves. He's good at his job, and he does it without complaint. We're working together for a piece of the future, Detective. We're working to make the world a better place. We're a family around here."

Novak smiled as he measured the man. "I understand all that. But let's get back to tricky."

Plashett sank into his chair and sighed. "They've been on the same schedule for the past ten days. I checked when you called. Last night he let his assistants go home early."

"What time was that?" Lena asked.

Plashett hesitated again, then lowered his eyes. "Around ten," he said.

9

Tricky . . .

Lena thought about it as she acclimated herself to the RHD car's loose, pinball steering.

The trick to a decent interview was to start off slowly and work your way to the big moment. That moment came when Plashett called Brant's assistants into his office and both employees admitted that they were the last to leave the building and couldn't really explain why they had been given the night off. Brant told them that they looked tired, that it was only Thursday and they would have to work over the weekend. Brant seemed troubled last night, as if he wanted to be alone.

Tricky.

Because the company was an extension of Plashett's work on campus, security was lax and offered no indication of when Brant had left the office and headed home. Even worse, when they checked Brant's computer, the last saved file matched the time the two employees had left for the night: 10:00 p.m., not five in the morning.

James Brant didn't have an alibi. The story he'd told Tito Sanchez couldn't be verified.

But then the real trick was to somehow find a way to keep an open mind. Follow the evidence and not ricochet off any one of its parts. Maintain your direction. Stay away from the fork in the road or risk being deflected off course.

Lena glanced at her partner, then back at the freeway as she exited off the 134 at Linda Vista. The college where Nikki Brant taught art history was just on the other side of Glendale in the hills overlooking the Rose Bowl. Novak was sipping another Diet Coke from a cooler he kept in the trunk and pretending to read one of his retirement brochures. She thought he might be pretending because the brochure covered a tract of land in Idaho, the graveyard state of choice for L.A. cops. Within a week of their first meeting, Lena had managed to talk Novak out of Idaho. He liked to fish but enjoyed the taste of salmon better than trout. Besides, he was only fifty-three years old, had successfully quit drinking and smoking, and still had at least a third of his life ahead of him. If he was going to make the great escape, the Northwest seemed like a better place to go. Ever since Lena mentioned her frequent trips to Seattle with her brother's band and described the way the water met the land, Novak became excited and ran new places by her as if he needed her approval now.

"Don't tell me you're reconsidering Idaho," she said.

Novak dropped the brochure and held up one of his fishing magazines, already opened to the feature article. Then he pointed to a picture of a flounder set on a bed of tomatoes rather than ice.

Lena shook her head. "I don't get it. Why did they put the fish on the tomatoes?"

"Tomatoes have a short growing season. They're sensitive to frost. But a flounder can survive in ice-cold water because it has a gene that enables it to. Once they found the gene in the fish, they put it into a tomato."

"Em," Lena said. "An antifreeze gene. That must be why the tomatoes I buy at the store taste so good. What's all this got to do with Idaho?"

"Exactly what you said. Tomatoes don't taste good anymore. I can't remember buying one that had any taste at all. Maybe they've already added the flounder gene and we don't know about it yet."

"Where are you going with this, Hank?"

"At least in Idaho you might be able to buy enough land and grow your own."

"Maybe. But my guess is you can grow your own tomatoes anywhere."

"What about the growing season? It's gotta be pretty short in Seattle. It's cold up there. What if I get started and realize I need that fucking antifreeze gene?"

She gave him a long look, saw the glint in his eye, the corners of his mouth bending into his cheeks.

"How many tomatoes do you plan on eating, Hank?"

"Plenty," he said. "As long as I'm not thinking about flounder when I take the first bite."

He started laughing. It was a game. A short break after a long morning spent with a dead body and a view of the world they were paid to see. When they arrived at the college, it would mean another notification. More sadness as the day slipped back into the grim, and darkness sank its heels in.

Lena passed the Rose Bowl and made a left at the light, cutting through another quiet neighborhood burrowed in the hills beneath lush vegetation. About a half mile up, the hill steepened and the real estate gave way to open land, the tall grasses a muted gold swaying in the breeze. As she turned into the entrance and started down the driveway, the San Gabriel Mountains on the other side of the valley appeared to rise up before her eyes. To the east several peaks remained snowcapped in spite of the late season. The view at this height was magnificent.

Lena heard Novak drop the magazine onto the floor and turned back to the driveway, the car rolling over a speed bump. As she glided around the curve, she saw an enormous black building begin to take shape behind the trees. The structure crested the tops of two hills, the road passing beneath it. Lena wasn't sure if it looked like a twenty-five-story building that had flopped down on its side, or a bridge made of black steel and black glass joining the peaks of both hills. All she knew was that she liked it. That the architecture stirred deep-seated memories from her past—who she thought she would be and what she wanted to become a long time ago.

She shook it off, pulling underneath the structure and parking in the visitor lot on the other side. But as they climbed out of the car, she couldn't help taking another look. The entire campus was composed of this single building, balanced on top of the world.

Elvira Gish didn't take well to losing her colleague. They were sitting at a table in the cafeteria. They had given her the bad news fifteen minutes ago, a first-draft sketch of the horror without much detail, and she still appeared shaken to the bone.

"Are you all right?" Novak asked.

Gish looked up from an unopened bottle of spring water, trying to compose herself. "Give me another minute, please."

Lena remained silent for now, studying the middle-aged woman's reaction. Everything about it was the way it should have been, except for the faint glow of anger hidden in her crystalline green eyes.

"Tell me what happened again," Gish said.

Novak lowered his voice. "We've told you everything we can. You worked with Nikki Brant for what—two years?"

"Two years," Gish repeated.

Lena noticed a group of six or seven students watching them from the other side of the room. The recognition in their faces that the news was bad and that the messengers were cops. She turned back to Gish, who couldn't stop fidgeting in her chair. Her hair was a light brown, streaked with gray and drawn behind her back in a loose ponytail. Her face was soft and round, her skin etched with laugh lines around the eyes and mouth. When Lena glanced at Novak, he nodded slowly and reached into his pocket for his notebook and pen.

"The student at the front desk," Lena said. "He told us that you were more than a colleague to Ms. Brant. He told us that you were friends."

"Yes, we were," Gish said.

"Did she ever mention having any trouble with a student or faculty member?"

"Everyone liked Nikki. She was one of the most popular members of our staff."

"And the two of you were close," Lena said. "She confided in you."

"Yes."

"What did you talk about?"

Gish turned toward her, the anger more visible now. "Her husband," she said. "Most of the time we talked about him."

"Was there a problem? Her husband described their marriage as perfect."

"Is that your word or his?"

"His," Lena said. "It's a direct quote."

Gish shifted her weight in the chair as she thought about it. She was tossing something over. Trying to make a decision.

"Nikki wanted to have a family and he didn't," she said finally.

"So they argued about it."

Gish nodded. "Nikki was an orphan and wanted children. She needed to be a mother. It was important to her."

"Lots of people argue. What are you trying to say?"

"I've been married for ten years," Gish said. "This was more than that. He scared her. Nikki was afraid of him."

"Was he abusive? Did he ever hit her?"

"I'm not really sure. About three months ago I saw a bruise. It was on her arm just above the elbow. When I asked her about it, she told me that she fell."

"Did you believe her?"

"At the time I didn't think anything of it. But now I do. Their marriage was about him, not her. At least that's the way it seemed to me."

"Did you ever see any other bruises?"

"The way she dressed. They could've been there and I never would've noticed."

"What about sick days?"

"She loved teaching. I can't remember Nikki ever missing a class."

Lena glanced at Novak, then pulled a card out of her pocket, wrote her name and number down, and handed it to Gish.

"They can't afford to give detectives business cards?" Gish asked.

Lena met her eyes and shrugged. "I've got another question."

The woman nodded, slipping Lena's card into her pocket.

"Did Ms. Brant say she was afraid of her husband? Or is that something you sensed on your own?"

Gish met Lena's eyes, her face hardening. "It's a direct quote."

"When did she say it?"

"Three days ago. After she confirmed her appointment with her gynecologist. I was in her office when she hung up the phone."

Lena tried not to show any emotion. "Would you happen to know her doctor's name?"

Gish nodded and looked down at the table, unable to speak as the reality of what might have happened to her friend seemed to pass over the building like a flock of black crows scouring the valley.

• • •

It was only a hunch, but the fifteen-minute ride to South Pasadena seemed worth it. Novak kept his thoughts to himself, remaining quiet and ignoring the travel brochures piled up by his feet. From the look on his face, Lena doubted that he was thinking about Idaho or Seattle or even tomatoes grown with flounder genes.

Their break was over. Novak may have been a detective, but he was also the father of three daughters.

She pulled up to the light on Orange Grove and made a left on Mission. Three or four blocks later, she spotted the building across the street from a bookstore and turned into the lot. Elvira Gish knew who Nikki's doctor was because they shared the same one. Close to work and not too far from the medical corridor supporting the hospital on Fair Oaks Avenue. Lena was familiar with the neighborhood because her brother had brought her to that bookstore across the street more than once. Book'em Mysteries was one of David's favorite mystery bookshops in the city, and over the years he'd become friendly with the staff. But as they crossed the lot and entered the building, Lena wasn't thinking about her brother.

Dr. Sarah Colletti sat behind her desk, trying to remain professional while they asked about her former patient. Colletti had interrupted her examination schedule without protest the moment they'd walked up to the window at the front desk and explained who they were. She didn't look much older than Lena and probably had a warm, confident smile on most other days. But that was long gone, shut down the moment the door closed and Novak told her that Nikki Brant had been murdered.

"Yes, she was pregnant," Colletti said. "I gave her the news yesterday, and she was thrilled."

The confirmation had a deadening feel to it that weighed down the room. Nikki Brant had been pregnant at the time she was stabbed to death.

"How often did you see her?" Lena asked.

"Once a month in the beginning, then every other week or so. Nikki really wanted a baby. She'd had a couple of false alarms."

Novak back-paged his way through his notebook and stepped in. "Did you ever notice any welts or bruises when you examined her?"

Colletti turned to him but didn't answer.

"A friend told us she noticed a bruise on her arm about three months ago," he said. "You just told us that you saw her as a patient at least once a month. We're wondering if maybe you saw the bruise as well."

The doctor shook her head.

"What about her vagina?" Novak asked.

"I never saw any bruising. No tears or abrasions or indications of rough or forced sex. If you're asking me if Nikki had a problem with her husband, she never mentioned it. When I told her that she was pregnant, she was dancing on air. I prescribed something for her nausea and that was it."

Lena wrote down the name of the prescription, wondering why they hadn't found the pills at the crime scene. "How far along was she?"

Colletti almost broke but caught herself. She pulled a sheet of paper from a file and handed it to her. Novak moved closer for a better look. It was an image from the ultrasound. A picture of a fetus with verifiable fingers and toes, curled up in the womb.

"Ten weeks," Colletti said. "She was hoping for a boy, but it was still too early to tell."

Novak stared at the photograph for a long time, then passed it back to the doctor. On their way through the lobby, Lena heard Colletti tell the receptionist to hold her next exam for another fifteen minutes and watched the doctor close her office door. The front she put up had been a good one, Lena thought. But it didn't take much to know what the doctor would be doing for the next quarter hour. Yesterday afternoon she had the pleasure of telling a young woman that she would be a mother, supporting that dream with pictures from an ultrasound. Today, both were lost in the void. Knocked out and gone.

10

Sixteen hours ago Nikki Brant had stood five feet two inches tall and weighed ninety-eight and one-quarter pounds. Now her small body was laid out on a cold sheet of stainless steel, the ultimate violation complete. Lena watched Lamar Newton take what would be the last photograph of the young woman. When the flash of light died out, the medical examiner moved in, pushing her chest cavity back together and lacing the childlike body up with a heavy black twine as if she were nothing more than an old, worn-out shoe.

Lena checked her notebook, making sure she had written down the main points of the autopsy so she wouldn't have to wait for a report.

The plastic bags that the perpetrator had wrapped around the victim's hands and face would be sent to the lab, but appeared to be a hoax. Pure window dressing. Nothing was found beneath Brant's fingernails. There were no defensive wounds on her palms or wrists, nor was any debris evident when they combed out her hair. Although enough ejaculate was found for DNA analysis, closer examination of her vagina yielded no bruising, rips, or tears.

No physical evidence supported that Nikki Brant had been raped.

Lena underlined the note and turned to the next page. Art Madina, the ME, confirmed what they already suspected by carefully inserting probes into the wounds and taking multiple X-rays. Cause of death came from a knife matching the exact size and shape of the one found in the Brants' dishwater. But the wound in her upper chest hadn't killed her, even though her right lung was punctured. It had been the wound to her abdomen that was ultimately responsible for her death. The twelve-inch blade had been driven upward, severing the aorta and piercing the young woman's heart.

Lena turned away to collect herself. Six autopsies were under way in the same room, the smell of disinfectant and decomposing flesh hitting her like a brick wall. It had been a long day. Removing her mask and safety glasses, she stepped out of her scrubs and left the room without looking at anyone. In the hallway, bodies were lined up on gurneys awaiting their turn. Some were covered in a translucent plastic. Others were laid out with nothing more than a toe tag. Lena shook it off and kept walking.

The wait for the elevator seemed endless—the fluorescent tubes in the hall blinking and buzzing and casting the walls in a sterile light without shadows. When she finally reached the front door, she gave it a hard shove and stepped outside into the chilly, night air. Crossing the lot to the next building, she sat down on the front steps and gazed past the guard shack to the street. An ambulance was speeding up Mission Road on its way to USC Medical Center just next door, its siren blistering the eardrums.

Novak sat down beside her without saying anything. Lena kept her eyes straight ahead, the immediate view reminding her of a third world shanty-town. The people drifting down the sidewalks in this neighborhood were dressed in rags, didn't speak English, and never would. Across the street a fast-food restaurant and a gas station gave way to a bleak industrial setting marred by layer upon layer of graffiti. And rising out of the muck about a mile in the distance was this beautiful city called Los Angeles—its buildings sparkling in the black sky, shimmering in reds and blues and surrounded by white electric beads of light from the thousands of cars stuck in traffic on the freeways. It you weren't trying to get somewhere, L.A. was a knockout.

Lena dug into her bag for a tissue and wiped the Vicks VapoRub away from her nose. In spite of the strong mentholated odor, the smell of death permeating the building had cut through. The scent had a certain density to it that took root in the body and was hard to shake. Lena had attended her share of autopsies before and never found them easy. But the smell was far worse than the view. Days would pass, the odor nearly forgotten, until one morning she might sneeze or cough after a shower and there it was again—

the smell of death lodged in the back of her throat. Nearly forgotten, she thought, but always close enough to taste.

"Give me one of those," Novak said.

She passed him a tissue and watched him wipe the gel away from the base of his nose.

"You know anything about erotic asphyxiation?" he asked.

"You mean the bag over her head."

"The drawer in the kitchen was full," he said. "They had an endless supply."

He flipped open his cell phone, entered a number, and clicked on the speakerphone. Rhodes picked up before either one of them heard a ring.

"Tito and I are still here," he said. "The house is sealed."

"What about Brant?" Novak asked. "How's he holding up?"

"Okay, I guess. He's still with us."

"Anything new?"

"Barrera came out and spent a couple of hours going through the house, then left to get started on the warrants."

Barrera was their lieutenant. He often came to crime scenes and liked to play an active role in as many investigations as he could.

"What else?" Novak asked.

"Their next-door neighbor told us that the perfect marriage wasn't so perfect. They argued a lot and sometimes it got loud."

Novak gave Lena a look and shook his head. "We're hearing the same thing. We need to keep things friendly, Stan, but we've gotta bring him in. You understand how to play it?"

"Got it," Rhodes said. "Keep it friendly. Maybe the piece of shit can help."

Lena thought about the game they were playing. The rules were simple: string Brant out for as long as they could and hope he didn't realize he was a suspect and lawyer up. They had stepped across the line, the investigation following the statistical average now and headed in a loose but single direction. No matter how bizarre, most murders involving a married couple still pointed to the surviving partner. Odds were that Brant had murdered his wife, then tried to make it look like something else with a chef's knife and three grocery bags. And it had almost worked. The way the body had been left. The missing toe that he had probably flushed down the toilet.

"How do you want to handle the interview?" Rhodes asked.

Novak turned to Lena as he considered the question.

"They've spent more time with him than we have," she said. "I'll get started on the murder book."

Novak nodded in agreement. "You hear that, Stan? Lena can fill you in on what we've got when you get downtown."

"See you soon," Rhodes said.

Lena watched Novak return the phone to his belt, her mind drifting back to the moment they showed Brant the Polaroid of his dead wife. The tears. The emotion. What seemed like nothing more than an act now. Last month Jose Lopez had been just as convincing over a period of thirteen hours before finally making the turn and admitting that he'd murdered his wife, Teresa. Now he was awaiting trial at Men's Central Jail. Lena found the building in the skyline. She could remember the rage in Lopez's voice as he spit his words out and confessed to stuffing an entire bath towel down his wife's throat and slashing her neck open with a box cutter from her own utility belt. She could still see the look on the man's face, his eyes burning with emotion as he finally admitted to painting a cross on the bed with his wife's blood and laying her body out as if she had been nailed down. The thought of it rattled Lena's nerves. That first glimpse at what some people were capable of. How they acted when they shed their humanity and poked at the end. She mentioned it to Novak at the time, who called it a warning sign. A sanity check. He told her that if she ever got comfortable working a homicide case, he hoped she had enough sense to quit. Lena wasn't comfortable, nor was she ready to quit.

"I need to ask you a favor," Novak said.

She glanced at her partner without responding. The handcuffs had been removed so that Lopez could sign his statement. Before anyone noticed, the man unzipped his fly and started urinating on Lena's leg. It took a moment before even Lena realized what was happening and the man was pulled away by his own attorney. Welcome to RHD.

"You with me, Lena?" Novak asked.

She nodded. She hadn't felt clean since that night. No matter how hard she scrubbed in the shower, no matter how often or what brand of antibacterial soap she used, she didn't feel entirely clean. Not yet anyway.

"I was gonna take Kristin out to dinner," Novak said. "She called me yesterday and we set it up for tonight."

Novak got to his feet. Lena grabbed her briefcase and they headed down the steps to the car. Kristin was Novak's eldest daughter. Twenty-one years old and the one he seemed to have the most affinity for in spite of her recurrent problems with drugs and alcohol. She had been in and out of rehab since she was sixteen. Novak blamed himself for not being there for her. His divorce and its timing for his daughter's shaky footing. From what Lena had gathered over the last couple of months, Novak and his daughter didn't speak on the phone often and saw each other even less. But things had recently changed. The girl was clean and sober and talking about another try at college. Lena had met her several times and liked her, even though she was a fan of her brother's music and seeing her often reminded Lena of her own loss. But that was Lena's burden, not the girl's.

"What's the favor?" Lena asked.

"We're working," he said. "I could easily bag it. But after all this, I don't want to bag it. I want to see my daughter and make sure she's okay."

"I'd do the same thing. Besides, we've got two teams. Go see her."

Novak raised his hand and she tossed him the keys.

"It'll only be for an hour or two," he said. "There's a new steak house downtown. I was thinking we'd eat there and I could bring you something back."

Lena got into the car, feeling her stomach bottom out. It was 7:00 p.m. They hadn't stopped for lunch, and she knew she needed something to snack on because two hours seemed like a long way off and there was a lot of work to do. But what she really wanted was a cup of hot coffee. Something with more octane than any coffeemaker at Parker Center could provide.

Novak pulled out of the lot, turning left at the light. Within five minutes, the shantytown was lost in the rearview mirror and they were cruising through the city of hopes and dreams. Three blocks from the Glass House, Lena spotted the Blackbird Café and grabbed the door handle.

"Drop me off here," she said.

"It's dark. I was gonna pull up to the front door."

"I want to stop first. My car's still on the Westside."

Novak pulled over. Lena got out, slinging her briefcase over her shoulder. The computer inside was getting heavy, but it didn't matter. The Blackbird served what might be the best cup of coffee in town. She would drink a cup there, she decided, then order another one to go.

"How do you want your steak?" he asked.

Lena didn't need to think about it. "Black and blue," she said, slamming the door closed and hurrying off.

Friday night at the factory. Parker Center or the Glass House. No matter what people called it, the building was a dinosaur. A symbol of the past set in a city that had spent more than four decades driving forward. Pipes leaked, the walls were cracked and paper-thin, and every time Lena plugged something into an outlet, she waited a beat for the lights to pop off.

She didn't like the building, nor did she think it safe.

The Glass House only survived the 1994 Northridge earthquake on paper, she figured. A technicality based on what it would cost the city to tear it down and replace it. Rather than condemn the six-story building with a red tag, city inspectors awarded the structure a yellow tag, meaning that the building had been heavily damaged and might just be unsafe. The city councilwoman who chaired the Public Safety Committee seemed to agree with that assessment, saying that the building would be replaced or renovated in the *reasonable near-term*. But the Northridge earthquake had stopped rumbling more than ten years ago, and no one who worked here, including the new chief, needed an inspection team or a politician to tell them which tag the building really deserved. Civilian employees only saw red and were fleeing. If they couldn't transfer out, they were starting to quit. Lena had no doubt that the next time the ground began to shake, the Glass House would collapse into a pile of rubble. Inspectors filing false reports would no longer be necessary, and all those politicians could finally end their foolhardy debate.

Lena took another sip of hot coffee, trying not to burn her tongue or think about how much time it might take to exit a building from the third floor. The brew was rich and strong and seemed to revive her. She was sitting at her desk, alone on the floor, but grateful for a seat by the window at the back of the room. It was less noisy here and she appreciated the view. RHD was composed of twenty-four desks pushed together in four groups of six. The captain's office was off the alcove down the center aisle behind her. Lieutenant Barrera's desk was at the head of the floor facing the entrance and separated by a partition and two sets of three more desks. It was overcrowded. The furniture was fifty years old. Asbestos had been found in the basement down the hall from the Property Room. Three people who'd worked in the building for more than fifteen years had come down with a rare form of cancer.

Lena looked at the preliminary reports on her desk but started thinking about that idiotic woman on the city council again. When the phone rang, she shook off the bad vibes and picked it up, recognizing the voice at the other end. It was Jimmy Kim, her contact at the phone company. Lieutenant Barrera had come through with the warrant for the Brants' phone records, and she'd spoken with Kim fifteen minutes ago from the Blackbird using her cell.

"I've got the list," he said. "You want me to fax it over, or would you rather use e-mail?"

"E-mail," Lena said. "How much activity was there?"

"They've got two numbers. One for voice and another for data. A call came into the Brants' primary line at nine forty-five last night, only lasting about eight minutes."

"Where from?"

"The number you gave me. Brant's office."

"What about the rest of the night?"

"That's it for the primary line. Just the one call. Nothing else went in or out. I'll send you a hard copy by mail."

"What about the second line?"

"You're in luck," he said. "It's used for data, and it's low-tech. They don't have a DSL line or a cable modem."

Lena had been hoping for this. If the Brants accessed the Internet with either a DSL line or through their cable company, the connection to the Web would always be on. In order to establish the time the computer was used, Lena would have to rely on the Computer Crime Section, which wouldn't reopen until Monday morning.

"It's a dial-up connection," Kim said. "Someone went online at three a.m. last night and didn't shut down until five in the morning."

An e-mail appeared on Lena's computer monitor. When she clicked it open, she saw Jimmy Kim's report. She reached for her coffee and took another sip, unsure if the buzz she felt came from the high dose of caffeine coursing through her body or the shot of adrenaline she picked up from the report. The medical examiner had confirmed what they'd learned in the field, narrowing Nikki Brant's time of death down to 2:00 a.m. The idea that a third-party intruder had spent two hours in the den surfing the Internet after committing the murder seemed ludicrous.

"Thanks, Jimmy," she said. "I've got the report. I owe you one."

"You sure do. It's Friday night, Lena. I don't know about you guys, but I'm going home."

She hung up, leaning back in her chair and wondering how her initial instincts could have been so wrong. The first suspect to be cleared in any homicide case was always the spouse. The first reason, a result of domestic violence. Why hadn't she seen it? Why hadn't Novak or Rhodes?

There was the Simpson case, she thought, but there were others. Too many others.

A case in northern California had been making headlines a little over a year ago. A man stood accused of murdering his pregnant wife and dumping her into the San Francisco Bay on Christmas Day. When the bodies of his wife and unborn child washed up onshore, the case went to trial and a jury found the man guilty. Lena had followed the story from beginning to end, along with just about everyone else in the country. Odds were that Brant was watching, too.

She thought about the Teresa Lopez murder and wondered if Brant got any ideas from that case as well. But there were others. A list so long it seemed unimaginable. Last year in Los Angeles a man had been arrested for an even more grisly night's work. He'd noticed on his phone bill that his wife had made several toll calls to a number outside Oxnard that she couldn't explain. When she told him that she needed to take a business trip and wouldn't return until late Saturday night, he grew suspicious and decided to follow her. Although she checked into a hotel, he tailed her to a ranch and, over two days, witnessed her riding horses with another man. The husband drove home and waited. By the time his wife returned, his rage had worked itself into a red-hot flame and he exploded. He used the bathtub and worked on the body with a carving knife for most of the next day. His plan was to flush her down the toilet. His mistake came when the toilet backed up and he called a plumber. The following day a pickup truck arrived at the crime scene towing a horse trailer. After interviewing the driver, detectives realized that it was the same guy the husband had seen riding horses with his wife. She had been planning to give her husband a special present for his fiftieth birthday, a palomino named Freddie. Rather than having an affair, she had been a savvy customer and wanted to spend two days getting to know the horse.

Lena sensed someone entering the floor and turned away from the window.

James Brant was staring at her as he walked down the center aisle with Sanchez and Rhodes. The interview rooms were off the alcove directly across from the captain's office. As they passed her desk, she tried to read Brant's face and noted his ghostlike appearance. His tears must have evaporated over the day. His eyes had that zombie look—lost and hollow and ice-cold. His mouth was clamped shut, producing a faint sneer.

For some reason Lena remembered the words Novak had used at the crime scene when she'd asked about notifying Nikki Brant's next of kin.

Other than us, he's the only one she's got.

James Brant didn't carry himself much like a family member of a victim anymore. Instead, he looked more like an actor, carrying a pocketful of memories in his wrinkled suit to be used as triggers just in case he needed to perform.

Kristin Novak stopped before Lena's desk, handed her the Styrofoam box from the steak house, and flashed a shy, anxious smile.

"You've brought me dinner," Lena said. "Thanks."

She opened the lid, eyed the steak and salad, and felt that crease working through her stomach again. She was hungry.

"It's a New York," the girl said. "We had the same thing and liked it, so Dad ordered you one without a baked potato."

Novak's desk was right beside Lena's. Slipping his jacket on the back of his chair, he remained on his feet and beckoned her for an update on what he'd missed.

"They're in room two," she said. "Tape's rolling."

"He ask for a lawyer?"

"Not yet."

"Then he hasn't figured it out."

"Maybe," Lena said. "Or he thinks he's smarter than us."

"You've been watching?"

She nodded, glancing at the blue, three-ring binder on her desk with Nikki Brant's name on it. It was the murder book she'd started compiling, sometimes called a blue book. Between bringing a deputy district attorney up to speed over the phone, updating the chronological record, and completing her preliminary reports, she'd slipped up to SID on the fourth floor and taken a look at the monitor. Unfortunately, the interview rooms were not equipped with observation rooms or mirrored glass, so often depicted in the movies or on TV. Once the door closed, the only way to observe an interview in progress was from the camera and mike hidden in the smoke detector mounted on the ceiling.

"What about DNA?" Novak asked.

"Hairs were found in his comb, but Tito got him that coffee this morning and kept the cup. Samples reached the lab before we got to Pasadena. I called to double-check. Barrera made sure everybody at Piper Tech knows it's a rush. We should have the results by Monday afternoon."

Novak seemed pleased by Barrera's assistance. The lab was overwhelmed with work and seriously understaffed. It took months to get results, not days. Lena could remember working a case out of Hollywood in which she'd sent a request for blood samples to be analyzed but didn't receive the results until one year after the suspect's conviction.

"Did you run him through the computer?" Novak asked.

"Two hits for drunk driving while he was a student. Nothing since."

Novak paused a moment, looking at his daughter, then at Lena. "I'll be back in a minute."

He walked off, leaving her with the girl and heading for that monitor on the fourth floor. Ordinarily, Lena wouldn't have minded taking a break and holding the girl's hand. She knew it would be a long night and that she needed to eat something to keep up her strength. Sanchez and Rhodes had been at it for more than an hour. At a certain point, she and Novak would take over, the teams switching back and forth until Brant either wore down or lawyered up. She also knew that for some reason Novak liked seeing her and Kristin together. That he thought it was important for his daughter to connect with others.

But tonight it felt like an imposition. Lena wanted to finish reading SID's preliminary report and think through what their findings implied. In spite of the soft ground, no tracks were found in the garden below the open bedroom window. A study of the parking lot at Rustic Canyon Park yielded no new information. Based on the physical evidence, no obvious point of entry or exit from the crime scene could be determined. From what she'd read so far, SID's conclusion seemed to mirror their own. Either the perpetrator flew through the open bedroom window like a vampire, or he gained access to the house using his keys.

Lena tore open the bag containing a set of plastic utensils and sliced into the steak as the girl watched.

"It looks like they burned it," Kristin said.

"Only on the outside. It's just the way I like it."

Lena took the first bite, the meat so tender she barely needed to chew. As she tasted the salad, the girl leaned against her father's desk. Her movements seemed awkward, her mind visibly racing as if she had something to say but was working from a list.

"Dad said you're busy and I can't stay very long."

"Sounds like a dad to me."

The girl smiled, still nervous, and Lena could feel her measuring her. Kristin had Novak's blue eyes and sandy blond hair. But any physical resemblance to her father ended there. Her face was angular, striking yet innocent. From the few times they'd met, Lena sensed that she'd inherited her father's natural curiosity and intelligence but hadn't had time to refine it. If she could get past her problems with drugs and alcohol, get through her twenties and beyond her parents' divorce, she would probably end up okay.

The girl checked out the room, then turned back. The bureau remained empty and they were alone.

"Can I ask you a question?"

Lena nodded, taking another bite of steak. The girl grabbed her father's chair, wheeled it closer, and sat down.

"How come you work here?"

Lena grinned. "That's a long story."

"I mean what made someone like you want to be a cop?"

"That's even longer. Sometimes things just happen."

"When I was growing up, all my friends hated cops. I was embarrassed about what Dad did."

"When I was growing up," Lena said, "I didn't like anyone I thought might tell me what to do. That's not necessarily bad, you know. And by the way, no one's here to tell you what to do."

"Dad keeps saying that it's better to get it out of your system early. That people who revolt late in life really get screwed."

Lena laughed, guessing that what the girl had just said was a direct quote. "I've never really heard it put that way. But now that you mention it, he's probably right."

The girl fell silent, thinking something over. Lena cut another slice of meat away from the steak, realizing she was almost halfway through. Either the slab of raw meat was smaller than she'd first thought or she was inhaling it.

"Was your brother embarrassed?" Kristin whispered.

The question had a certain sting to it. Lena lowered her plastic fork, the thought of her brother prodding a nerve with deeper roots than hunger.

"I'm sorry," the girl said. "I shouldn't have asked. I was just wondering."

"That's okay." Lena turned to the girl, saw her staring back at her. She was leaning forward with her elbows on the desk, poised for Lena's answer. The question had been an honest one, asked by a curious twenty-one-year-old.

"He thought it was funny," Lena said after a moment. "He used to tease me and call me his personal bodyguard."

"But he was a musician. I have every one of his CDs. I read the story in *Rolling Stone.*"

Lena knew what the girl was straining to get to. Her brother's bohemian lifestyle. His use of drugs. But she wasn't listening anymore. She was thinking about the first day she came home dressed in her uniform. How David laughed when he saw her and hugged her. She found him out by the pool, lounging in a chair with a book and a beer and wearing a tattered pair of jeans. He must have just taken a shower, and she could remember the clean smell of his skin as she held on to him. How he told her that she should take notes and write crime novels the way Joseph Wambaugh, another LAPD cop, had. Her brother had been an avid reader of crime fiction his entire life and named three more cop-turned-mystery-writers he admired. But after an hour, David's imagination kicked in and he suggested they were the perfect brother-rock/sister-cop team to rob banks. For the next three days he ran wild scenarios by her, and all they did was laugh. Then he came up with an idea for the movie version of their exploits that he thought might go over well in France. In the end, like everything else in her brother's life, the story became a song. One of his few ballads. One of his best. Three and a half minutes of music she could no longer listen to.

David hadn't been embarrassed.

Instead, he liked the idea of his sister being a cop, called it outrageous, and kept his worries about her safety to himself. He even attended a department fund-raiser for abused children with her. It was the day Lena had first met Stan Rhodes. A picnic on the lawn at the Police Academy across from Dodger Stadium. She could remember her brother whispering in her ear that he had a joint in his pocket, and laughing at his own joke. She could still see him zeroing in on the homicide detectives, hitting them with questions from all the novels he'd read and listening to their stories. He had a good time, particularly when he found the bar and realized that cops drink beer, too.

"We're up next," Novak said.

Lena surfaced, watching her partner cross the floor. His daughter got out of the chair, rolling it back to her father's desk.

"Sorry, honey," he said. "You're gonna have to split."

"Thanks for dinner, Daddy. Maybe we could get together again next week."

"I'd love to. You know that. Just pick the day."

Lena watched them hug. Then the girl turned and smiled at her.

"Thanks for talking to me, Lena. Hope I didn't say anything wrong. It was great seeing you."

"You, too," she said. "Take care."

She watched Novak walk his daughter out the door to the elevators down the hall, then closed the lid on her steak, thinking about the words *black and blue*. Charred on the outside, but raw underneath. She wondered if the memories she harbored all these years would ever stop. If her skin would ever thicken. She reached for her coffee. What was left tasted bitter and cold. She was ready to meet James Brant, she figured. Pumped and in the mood.

L ena stepped through the alcove, passing the captain's office and entering Room 2.

"Is there anything you need before we get started, Mr. Brant?"

Brant's weary eyes rose from his empty Styrofoam cup, bounced off
Lena, and slid over to Novak closing the door. It was 2:00 a.m. He was
slumped over the wooden table holding his head. He had missed a night's
sleep, was about to miss another, and was showing it.

"I'm fine," he said, slurring his words. "Where did those guys go?"

"They thought you might want something to eat. You've been so helpful,
they thought it was time for a break."

"Then what are you doing here?"

"We just have a few follow-up questions. It won't take long."

Brant lowered his hands. "Come to think of it, I am getting hungry. And
I could use another cup of coffee, too."

"It's on the way," Lena said.

Novak sat down, blocking the door and remaining quiet. Lena glanced
at her notes, intentionally letting the silence take over the room. The mo-
notonous late-night hum of the overhead lights. It was part of the play.
Sanchez and Rhodes had spent an additional four hours working with
Brant, going over the details in a friendly manner and not getting anywhere.
Now it was time to shift gears and see what floated to the surface. Lena had

finished reading SID's preliminary report on the fingerprints picked up at the crime scene. Because it was a Friday, because they only had about six hours during the day to work with the evidence, the findings remained incomplete and covered only a partial sampling of the prints found in the bedroom and bath. Thus far, every print belonged to Brant or his wife. There was no evidence indicating a third party had entered either room.

Brant suddenly laughed. "You think I did it, don't you?"

"What makes you think that?" Lena asked.

"The way you're looking at your notes. And why else would Tito have read me my rights?"

"He does that for everybody, Mr. Brant. He was just doing his job."

"Yeah, I get it. That's why that other guy asked me to take a polygraph. Just doing his job."

"It would've saved time. Why should you be worried? You don't have anything to hide."

Brant nodded, then leaned back in the chair and yawned. As he stretched his arms over his head, Lena realized it was a ploy. He was peeking through his arms for a look at her body. In spite of his wife's murder, he was checking out her boobs.

"You're a beautiful woman, you know that?"

"And you've spilled your coffee."

His eyes followed hers to his wrinkled shirt. He looked at the stain, rubbed it with his thumb, and seemed embarrassed by his disheveled appearance. Smoothing out his jacket, he covered the stain with his palm.

"We've read your statement and found a few discrepancies," she said. "We were hoping you might help us clear them up."

"What discrepancies?"

"Your marriage. You called it perfect and we're trying to understand why."

"But it was," he said.

"From what we've heard, it sounds more rocky than that."

Brant straightened up in the chair and tried to focus. "Who have you been talking to?"

"Friends and neighbors."

"Do me a favor and tell my friends and neighbors to go fuck themselves. What are we doing here anyway? Why are you wasting time on me? That guy's still out there."

"Which guy is that, Mr. Brant?"

He sat back and shook his head in disbelief. "The sick bastard who did this. He's out there and we're in here. How stupid is that?"

"Then let's go upstairs and take the polygraph."

He shook his head, unwilling to move. Lena remained quiet, waiting the man out. It was a small room with poor air circulation, and she imagined the walls were beginning to close in on him now.

"Okay, so maybe it wasn't perfect," he said finally. "Maybe if you were watching from the outside, we had our moments. From where I stood, it was still good for both me and her. Real good."

"What did you fight about?"

His eyes stirred. "They weren't fights. They were discussions."

"Okay," Lena said. "Then what did you discuss?"

"Nikki wanted kids."

"And you didn't."

He turned to Novak as if trying to recruit an ally. "Why is she putting words in my mouth?"

Novak stared back at the man, his eyes steady but dead, not saying anything for a long time. When he finally spoke, his voice was so restrained that Lena felt a slight chill.

"She's not putting words in your mouth, Mr. Brant. Detective Gamble asked you a simple if not obvious question. You've already told Detectives Sanchez and Rhodes that you can't think of anyone who would want to hurt you or your wife. No one at work. No one you knew. We thought you wanted to help us find out what happened. It's in your best interest to help us find out what happened. It's in everyone's interest that you assist us any way you can."

Brant quickly looked away from the detective as if he might be dangerous. Clearly, Novak was holding in his anger at considerable effort.

Lena cleared her throat before continuing, "She wanted a family and you didn't."

"Whoever told you that is a liar. I knew where Nikki was at. I knew why she wanted it so bad. You think I'm an idiot? It was all about money. We couldn't afford to have a family. We needed to wait until the deal went through. I wasn't sure I'd still have a job, and my paycheck only covers gas and groceries."

"Your boss seems to think a lot of you. Why would you be worried about losing your job?"

"My boss wouldn't be making the decision. We're merging with a Fortune 500 company based in Chicago. That's two thousand miles away. All I'll be is a number. Numbers don't have faces. They come and go."

"But you're going to benefit from the merger."

"So what? Everybody is."

"How much money will you receive in back pay?"

"I haven't had time to add it up."

Lena smiled. "In other words it's a lot of money and you're afraid to tell us how much."

"I haven't had time to add it up. And it won't be that much. Not enough to cover my place in the unemployment line."

"Did you know your wife was pregnant?"

Brant didn't bat an eye. He should have, but he didn't.

"Where's that coffee?" he asked.

Lena repeated the question, then watched him think it over. After a few moments, he slid down on the seat and sighed with resignation.

"Yeah, I knew," he said. "I knew, but I didn't know. I've been thinking about it all day. Nikki had been acting weird for almost two weeks—hinting at it but not saying anything."

"Then she didn't tell you directly. She didn't say anything when you called last night from the office."

"No. When I called, she just told me she was going to bed."

"For a man who's just learned that he was about to be a father, you're not showing much emotion."

"That's because I'm having such a wonderful day."

"Why did you give your assistants the night off?"

He smiled. "So I could go home and kill my wife."

"Do you think this is funny, Mr. Brant?"

"No. I think it's a fucking waste of time."

"Why did you give them the night off?"

"Everyone was tired and they were screwing up. I knew we'd be working the weekend. I thought they needed a decent night's rest."

"What did you do when they left?"

"I tried to get something done, but must've lost it. I woke up in my desk chair."

"What time was that?"

"Around five. I woke up and drove home."

"What about your sex life?" Lena asked. "How would you describe it?"

"On a scale of one to ten?"

"How would you describe it?"

He thought it over and flashed a lazy smile. "Perfect."

Lena ignored the jab. "Describe perfect."

"Perfect is a world where this kind of bullshit doesn't happen. If you think I get my rocks off covering my wife's face with a trash bag, then you can stick it up your ass."

"When was the last time you had sex with your wife?"

He shook his head. That smile was back.

"Last weekend," he said. "About seven in the morning before I went back to work. If I remember correctly, she was on top and I sucked her tits."

"Then the seminal fluid found at your house isn't your own?"

His eyes lost their focus as he considered the question. He glanced at the ceiling briefly, then back at Lena.

"No, Detective. The cum found at my house isn't my own. If it was, we wouldn't be here."

He reached into his pocket for a pack of cigarettes and lit one. When he tapped the ash into an empty Styrofoam cup with his right hand, Lena noticed that he was trembling. Novak glanced at the smoke detector and cracked the door open. Then she checked her notes, deciding to move on.

"Do you like to play around, Mr. Brant? Do you have a girlfriend on the side? Maybe someone at the office?"

"You're really good, you know that. You think I'm like that guy in the papers."

"What guy in the papers?"

"The one that killed his wife because she was pregnant. You think I'm just like that."

"Were you keeping up with the story?"

He nodded, blowing smoke out the side of his mouth. "They say that when he threw her into the bay, she was eight months pregnant. That her body decomposed and that's what caused the birth. There's a name for it."

"It's called a coffin birth."

"That's it," he said. "A coffin birth."

His eyes glazed over. Lena took a moment to get a read on him. He was smart, tough, seemingly impenetrable.

"How often did you hit your wife, Mr. Brant?"

The smile finally vanished, along with the attitude. Brant stared at her without responding.

"It's a simple question," she said. "You seem to have answers for everything else."

She glanced at the coffee stain on his shirt just long enough for him to notice. When he did, he quickly covered the spot with his free hand.

"I never touched her."

"That's not true," she said. "We know about the bruise on her arm because people saw it. How often did you hit her?"

He looked away, trying to avoid her eyes. "Just that one time," he whispered.

"Just that one time," Lena repeated. It had been a guess, but somehow she knew. "According to the medical examiner your wife weighed ninety-eight pounds. You look like you're about two-thirty. Did you hit her with a closed fist?"

He started to nod, then caught himself. "It was a mistake. I didn't mean to do it."

"I'm sure you didn't. Did you seek counseling?"

"I didn't need to. All I had to do was remember the way she fell. She wouldn't let me help her up. And there was that bruise on her arm, but there were bigger bruises on her shoulder and hip. They didn't heal for six weeks. I could see them every time she got in the shower."

Novak leaned forward, clasping his hands on the table. "You're right, kid. It all sounds so perfect."

Brant's eyes shut down, narrowing into two tight beams of darkness. When he dropped the cigarette into the empty cup, Lena heard the head fizzle out.

"Fuck you," he said, pointing his finger at Novak. "I loved her, and when I hit her, it was a mistake. People shouldn't judge other people by their mistakes. A mistake only happens once. That's why it's called a mistake."

"Do you consider murder a mistake?" Novak asked.

Brant jumped to his feet and lunged toward him. When Novak gave him a hard push back into the chair, he started screaming.

"Who the hell do you two think you are? I've done everything I can to help. Now I want my fucking lawyer."

He said it. The magic words.

Now I want my fucking lawyer.

Lena got up from the table. "Who's your attorney, Mr. Brant?"

"Buddy Paladino."

Buddy Paladino opened the glass door to the captain's office and flashed that million-dollar smile. It was a big, wide-open spread that exposed his capped teeth and had become the man's trademark. Lena guessed that over the past decade that smile appeared in every newspaper in the country, every cable channel on TV. The gesture wasn't really directed at anyone in particular. Instead, Paladino flashed his dental work at anyone and everyone who looked his way. It was a smile, but it was also a warning, like a domesticated animal that appears tame but bites just as you reach down to pet it.

"Have you had a chance to speak with your client?" Barrera asked from behind the captain's desk.

"I have, Lieutenant," Paladino said in a smooth and creamy voice. "I have."

"Then take a seat."

The entire team had been waiting with Lieutenant Barrera in the captain's office for over an hour, along with Roy Wemer, the deputy district attorney assigned to the case. Captain Dillworth was away on an early vacation, cruising the Mediterranean with his wife in anticipation of murder season, which usually got under way in June. But even when the captain was in town, his office was regularly used by detectives and never locked. The only conference table on the third floor was in this office, the end of the table pushed against the front of his desk. And the homicide logs were here—a library of bound ledgers summarizing every murder that occurred in the county dating back to the nineteenth century. Lena found these books fascinating. Over the past two months, she'd examined the logs whenever she had a few minutes' downtime or decided she needed a break. The books were split into two sections, the first amounting to a list of homicides kept in chronological order and filled in by hand. Beside the victim's name was a page number referencing the case summary. The summaries were no longer than a paragraph or two, detailing the major components of the crime. And every time Lena read one she was reminded of how much the world had changed. How neurotic things were becoming with the march of progress in the so-called Technological Age. Between 1899 and 1929, the entire homicide log filled a single book. By the 1960s, a new volume was required for each year.

Buddy Paladino entered the room.

Lena watched the defense attorney settle into the open chair at the head of the conference table. His dark hair was cropped short and combed so neatly it could have been painted on his narrow skull with an airbrush. His suit and shirt were obviously handmade. She noted the manicured fingernails, the silk tie and gold watch, trying to calculate how much money it might take to get Buddy Paladino dressed and ready for the world every morning.

More than the value of her car, she figured. Maybe twice that.

It was 10:00 a.m. Saturday morning. Paladino had returned to Los Angeles from San Francisco on the first plane out. He arrived at Parker Center an hour and fifteen minutes ago, ordered coffee and croissants for his client, then closed the door to Room 2. Now he sat before them with his legs crossed, beaming from head to toe like a man who thrived on having an audience. Any audience, Lena imagined. Even a room stacked heavy with cops.

Buddy Paladino had made his mark as a criminal defense attorney after the 1992 riots. Most of his clients in the early days were underdogs. Most of his cases, pure fiction. He began by targeting the department and soaking the taxpayers for hundreds of millions of dollars in damages. Although his courtroom antics were oftentimes outrageous, his techniques were flawless. A rumor was circulating through the department that Harvard Law School was devoting an entire course to his work next year and calling it "Precision: A Trial Attorney in the Real World."

Once Paladino started to make headlines, however, he switched gears and began representing only those clients who could afford his burgeoning fees. Lena remembered reading about a case he handled five or six years ago. A college student stood accused of plowing his car through a crowd of people on a street that was shut down for Octoberfest. Three people died, fifteen more were injured, and a blood test indicated that the boy behind the wheel was using PCP. A bystander recorded the crime on videotape, and more than ten witnesses, including the student's roommate, claimed the act had been deliberate. But the boy's father was the CEO of TEC Energy Group and started writing checks payable to Buddy Paladino the night his son was arrested. In spite of the evidence, Paladino zeroed in on the car and its maintenance history. The mechanic owned a successful business but was a reformed alcoholic, and the attorney used his frequent meetings with a recovery group to destroy the man's good reputation. Once Paladino tainted the car his client was driving, he focused on the condition of the street and a pothole that seemed particularly deep. When he was finished, the crime had the feel of an act of God, and the jury delivered a not-guilty verdict to the surprise of no one but the families of the victims. Two years later when the boy's father stood accused of redirecting money earmarked for the pension fund to an account in the Bahamas, Paladino got him off as well with nothing more than a fine. A large fine, worthy of headlines on most business pages, but one the man could easily afford.

Buddy Paladino was a special kind of attorney, and his presence in the room made Lena feel uncomfortable. He was slippery, but he was also extremely smart. No matter how good a case might seem on paper to the prosecution, Paladino was a genius at finding the loose end, unraveling it before a jury, and making everyone look like a fool.

He cleared his throat, his dark eyes sparkling as he ignored DDA Wemer and directed his full attention to Lieutenant Barrera.

"I've had a chance to speak with the young man," he said. "Yes, I have. And I've read that statement you good people took down before he had the benefit of conferring with an attorney, which is his legal right."

Barrera cut in, "Wait a minute, Counselor. He waived his rights and we've got it on videotape. When he asked for an attorney, we made the call. That was seven hours ago."

"Yes, yes," Paladino said. "It's unfortunate that I was in San Francisco when I received the message. My flight was delayed because of fog. You have my apology, Lieutenant. All of you do."

Lieutenant Frank Barrera's approach to life was straightforward. He began his career in uniform, rose in the department by avoiding politics as best he could and downplaying the petty games that went with it. He was fair-minded, a good judge of character, and from what Lena could tell, had the support and respect of the detectives he supervised. But Frank Barrera was a busy man and liked people who got to the point. Buddy Paladino was a ball-room dancer—a magician—who may have risen from the streets but had also mastered the art of the shell game. From the guarded expression on Barrera's face, it seemed to Lena that her supervisor had already lost his patience and was repulsed. Still, Lena had never seen Paladino in real life before and couldn't keep her eyes off him.

"Is there a problem with the way your client has been treated?" the DDA asked.

"I'm not exactly sure, Mr. Wemer. I'm just not sure. Mr. Brant told me that he waived his rights because he thought he was assisting with the investigation, not a person of interest. The young man didn't believe he was a suspect and wanted to do everything he could to help."

Paladino stressed the word *help,* glancing at Lena. Had he been wearing a hat, she was sure he would have tipped it.

"Then what's the problem, Counselor?" Barrera asked.

Paladino cleared his throat again. "It seems the young man wants a polygraph test."

No one said anything for a long time. Barrera and Wemer smiled, and so did Paladino, though in a different way. But not Lena. And when she traded quick looks with Novak and Rhodes, they weren't smiling either. Something was going on. Something they weren't aware of or missed. She had never heard of a defense attorney agreeing to a polygraph performed by the police without first hiring an expert and trying it out on his own. Particularly an attorney of Paladino's stature and experience.

"I've advised him against it, of course," Paladino said. "But he insists. It seems the young man thinks he's innocent of all charges. He'd like to clear

up any discrepancies there might be between his statement and the statements of others. He'd like to dot the i's and cross the t's, so to speak. I never
had the pleasure of meeting his wife, Lieutenant, but I understand that she
was quite lovely. Everyone in this room knows exactly what will happen
when the press picks up on this most unfortunate situation, particularly in
light of its similarity to other crimes of the same nature making headlines
these days. The young man would like the story to include the fact that he's
not hiding from anything or anyone. Far from it, he's doing everything he
can to cooperate with you good people and help find the poor soul who actually perpetrated this egregious crime."

Paladino was slippery. For some inexplicable reason Lena thought about
her car. It needed an oil change.

"The investigation is just getting started," Barrera said evenly. "Mr.
Brant has the opportunity to lower our suspicions. Taking a polygraph
would be a great help."

"I'm sure you realize, Lieutenant, that based on the evidence you have at
this time, you have no right to hold Mr. Brant against his will. That his
presence and participation is a voluntary act on his part. And that after the
test, he will walk through that door with me no matter what the outcome."

Barrera's eyes flicked to the door and back. When he nodded, Lena
thought the gesture appeared tentative.

"When can you be ready?" Paladino asked.

"It's Saturday," Barrera said. "We'll have to bring someone in."

"Two hours," Novak said.

Paladino checked his gold watch and looked back at Barrera. "Noon," he
said. "We'll be ready at noon then."

Paladino flashed that smile again, then rose from the chair and slithered
out. Lena watched him cross the alcove, heading toward the interview
rooms. When he shut the door to Room 2, Barrera shook his head and
slapped the captain's desk.

"I need a fucking bath," he said. "What's an accountant doing with a
slime-bag lawyer like Paladino?"

"It turns out that Paladino knows the family," Rhodes said.

"Brant's father," Sanchez added. "They grew up together."

Barrera turned to Novak. "Why do you think Brant's changed his mind
and wants the polygraph?"

"Maybe he thinks he can beat it."

"You better make sure he's not on anything."

DDA Wemer got out of his chair and started pacing by the window. He was a small, wiry man who had spent ten years as a prosecutor. They were working together on the Lopez case as well. As far as Lena knew, he hadn't yet made a name for himself. When Wemer turned to Novak, he looked drained and particularly worried.

"You're absolutely sure you've got the right man?" he asked.

Novak shrugged. "There's a history of abuse pointing to motive. We found no signs of forced entry. There's evidence to support that the victim wasn't raped and knew the doer. That the doer spent at least three hours in the house after the murder, and that the murder weapon wasn't brought in from the outside. Brant offered an alibi, but we picked it apart and what's left doesn't make sense and can't be verified."

"It's worse than that," Rhodes said. "The doer attempted to wipe his semen off the dead body. If he'd come from the outside and was concerned about his DNA, he would've worn a condom. Instead he made the decision to clean her up after the fact."

Barrera sat back in his chair, thinking it over. "The blood work comes in on Monday?"

"Late afternoon," Novak said. "If we're lucky."

"What about fingerprints?"

"It's early," Novak said. "We've only had time to compare the prints in two rooms, but there's no evidence of a third party."

"So what you're saying is that we can't hold him until Monday. You heard Paladino. They're out of here this afternoon no matter what. How bad's it gonna be when he walks?"

While they had waited for Paladino to show up, Lena met with Lamar Newton and added the crime scene photos to the murder book. Now she opened the binder and laid it out on the desk. Barrera flipped through the pages with Wemer, eyeing the collection of images from yesterday's visit to hell. Nikki Brant's childlike body lying in a sea of blood. Her face poking through the rip in the grocery bag. Her breasts disfigured with bruises, and the semen wiped away from the sheet between her open legs.

"He's a possible flight risk," Lena said. "He's no longer showing any remorse. His behavior appears erratic and unpredictable."

Barrera reached the shot of the victim's missing toe and pushed the binder away. "What's wrong with these guys? Why don't they just get a fucking divorce?"

It may have been the question of the century, Lena thought, but no one said anything. No one in the room had an answer.

"Who do you guys want to call in for the polygraph?" Barrera finally asked.

"Cesar Rodriguez," Rhodes said.

Novak agreed. "If they're trying to beat it, Cesar gets the call."

"Then get him in here in a hurry," Barrera said. "I want to get this over with before these shit heads change their minds."

Lena watched Brant step out of the men's room. His eyes were clear, his face washed. In spite of his rumpled clothing and two-day beard, he looked remarkably fresh.

"My client's ready," Paladino announced.

She didn't react or say anything as they walked down the hall to the elevators. It was 6:25 p.m., more than six hours after the time they agreed upon, and Lena now considered herself immune to the real-life aura of Buddy Paladino.

The attorney had been stalling since noon with a variety of excuses.

At first she thought the delay might be a legitimate attempt by Paladino to talk his client out of taking the polygraph. Brant was under no obligation, and the results could easily be more damaging than not taking the test at all. But an hour ago Lena had finally lost her patience, convincing SID to switch the camera back on in the interview room. When the tech walked out, her hand *inadvertently* knocked against the audio button and up came the sound.

Paladino was seated at the table, conducting an interview over his cell phone while sipping a Coke and adjusting his $300 tie. His client was sprawled out on the floor, mouth open and eyes closed, in what looked like a deep, untroubled sleep.

It had been a waiting game. A play. The entire day had been wasted so that Paladino could frame his story in the media and give his client a chance to rest.

Half an hour later, the attorney stepped out of the interview room insisting that the test be conducted in a neutral setting, the battery on his cell phone apparently dead. But it was another game. When a brief tour of Parker Center yielded nothing close to neutral, Paladino finally agreed that the test should be conducted in one of the regular examination rooms on the fourth floor. Not that Cesar Rodriguez, the forensic psychophysiologist who got the call, would particularly have minded. His equipment was digital, amounting to a computer, two rubber tubes with bellows that calculated a subject's respiratory rate, a simple cuff to measure heart rate and blood pressure, and two finger plates to assess skin moisture. A notebook version of the package was completely portable and easily fit inside a briefcase. The test could be performed anywhere.

Lena escorted the men into the examination room, introducing them to Cesar Rodriguez, who shook their hands and greeted them with an affable smile. Rodriguez was of average height and had a quiet, almost fatherly way about him that seemed to set people at ease. Over the years he'd examined thousands of subjects. He was methodical, liked to explain the process as he went along, and had a reputation of becoming a subject's advocate if he thought the test revealed a lack of deception.

But he was also known for being extremely thorough. And he had to be, Lena thought, because of the countermeasures some people used when trying to beat the test. Antiperspirant sprayed on the fingertips to prevent sweating, antihistamines or sedatives to raise or lower blood pressure, tacks placed in shoes and stepped on after every question to equalize the physiological response. Ever since corporations started using polygraph tests on employees, Web sites had sprung up on the Internet detailing countermeasures for anyone with a problem who might be facing the box.

Rodriguez pointed to the chair on the other side of his workstation, removing his glasses and digging into his pocket for a handkerchief. The room wasn't much bigger than an interview room but was decidedly more comfortable. The lights were on a dimmer switch. The subject's chair was padded and reclined.

"We'll spend an hour or so just getting to know each other," Rodriguez said to Brant. "This is your chance to tell me about yourself. Your chance to tell me your side of the story, James."

Brant slid into the chair, visibly anxious but determined.

"After we get to know each other, I'll make up a list of questions. The list will be short. Ten, maybe fifteen questions at the most. Then we'll go over each one before the test until both of us feel comfortable."

"Before the test?"

"The way we phrase the questions is as important as the questions themselves."

Brant appeared confused. Rodriguez huffed on a lens and wiped it dry.

"Let's say I asked someone if they ever used cocaine, James. Let's take it even further. Let's say I asked them a blanket question like that and they said no because they really never had. But let's say the question triggers a memory. Two years ago they saw friends use the drug at a party. In this setting just the thought of that party makes them feel uneasy. If we didn't talk about it first, if I didn't know about that experience and rephrase the question, there's a good chance the result would be a false positive. In other words, they answered the question truthfully, but it read like they didn't. That wouldn't help anyone. See what I mean?"

Brant nodded, eyeing the computer on the table. Rodriguez slipped his handkerchief into his pocket and continued.

"We won't do the actual test until we've gone over each question and determined your comfort level. And then we're ready. I ask the questions, you answer them as best you can, and we're done. It's as simple as that, James. So why don't you slip out of those shoes and relax."

Brant reached down for his laces.

"I'd like a chance to review those questions," Paladino said.

Rodriguez ushered the attorney and Lena out of the room.

"You will, Counselor, you will. When we're finished, it would be my pleasure to print you out a copy of the results."

Rodriguez smiled and closed the door. For the next two hours, he and Brant would be working alone. Lena turned to Paladino as they stood there, surprised by the faint presence of fear she saw in the attorney's eyes. It lasted for only a split second, but it was there. A momentary scratch in the man's polish and a measure of the risk he was taking. Then the attorney shrugged, excusing himself and heading briskly down the hall toward the elevators.

Lena chose the opposite direction, using the stairs. As she entered the bureau floor and sat down at her desk, Rhodes gave her a look from the other end of the room. He was speaking in a low voice to someone on the phone. Probably his girlfriend. Lena nodded back at him and turned away, fighting off a yawn.

The bureau was empty.

Barrera and Wemer had left after their initial meeting, requesting the results from the polygraph once the exam was completed. Novak and Sanchez were making a food run and hadn't balked when Lena asked for two cups of coffee from the Blackbird Café. She thought they might. In spite of its proximity to Parker Center, the Blackbird wasn't exactly a cop hangout. The café catered to artists migrating downtown as loft space became more available. Musicians mostly, seeking a quiet place to sip coffee and talk in subdued lighting. Lena had never entered the café without catching a hint of grass wafting from the alley, but always ignored it. She wasn't sure how Novak or Sanchez might react, though they seemed well aware of the café's reputation and knew they would be spotted as cops the moment they stepped through the door.

She checked her watch, guessing they wouldn't return for another ten minutes. Fighting off another yawn, she realized that she had been up for almost forty hours. The length of most people's workweek. She needed something to keep her mind occupied while she waited on the caffeine fix. Something to beat back the sleep weighing down her eyelids. As she settled into her chair, she looked at the murder book with Nikki Brant's name on it. But another blue binder was leaning against her computer monitor, similarly labeled, though with a different victim's name.

Teresa Lopez.

The case still merited pause. The condition of the body when they'd found it still seeped into her dreams. Teresa Lopez had been employed for ten years by Global Kitchen & Bath, a plumbing supply store located three miles from her home in Whittier along the San Gabriel River. Her husband, Jose, drove a bus for the city and claimed early on that he had been delayed at work on the night of the murder.

But a polygraph hadn't been necessary to turn Jose around. Proof of his wife's infidelity had finally broken him down. The statements they showed him during the interview from numerous men Teresa worked with claiming that she liked to fool around. Rumors of several affairs she had with other men from their neighborhood who refused to come forward. A lab report indicating that the cum they found inside his wife was from a third party. An eyewitness who stated that he saw her lover leap from the bedroom window when Jose returned home from work earlier than expected. The man seen running away was thought to be Teresa's manager at Global Kitchen & Bath, Terrill Visconte. Unfortunately, Visconte was married, and Lena held little hope that he would cooperate with them before the trial. At the crime scene they found Beethoven's Symphony No. 6 in the CD player on the bedside table, along with a copy of *The Times*. The crossword puzzle was partially filled in. During an interview at the plumbing supply store, Visconte acknowledged that while he liked music, even puzzles, he wasn't about to ruin his marriage and admit to something he hadn't done over a piece of music or a stupid word game.

In the end, they probably wouldn't need his statement.

Lopez had confessed, and Lena could still remember the moment he did as if it had happened that very day. They were sitting in Room 1 with Lopez and his attorney. Novak pulled a crime scene photo out of the murder book and threw it down on the table. As Jose stared at the picture of his wife lying on the bed with her throat slashed, Novak told him that the case was simple. As old as time itself. Teresa Lopez was a beautiful woman full of life, and that night Jose caught her with another man. When he realized the rumors were true, when he saw with his own eyes that his wife was a whore, his anger reached a fever pitch and he blew.

It happened in a heartbeat, Novak told the man.

Lopez was caught in an emotional overload, caught in a rush of despair, and so it was no wonder he lost control. It was a crime of passion, and his wife had committed a great sin. Something anyone who was married could understand. That was why he used the box cutter from her tool belt and painted the cross on the sheet with her own blood.

16

Buddy Paladino eyeballed the graph on Cesar Rodriguez's computer, working on his game face but looking more like a man who was just struck by lightning. He remained silent, huddled with the others around Rodriguez's chair at the workstation as he took the jolt.

Lena didn't need to see the monitor to know that Brant had failed the polygraph. She could tell the outcome the moment Rodriguez opened the examination room door. It was written in his body language. The way his eyes appeared to be poking through his glasses and bumping off the ground.

"Mr. Brant didn't miss a question here or there," Rodriguez was saying. "He spiked out on every single one."

Paladino grimaced, his gaze riveted to the screen. As Rodriguez continued, Lena glanced through the doorway at Brant, fidgeting in a chair at an empty desk in the room across the hall. Unaware that he was being watched, he seemed preoccupied with that coffee stain on his shirt, and she thought he might even be talking to himself. After a while, he gave up on the stain and opened a bottle of spring water.

As he took a long swig, Lena tried to reconcile the differences between the man she'd met yesterday morning with the one she was staring at now. When she showed him that photo of his wife, he was upset, a grieving husband. Even though most murders of a spouse still pointed to the surviving partner, the crime had been horrific enough, even strange enough, that Lena had thought it would end in a much different way. She remembered sitting on the steps at Rustic Canyon Park, her first thought upon entering the bedroom and seeing the corpse—the idea that only a madman could have committed this murder.

But then she found the drops of semen in the den, and Rhodes discovered the murder weapon in the dishwasher. Brant's alibi fell apart, his wife's colleague opened the door to spousal abuse over an unwanted pregnancy, and Lena caught Brant in a lie during their interview. Thinking it over, she realized that she didn't want Brant to be the one. That she secretly hoped he wasn't the one as each new piece of the puzzle fell into place. This was a crime on the list of many other crimes that didn't need to happen. Brant may have been prone to domestic violence but, like Jose Lopez, was not a psychopath and could have taken a time-out and sought counseling. He could have walked away.

She looked back at the man, struck by an overwhelming feeling of disappointment. As he drained the bottle of water and tossed it in a nearby trash can, she studied his face, comparing it with the face of the man who had been found guilty of dumping his pregnant wife into the San Francisco Bay. Outward appearances yielded nothing, she thought. In both cases, they could have been neighbors, friends, even relatives, and Lena would never have guessed what was really going through their minds. She wondered at what point in their lives they crossed the line. She wondered what the experience might have been that set them off. How their thought processes worked from thinking about the crime to actually performing it. How much time they spent wondering if others could read what they were thinking.

It defied explanation, yet it was there. James Brant thought he could beat the box but failed.

"What about the control questions?" Paladino blurted out.

Lena turned away from the door and moved in beside Novak. Rodriguez was scrolling forward on the time line.

"Here's the first control question," he said, pointing at the screen. " 'Have you ever stolen anything?' Your client answered yes, and you can see his lack of response. His blood pressure and heart rate, everything remains stable. He stole candy from a drugstore as a child and answered truthfully."

Paladino shrugged it off. "So did everybody else. What came next?"

" 'Have you ever been arrested for anything other than drunk driving?' "
Rodriguez said. "He answered no, and again there's no sign of deception.
There's no overt physiological response."

"I should have been given the opportunity to review the questions before
they were asked."

"I'm sorry, Counselor, but I understand why you're disappointed with
the results. Every time I repeated a question specific to the crime, I got the
same response. Look at his perspiration level jump when I asked him if he
ever struck his wife."

"How did you phrase the question?"

" 'Other than last January, have you ever hit your wife?' Your client answered no. It's a fair question and it's specific enough to exclude the incident
he mentioned in his statement. If we dig into his past, I think you'll find a
history of spousal abuse. I think we'd learn that he struck his wife several
times. Look at his heart rate and blood pressure. When I asked if he murdered her, they're off the chart."

Paladino's anger was out in the open now. "Hey, wait a minute. This test
was performed on a computer, not a polygraph instrument."

"It's digital," Rodriguez said. "It's more accurate than an analog system."

"What if there's a software problem?"

Lena looked at Novak and caught the faintest of smiles. Paladino was
doing Paladino, dancing his way through another shell game as if getting
ready for court.

"This equipment is working perfectly," Rodriguez said.

"Maybe it is," the attorney said. "But maybe it isn't. I can't tell because
I'm not an expert in computer science. All I know is that I see a heart rate
and some indication that my client is breathing. But can this machine detect
a lie?"

Everyone remained quiet.

Rodriguez narrowed his eyes. "You know the answer to that question
without asking, Counselor."

Paladino shook his head. "All I know is that there's a reason why the
ACLU calls this stuff voodoo science."

"Call it what you want, Counselor, but your client was most likely attempting to be deceptive when he answered these questions. If you'd like a
copy of the results, I'd be happy to print them out."

Paladino flashed that vicious smile of his, stepping away from the table and checking his watch. "I'll take a pass on that, Mr. Rodriguez. Unless there's any objection, I think I'll show my client the door."

He waited a beat with his back turned. When no one said anything, he stepped into the hall. Lena's eyes flicked to Brant, sitting at the desk in the other room, trying to get a read on him. Their eyes met and she realized that Brant had been staring at her.

"Let's get out of here," Paladino said.

Brant looked away from her and jumped to his feet, his face flooding with relief. Lena watched with the others as Brant exited the section with his attorney and vanished around the corner. When she heard the elevator open and close, she glanced at Sanchez and Rhodes, then turned to her partner, still staring through the doorway.

"He's loose," Novak said. "He's free."

The marine layer was so thick, the night so dark, Lena couldn't see the ocean as they made a right on West Channel and started working their way into the hills. Sanchez lived at the beach in Playa Del Rey and had offered to give Lena a lift back to the crime scene where she'd left her car. The clock on the dash read 10:15 p.m., but as she looked out the windshield at the bright wall of fog, it felt later than that. Maybe two or three days later.

She had reached the point where caffeine no longer had an effect. The entire team had, and she wondered how Sanchez was managing the narrow road. He looked exhausted and hadn't said a word for the last twenty minutes. As she thought it over, she realized that he had been quiet for most of the day. While they'd waited on Paladino, she'd seen Sanchez walk away from his desk two or three times with his cell phone.

Sanchez made a left on Oak Tree and rolled over the wooden bridge. Idling past the death house without looking at it, he pulled over and stopped behind Lena's car.

"You okay driving, Tito?"

"Sure, Lena. How 'bout you?"

"I'm good," she said. "But you've been pretty quiet."

He paused a moment, thinking it over. "Problems at home."

"Bad?"

"Bad enough."

Lena knew that Sanchez was three years in on his second marriage. She had never met his wife but heard that they were particularly close.

"I love my work," he said. "And I love my wife. It pisses me off sometimes when I think maybe I can't have both."

"She doesn't like the long hours."

He laughed. "She'd be happier with a nine-to-fiver, but she'll get over it. She always has. One night with a banker and she'd be crying foul." His eyes moved to the clock. "I better drag my ass home."

Lena grabbed her briefcase and climbed out, watching him turn the car around. As the taillights faded into the night, she spotted the parking tickets on her windshield. There were three, stacked neatly beneath the wiper. Fighting off the urge to tear them up, she stuffed the tickets into her briefcase and glanced through the fog at the death house. She could barely see it and was about to turn away when she noticed the light in the trees.

It was a beam of light, rippling across the treetops, then vanishing into the backyard. She kept her eyes on the canopy, wondering if the stray shaft of light wasn't from Sanchez's car as he made the turn and drove back down the hill on the other side of Rustic Canyon Park. But when the beam reappeared, the path it cut was too narrow and jittery to be from any car.

Someone was on the property.

She popped open the trunk, dumped her briefcase inside, and grabbed a flashlight without turning it on. Legging it down the street, she stopped before the house and listened. She could hear her heart beating, the sound of the stream behind her, but nothing else. Only silence coming from the back of the house, and the sight of that intermittent light jiggling overhead.

She stepped beneath the crime scene tape, walked to the end of the drive, and started into the yard.

She moved slowly, one step at a time, estimating her range of vision through the fog at less than twenty yards. When she reached the backyard, she heard someone mutter something and stopped for a look around the corner.

Someone was standing on the rear terrace fiddling with the lock on the back door. The light she'd seen had come from a flashlight cradled in the figure's arms.

Lena reached for her gun, drew the weapon from her holster, and stepped around the corner. Eyeballing the figure, she inched her way along the back of the house. The figure was taking on detail now. It was a man and he had his back turned. A large man with brown hair wearing a wrinkled white shirt.

It was Brant, fumbling with a set of keys. Apparently, he didn't use the back door often and couldn't find the right key.

She stopped just short of the terrace. Her flashlight was a high-powered model that could produce a light almost as oppressive as the sun. She pointed the lens at the man and switched it on. Brant nearly jumped out of his skin. Jerking his body around, he shielded his eyes with outstretched hands and started shaking.

"Who's there?" he shrieked. "Who is it?"

"What do you think you're doing, Mr. Brant?"

He picked up on her voice. "It's you," he shouted. "What the hell are you doing here?"

"You've got the question right," she said. "And now I need an answer."

She could see his eyes trying to penetrate the light. After a moment, he noticed the gun in her right hand. A .45-caliber semiautomatic with a black finish that weighed a mere 25.6 ounces but held nine plus one rounds when fully loaded.

"Why are you pointing that at me?"

"This is still a crime scene," she said. "Maybe you didn't notice that the house is sealed. Or maybe you've forgotten why. I don't really give a shit."

He took a step toward her. She pushed the business end of her gun into the light so that he could get a better look at the weapon. She wished her heart would stop beating so fast.

"Easy, Mr. Brant. You probably don't want to do that."

He stepped back and lowered his hands. "This isn't necessary. This is crazy. Put that thing away."

"You haven't answered my question," she said. "And I'm no mind reader. I don't know why you're here or what you're up to. I can only tell you what I know for certain."

"What's that?"

"If anything happens here tonight—if you should lunge toward me, if you should accidently trip or fall—you're going to die, and I'm not."

She tightened her grip on the gun. His eyes flicked to the muzzle, then rocked back as if he knew it was a .45.

"Nothing's gonna happen here," he shouted.

"Then take a deep breath and tell me why you're trying to break into the house."

"It's my house. Everything inside it belongs to me."

"You're committing a crime, Mr. Brant."

"All I want are my clothes. It's the truth. That's why I'm here. I'm sneaking into my own fucking house for a clean pair of underwear."

Lena paused a moment, appraising the man. That crazy look in his eyes. His sleeves were rolled up, and she noted the muscle definition in his forearms. There was no question in her mind that he was stronger than her. More powerful than her.

"That's what friends are for," she said calmly. "Why don't you go to a friend's house, borrow a change of clothes, and get some rest?"

"Friends? That's a good one. Every friend I've got thinks exactly the same thing you do."

"And what's that?"

He paused a moment, then spit on the flagstone. "That I murdered Nikki. Fuck those assholes. I don't have any friends."

"Then get a room at a hotel."

He lowered his eyes and didn't say anything. Lena took one step onto the terrace and stopped, estimating the distance between them at ten feet.

"Where's your car?" she asked.

"In the lot at the park. I've been driving around ever since my lawyer dropped me off."

"I want you to remove your car key and drop the ring on the ground."

"What about my keys to the office?"

"Like I said before, I'm no mind reader. I don't know which key goes where. You'll have to get another set from somebody at work."

He gave her a long, pissed-off look and shook his head, then removed the key with his right hand and tossed the ring onto the flagstone. Lena took another step to her left, offering the angry man a wide path to the backyard.

"You can leave now, Mr. Brant. Someone will let you or your attorney know when you can come back. When they do, you'll be able to use the front door."

He didn't say anything. He started to, but stopped. Then he closed his fist around the key and marched toward the rear fence with his flashlight.

Lena switched off her own, watching Brant's ghostlike figure vanish into the fallen clouds. She heard him climb the fence, drop down on the other side, and swear. When the beam of light started up the hill toward the park, she holstered her gun and filled her lungs with a load of fresh air.

She paused a moment to take it in. She could smell the ocean, but also the earth.

She knew that she was shaking. She also knew that she had never once fired her gun in the line of duty. That she had never killed a human being.

She grabbed the keys and checked the lock. Satisfied that the house was secure, she switched her light back on and retraced her steps into the front yard. As her car became visible in the mist, she thought about the drive home. Caffeine might not be working anymore, but that hot shot of adrenaline she'd just swallowed sure seemed to do the trick.

She heard the phone ringing from the counter between the kitchen and living room before she pulled the key from the lock.

Lena swung the front door closed, tossed the unread copy of the Saturday paper on a chair, and rushed across the room in the darkness. As she grabbed the cordless handset, she switched on a small table lamp set beside the phone's cradle.

"Channel Four," Novak said.

"I just got home. Hold on."

She spotted the remote on the counter, hit the POWER button, and heard the TV fizz from the other side of the couch. When the screen lit up, she toggled up to Channel 4.

"What is it?" she asked.

"Just watch."

Lena had missed the opening, but the story appeared to be a condensed version of the Nikki Brant murder. As the newsreader ran down the case, the station cut to close-up shots of the death house. The images must have been taken sometime after the investigation team had left the location and reopened the street. Recorded in daylight, the camera was set on the curb with strands of crime scene tape stretching across the frame.

Listening to the summary, Lena was surprised by the amount of detail the writers had been able to collect. It didn't sound like a leak. The station had obviously jumped on the story and mirrored their own investigation. They had an approximate time of death. They knew where Nikki Brant grew up, went to school, and how she met her husband. They'd found out where she worked and knew that she was pregnant. But they also knew about her marriage difficulties and that the murder had been particularly bizarre. For some reason, the report stopped short of its own obvious direction and didn't point the finger at James Brant. Lena wondered if it was a result of Buddy Paladino working the press this afternoon with his cell phone.

She got her answer when the picture cut to a live feed. The newsreader's case summary had only served to set the table for an exclusive interview by a reporter in the field. But the conversation wouldn't be with Brant's smooth-talking attorney. Instead, the reporter had uncovered a witness. A neighbor, George Smythe, who claimed that he'd seen James Brant park his car in the lot at Rustic Canyon Park and slip into the woods at 1:00 a.m. on the night of the murder.

Lena walked around the couch for a closer look at the witness.

Smythe was sitting in a chair on the front deck of his house, the community center in soft focus behind him. He was introduced as a screenwriter. Although Lena had never heard of or seen any of the films he wrote, Smythe lived across the street from the park and looked to be in his midthirties with light features and an intelligent face. As he spoke about sitting on the deck that night and watching Brant pull into the lot, she sifted through her memory of the preliminary reports and field interview cards she'd added to the murder book over the past twelve hours.

"I didn't think anything of it at the time," Smythe was saying. "When I woke up, his car was gone."

The picture cut to another live shot from the parking lot. This time the camera was handheld, and Lena knew what they were going for. A shot of the death house through the trees from the murderer's point of view. Unfortunately for the producers, the fog was so thick that the image didn't render beyond a blurry, smoked-out screen. When they cut back to the studio, Lena muted the sound and spoke into the phone.

"We canvassed the entire neighborhood, Hank."

"Maybe he wasn't home at the time."

"He was home," she said. "An FI card was filed by a West L.A. officer knocking on doors. Smythe never mentioned that he saw Brant. I read his statement on the card. It's in the murder book."

"It probably didn't register until he thought it over. I just wish we'd talked to him first. It might have been enough to hold Brant until Monday. He wouldn't be on the streets."

Deciding that this was as good a time as any, Lena told Novak about her encounter with Brant at the house. She didn't embellish what happened, and she didn't leave anything out. After she finished, Novak didn't speak for a long time. When he finally did, all he wanted was verification that she was okay.

"What do you want to do about Smythe?" she asked.

"Rhodes worked the neighborhood when we left on Friday. He may have spoken to someone who knows Smythe. I think we should let him handle it in the morning."

"You want me to make the call?"

"I'll take care of it," Novak said. "You deserve a decent night's rest. Everybody does."

"Hank?"

"What?"

"When did you know?"

"That it was Brant?"

"Yeah."

"I'm not really sure," he said. "This one's not exactly off the lot, Lena. I guess the answer is late. Too late to have made a difference."

He hung up. Lena clicked off her phone, then the TV, thinking it over. Novak sounded as disappointed as she was.

Too late to make a difference.

She unzipped her boots, pulled them off her aching heels, and tossed them onto the floor. She felt ragged. A notch or two beyond the dial. Still, she wasn't sure she could really sleep. The shaking had stopped, but that anxious feeling in her chest had followed her home.

Too late to make a difference. The concept felt like a snake bite.

She got up and switched on the tuner, scanning through the albums loaded in her CD player before the murder. Classical probably wouldn't be enough, and rock might sharpen the edge. Nothing jumped out at her as the way to go. She needed a jazz fix. But listening to CDs seemed too isolated, and 88.1 out of Long Beach was too far away to make the twisted climb through Hollywood Hills.

Her audio system was connected to the Internet via a cable modem. Firing up the monitor, she scrolled through her bookmarks until she found WRTI, a station she liked out of Philly. According to the playlist, a retrospective on partnerships would begin at the top of the hour. Ellington and Strayhorn. Parker and Gillespie. Until midnight, it would be Larry Coryell on guitar. Side 2 from *Barefoot Boy*.

Her brother had the album on vinyl, but she hadn't listened to it for a long time. When the music started, she adjusted the volume and headed for the kitchen.

Three bottles of chardonnay were left in the fridge from a case she'd bought six weeks ago at a warehouse on San Fernando Boulevard. Popping the cork, she poured a glass and took two quick sips. It was a good wine, Chardonnay–Les Pierres from Sonoma-Cutrer, and it tasted clean and particularly fine right now. As she savored the wine and listened to Coryell's haunting rhythm build, she noticed the light blinking on her answering machine. She hit PLAY, recognized the caller, and would have smiled at the irony if she hadn't been so tired. Tim Holt had been her brother's best friend, played keyboard in the band, and cowrote many of their songs. She hadn't heard from him in nearly six months.

"Hey, Lena, this is Tim. It's been awhile. I've been out of town, but I'm back now and thought I'd try giving you a call. Maybe we could grab a bite to eat this week. I'd like to meet up and talk."

The phone number he gave was new and she jotted it down. His voice sounded strong and she thought maybe he was clean again. But she also guessed that Holt wasn't calling just to catch up. Since her brother's death, there had been many calls. Over the past couple of years they usually ended with a request to reopen the studio. Like her brother, Holt was convinced that the place offered a special sound. Lena wanted to help and felt guilty that she couldn't. She considered Holt a good friend, but she wasn't ready yet. The idea of hearing music, the thought of walking into the garage and seeing someone else on guitar, someone other than David at the mike, stirred up too many memories and brought back too much pain.

She finished off the wine, then filled a second glass to the top. Crossing into the bedroom, she peeled off her clothes, turned the shower on, and stepped beneath the warm spill. It was a long shower. One that lasted until the hot water ran out. Slipping into a T-shirt, she worked the hair dryer for as long as she could stand the noise. Then she carried her wineglass over to the bed and set it down beside her gun on the table. She cracked the window open, reminding herself as she always did to fix the small rip in the screen before switching off the lights. As she got under the covers and leaned against the cherrywood headboard, she sipped her wine and looked outside. She was feeling it now. The grapes, the music, maybe even a deep sleep lurking at the end of the tunnel.

But the view from the window beside her bed was remarkable. Almost heavenly. The clouds had swept in from the ocean blanketing the city and filling the basin to the tip of the hill like a bowl of soup. The surface was below her, stretching as far as the eye could see and appearing soft but sturdy enough to walk on. Above the base of clouds, the full moon dangled hypnotically from a clear sky over the Westside.

She had never seen the marine layer roll in below eye level before. She had inherited the house, the room, even the bed she slept in, from her brother. She remembered him saying that he once saw this, too. That he stayed up all night, watching the moon burrow into the clouds from this very window, and waiting for the sun to pop through from the other side, on this very bed.

She took another sip of wine. Then another. Setting the glass down, she rested her head on the pillow and gazed outside again.

It wasn't her confrontation with Brant that was keeping her awake, she decided. It was the fact that he tried to beat the box. That he thought he could lie and get away with it. When she caught him trying to break into the house, his explanation had come so effortlessly. So smooth and fast.

He wanted a change of clothes, he said. All he wanted was clean underwear and a fresh shirt.

Lena rolled over on her side, her face bathed in moonlight, thinking about the truth. She closed her eyes as a loose plan for tomorrow began to take shape, her mind untethered and ready to drift. She would get a couple of hours' rest, she told herself. Then wake up early and drive out to the death house for another look on her own.

19

Lena slung her briefcase over her shoulder, pausing a moment by the car to take in the death house through the web of yellow tape. The trees were swaying from a cold offshore breeze, the sun leaking through the leaves and spilling as if from a kaleidoscope onto the lawn. But her eyes were fixed on the Sunday paper on the front doormat. It seemed so odd seeing the paper lie there. She wondered what the person was thinking when he delivered it to the crime scene. Maybe he heaved it from the car without looking, or maybe he made the delivery as some kind of sick joke.

She checked her watch. It was 7:25 a.m. Somehow she'd managed to get five hours of dreamless sleep and felt revived. She was ready, she decided, mentally prepared for what lay ahead.

She crossed the street and stepped beneath the tape. When she reached the front door, she dug into her pocket and fished out the key ring. Brant had taken the car key with him last night. Six keys remained, and she worked through them until the lock finally clicked.

She pushed the door open and heard the hinge creak. Then she picked up the newspaper and stepped inside, greeted by the oppressive smell of Nikki Brant's tainted blood. In spite of the chilly air, the foul odor had permeated the entire house. Lena ignored it, closing the door and setting the newspaper down on the kitchen table, along with her briefcase.

Brant had tried to break into the house last night, claiming that he only wanted a change of clothes. The more Lena thought it over, the more his explanation troubled her. But what was he looking for? His computer had been taken to Parker Center. The murder weapon was already logged into evidence, and the investigation team had spent most of Friday searching the house.

What could Brant want that he didn't think they already had?

She crossed the foyer to the study, noting the fingerprint powder on the desk. The semen stains on the white carpet had been snipped away. What little remained on the carpet pad was no longer clear but had taken on a reddish hue easy enough to spot. Stepping around the stains, she slipped on a pair of vinyl gloves and got started. The files in the lower drawers appeared work-related, the subject matter limited to the courses the victim taught at college and personal notes Brant kept from meetings at the office. When she opened the top drawer, she found the Brants' checkbook beside a stack of unpaid bills and slowed down to take a closer look. Flipping through the register, nothing stood out except for the balance. The Brants were between paychecks. Only $159.62 remained in their bank account.

She tossed the checkbook into the drawer and moved to the closet, avoiding the fingerprint powder on the door handle. The house must have been short on storage space because she found Brant's clothes here. On the shelf above she saw a beat-up 35 mm camera set beside three eight-by-ten manila envelopes. As she slid the envelopes out, she spotted a shoe box hidden in the back. Lena inched the box forward with her fingertips, then sat down on the floor and opened the lid.

It was a collection of memories. Letters and snapshots from his past. Brant's family, his friends, and what looked like a number of women he'd dated from high school through college. But what caught Lena's eye was the house Brant grew up in. Brant hadn't come from poverty, or even a middle-class home. The fleet of Mercedeses parked before a tennis court and swimming pool added up to a life of privilege. His parents were wealthy.

Lena hadn't expected this. Nikki and James Brant had obviously been struggling to make ends meet. She saw the balance in their checkbook, less than $200, and assumed that they were on their own. During the interview, she remembered Brant saying that he wanted a family but couldn't afford one right now. Given the situation, she wondered why Brant hadn't gone to his family for help. But perhaps he could, she thought. Maybe it was just another excuse. One more lie on the list of many. After all, he had enough money to buy Buddy Paladino, one of the most expensive criminal-defense attorneys in the business.

She closed the box and went through the manila folders. The first two were filled with black-and-white photographs. The third contained proof sheets taken from the negatives. Lena turned toward the window, examining the images in the light. Although there were some portraits of family members she recognized from the snapshots in the shoe box, most of the photographs were carefully framed landscapes. She shook her head as she went through the pile. At one point in his life, Brant had been interested in photography and art. Maybe he could take it up again in prison.

She got to her feet, returning the items to the shelf and entering the bath, which was attached to the study and master bedroom. The sour smell of rotting blood was stronger here. Again she ignored it, carefully examining the small room. Most of the plumbing had been ripped up from the floor and carted off to the lab as SID searched for the victim's missing toe and any residual evidence that this was the place where the doer had cleaned up. Lena started with the medicine cabinet. She thought she might find Nikki's prescription here, but the only medication turned out to be a muscle relaxant dated two years ago. She shook the bottle, holding it to the light. It still looked full.

It would have been easier, of course, if she had some idea of what she was really looking for. A feel for the shape of the thing and its relative size. She opened a narrow linen closet, sifting through towels. She searched the cabinet below the sink and found nothing here as well. Then she crossed the room to the open bedroom door.

The curtains were drawn, masking the view from any neighbors who might wander onto the property for a nervous peek through the windows. Even without a dead body, the sight of the enclosed space rattled the nerves. The bedding had been taken downtown, but enough blood had seeped onto the mattress and remained on the walls to reawaken her memory of the day she'd first laid eyes on Nikki Brant. She could see the young woman on the bed with her eyes open even though she didn't want to see it. She could still see the young woman's foot and those horrific chest wounds.

Lena gritted her teeth and stepped into the room. The closet was on the other side of the bed. Tiptoeing around the bloodstains, she felt a sudden chill ripple between her shoulder blades as she opened the door and went through the victim's clothing. The smell of the room was disgusting, as dense and confining as a hood. No longer able to ignore it, she sucked the vile odor into her lungs and made it the reason to keep going. To keep pressing forward.

She went through a long line of slacks and skirts. When she spotted a jacket, she reached into the pocket, felt something, and pulled it out. It was the prescription pills for nausea. Nikki Brant had been keeping them a secret, hiding the bottle in a place her husband was unlikely to look. The label indicated that five pills had been prescribed by her doctor with no refill option and warned that the drug could cause drowsiness. She opened the bottle. Only four pills remained, and it was a safe bet that Nikki Brant had been using the drug at the time of her death.

She wondered how strong it was. Whether the drug might be in play. She thought about the question Novak had asked her outside the coroner's office.

Do you know anything about erotic asphyxiation?

She wondered if the two were connected in some way. If maybe the Brants were into something kinky and the victim had been under the influence when it went down. If maybe the events leading to the murder were accidental, the window dressing added to cover up the result.

Lena shook it off, thinking it seemed unlikely, but making a mental note to bring it up with Novak.

The evidence bags were in her briefcase in the kitchen. Opting to log the pills in later, she slipped the prescription into her pocket and moved to the bedside table for a look inside the drawer. If the Brants were into kinky, she might find some sign of their varied sex life here, even though Novak had been through the room on Friday and hadn't mentioned any unusual toys. Instead, what she discovered beneath a tablet of paper was anything but aberrant. From the vitamin bottles containing iron and folic acid, she figured this was the victim's side of the bed. When she spotted the basal body thermometer, her guess was confirmed. The temperature increments were graduated by one-tenth of a degree, the device used to calculate a precise waking temperature. At the bottom of the drawer, Lena found a pocket calendar and opened it. The notations began in January. Nikki Brant had been charting her menstrual cycle—her fertility—taking her temperature every morning and recording the changes in her cervical secretions until she found the right time. The right moment.

Lena stared at the woman's notes—her hopes and dreams for a family that came to fruition but lasted only a single day. She listened to the house. The oppressive silence. Willing herself out of the black, she stepped around the bed and quickly sifted through the chest of drawers. The woman's T-shirts, her stockings and underwear. When she found a tattered snapshot of Nikki as a young girl, her hand started shaking. Brant didn't look more than seven or eight years old. She was standing shoulder to shoulder with a boy in front of the orphanage. Both sported bittersweet smiles, their eyes hiding fear and loneliness. Lena dropped the photograph on the chest and walked out of the room.

She took a moment to pull herself together. Then another to regain her focus.

Except for the boom box and TV, the living room was empty. She spent the next twenty minutes in the kitchen, going through the cabinets and drawers. She worked quickly, thoroughly. She wanted to get out of the house. She needed to get away from the smell. Away from that snapshot of the victim as a girl. When she finished, she realized that she was as far away from discovering anything new or even relevant as when she began.

She glanced at her briefcase and the newspaper on the breakfast table, then pulled a chair out and sat down. What could Brant have wanted out of this nearly empty house? What was worth the risk of committing another crime and appearing even more guilty?

Her eyes rocked about the room until they came to rest on the bulletin board fixed to the wall. She hadn't really noticed it before. A schedule of events at the art college was posted, along with lists of errands to be done and groceries needed at the store. Several notes were also tacked to the board. Back-and-forth notes written over the past ten days when James Brant claimed to be working night and day.

Lena read them, deciphering the loose script from both sides. If they were in the midst of an argument, one that would end in murder, it seemed extraordinarily civil.

She turned away, ready to leave and disappointed that her effort hadn't paid out. Reaching for her briefcase, she glanced at the stack of newspapers on the seat beside her and guessed that it was easily a week's worth. The section on top was opened to that idiotic story about a pregnant woman from Santa Monica who claimed she hadn't had sex in two years. Lena flipped it over in disgust, noticing the crossword puzzle underneath. It was the same puzzle she had trouble with earlier in the week, and either Brant or Nikki had filled it in. Her eyes drifted to the bottom right section—51 DOWN—and she reread the clue referring to a contestant who won a million dollars in a reality series on TV. The answer was written in ink and seemed to fit. She tossed the paper on the pile and stood up, wondering why anyone in search of reality would seek it out on television.

And then it hit her. Her heart started pounding and that shake came back—a second hot load of adrenaline exploding through her body.

She slid the newspaper off the pile and carefully laid it out on the table.

She noted the date at the top of the page. Not sometime last week, but Friday morning.

She studied the puzzle—the words, the lettering, the machinelike precision of the handwriting that didn't match either the victim or her husband yet seemed so familiar now.

She rifled through the stack of newspapers on the chair. Every other puzzle remained blank.

Her eyes flicked past the kitchen counter to the boom box sitting on the living room floor. She sprinted toward it, her mind jetting ahead of her body in a jumbled blur. What she was thinking was absolutely impossible. They'd followed the evidence without bias. Brant's alibi had fallen apart and he blew the polygraph. An eyewitness even came forward. She saw the interview last night on TV.

Memories of the Lopez case began to surface—one after the next in rapid succession. The newspaper by the bed. The CD player. What she was feeling in her gut was totally ludicrous. The MOs were entirely different. There could be no connection between the two murders. Jose Lopez was in Men's Central Jail where he belonged. While it might be true that Lopez had been under extreme emotional distress, that he started weeping when Novak showed him the picture of his dead wife and called the woman a whore, Jose Lopez had murdered his wife and confessed.

She switched the boom box on and hit the EJECT button.

The tray slid out.

When she read the title on the CD, her skin flushed and the room seemed to ignite in a fiery haze. But it wasn't Beethoven's Symphony No. 6 spewing out the heat.

This time it was one of Lena's personal favorites. No. 7.

20

Lena flipped open her cell, keeping her eyes on the road as she hit her partner's speed-dial number and bulldozed her way through weekend traffic on the Santa Monica Freeway. Novak picked up on the second ring.

"We've got a problem," she said, her voice cracking.

"How big?"

"What are you doing right now?"

"Talking to Officer Marwick out of West L.A. He took the witness's statement on Friday. Sanchez and Rhodes brought in that screenwriter. We're trying to straighten things out. I was starting to get worried. I was just about to call you at home."

She glanced at the clock on the dash: 10:15 a.m.

"Do you remember Terrill Visconte?" she asked.

"Teresa Lopez's boss. The guy who won't admit that he was doing her the night of the murder."

"We need to find out where he was on Thursday night," she said. "I'm thinking he'll be clear, but we need to know for sure."

A long moment passed. Lena thought her phone had gone dead and checked the screen for a signal. When Novak finally spoke up, his voice was low and riddled with concern.

"Where you going with this, Lena? What's happened?"

She steered around a slow-moving Buick, working her way into the left lane as she thought it over. The implications of her discovery were ominous.

"I made another trip out to the house," she said. "The DNA results we get tomorrow probably won't come back to Brant."

It hung there. Big and heavy like a stone dropping out of the sky.

"You bringing something with you we can see?" he asked.

"Enough to ruin your day."

Novak didn't hesitate. "I'll make the call. What else can I do until you get here?"

"Don't let that witness walk. We'll need to pull the newspaper from the Lopez case. The one we found on the bedside table. I know it's Sunday, but I think we'll need Barrera."

"You sure about this?"

She nodded, then realized he couldn't see her. "I'm sure," she said.

"If you're gonna ruin my day, we might as well take a shot at his. Let me get started on these calls."

She clicked off the phone, glancing at her briefcase on the passenger seat. It was more than a gut feeling now. They'd followed the evidence and made a wrong turn. But it was worse than that. Almost a perfect storm conspiring against them. They had an eyewitness whose claim now seemed dubious at best. A confession from Lopez that made even less sense. And what about Brant's polygraph? Lena tried to stem the riptide, concentrating on the road and heavy traffic. Still, their mistake was on paper and a matter of record. Innocent people were getting hurt.

Ten minutes later her cell phone rang. It was Novak, filling her in on Terrill Visconte. Apparently the man had been in Miami for the past week, seeing his father through an appendectomy. Novak had spoken with Visconte at the hospital and confirmed his conversation with the desk nurse. Visconte had been out of L.A. for a week, visited the hospital in Miami daily, and was clear. Under the circumstances, he readily agreed to give a DNA sample immediately upon his return. Lena listened as Novak went through the details, but she was thinking more about what he'd said to her on the phone last night.

This case wasn't exactly off the lot. The track they were racing down was mired with potholes and a collection of illogical events that didn't add up.

When it seemed that Novak was finished, her mind surfaced and she looked out the windshield. She was closing in on the city. Hitting the 110 freeway fast.

She told her partner that she would see him in ten minutes. He told her that he was headed down to the basement. The labs might be closed, but the Property Room was open 24-7.

The elevator doors opened onto the third floor. Lena stepped out, legging it around the corner to the bureau floor. As she entered, she found Novak waiting with Barrera at the lieutenant's desk, the Calendar section of the *Times* laid out before them. Barrera had a pair of golf shoes on, and his face looked sweaty and sunburned.

"It's the crossword puzzle," she said.

Novak was already wearing gloves and reached for the paper. Lena slipped on a pair of her own, opening the evidence bag and laying out Friday's paper beside the one they'd found in Teresa Lopez's bedroom. Everyone eyeballed the handwriting samples. Although no one was an expert, it seemed obvious enough that the machinelike lettering had been stamped out by the same hand.

Lena fished another evidence bag out of her briefcase—Beethoven's Symphony No. 7—and lowered it to the desk.

"I found this in the CD player," she said.

Novak's eyes rolled off the newspaper, hit the CD, and rolled back to the handwriting samples.

"Number seven," he whispered.

From the look on his face, she could tell that he was blown away. But it was more than that. His mind had slipped from its moorings and appeared to be under full sail. There was a certain joy on his face at the revelation, a certain wonder he couldn't hide. An hour ago, Brant and Lopez had been guilty of murdering their wives. Now another possibility was unfolding before them. Something darker and far more hideous, but amazing nonetheless.

"Number seven," Novak repeated.

"This may be a stupid question," Barrera said, "but what are the chances Brant murdered Teresa Lopez?"

"Zero to none," Novak said.

"Why?"

"Buddy Paladino. No attorney would have agreed to the polygraph unless he knew something we didn't. It wasn't that he thought Brant could beat the box. It was the fact that he knew we were off track. He knew it and he was digging it. He knew Brant didn't do the crime."

"Then why did Brant fuck up the test?"

"I've got no idea," Novak said. "Paladino was overplaying his hand. He got burned."

"These murders occurred thirty miles apart," Lena said. "When you put them together, they look random. And Brant doesn't strike me as a serial killer. If he's living a secret life, it's unlikely he'd bring it home and do his own wife."

"But there's no evidence of rape," Barrera said. "No vaginal bruising. No rips or tears or even any bleeding. She knew who she was having sex with."

"I think there's another explanation," Lena said.

She had been thinking about it ever since she'd left the death house. Mulling over the details of a new case theory as she worked the road. She pulled a third evidence bag from her briefcase and dropped it on the desk. The meds.

"I found these hidden in the bedroom closet," she said. "On Friday her doctor told us she prescribed them to help with nausea and vomiting. But there's a side effect. A chance the drug made her drowsy. I think her judgment was off, at least when things got started. I think she was confused and thought she was with her husband."

Lena tried not to spend too much time thinking about the moment when Nikki Brant finally realized that the man on top of her wasn't really her husband. It seemed to her that both Novak and Barrera were troubled by the same thought. A view of something so horrific it shook the core and forever changed it.

Barrera rubbed his hands over his face, suddenly appearing tired. "What about Lopez? You got a confession. He's in jail, for Christ's sake."

"There's no answer for that except to say that the pressure was on," Novak said. "He was upset. He'd just learned that his wife was fucking around. It must have pushed him over the edge."

Barrera sat back in his chair, thinking it over. "Okay," he said. "Let's assume that the crimes are random but related. Let's say for the sake of argument that the doer is a third-party motherfucker from planet X. Tell me why he's hanging around. What's he doing at the crime scene after the murder? And don't tell me that it's because he likes to play with puzzles or listen to music. If he's a third party, then he's taking unnecessary risks. He was nearly caught by Jose Lopez when he got home that night."

"It's in the report," Novak said. "A witness saw someone jump from the bedroom window. We thought it was Visconte."

"But now it's not Visconte," Barrera said. "Now it's someone else. At Brant's house he raped and murdered the woman—he cut off her toe— then hung around for two hours with his dick in the Internet. What the hell was he doing?"

It was another one of those million-dollar questions, Lena thought. A question no one had an answer for. Then Novak picked up the plastic bag containing the CD and added another. Something that was already out there but had been left unsaid.

"If Teresa Lopez is number six and Nikki Brant makes seven, then what about the previous five?"

Barrera pushed his chair away from the desk and stood up as if he were just served tainted food at a restaurant. Lena thought she noticed his hands trembling slightly before he slipped them into his pockets.

"I want to slow this down," he said. "The captain's away. I'm gonna have to take this up to the sixth floor. No one mentions the Lopez connection to anybody, okay? Everything sits on hold until we get the blood work back tomorrow and we know what we're dealing with. Who's the DDA on Lopez?"

"Same as Brant," Lena said. "Roy Wemer."

She hoped her voice didn't reveal her disappointment. The chief was on the sixth floor, along with his deputies. It would mean more meetings, more reports, the chance that someone might be watching over their shoulder. In the end, ringing the bell upstairs would wake up the bureaucracy. Decisions would be made by committee, slowing everything down.

"Okay," Barrera said, thinking as he spoke. "We'll call the lab and make sure they compare the DNA samples with the Lopez case. If we get a hit, I'll talk to Wemer and let him know where things stand." He eyed Lena's briefcase, then looked at her. "Did you pull samples of Brant's handwriting?"

She nodded.

"What about his wife?"

"I've got those, too."

"Good. Then you two better spend the rest of the day verifying these samples. They may look the same to us, but what the hell does that mean?"

"It's Sunday," Novak said. "The store's closed. You'll have to authorize the overtime."

Barrera nodded. "Just get someone in here. Where are Sanchez and Rhodes?"

Novak raised his eyebrows. "With the eyewitness who says he saw Brant on the night of the murder."

It had been happening with greater frequency over the past couple of years. People stepping forward and claiming to have witnessed a crime in order to bask in the limelight. They looked at the situation as an opportunity to be noticed. A chance to get on TV. In this case, Lena thought it might have something to do with the fact that she didn't recognize any of the movies credited to the man. That his foray into the dim light of a television audience was an attempt to get his name out there and boost his career.

"Sounds like obstruction of justice," Barrera said. "Tell Rhodes to arrest the son of a bitch. Give him a room over at Men's Central Jail. And get Sanchez started on the database so we can find those first five kills. Any objection to bringing Bernhardt in?"

Novak shook his head.

"Good," Barrera said. "Then everybody meets here tomorrow morning. Eight sharp in the captain's office. I'll call Andy and bring him up to speed."

Dr. Andy Bernhardt was a staff psychiatrist and an experienced profiler. Unfortunately, most of his time was spent working with the Professional Standards Bureau, the new name for Internal Affairs. There wasn't a working cop in any division that didn't have a natural distrust for the unit no matter what they called it these days.

Lena collected the newspapers, returning them to the evidence bags. As she walked to her desk with Novak, she glanced at her partner's face. The wonder was gone, the joy of the revelation replaced with exhilaration, but also fear.

They had wasted the first two days, she thought. The most important period in any investigation. But it felt like maybe they lost more than that. Not two days on Nikki Brant or even thirty on Teresa Lopez. It felt more like they were in the weeds and had lost the better part of a year.

He's left-handed."

Irving Sample snapped the magnification lens closer to his worktable as he began a side-by-side comparison of the two crossword puzzles. The notes Lena had collected from the Brants' bulletin board were laid out on the light box off to the side, along with other examples of their handwriting she'd pulled from the files in their desk, just in case.

Sample hadn't wanted to come in. And in the end, he didn't. They were sitting in his study at his home in La Cañada, a small, affluent town in the hills overlooking Glendale. When Lena had made the call, he told her that he would prefer to examine the documents here. It was Sunday, his children were visiting from out of town, and he had everything he needed at the house to give them a preliminary finding.

Lena didn't mind, nor did Novak. La Cañada was only a twenty-minute drive from Parker Center and both of them needed to get some fresh air. What she didn't expect when they arrived were the peacocks roaming freely about the neighborhood. Two were standing on a neighbor's roof squawking at something in the hills behind the house. Another three were devouring a garden three doors down the street.

Lena gazed out the window from her seat at the worktable. A peacock had just landed in Sample's backyard and was giving her a funny look through the glass. Had it been an earlier time in her life, she would have sworn she was hallucinating.

"Don't mind the birds," Sample said over his shoulder. "They actually make great watchdogs."

"I'll bet," she said.

"Someone moved away and left them behind. The flock grew and, for whatever reason, decided to stay. There hasn't been a robbery in the neighborhood since we've lived here."

"The noise would drive me crazy," Novak said.

"You get used to it."

Sample pulled a clean sheet of paper from a drawer and began copying letters from the crossword puzzles, mimicking their shape and style. As he worked, Lena looked at the equipment on the table, the collection of inks kept in a glass cabinet away from the light of the window, the number of books dedicated to the subject of forgery on the shelves. She didn't mind the drive at all. Instead, she felt lucky to have access to a forensic document analyst with Sample's reputation and experience.

Sample had begun his career in the Questioned Documents Section of the Secret Service. When he was asked to teach at U.C. Berkeley, he accepted the job largely because his children had moved to northern California. But as much as he enjoyed living close to his family and working with students, he missed the thrill of the hunt. The pressure of a life spent in the real world. To the LAPD's credit, the examiner was openly recruited until ten years ago, when Sample agreed to move to Los Angeles and head the Questioned Documents Unit.

Lena had worked with Sample on two occasions during her stint in Bunco Forgery as a detective in Hollywood. They liked each other immediately.

"I've found something," Sample said in a voice charged with emotion. "An anomaly."

He grabbed the notes from the bulletin board, comparing them to the hand that filled in the crossword puzzles.

"It's the way he forms the letter *P*," he said. "It's unusual. Very unique."

Lena and Novak moved in for a closer look.

Sample beckoned them even closer. "Most people form the letter *P* in one of two ways." He pulled a fresh sheet of paper from the drawer and grabbed his pen. "The letter *P* is essentially a line connected to a half circle. If they use two strokes to form the letter, they start at the top and make the line, then draw the half circle. If they form the letter using a single stroke, they start at the bottom, form the line, and continue around until they complete the loop."

Lena watched Sample form the letter *P* using a double stroke, then a single stroke. There didn't seem to be a third possibility.

"What's the anomaly?" she asked.

He smiled. "Most people start with the line. The man you're looking for doesn't." He slid the piece of paper closer and demonstrated the technique. "It's a single stroke that begins at the bottom of the half circle and loops around to form the line."

"How rare is it?" Novak asked.

"As good as a fingerprint. Whoever filled in this puzzle did that one, too. There's no question about it. Every letter *P* was formed in the same unusual way."

Lena glanced at the notes she'd pulled from the Brants' house. "What about them?"

Sample shook his head. "Both Nikki and James Brant are right-handed. They form their *P*'s the way everybody else does. She used the single-stroke method. He forms the letter using two strokes. If the crossword puzzles are in play, then James Brant is clear."

It hung there. Hearing Sample say the words.

James Brant is clear.

Lena's stomach began to churn. She thought about her dealings with Brant. The way he'd played with the coffee cup and held a cigarette during their interview. The hand he used to remove the car key from his key ring when she'd confronted him at the house. Brant definitely favored his right hand. She looked at Novak and could tell that he was feeling it, too.

The heat. The fire. The train rolling down the tracks into the black.

Their eyes met and Novak grimaced. Then he mouthed those words again.

Number seven.

22

Three things had kept Lena awake through the night. Three thoughts that hounded her and wouldn't let go.

The first was that tomorrow would be a Monday, the forensic labs would be open, and they wouldn't be working with one hand tied behind their backs. Second, they had spent yesterday afternoon searching through the RHD database for the first five kills. The effort had yielded nothing and, as a result, sparked new waves of fear that the doer remained hidden and they still didn't have a single lead. But perhaps the real reason she'd spent most of the night tossing and turning and staring out the window was that Irving Sample's findings offered a faint glimmer of hope.

Lena knew that it had been the work of the Questioned Documents Unit that clinched the Ennis Cosby murder case and sent Mikhail Markhasev, a nineteen-year-old Ukrainian immigrant, to jail. That it had been the side-by-side comparison of incriminating letters with known examples of Markhasev's handwriting, the unique way Markhasev formed the letter *S,* that had turned the case in the mind of the investigators and, in the end, the jury.

If they could just find a suspect, Lena felt certain that Irving Sample had enough information to link the man to two murders. At the very least, the suspect would be off the streets long enough for them to issue a search warrant and see what turned up.

It was 6:30 a.m. The bureau was still quiet, and their meeting with Dr. Bernhardt wasn't for another hour and a half. Lena had come in early because she'd noticed over the past two months that the Computer Crime Section kept odd hours, getting a head start on the day and sometimes working late into the night. She already knew from phone records that the Brant's computer had been used to access the Internet at 3:00 a.m. on the night of the murder. The doer spent two hours on the Web before the newspaper arrived and he logged off. Figuring out what he was doing on that computer seemed like the next logical step. Maybe even their only step.

Based on the same floor as RHD, the Computer Crime Section was a subsection of the Financial Crimes Division, known before the new chief arrived as Bunco Forgery. She walked down the hall to the other side of the building. The door was open, the overhead lights switched off. As she entered the darkened room, a tech looked up from a nineteen-inch flat-screen monitor and grimaced as if he didn't want to be disturbed. He was about her age, maybe even younger, with a sullen face and hair so short she couldn't really identify the color. He wore a cheap pair of reading glasses— the kind sold at a drugstore or bookshop—with remnants of the sticker still marring the right lens. His jeans looked as if they could use a wash, his denim shirt, a steam iron. A skateboard would have made the picture complete but she didn't see one.

"You look lost," he said in a snarly voice. "And I'm really busy. If you need directions, ask someone down the hall to help you out."

His eyes snapped back to the monitor and his back stiffened. He was blowing her off.

Lena remained undaunted. She spotted the Brants' computer on a shelf, wrapped in plastic and sealed with an evidence tag, then looked back at the tech. She had never met the man, but knew his name and had heard the rumors. Keith Upshaw had been arrested for hacking into AT&T's computer system at the age of fifteen. The following year he found his way into American Express but was turned in by a friend before he could do anything stupid. Whether it was his age, his fear of prosecution, the private conversation he had with the judge in juvenile court, or the fact that both AT&T and American Express offered to pay his way through college, at some point Upshaw crossed back over, graduating with honors and a degree in computer science. Now he was here, nervously tapping his sneaker on the floor and appearing totally disagreeable, yet sipping high-octane coffee from the Black-bird as he concentrated on his work.

Lena noted the logo on the coffee cup and took it as a good sign. Grabbing a chair from a second desk, she rolled it over to Upshaw's, then moved it even closer so that she could see what was on his monitor.

"I'm busy, too," she said. "And I'm not looking for directions. That's my case you're working on."

He lifted his hands off the keyboard and shot her a close-up look. After a moment, a dark smile overtook his grimace and he laughed.

"Now I know you're really lost," he said.

The smile didn't fade, and they introduced themselves. Then Lena turned and looked at the monitor.

"How far have you gotten?"

"What you're looking at is a perfect copy of the Brants' hard drive. A picture of their computer taken the moment the last user shut it off."

"That's what I'm interested in," she said. "The last user."

"All I can tell you right now is that he knows something about comput-ers. The browser he was using to surf the Internet. He knew enough to delete the history and wipe out the cache. It's gonna take some time to find out what he was doing."

"What do you think he was looking at?"

Upshaw gave her a look as if she were crazy. "Porn. I found remnants of pictures in the system files."

He clicked through several windows, revealing pieces of a woman's face. An eye, a nose, and a mouth with lips so bloated from collagen injections that they looked as if they might pop.

"It's part of a graphic," he said. "The pieces come together to make the whole."

"How do you know it's porn?"

His smile deepened and he clicked open the next window without saying anything. Lena looked at an image of the woman's swollen breasts and thought they might pop, too. She got the point, and Upshaw closed the window.

"The Web provider the Brants use is on the East Coast," he said. "I gave them a call when I got in this morning. They promised a report within the next hour."

"What else?"

Upshaw pulled the keyboard closer and grabbed the mouse. "He spent at least half an hour accessing files on their hard drive before he logged on to the Web."

"What kind of files?"

"The Brants use an accounting program to keep track of their money and credit cards. The program requires a password on start-up. The last user knew the password and got in."

"How can you tell?"

"Look at the time and dates." He pointed to the screen. "That's the data file. The program automatically saves your work when you exit."

"Did you figure out the password?"

"On the first try. It was so easy anybody could have figured it out. They used their address. Nine thirty-eight. By the way, they're broke. Thirty thousand's riding on plastic."

Lena thought it over. Twenty-four hours ago, hearing that someone had typed the correct password into the computer would have been another strike against Brant. But now all it meant was that the person they were looking for was educated, knew something about technology, and demonstrated a certain degree of curiosity toward his victims.

"I'm guessing it didn't end there," she said.

Upshaw nodded. "He went through their word processor."

"He opened personal files," she said. "Letters to friends and things like that."

He laughed. "Are you a fortune-teller or what?"

She shrugged it off, wondering if she hadn't just put her finger on a small piece of why the doer hung around the crime scenes after committing the murders. In the Brants' case he had access to the documents stored in their computer. With Teresa Lopez, a journal had been found in her chest drawer that was thought to be insignificant at the time. Maybe the doer got off on the intimacy, she thought. Maybe reading the private ruminations of the women he killed brought him closer to his victims and gave him a thrill.

"Teresa Lopez was raped and murdered in her home in Whittier," Dr. Bernhardt said. "Nikki Brant was found thirty miles away in her home bordering a public park. If we knew where the previous five homicides occurred, assuming they happened at all, then we could make an educated guess as to where he's from and which side of the city you might focus on. Until then, or until he strikes again, I'm afraid all we have are snapshots of his personality based on his psychopathic behavior."

They were sitting at the conference table in the captain's office—the entire team, plus Lieutenant Barrera and Deputy Chief Albert Ramsey, the chief's closest ally and the second-highest-ranking officer in the department. It was 8:30 a.m. To Ramsey's credit, he hadn't said a word since entering the room. Still, his presence tightened things up. Lena could feel him behind her back, sitting at the captain's desk so that he could keep his eyes on everyone without moving his head. The bureaucracy had risen from its slumber.

"He likes to poke things," the psychiatrist was saying. "He likes to probe his victims and torture them. And when he's finished, he goes for the shock value by posing his victims with you in mind. Teresa Lopez was nailed to an imaginary cross. Nikki Brant was entombed in a sea of blood. This is about a guy who's trying to make some kind of insane point that's lost in translation. Just remember that it starts with his penis. In Romeo's mind, his penis and the weapons he chooses have become one and the same thing."

It was the second time in the past half hour that Dr. Bernhardt had called the man they were looking for Romeo. She wondered if the name would stick, and from the look on Barrera's face, thought it might.

Romeo.

"I think we're looking for a white male between the ages of twenty-five and thirty-five," Bernhardt said. "A voyeur who's graduated from rape to murder."

Lena took notes as she listened, even though she knew Dr. Bernhardt was giving them the boilerplate definition of a serial killer. Someone who was abused by his parents as a child. Someone who probably practiced animal cruelty as a teenager. A former victim whom no one noticed and who finally reached the point of striking back.

"He was probably hurt," Bernhardt said. "He was probably wounded in some way or faced a severe emotional trauma he couldn't deal with or understand."

He glanced at Lena for a moment, then turned back to his notes.

Dr. Andy Bernhardt was a large, vigorous man with clear gray eyes, a short-cropped beard, and a tanned skull. They had met after her brother's murder when her supervisor sent her down to the psychiatrist's office for what he called a *tune-up.* A routine checkup. A chance to chase the blues away without the pressure of having to work. But no matter what anyone called it, Lena knew that it had gone down as an ISL in her records.

Involuntary stress leave.

She played the words back in her head as she thought it over.

Unfortunately, Dr. Bernhardt had wanted to know more about her than how she might be experiencing the loss of her brother. He wanted a complete picture for his psychological evaluation. The entire list of bumps and bruises and dark spots.

The sessions lasted for six weeks. Every Tuesday and Thursday afternoon for one hour at his office in Chinatown. Lena resisted for as long as she could, then shut down. Not because there was anything wrong with Dr. Bernhardt. In spite of his size, he was a gentle, soft-spoken man whom she actually grew to admire. It was the fact that he worked for the department that concerned her. That his role as a psychiatrist often meant working closely with the Professional Standards Bureau, which she didn't trust. The idea that anything she said would be written down and placed in a file that might be used against her in the future.

While Dr. Bernhardt tried to assure her that her personal file was indeed personal, and therefore private, Lena noticed that his filing cabinets were as old as the furniture at Parker Center and didn't include locks. Besides, she told the psychiatrist, everyone who's anyone gets at least one *existential moment* along the way. She could get through this just as she always had in the past. Getting back to work would keep her mind off things and speed up the process. In the end, Dr. Bernhardt agreed, they found middle ground, and their last two weeks of meetings actually proved beneficial.

She heard Novak speak up and the memory vanished. Her partner was asking the psychiatrist why he thought the MOs differed between Teresa Lopez and Nikki Brant.

"His method is changing because he's growing," Bernhardt said. "He's evolving."

"Into what?" Novak asked.

"Into someone who can't stop himself, Detective."

"What about the missing toe?"

Dr. Bernhardt shook his head. "He likes what he's doing. He's thinking about it. Learning as he goes along. The problem is that he can't control his hunger. His behavior is a reaction to his primal urge. I think he sees the toe as a trophy or keepsake."

Lena thought about the press. When she'd checked *The Times* this morning, the reporter working the crime beat was still playing with the idea that maybe Brant murdered his wife.

"What about when the story breaks?" she asked.

"I'm split on that," Bernhardt said. "I think the perpetrator could go either way. Either he's going to like it because he's finally been noticed. Suddenly, he's king of the jungle. He's famous, and he's holding his identity a secret over everybody else. Or it goes the other way and he gets pissed off because part of his secret is out of the bag and he likes working in the dark. I'm split because of the letters you mentioned, and Teresa Lopez's journal. But also because of the way the bodies were posed."

"The intimacy," Sanchez said. "The shock value."

Bernhardt nodded. "Either way, I'm afraid there's a chance that going public may accelerate his behavior."

Lieutenant Barrera interrupted with an announcement. "Everybody checks their mail before they open it. If you don't recognize the return address, open the envelope carefully and use gloves."

"I agree," the psychiatrist said. "There's reason to expect some degree of contact."

Rhodes dropped his pen on the table and started rubbing his temples. Like the deputy chief, he hadn't said a word since entering the room.

"I realize we don't have much information," he said finally. "But I've got two questions. Two problems I can't get past, so I'm throwing them on the table. I don't understand why he's hanging around. I don't think it's just so that he can go through the victim's journal entries. And if it turns out that he's into porn, why look at it there? Why not limit his risk and go home?"

"I'm troubled by that, too," Bernhardt said. "All I can say is that it probably adds to the thrill. But it also points to a certain degree of arrogance on his part. What else is on your mind, Detective?"

"He tried to wipe his semen away," Rhodes said. "All of this was shaky enough when we were looking at Brant. But now it doesn't make any sense at all. If he's cleaning up after himself, why not wear a condom? If he's smart enough to delete files on a computer, then he's got to know that he couldn't possibly clean up the body well enough to erase his DNA."

Rhodes had thrown them out on the table. Two questions with jagged edges. Dr. Bernhardt appeared uncomfortable and took a moment to consider them before speaking.

"I would answer your second question the same way," he said finally. "There's no condom because it's all about the thrill. Perhaps he thinks it's possible to degrade the DNA. But the more likely scenario is that he's so arrogant he doesn't give a shit. He thinks he can beat you and not get caught, so he leaves a piece of himself behind. What's important for you to understand is that the man you're looking for is a world-class monster. Someone who's so consumed by his own anger that he no longer resembles a human being. If we were to draw an analogy from nature, I'd say he works something like a shark in a feeding frenzy. Romeo kills to live just as much as he lives to kill. When he's full, he drifts to the bottom fantasizing about the day he can swim back to shore and do it all over again."

Lena heard a noise. A chair moving.

She turned and watched Deputy Chief Albert Ramsey march toward the door. She could hear him breathing as he passed behind her back, the sound of his heels digging into the thin blue carpet. Somehow his white hair looked a shade whiter than an hour ago, his jaw more square. He left the room, closing the door without making any sound. Lena imagined that it was time for Ramsey to report to the new chief. Time to tell him that Romeo was a lover and a motherfucker and the case wasn't going well.

He could smell her vagina. He was trying to concentrate on his work, but he could smell it. He was sure he could. The odor was hidden in the recesses of her perfume. Lost but not forgotten in the attempt by the perfume designer to replicate the scent of lavender flowers hovering over a garden and wafting through crisp morning air to the end of his nose.

Martin Fellows liked the smell of lavender.

He looked up from his notebook. Harriet Wilson smiled at him from the other side of the lab table. He smiled back the way he usually did. At least he tried to duplicate the gesture even though he understood that everything was different now.

Everything changed the moment he found out who she really was.

Even worse, he had been the last to know. The last one in the entire company to find out, so the revelation stabbed at him, keeping him awake at night and feeding on his frenzied soul. Ever since gaining this knowledge, he'd become aware of people sneering at him and making a joke of it whenever he entered the offices on the second floor. Upon his exit, he could hear them giggling behind his back.

Martin Fellows was in love with a whore. And he felt like a fool.

His eyes drifted about the lab, searching for No. 3 in as casual a manner as he could muster. He could feel his heart racing. In spite of the change, his jealousy reawakened with new fervor, triggered by the fear that maybe No. 3 could smell Harriet's vagina, too.

Fortunately, the man was working on an experiment at the far end of the room. His back was turned and he appeared to be diligent in his approach, a rare quality for a minority. Actually, Martin Fellows wasn't sure how to classify No. 3. His name had an Asian ring to it, not Hispanic or Eastern European, and No. 3 had that mixed-breed look just like the people Fellows saw wandering about the mall. None of them carrying packages, he observed. None of them buying anything at all. Just taking up space like alien drones and making the shopping experience more difficult for people who still spoke English and could afford to buy what they wanted.

Fellows didn't like No. 3 and he never would.

He didn't like the good-natured smile the biologist continually wore, the naïve way he looked at the world with both eyes open, or No. 3's incessant attempts at camaraderie. It was a small lab, just the three of them working here, when Fellows was certain that two would have done just as well. He didn't want to be No. 3's chum, nor did he want to play with the heathen on the company's stupid softball team.

Fellows wished that management would spend less time thinking about the company's idiotic softball team. Then maybe they would see it the way he did and demote No. 3 to the lab down the hall. But management wouldn't listen. No matter how many times Fellows made the suggestion as lab supervisor, they dismissed his proposals as if they'd forgotten who he was or failed to read his résumé all the way through. The last time he broached the subject, the response remained cordial but seemed unnecessarily curt.

Forget it, Marty. Tommy Tee's a long-ball hitter.

Fellows wasn't exactly sure what that meant but thought it might be a veiled reference to the size of No. 3's anatomy. While the man who said it may have been the team coach, Fellows had always suspected that he was a homosexual, still locked up in the proverbial closet despite the times.

He kept his eyes on No. 3 for another long moment. Satisfied that the long-ball hitter wasn't watching him or sneaking peeks his way, he turned back to Harriet Wilson for a more careful look.

She was a whore, but she was also the most beautiful woman he had ever seen. So striking that he could see her face whenever he wanted by merely closing his eyes. Her hair was a mix of blond on blond draped just below her shoulders. Her eyes, a windy blue, reminding him of the color of rain an hour before nightfall. Her skin was so soft and smooth that any incidental contact in the lab gave him an erection. But then, so did the way she looked at him sometimes. That lazy glint she could muster in those eyes. The rings she wore on her thumb and first finger. The way she walked around the lab trying to hide her limp.

Harriet Wilson was more than ten years younger than him but had been born in the same month. She was a lovely, twenty-eight-year-old Taurus, ruled by the planet Venus and the ways of love. And she would be celebrating her birthday this coming Friday. Fellows had jotted down a reminder over the weekend and clasped it to the file he kept on her by his bed. A file that included several pictures, along with photocopies of her employment records he'd lifted from the office one night when everyone else went home. He wanted to do something special for Harriet, even though she hadn't remembered his own birthday just last Thursday.

Harriet stepped around the table gripping a large male cockroach in her hands.

Gromphadorhina portentosa. The Madagascan hissing roach.

The four-inch-long insect seemed to know that he was about to die, hissing at them and tucking his head and antennae under his thorax so that his chest resembled a second head large enough to scare off a rival. As Fellows watched the insect, he thought about the pain he had been forced to endure last Thursday night. The look on Nikki Brant's face as she was downgraded to the role of specimen.

"They can always tell, can't they," Harriet said, turning the roach over in her hands and stroking its belly.

Fellows selected a scalpel and nodded. "Yes, I think they can. Let's get him in the glove box."

She placed the insect in the air lock. As she slipped her hands inside the second set of gloves, Fellows could feel her hip rubbing against him but filed the sensation away for later.

Of the thirty-five hundred known species, it was the hissing roach that they hoped would be the missing ingredient in creating the perfect apple. The large insect was a native of Madagascar, an island in the Indian Ocean off the eastern coast of Africa. On the plus side, it had no odor and could survive in a warm climate without food for as long as a month. Often known as living fossils, the insects were the size of rodents and remarkably similar to the cockroaches that inhabited the planet long before the appearance of dinosaurs. Fellows had isolated the gene enabling the roach to resist heat and inserted it in various types of apples, hoping the plant might flourish in tropical climates. His initial experiments had proven successful. But Fellows was less satisfied with the color of the fruit's skin and wanted to refine it. He thought a red apple with zebralike stripes would stand out. Something he could easily identify if it ever turned up at the grocery store so that he wouldn't buy or eat one by mistake.

He might be a molecular biologist, but he wasn't about to begin eating anything that came out of a lab. Even if it carried the label *All Natural*.

The roach hissed at them from within the glass box, rocking its head up and down and wiggling its legs in Harriet's hands.

"It won't hurt," she said in a soothing voice. "It won't hurt, I promise."

Fellows slid the razor-sharp blade down the insect's chest and belly, the roach still flailing its legs and hissing at them. After prying open the exoskeleton, Fellows scooped out its viscera with a spoon and flicked them into a petri dish.

"See," Harriet said to the dead cockroach. "It didn't hurt at all."

Fellows smiled, taking in the scent of her body. Every aspect of the scent in all of its wondrous parts.

"If it did," he whispered, "the hurt didn't last very long."

The meeting with Dr. Bernhardt had ended ten minutes ago. Now they were huddled around Novak's desk. Lieutenant Barrera was at the other end of the floor, speaking with DDA Roy Wemer on the phone. Apparently Wemer found out about their lab request for a side-by-side on the DNA samples found at the Lopez and Brant crime scenes. From the look on Barrera's face, Lena imagined Wemer was pissed off for not getting a heads-up and being out of the loop.

"Here's what I think we need to do," Novak said. "You guys have a better idea, just say the word."

He glanced at Lena, then grabbed a pen and paper.

"I want you to call Dr. Westbrook, Lena. Bernhardt's okay, but we're high and dry and we're four days in on a trail that could be seven months old."

She looked at the area code and phone number Novak was jotting down from his address book.

"Who is he?"

"A criminal psychiatrist with the FBI's Behaviorial Science Section. Use my name and give him whatever he needs to get started. Just make sure he understands that we're late on this."

Novak spotted the Lopez murder book on Lena's desk, snatched it up, and handed the three-ring binder to Rhodes.

"It's the Lopez case, Stan. You've never seen it before, so everything should read like new. Maybe Lena and I missed something. Maybe you can find something we didn't."

"Anything you think you might have overlooked?"

"No," Novak said. "It seemed righteous, but so did everything leading to Brant."

Rhodes nodded. Novak turned to Sanchez.

"You need to get back on the computer, Tito. But this time, limit your search to sexual assaults, not homicides. Any woman who's been raped over the past two years."

"What about ages?" Sanchez asked.

"Sixteen to dead," Novak said. "Pull everything."

Sixteen to dead. The words hung there.

Novak glanced across the floor at Barrera, still on the phone with Wemer, then turned back and met Lena's eyes.

"I'm heading over to Piper Tech," he said. "Wemer might be holding things up. I want to make sure the lab still has us up on top. I'll be back in an hour. You need to reach me and can't get the cell, call SID. We cool?"

Lena nodded. So did everybody else.

A new brand of urgency was in the air. Lena wasn't sure if the energy emanated from their briefing with Bernhardt, or the dread she felt in her stomach as she went through the case from the very beginning with Dr. Westbrook over the phone.

Halfway through, Dr. Westbrook was interrupted by someone in his office, and Lena heard him say, "Hold all my calls." A door closed and the background noise quieted. When he got back on the phone, he said they wouldn't be interrupted again.

He seemed particularly interested in the way the bodies were posed. The grocery bag covering Nikki Brant's face and her missing toe. The cross painted on the sheet with Teresa Lopez's blood. He asked Lena to describe these findings twice, pressing her for details and writing everything down. When she told him that Brant failed the polygraph, he didn't say anything. When she described the hit made by Irving Sample after studying the writing samples found at both crime scenes, any doubt he might have had that the murders were related completely vanished.

"So what you're looking for is a left-handed alien from another planet," Dr. Westbrook said. "In L.A. that narrows the field down to what?"

Lena hesitated. She didn't know the man and wondered if he was making an ill-timed joke. But when he spoke up again, she realized that he was merely thinking out loud as he did the math.

"About a million," he said. "Approximately ten percent of the population is left-handed. What about hair and fiber?"

"Nothing was found at either crime scene."

"What about the ME?"

"He combed both victims out. No pubic hairs were found on either body."

Dr. Westbrook became quiet again. It didn't take much for Lena to know why he seemed so troubled. The lack of pubic hairs in a rape case was unusual.

"Are your reports digitized?" he asked.

"No," Lena said.

"Then here's what I'd like you to do. E-mail me a short summary of each case. Just the main points, but make sure you include everything we discussed and the observations made by Dr. Bernhardt. Attach a photo of each victim. What I'm looking for are shots of the crime scenes before anything was touched. The way he left them for you to see. Then copy everything you're sending me to Teddy Mack."

Lena jotted the name down, wondering why it seemed familiar as Dr. Westbrook gave her Mack's e-mail address and cell phone number.

"Give Teddy a call and let him know it's coming. He's in California right now, about three hours south of L.A. on the border by the New River. We're working on something I can't really talk about, but I think he's got time to take a look. Not much goes on in the desert during the day. At least not the kind of thing we're looking for."

Lena glanced at Rhodes, studying the Lopez murder book at his desk. The intensity in his eyes made her feel a little sad. They were grabbing at straws, and all of a sudden it sounded as if Westbrook might be blowing them off on a field agent.

But she remained undaunted, thanking the psychiatrist for his time and getting started on the report. It took only twenty minutes to complete the summaries. When she was finished, she gave Lamar Newton a call, requesting digital scans of the crime scene photos. As the files appeared on her monitor, she found Teddy Mack's cell phone number in her notes and grabbed the phone. After half a ring, the call bounced over to his service. But his message was personalized, and Lena listened to his voice, still wondering why his name seemed so familiar.

She left a short message that included her contact information and hung up. Then she turned back to her computer for a look at the photos Lamar had chosen. The horror depicted in living color. Each one was worth more than a thousand words, she imagined. Even for someone working in the Behaviorial Science Section at the FBI.

After double-checking the e-mail addresses Westbrook gave her, she clicked SEND and watched her report get sucked into the digital pipeline. Checking her watch, she realized that it was only 9:45 a.m.

Upshaw hadn't tried to reach her with an update on the Brants' computer and she didn't want to hound him. Deciding to give him another ten minutes, she grabbed her empty coffee mug and headed for the door.

There were only two choices for coffee on the third floor. The closest was kept in the janitor's closet beside the sink and mops outside the captain's office. The better choice was on a detective's desk in the Cold Case Unit, an office not much bigger than a closet staffed by six detectives just down the hall. But as Lena reached the doorway, she saw Rhodes inside and stopped. He was holding an empty mug and flipped it upside down.

"They've moved," he said. "No hot java."

Lena read the note taped to the door. "Looks like they're on the fifth floor. Better digs."

"Bigger, you mean."

"Yeah, bigger," she said. "I forgot where I was."

The new chief was doubling the size of the unit, and the ten-by-fifteen-foot space would no longer do. Lena had been here for only three weeks when she realized that in spite of the working conditions, her goal was to eventually make the transition to this unit. The detectives were some of the department's best and brightest and had a sense of humor whenever she showed up with her empty mug. Because her brother's murder remained unsolved, she had a personal affinity for the work they did. This was the last stop for the victims' families on the hope train. This was where the forgotten bought their ticket, took a seat on the bench, and waited for news that just maybe they could start life over again.

She followed Rhodes down the hall.

"Who's Teddy Mack?" she asked.

He thought it over a moment, then gave her a look. "The E.T. murders. Five or six years ago in Philadelphia. Don't you remember last year when that guy finally got the needle? Cable TV wanted to air it live."

An image surfaced. She remembered seeing Mack's picture on the front page of *The Times* and reading the story.

"Twenty or thirty bodies," she said. "But I thought Mack was an attorney."

"He worked the case and closed it. Why are you asking?"

"Westbrook had me copy everything to Mack. He must be working for the Bureau. He's in California somewhere near the New River."

Rhodes gave her another look, different this time. "It sounds like maybe Westbrook said more than he should have."

It dawned on her what Mack was doing along the New River. Over the past ten years the bodies of more than three hundred young women had turned up on the Mexican side of the border. Because of the number of victims and the duration of the crime, because each woman was sexually assaulted, each body mutilated, the crimes were thought to be perpetrated by an organized group that warranted an American response. But the official line from the Department of Justice was that the United States wasn't involved in the investigation.

Rhodes was right. Westbrook had said more than he should have.

They reached the janitor's closet outside the captain's office. Rhodes opened the door to reveal the coffeepot of last resort, set on a plywood shelf overtop a bucket filled with gray water and a heavy dose of ammonia. Lena ignored the harsh odor, filling Rhodes's cup and then her own.

More curious than ever, she returned to her desk thinking about the E.T. murders and Teddy Mack. But as she sat down, she noticed the e-mail waiting for her on the computer.

Upshaw had come through without being rousted.

She clicked open the message and read it carefully. The doer had spent two hours surfing the Internet. According to the Brants' Web provider, the computer had been used to visit two sites. The first for roughly fifteen minutes. The second, for an hour and forty-five. Upshaw included links to the Web sites in his note, promising contact information within another half hour. As Lena read the Internet addresses, it was obvious that both were porn sites.

She checked the bureau floor, conscious of the detectives working in the room around her and grateful that her back was to the wall. Then she moved her cursor over the first link and clicked the mouse, waiting for the home page to render on her outdated computer.

Lena had grown up with a brother. As the images began to register before her eyes, she didn't see anything she hadn't seen before. But as she scrolled to the bottom of the home page, she noticed a password was required to continue.

She looked at the menu and noticed that a visitor's section was available, promising free sample images for the viewer to download. Lena clicked through the screens, eyeing the samples. The women were young, some maybe even too young, posed in various states of undress and leaving nothing to the imagination. Inside a box at the top of the screen she read the sales pitch. For $19.95 a month, a member could have unlimited access to the hard-core section and see these same young women in action.

Lena checked the bureau floor again, saw Rhodes glance her way, then looked back at her monitor. From the quality of the graphics and high-resolution photographs, the Web site appeared to be making money. But what interested Lena most were the sets the women were posed in. The furniture and appliances. Even the shower fixtures and electrical outlets. She looked back at a model's face, noting a smile that appeared forced. These pictures had obviously been taken outside the United States. Probably Russia or Albania or some other Eastern European country where posing nude and the life that went with it wasn't necessarily a matter of choice. Lena remembered reading a department bulletin sponsored by the FBI while still working out of Hollywood. It was all about moving the model out of her own country. Once her passport was taken and she couldn't escape, she was bought and sold and forced to repay debts for her estimated street value by the people who owned her.

Lena closed the window and reopened Upshaw's e-mail, moving her cursor over the second link.

Mounds-A-Plenty.com.

She paused a moment, thinking about the name of the site and the deadbeat who'd thought it up. Then she clicked the link and waited for the home page to render on her monitor. Mounds-A-Plenty was decidedly more crude than the first. But as she read the menu, she understood why Romeo spent more time here. This site was devoted to amateur hard-core movies and didn't offer sample photographs. Like the previous site, a password was required to enter. The only free section appeared to be a live feed from a webcam.

Lena moved her cursor over to the icon depicting a movie camera and clicked it. A small window about two inches wide appeared on her screen. Below the window a caption read, *Visitor's Section: Image changes every 30 seconds. For hi-res quality, join Mounds-A-Plenty.com!*

Her eyes rose to the image inside the small box. A woman with black hair, maybe twenty-nine or thirty, sat on a couch removing her bra. When the next image appeared thirty seconds later, the couch was empty. When a third rendered, the woman was back on the couch with a middle-aged man dressed in a suit and tie and with a full head of curly brown hair. Lena eyed the background, noting the sliding door behind the couch. The image was hazy, the quality, degraded. Still, the hills outside that door were unmistakable.

The source of the webcam was Los Angeles.

Lena slid her cursor across the menu, clicking open a hot button that read JOIN NOW. As she read the membership application, she felt a slight chill tickling her spine. Then she found Upshaw's number in her notebook and grabbed the phone. After five rings, he picked up without a hello, stating in a disagreeable voice that he was busy. Lena couldn't explain it, but she found something about the guy endearing.

"It's Gamble."

He laughed. "I was just about to give you a call."

"It's not the images. It's the passwords."

"Don't be fooled into thinking that because it's porn, these guys are idiots. They're not. Their brand of computerese is more sophisticated than any high-tech stuff out there. These guys know as much about hacking as any hacker. Maybe more. It's gonna take me time to break through."

"That's the point," she said. "I'm looking at the second site right now.

Romeo didn't hack his way through the front door, and he didn't spend an hour and forty-five minutes staring at a garbled thumbnail image that recycles every thirty seconds. He's a member."

She looked up. Novak was standing behind her, gazing at her monitor. Inside the two-inch box it looked as if the middle-aged man in the business suit was getting down to business without his suit.

"That's why he deleted the files on their computer," Upshaw said excitedly. "He's a member. The computer would have recorded his password."

She looked back at Novak. Their eyes met.

"And to get a password," she said, "you'd need to use your credit card."

It settled in. Their first lead. Novak's face took on a glow as he realized what had just happened.

"That site you're looking at is based in L.A.," Upshaw said. "I've got their address."

"Send it over."

She could hear Upshaw typing furiously in the background. When he stopped typing, she heard a hard click.

"It's on its way," he said.

"Thanks."

She hung up the phone and clicked open her mailbox. Within a few seconds Upshaw's message appeared, along with the Web site owner's name and address. Charles Burell did business in the Valley.

Novak shot her a look. "We'll have the DNA results in two hours," he said. "Let's roll."

26

Lena caught the look on Charles Burell's face and knew he read them as cops the moment he cracked open the front door. The address Upshaw had given them wasn't a business location. Instead, they were standing on the front porch of an upper-middle-class home in Sherman Oaks. Children were playing hopscotch on the sidewalk. Another two were riding bikes in the cul-de-sac at the end of the block. Novak flashed his badge to make it official and looked pumped.

"Mr. Burell?" he asked.

The man nodded, eyeing them suspiciously.

"We need to have a word with you," Novak said. "May we come in?"

"I'm busy," Burell said in a gruff voice. "What's this about?"

"Do you own and operate Mounds-A-Plenty dot-com?"

"If I did, it's perfectly legal. Every model is over eighteen."

"That isn't the issue, Mr. Burell. This is a homicide investigation."

Charles Burell didn't bat an eye. Nor did he make a move to unlatch the safety chain and open the door. Although half his body remained hidden, Lena guessed from the lines on his face that he was in his early fifties and that the hair clinging to the sides of his shiny scalp was dyed from a bottle purchased at the grocery store. Every hair was exactly the same color, a dull shade of brown that reminded her of wood stain. He was a short man with a clean shave and what looked like an artificial tan. From the way he was dressed, Lena couldn't help but think of the directory at the mall. She caught Ralph Lauren's name on the jeans and Tommy Bahama's on the shirt. His bare feet were sheathed in a pair of Gucci loafers, his belly hanging four or five inches over a belt with Calvin Klein's name engraved on the buckle.

"I don't know anything about a homicide," he said. "I can't help you."

Burell started to close the door. Novak stopped it with his fist.

"We'd like to speak with you inside," he said, glancing at the children within earshot on the sidewalk. "You can make it easy, or you can force us to take the long way around the block. Easy works both ways, Mr. Burell. It's your choice. We're not going away."

Burell met Novak's eyes, considering his options with a well-worn grimace. Then he closed the door long enough to free the safety chain and finally opened up.

"I used to be an attorney, you know."

"Good," Novak said as they entered. "Then maybe you'll understand why we think you can help."

"My office is downstairs."

Burell closed the door and flipped the lock. As he led them through the house, Lena glanced at the living room, noting the absence of color. The white carpet and white walls, the white couch and chairs, the glass coffee table and a grotesque sculpture of Cupid on the mantel over a gas-burning fireplace. The cheap, sterile feeling only intensified as they reached the kitchen and she picked up the scent of disinfectant in the air. The counters were bare and she figured Burell didn't eat many meals here. As they reached the steps, she noticed a photograph on the windowsill above the sink. A picture of Burell with a woman and two young children.

"You have a family," she said, following the man downstairs.

"No," he said. "We're divorced."

"Where do your wife and children live?"

"Phoenix. I don't see them anymore."

Lena sensed the bitterness in his voice and wondered why he kept the photograph around, then lost her train of thought when they reached the lower level and the smell of disinfectant became oppressive. The floor wasn't divided into rooms. Instead, she counted four different movie sets separated by removable walls. A living room was directly before her and she recognized the couch and sliding door from the webcam she'd seen on the Internet. To the left was a makeshift hospital room beside the furnishings for an office. To the right, a bedroom complete with a king-size mattress sealed in a plastic cover. Outside the glass door, she saw a pool and hot tub. She looked around for the nude model with black hair and the businessman who'd lost his suit, but didn't see either one.

"Is there a problem?" he asked.

"The smell," Lena said. "You use a disinfectant. I couldn't help noticing."

"I like to keep things clean," he said. "Very clean. Now follow me, and please don't touch anything."

She watched him push a wardrobe rack out of the way. As they crossed the bedroom set to a door, she traded quick looks with Novak. All things being equal, Charles Burell's entry point into the World Wide Web had exactly the same feel as a public restroom at the bus station.

Burell opened the door, ushering them inside and then closing it behind them. It was more of a control room than an office. Workbenches lined the walls, supporting three computer terminals and what looked like the Web site's server by the window. And the air was noticeably cooler here and almost free of that strong smell.

Novak cleared his throat as they sat down. "You work here alone, Mr. Burell?"

"It's a small business, but extraordinarily profitable. Like I said, I used to be an attorney. The hours are about the same, but this line of work has more perks."

"Do you practice safe sex?"

He shook his head. "It doesn't sell. But every model gets checked out."

"What about you?"

He wouldn't answer the question. Novak moved on.

"Is this Web site your only source of income?"

"I bought this house with cash," he said impatiently. "I own two Mercedes and a condo at the beach. I paid three grand for this ring I'm wearing. This Rolex cost me ten. You bet. This is my only source of income. It's all I need."

"Besides the money and women, what are the perks?"

His beady little eyes drifted over to Lena, then flicked back to Novak. "What else is there, Chief?"

Novak winced but didn't say anything. Burell's eyes lost their focus, staring into the Rolex as if it were a magic looking glass.

"I can go out with any babe I want," the man was saying. "They see the things I own, the way I dress and tip at clubs, the presents I buy them. It doesn't take long before it sinks in. If they give me what I want, I'll give them what they want."

Burell must have sensed Novak's disgust. He had become defensive and was about as warm and appetizing as a dead fish. And something about his crimsoned skin hinted at an illness. Lena's eyes drifted over his shoulder to the bottle of prescription pills on the counter behind him. Although she couldn't make out what was written on the label, she recognized the little blue pills as Viagra. When she spotted the hairpiece on the counter, the curly brown hair, she looked back at Burell's face and realized that he didn't really have a tan at all. He was wearing makeup, his skin still blushing from the drug. Beads of sweat were bubbling out of the man's forehead. Whatever he was using to highlight his eyes had begun to drip down the bridge of his nose. It had been Burell playing the businessman with the naked woman on the couch.

Before the image could take root in her mind, Lena sketched out the reason why they were there in three or four quick sentences. She left out the names of the victims. And she made every effort not to look at the makeup smeared against the little man's nose.

"What we're looking for is a list of members who logged on to your Web site between three and five a.m. on the night of the murder."

"What about privacy issues?" he shot back.

"We're trying to save time," Lena said. "If it gets that far, we've got enough evidence to convince a judge that the man we're looking for logged on to your Web site. We can provide the paperwork for a warrant, but it'll take a couple of hours."

"You said you used to be an attorney," Novak added. "Maybe we'll hit a judge you know."

Burell's eyes widened a little and he fidgeted in his seat. They had found a soft spot in the man's façade. It seemed obvious to Lena that there was a disconnect between Burell's former life and the one he lived now. Something he wanted to keep hidden in his basement and didn't necessarily want to advertise.

"Let's see what's out there before we bother a judge," Burell said.

He swiveled his chair around to the computer. Opening a window on the screen, he began scrolling through what looked like a spreadsheet. Lena and Novak moved their chairs closer to the workstation. Burell pointed at the screen.

"This program is really nothing more than a time line. When a member logs on to the Web site, the time and date is recorded beside their user name and password."

"What about their account information?" Novak asked.

"We'll get to that in a minute," Burell said. "If you're lucky. But I wouldn't get my hopes up if I were you. Most people don't log in. Only about five percent ever join. Most people just open the visitor's webcam because it's free."

The information on the monitor was going by too fast to read. Lena realized that the number of people who accessed the site over the past four days was well into the thousands. At $19.95 a month, it added up to more than a gold watch.

"Thursday night," he said, scanning the monitor as he got closer. "Friday morning. Okay, we're here. Now what?"

Maybe it was the lawyer in him, but Burell was trying to be difficult again. He would do what they asked, but nothing more. Lena opened her notebook, checking the times she'd jotted down from Upshaw's e-mail.

"According to the Web provider, the computer we're examining hit your home page at exactly three-sixteen on the night of the murder."

"How come you won't tell me the victim's name?"

Novak stared back, deadpan. "We don't have all day, Burell."

The man turned toward the monitor, wiping a speck of dust off his keyboard before toggling down the time line. Unfortunately, no one logged on to his Web site until 3:18 a.m.

"You understand that the times will differ," he said. "The time he arrived at the site will be different than the time he logged in."

"By a minute or two," Lena said.

"Sometimes it's longer if they forget their password."

"Let's try everyone who entered the site within the first five minutes."

"Whatever you say."

Burell highlighted the first user name, then paged down the time line. "Looks like we've got fifty-seven names."

Once he blocked out the user names, he moved the cursor to the menu at the top of the screen and clicked on the word CREATE, then ACCOUNT. A new window appeared on the monitor and another spreadsheet opened. Lena moved in for a closer look. Beside the time was a name and an address for every user name highlighted on the log. As her eyes rolled down the list, she recognized three names and gave Novak a quick nudge. Then she checked the duration of their stay recorded in the last two columns of the spreadsheet. None of the three had spent more than fifteen minutes at the site and probably had no relevance to the case. Still, seeing them listed as members of Burell's porno site was enough to give her pause.

They were lifelong members of the holier-than-thou club. A senator from Pennsylvania. A radio talk-show host who talked about morality from his front-row seat somewhere to the right of Neptune. And that weird guy on God TV who thought he was Jesus and dispensed miracles to the little people if they sent him big enough checks.

The Holy Trinity.

She shook it off. "The list is bigger than your screen," she said. "Can you sort it by city and state?"

"Of course I can. I wrote the fucking program."

Within a few seconds, the list reappeared on the screen. As he paged down, Lena was surprised by how many members were from Asia and the Middle East. Burell stopped when he reached California. Of the fifty-seven names, only three were from the Pacific time zone. She found Los Angeles on the list, then compared the log-off time with the one she'd written down in her notebook that the Web provider had given them.

The times were an exact match and she read the name.

But it took a moment to register. It wasn't a man's name. It was a woman, and Lena copied the information into her notepad. According to the address, Avis Payton lived in Marina Del Rey.

The carpet was threadbare, the grimy walls, in need of a double-coat paint job. Legging their way down the hall, they followed the muffled sound of a canned laugh track from a TV sitcom directly to Avis Payton's front door. Novak tried the bell. When that didn't work, he knocked with an open fist. A minute or two later the peephole darkened as someone pressed their eye to the lens.

"Who is it?"

"Police, Ms. Payton," Novak said. "We'd like to have a word with you."

"You got ID?"

Novak held his badge up to the peephole. After another long moment, they heard the dead bolt disengage and the door swung open to reveal Avis Payton dressed in a heavy pair of sweats.

"How'd you get into the building?"

"Someone was walking out," Lena said.

"Well, it's your lucky day," Payton said. "Enter at your own risk. I'm only home from work because I'm sick and can't hold my food down."

Without asking why they were here, the young woman stepped away from the door and headed for the blanket on the couch. Lena followed Novak into the living room, noting the balcony and second-story view of the marina on the other side of the bike path.

Payton grabbed the remote and switched the TV off. "I'm sorry. I didn't even ask you guys why you're here. I'm really out of it. I've got some kind of flu bug. Have a seat. If I've gotta make a run for the bathroom, I'll let you know."

From the background check they'd run on the way over, Lena knew Payton's age and that she didn't have a record. At a glance, the woman appeared innocent. From the way she spoke, educated. Her hair was short and tinted in an unnatural shade of red that bordered on metallic maroon. Her body was on the small side without being girlish. In spite of the black circles beneath her eyes, her face radiated a certain glow. But what struck Lena most about the woman was her composure. Most people were uncomfortable when the police showed up at their door. Avis Payton appeared relieved.

Why?

Lena looked about the apartment. It was a small one-bedroom, sparsely furnished but clean. As Lena turned, she saw Novak reach down for his pager and check the LCD screen.

"It's Barrera," he said. "I've gotta return the call."

A security bar was attached to the slider. Novak released the device, slid the door open, and stepped out onto the balcony. When he flipped open his cell, Lena turned back to Payton.

"Have you missed much work?"

"I got sick over the weekend. Hopefully I'll be okay by tomorrow. I'm an account rep for MBC advertising. We do print work for newspapers and magazines. Tuesdays are always a big day because we have to get ready for the Sunday papers. I'll have to go in no matter what."

"May I call you by your first name?"

"Sure."

"Do you have a boyfriend, Avis?"

The woman flashed a crooked smile. "What's this about?"

Lena didn't really want to say. At least not for now. Not until she had a better feel for who the woman actually was.

"I'm just asking. It looks like you live alone."

Payton seemed to relax, wrapping herself up in the blanket. "I haven't seen anyone since I moved to California."

"How long ago was that?"

"It's kind of embarrassing."

"I'm okay with embarrassing," Lena said.

Payton smiled again, then lowered her voice. "It's been more than a year."

She turned toward the balcony. Lena followed her gaze over to Novak. He was staring at the boats lashed to the docks and tapping his foot as if someone had put him on hold. When Payton began fidgeting on the couch, Lena thought she might lose the woman's goodwill and decided to keep going on her own.

"We stopped by because we're investigating an unrelated crime and your credit card number came up."

"Is that what this is about? But that was almost a month ago."

The woman's face burgeoned with surprise, but more of that free-flowing relief as well. Lena nodded slowly, disappointed that what had looked like a fertile lead was falling apart.

"What happened a month ago?"

"My purse was stolen. I left it in the car when I ran into the post office. I was only gone for maybe a minute or two. When I got back, it was gone."

Something crossed the woman's mind and she got off the couch, heading for the pile of mail on the dining room table. As she sifted through the envelopes, Lena sized her up. Payton was going out of her way to please them. Her easy manner stood out.

"What's your father do?" Lena finally asked.

Payton smiled and her eyes got big. "He's a cop. Salt Lake City, Utah."

It had been obvious. Out in the open all along. She was comfortable around cops because she'd grown up with one.

Payton returned to the couch clutching an envelope, then passed it over. "And he keeps calling me. He wants to know if I'm ever moving back. Go head and open it. The account should've been closed."

Lena checked the return address from the bank, tore open the envelope, and read the statement. The account had been closed two weeks ago. A charge of $19.95 from Charles Burell Enterprises had been included, then credited to the account. Below the charge was a note indicating that a new card and account number would be issued sometime within the next ten days. Their lead was no longer a lead and had officially burned out. Avis Payton was not a suspect but the victim of a theft.

"Was there just the one charge?"

"I called the bank as soon as I realized what was missing. You seem disappointed. Is there a problem?"

Lena's eyes moved back to the security bar on the slider. The device looked new and she was glad that it was there.

"Was your license in your purse?" she asked.

Payton nodded, acknowledging the balcony and that whoever stole her wallet knew where she lived. Her voice became more subdued. "I'll be okay. I haven't told my dad about it because all I'd hear is I told you so. Either that or he'd do something stupid."

"He worries about you living here."

"And he's real good at it. That's why I haven't said anything. He'd go crazy."

"Then you never filed a report?"

She shook her head. "There was only fifteen dollars in my wallet. It didn't seem worth it."

Although Payton's story seemed righteous, Lena wrote down the account number so that she could verify it with the bank. Setting the statement on the coffee table, she glanced at Payton as she thought it over. She didn't feel the need to tell Payton who they thought had been using her credit card. It had been a month since the theft. Nothing had happened thus far, and their suspicions would only terrify the young woman. Instead, Lena decided to make a call from the car and bring Pacific Division up to speed on the case. Patrols would be stepped up, the building and neighborhood watched more carefully.

"We've gotta go," Novak said.

Lena looked up. Her partner had been standing in the doorway watching them. His cell phone was back on his belt beside his badge. From the look on his face, he'd heard enough of the conversation and was anxious to leave.

Lena left a business card on the table and they let themselves out. But once the front door closed, Novak started rushing for the stairway down to the lobby. When he turned back, his eyes sparkled with excitement.

"The science is in," he said. "We got a hit."

The press conference couldn't be avoided because an innocent man was about to be released from Men's Central Jail.

The preliminary DNA results proved that the seminal fluid found inside Teresa Lopez's body matched the samples found inside Nikki Brant, on the sheet between her legs, and on the floor of the Brants' den. Romeo had raped and murdered both women, and Jose Lopez and James Brant were clear.

The new chief was standing at the mike with Deputy Chief Albert Ramsey, fielding questions from an energized press core who wanted to know why Lopez confessed to a crime he couldn't possibly have committed. Even though Lena was forced to attend the press conference and stood behind the podium with the rest of the team, she couldn't help but admire the new chief for his ability to take a punch and remain unfazed.

What the press was implying seemed obvious. But when a reporter from Channel 2 finally got the nod, the question was out in the open.

Did LAPD detectives beat a false confession out of Jose Lopez?

Lena looked through the bright camera lights into the audience as the chief took a moment to consider the question. She couldn't find DDA Roy Wemer or Lopez's attorney, but a beaming Buddy Paladino was sitting in the last row flashing those teeth.

"I'm not sure how much you know about modern methods of interrogation," the chief was saying to the reporter. "But what you're alluding to isn't in our playbook for many reasons, the first being that it doesn't work. No one from this department ever touched Jose Lopez. Mr. Lopez confessed to his wife's homicide of his own free will. I'd say that's a question you might ask Mr. Lopez when he's released. If I were a reporter, I'd give his attorney a chance to answer the question, too. He was in the room with both detectives when his client confessed."

Lena wondered if the chief would mention what she'd heard an hour ago on the bureau floor. That despite the evidence clearing Lopez, the man had barricaded himself in his cell, refusing to come out and shouting that he couldn't live without his wife, Teresa, even if she was a no-good whore. Lopez wanted a guilty verdict and the needle to kill the pain. Or even worse, it sounded as if he wanted to end it all tonight by baiting a guard into pulling the trigger.

She waited for the chief to mention it, but he never did. Instead, he spoke about the role forensic science played in uncovering the man's innocence and moved on. When he was asked to describe how Nikki Brant was murdered, he told the reporter that the investigation was less than a week old and left every detail out except for the DNA report linking the two crimes.

The give-and-take went on for another ten minutes before the chief finally walked off. Then Lena followed Novak through the crowd, ignoring stray questions thrown their way, until they reached the elevator behind Sanchez and Rhodes.

Novak glanced at his watch and turned to Sanchez. "How'd you make out on the computer?"

"You wanted every sexual assault from sixteen on up. I'm just getting started."

The elevator shook and groaned all the way up to the third floor. The doors vibrated, then opened, and Novak led the way down the hall to the bureau floor.

"It's six-thirty," he said. "Let's divvy them up and get the hell out of here."

Sanchez nodded with relief, crossing to his desk. It looked as if the stack of case summaries was four to five inches thick. Lena slipped her share into her briefcase, then sat down before her computer and quickly checked her e-mail. When she had stepped off the elevator, she noticed that the door was closed to the Computer Crime Section. She hadn't spoken with Up-shaw since he'd come up with Charles Burell's address and was hoping that he had a better day hunting than she did. But as she weeded through the junk mail, she didn't find anything related to their case. By the time she logged off, the only one left on the bureau floor was Novak, hovering over an open file on Lieutenant Barrera's desk.

"What is it?" she asked.

"The DNA report."

Novak grabbed the file, shaking his head as he returned to his desk and sat down beside her.

"Is there something wrong?"

"I don't think so," he said. "What's a CCR5 gene?"

She had never heard of it and shrugged.

"It's mutated," he said.

She rolled her chair over and leaned in for a closer look. When her eyes hit the words *Black Death,* she started reading. Romeo's CCR5 gene had mutated into something molecular biologists were calling delta 32. Accord-ing to the report, the mutation was rare and had occurred somewhere in Romeo's lineage 350 years ago as members of his family struggled to survive the Black Plague. Those who carried the mutated gene survived the epi-demic. Those who didn't suffered a particularly hideous and lonely death. The discovery of delta 32 was related to present-day HIV research because the two diseases attacked white blood cells in a similar way. For some rea-son, anyone who inherited the mutated gene was immune to HIV. But what struck Lena most was the shadow that the plague had cast over the world. It was limited to Europe. Thus Romeo couldn't be Asian or African because only Europeans carried the mutated gene.

Lena gave Novak a look. "Why didn't Barrera say anything?"

"He probably didn't get this far in the report. He was looking for a match. When he saw the DNA hit, he knew we were in trouble with the Lopez bust and went upstairs to work things out with the chief."

Lena thought it over. It was a case without clues, yet vague pieces of the puzzle were unfolding before their eyes. A portrait of the doer.

"Romeo carries the delta 32 gene," she said, "so now we know for a fact that he's Caucasian."

"What else?"

"He's not leaving any hairs behind. Could be a serial rapist who shaves."

Novak swiveled his chair toward the window, his eyes turning inward as he stared outside at the marine layer sweeping in between the buildings like smoke.

"His features could be light or dark," he said. "Let's stick to what he know."

"He's a lefty," she said. "From the severity of the wounds, he's young and strong."

"I would agree with that."

"But he's educated as well. He works the crosswords with a pen. He listens to classical music and knows something you don't."

Novak glanced at her. "What's that?"

"How to use a fucking computer."

He flashed a tired grin, then sank back into himself. "What about his penmanship?"

"Extremely neat," she said. "But he's got an odd way of writing the letter P. So odd that Irving Sample says it's as good as a fingerprint."

"Keep going."

"There's not much left. He gets off on porn. He's showing an unusual interest in his victim's lives. How much money they make and what they think about. He's posing his victims using religious themes so there's a moral angle. And he doesn't seem concerned about his DNA. He's tossing his body fluids around like a calling card."

A moment passed. When Novak finally turned away from the window, he looked a day older and shook his head.

"What is it?" she asked.

He stood up and started gathering his things. "Nobody wins in cases like this, Lena. We may know how to ID Romeo if we ever meet him. If we ever get the chance. But that won't happen until he makes a mistake or we catch him in the act. It could take awhile."

Lena got the drift and didn't say anything. She could see the disappointment in her partner's eyes. The frustration. As he said good-bye and walked out, she sat back in her chair and gazed at the empty room. It didn't take experience to realize that the price of catching Romeo would be another innocent life. Maybe two or three leading to nine or ten, and there was nothing either one of them could do right now to prevent it.

She grabbed her briefcase, fighting off a mix of depression cut with panic. She needed to clear her head. As she waited for the elevator, she decided to get some fresh air before driving home and thought about walking over to the Blackbird.

The doors opened. Rhodes was standing in the elevator alone. Maybe it was the glint in his eye or the way she was feeling tonight. Whatever the reason, she hesitated a moment before stepping inside and leaning against the rear wall. He turned away and pressed the button to the ground floor. She noted the Lopez murder book under his arm and the worn-out leather briefcase, guessing that he stopped off at SID on the fourth floor before leaving for the day. Once the doors finally shut, he turned slightly without looking at her. Thinking something might be on the floor, she followed his gaze and realized that he was staring at her hand. He was examining it. Probing it. She could feel his dark eyes tracing an outline around her fingers until they reached her palm and slid over her hips and legs. He was undressing her.

She didn't move, and he didn't say anything.

When the doors opened on the ground floor, a moment passed before he even noticed. Then he gave her a fleeting look in the eyes, stepped into the hall, and hurried off.

29

Martin Fellows lay back on the bench, lifted the bar off the rest, and heard the weights jiggle. He had reached his limit and wanted to laugh, but knew it was too dangerous. Tightening his grip, he glanced at the three hundred pounds teetering above his head, then looked over at his friend and spotter, Mick Finn.

"Ready?" Finn asked.

Fellows nodded with determination.

"Then give me five reps so we can start backing down again."

"I'm not sure I can do it."

Finn let go and gave him the nod. Fellows steadied the weights, then lowered them to his chest, gritted his teeth, and pressed the bar toward the ceiling. He had been pumping iron three nights a week ever since he was a teenager. On his own in the basement at the house until Finn finally convinced him to join a gym. It had been Finn's idea to begin increasing the weight, just as it had been Finn who suggested that they were now in training and Fellows needed to add bulk to his already hard and lean physique. Tonight Fellows was working the great pyramid. He'd begun with ten reps of two hundred pounds, adding weight in twenty-pound increments while decreasing the number of reps by one until he reached the pinnacle. After five reps at three hundred pounds, Fellows would have to perform five more sets, steadily decreasing the weight and increasing the number of lifts until he returned to where he'd begun.

Fellows couldn't help but admire his forearms, trembling as he strained to lift the weights upward again. It was the feeling of power and invincibility. Like a fine-tuned machine catapulting forward under the watchful eye of his trusted spotter.

They had met nine months ago at the Pink Canary, a diner run by an Italian family just around the corner from the promenade at Venice Beach. Fellows had been a lunchtime regular since he'd begun working nearby. He liked Italian food, and the old lady who worked the kitchen assured him that she used natural ingredients and made everything from scratch. Although Finn stopped by only once or twice a month in the beginning, Fellows noticed early on that the man seemed to be drawn to the same table he was. A table set apart from the others in the shade below a pair of palm trees. Fellows's sensitivity to light required that he eat lunch at that table. Rather than get into an argument over it, one day he asked Finn if he could join him, and they struck up a conversation. Finn's visits soon became more frequent, and Fellows realized that he had gained something he'd never possessed in all his life. Someone he could share his darkest secrets with. Someone who would never judge him but push him forward. A spotter and a partner. A true friend.

Finn grabbed the bar, helping him lift it onto the rest. As Fellows sat up and caught his breath, he looked about the weight room. He was free here. No one stared at him and no one laughed. Not even the brunette with the man muscles and pockmarked skin pumping fifty-pound dumbbells on the other side of the room. Finn had been right when he said that this was the one place in the city where they would *blend*.

Fellows almost teared up as he thought about it, removing twenty pounds from the bar and returning to the bench. Working his way down the pyramid always took more effort than the climb upward. If the going got tough, he might need an adrenaline boost and be forced to think about Harriet Wilson and what she had done to him.

"You sure you don't need a longer break?" Finn asked.

"Not tonight. We're going out later, right?"

For some reason Finn hesitated. He seemed preoccupied tonight, distracted, as if he wasn't all there.

"We'll talk about it after your reps," Finn said. "What about a swig of water?"

Fellows tried to get a grip on his anger. "I'm good. Just help me with the weights."

Finn grabbed the bar, lifting it over the rest. As Fellows took control of the weights and began his next set, he watched his friend watching him back.

Finn didn't want to do it—that much was clear—and he wondered why. Charles Burell needed to be punished. It seemed so obvious now. Even worse, Fellows had already done all the legwork. He'd found Burell's address and even scouted the location several times. Most nights Burell was home alone working at his computer or crying like a fool over the kitchen sink. When he wasn't alone, the wretched little cretin was doing the wiggly giggly with one of his leading ladies in the hot tub. Fellows had managed to work his way to within ten feet of the tub, hiding behind the trellis and listening to the horrible man moan and groan like some kind of animal as he received his daily blow job. Because they were playing to the camera set just outside the sliding door, neither one of them ever looked behind their backs or noticed that he was watching. Curiously, Burell never used a cameraman. Every time Fellows stopped by, the camera sat by itself on a tripod with the wires feeding into the house and directly onto that outrageous Web site.

Charles Burell was what came next because he deserved what came next. He was feeding on Harriet's low self-esteem. He had been fucking her for at least the past two months and doing it for the whole world to see. His fate was pure, clean, and true.

So why couldn't Fellows convince his friend?

It had taken nothing to win Finn over on his birthday last Thursday night. A single sentence coupled with a three-word description of their quarry, Nikki Brant.

Fellows hurried through his sets, then lifted the bar onto the rest and grabbed a towel. The accomplishment of performing the pyramid had been ruined.

"So now it's time to talk," he said.

"About what, Martin?"

"You know what I'm saying. Charles Burell. He's a heathen and it's righteous. He's taking advantage of Harriet."

"I can't tonight," Finn said. "I've got work to do. That's why I was late."

Fellows thought it over. When he arrived at the gym, he waited on Finn for a good thirty minutes. Thinking his friend might be a no-show, he got changed and walked upstairs to the weight room on his own. He didn't see Finn until after he'd sprayed the bench with Windex and carefully wiped everything down. It was Fellows's practice to work only with equipment that was properly sanitized. As much as he liked the gym, the staff was an international collection of losers who undoubtedly had no conception of how ugly a bacterial infection could become or how fast it might spread.

"That's just an excuse," Fellows said. "You don't want to do it."

"It's not an excuse. And I'm not going to get into an argument about it here at the gym. I can't do it tonight. Besides, precautions need to be taken. You know that as well as I do, Martin. This one's different."

"You mean because of who Burell is?"

Finn nodded. "Why are you in a rush? What's the difference between tonight or tomorrow night?"

Fellows shrugged, then smiled, thinking about tomorrow. Reaching for his three-inch stainless-steel cross, he clasped it around his neck. Life before he'd met Finn had been so complicated. So fucking lonely.

He checked the cross in the full-length mirror, admiring his body. His prowess. When he turned back to the room, his friend was halfway down the stairs. Fellows watched him exit, then gathered his things and headed for the locker room. Five minutes later, he was in the shower lathering up with a can of shaving cream. Like the bodybuilders he grew up watching at the beach, Martin Fellows shaved his entire body once a week. To the outside world, to his fellow students when he attended graduate school, even to himself in the beginning, his hairless appearance took some getting used to. But as with everything else he was forced to endure over the years, he found a way to manage.

Fellows rinsed himself off and reached for the towel. As he got dressed, he couldn't help thinking about Finn's plan for tomorrow. He thought Burell deserved an end that inspired anyone and everyone that gazed at the result. Something that stood out as special and made a statement. But he was also wondering where Finn had run off to without even saying good-bye. Finn seemed to enjoy keeping secrets and living a life of mystery. To this day Fellows still didn't know what his friend did for a living and even had doubts that he was using his real name.

Was it Mick Finn or was it something else? As much as the name brought a smile to his face, what parent would name their kid after a drink that was doctored? Even poisoned?

Fellows shook it off as he slipped on a shirt and felt the fabric rubbing against his hardened biceps and baby-smooth skin. He always thought that Finn had something to do with the security business. Maybe that's why he took off so quickly. Something had gone wrong in the security business tonight. When they'd first met, Fellows thought he made a mistake talking about his fantasy life because Finn looked like a cop. His eyes were dark and serious and stared back at him with a certain coplike reach. But after Fellows broke the ice, Finn opened up, revealing their common purpose. Over the nine months they had known each other, he'd never seen Finn dressed in a uniform or carrying any of the usual paraphernalia that went with a coplike job. Just that old briefcase.

Fellows zipped up his gym bag, strode through the lobby, and stepped outside. The fog had rolled in and he could smell the ocean in the cool night air. As he started down the sidewalk, a woman passed by with her eyes riveted to the ground. She seemed to be in a hurry. Too preoccupied with something to stop and talk. Fellows paused to look at her figure. Her long legs. But when he caught the scent of her perfume, all he could think about was Harriet Wilson. The smell of her skin and the way she'd brushed up against him in the lab today.

His heart started pounding. By the time he reached the car, he thought it might break through his chest. He pulled into traffic, ignoring the BMW with the quick horn and pulling up to the light. His house was to the left, a mile down the road, but it might take hours before he finally got to sleep. When the light turned green, he made a right and headed for the hills. Then he switched on the radio, found the news station, and lowered his windows. He could feel the air swirling about his shaved head. He could feel the tingle.

A man has needs, he told himself. Particularly a man in love with a fallen angel. Maybe the drive would ease the pain. Maybe the wind would cool him down. If not tonight, then tomorrow.

30

It had taken four hours, but Lena managed to get through her share of the case summaries. A share that amounted to 141 sexual assaults of women between the ages of sixteen and eighty-four living in Los Angeles County. It had been exhausting. Another long night.

She popped open the fridge and poured a glass of wine. Taking a quick sip, she glanced at her answering machine. When she got home, there had been a message waiting for her from Deputy District Attorney Roy Wemer, and she still found it disturbing. It had been an angry message, an insane message, something Wemer would never have left at the office. At first it sounded as if he was reprimanding her for being out of the loop on the DNA hit. But as he worked himself into a frenzy and began shouting, she realized that he was blaming her for losing the Lopez case. At one point toward the end he even claimed that he could still put Lopez away in spite of the science. When Wemer called her a stupid cunt, she looked back at the machine and hit STOP.

Unfortunately, the district attorney's office in Los Angeles kept a record of wins versus losses. They kept score, usually dragging out the results for Election Day. It was a dangerous statistic to keep because it encouraged people like Wemer to go for the win above all else. But it was also a meaningless statistic that many cities had long since abandoned in favor of getting it right. For Lena, keeping score pointed to the darkest side of her job. Something she'd talked about with her friend in the Cold Case Unit on more than one occasion.

DNA analysis of cases closed prior to the use of the technology indicated that 25 percent of the time they got it wrong. The reasons varied. Whether the problems originated at the investigative level or pointed to the prosecution and defense, an informant or eyewitness that lied or just got it wrong, or even a bad jury or an incompetent judge, the problems were systemic. While every inmate Lena ever met claimed to be innocent, one out of every four people locked up in a cell might actually be telling the truth.

Wemer was out of control. And his message might be worth keeping.

Ejecting the tape, she flipped the cassette over and snapped it back into the machine, rewinding Side 2 to the beginning. But as she closed the lid, she noticed a number jotted down on the pad by the phone and tried to place it. It took a moment before she remembered the message she'd picked up on Saturday night. Tim Holt, her brother's writing partner, wanted to get together. She had been too busy to return the call.

She checked the time. Just after midnight. Odds were that Holt would be out, either hitting the clubs or playing at one. It was the perfect time to leave a message. They wouldn't have to talk, and Lena wouldn't have to say no when Holt asked to reopen her brother's studio again. She dialed the number. After four rings his answering machine picked up. Holt sounded as good as he did when he'd left that message two days ago. He sounded *clean,* and she suddenly felt guilty for playing phone tag with her brother's best friend.

"Tim, it's me," she said after the beep. "Sorry I wasn't here when you called. I'm working on something right now, but maybe we can get together next week. I'll try calling you back tomorrow around lunchtime. If not, let's talk this weekend."

Her CD player shifted from John Coltrane's *My Favorite Things* to Pete Jolly's *Little Bird.* After switching off the phone, she listened to Jolly crank it up on the piano and made a mental note to call Holt back when she knew that he would be in. Then she walked around the counter to the table by the window in the living room, sipping her wine and glancing at the summaries she'd set aside for further inquiry. She hadn't expected to find any, but three stood out. In each case the rape was interrupted before it got started, so DNA evidence wouldn't be available. All three women were under thirty-five and lived alone. But what caught Lena's eye were the MOs, which seemed to mirror their working theory of how Nikki Brant had met her end.

Each victim had been awakened in the middle of the night by a man entering her bedroom.

In the first case, the perpetrator was chased off by the victim's dog. In the second, the victim switched on the light after hearing the window open and the man ran off. Unfortunately, he wore a ski mask and no identification could be made. But it was the third case that Lena found the most horrific. The doer had actually removed his clothing and was slipping beneath the covers on the other side of the bed when the woman fled the room and her house and started screaming for help on the front lawn.

All three cases had the look and feel of a match. Something she couldn't ignore or deny, particularly in light of what Dr. Bernhardt had said this morning. Romeo had graduated from rape to murder and was just getting started.

Lena set her glass down, lining up the summaries in chronological order. Like the murders, two of the three rape attempts had occurred a month apart. And in all three cases the assaults took place over the six months prior to the first murder. Flipping open her weekly planner, she paged forward until she reached the calendar. The first sexual assault attempt covered October of last year. While November remained blank, the second and third attempts occurred in December and January. February was blank as well, but Teresa Lopez had been murdered in March, and Nikki Brant was killed one month and three days later. If the CDs found at the murders were in play, the only symphonies she couldn't account for were No. 2 and No. 5, which might be in the stack of summaries Sanchez had handed out to the rest of the team.

Lena reached into her briefcase and fished out the *Thomas Guide,* a book of street maps that covered the entire county. On the back of the front cover was a foldout map that she had never used before. Pushing her wineglass aside, she laid the map out on the table and grabbed a marker. Maybe it was more than a theory. Maybe they weren't late on the investigation, but so early that no pattern could have been established before this moment.

A serial rapist in transition, she told herself. Romeo graduating to murder.

She found the approximate location of the first rape attempt on the map and wrote down the date and victim's name. After locating the next two, she added Teresa Lopez and Nikki Brant to the map and stood up for a better look.

The Lopez murder was the anomaly. It stood all by itself thirty miles on the other side of town. Although she wouldn't discount it, she could feel the weight of the map speaking to her. Nikki Brant's murder and each of the attempted rapes had occurred within two miles of each other on the Westside. If she joined the dots, the intersection was Venice Beach.

Lena didn't have much experience with sexual assault cases, but she had worked enough robberies to know that the locations of the crime scenes represented the doer's *comfort zone*. She also knew that what she was thinking right now wasn't based on a guess, a feeling, or even the wine she'd consumed.

The doer got started at the beach because he lived there. He knew the escape routes if something went wrong. He knew the quickest way back home if he was being chased. And that's exactly why in at least one case he wore a ski mask. The doer had concealed his identity because he was afraid someone might recognize him in his comfort zone. The place where he walked the streets, got out of his car to fill it with gas, and pushed a cart through the grocery store.

The doer, perhaps Romeo himself, lived somewhere near the beach. And if the doer really was Romeo, then something happened two months ago that had pushed him over the edge.

She looked back at the map. Something was troubling her, but she couldn't put her finger on it. When her eyes glided over the marina, it dawned on her what it was.

Avis Payton lived within the doer's comfort zone.

Although Novak agreed with her, Lena wondered if she'd made the right decision. After confirming the woman's story with the bank and verifying that her father was a cop in Salt Lake City, Lena made the call to Pacific Division rather than requesting a surveillance team from the Special Investigation Section. SIS was their primary surveillance unit but didn't usually get the callout unless they had a confirmed suspect to watch or tail. Keeping an eye on a location based on a one-month-old purse snatching seemed like a waste of resources. Even so, as Lena found Payton's street on the map and estimated the short distance to Venice Beach, she couldn't help but worry.

The phone rang. It was 1:00 a.m., and she wondered if it might not be Novak or even Rhodes. She glanced at her hand as she reached for the phone and thought about what had gone down in the elevator with Rhodes. His eyes probing her fingers. What she was thinking when he zeroed in on her hips and legs. Something inside her was hoping that it would be Rhodes.

"Sorry about my timing," a man was saying. "Hope I didn't wake you. But this is Teddy Mack with the FBI and it's the only time I've got."

She sat down on a stool at the counter. The slider was open and a breeze was playing with the map on the table.

"I can barely hear you," she said. "Where are you?"

"A place you never want to go. It's the middle of the night and it's still over a hundred and ten degrees. I'm standing outside my motel. The only place I can get a signal down here is a three-foot section in front of the lobby. If I lose you, I'll call back."

He sounded uncomfortable and tense. She could hear papers rustling in the background and thought about the heavy wind. Life in the desert required a shell.

"Have you had a chance to look at the report?"

"I've made some notes," he said. "I think you've got a problem and wanted to talk."

The FBI was calling it a *problem*. Lena eyed the three summaries laid out on the table.

"I guess you could call it that," she said. "A problem."

"Whatever it is, you got it. Let's start with the porn and why he accessed it at Nikki Brant's house."

"He used a stolen credit card to enter the Web site," she said. "We can't figure out why he's hanging around after the murder."

"We'll get to that," Mack said. "But don't you think it's curious that he would hide behind a stolen credit card when he could have easily joined the site and looked at it on his own turf without risk or consequence?"

Rhodes had asked the same question at their meeting with Dr. Bernhardt.

"You think it's a mistake," she said.

"Not necessarily. But I think it's proof that what we're looking at could cut both ways. Either this guy's into porn, or he's on some kind of bent mission and wants to keep it at a distance. The religious themes he's using to pose the bodies make me think he wants to keep the stuff at a distance. He doesn't want it in his home. What I'm saying is that it's possible Romeo was drawn to those two Web sites for a reason that might not be so obvious. Did you find the cardholder?"

Lena gave Mack a quick update that included how she'd spent the last five hours and that just maybe Teresa Lopez and Nikki Brant were the first two women Romeo had murdered.

"Now we're back to the way he's posing the victims," Mack said. "I think it's possible that you've hit on something. Your report says that you went through the homicide logs and nothing clicked. If there was anything else out there, it probably would've jumped off the page. Westbrook's going through our database as well. Hold on for a second."

She heard Mack cup the mouthpiece and whisper something to someone. After a moment, he was back.

"Sorry," he said. "Here's why I wanted to call. Bernhardt's got it right, but he left a few things out."

She reached for the pad by the answering machine and grabbed a pen. "Go ahead."

"The trick to Romeo is that he *observes*. For whatever reason he observes."

"Where's that coming from?"

"I'll get there in a minute."

"Okay," she said. "The key to the guy is that he likes to watch."

"That's right. He lives on distance. For the moment, let's say you're right. The MOs match and Romeo attempted to rape the three women you just mentioned. Rape is about a lot of things, but most often it's about control. When he couldn't control the situation, he didn't attack the woman who turned on the light and he didn't chase the next victim through the house. He ran away because he lost control. But the murders signify a pathological change. A new start. His evolution or need to commit the ultimate violation. His desire to take absolute control and do it at all costs. You with me?"

"I'm writing it down, Teddy. But it sounds a lot like what Bernhardt was saying."

"Here's what I think you need to keep in mind. You're looking for someone who blends perfectly with their environment. Someone who looks like he belongs there until you single him out and realize how truly odd he is."

"We're talking about Venice Beach."

"I get it, Lena. Venice Beach. But here's the thing. The guy you're look-ing for has been hurt in some fundamental way and is searching for some-one who feels what he feels. The ultimate kick for this guy would be to actually do the murder while someone watched."

"You're getting all this from what I sent you?"

"Some of it," Mack said. "But it really hit when I figured out the reason why he spends so much time at the crime scenes after the murder."

Lena raised an eyebrow. "What's the reason?"

"The trick to this guy is that he observes, right?"

"I've got that. Why is he hanging out at the crime scene?"

Mack lowered his voice. "Because he wants to see the husband's reaction to the kill."

A moment passed as the revelation cut through. Deep and fast like a bul-let penetrating human flesh.

Romeo read his victims' journals, went through their financial records and personal notes. He spent time looking at pornography on the computer. He listened to music and had a thing for Beethoven. When the paper ar-rived, he worked the crossword puzzle.

Romeo was waiting for the spouse to come home. He posed his victims to shock the first person who found them, not the police.

Mack cleared his throat. "The husband's reaction to finding his loved one is the key. It's as important to him as the rape or even the kill. It may even be the very reason he's making the kill. That's why I said you've got a problem. This guy's from another planet. He's off the charts."

Lena wasn't sure she could speak right away. Her mind was locked on Jose Lopez and James Brant. What they were forced to see and what they would never be able to forget. Perhaps that's why Jose Lopez wanted to die in prison rather than be set free. Maybe that's why Brant failed the poly-graph. No matter how the question was posed, he couldn't forget.

When Lena finally spoke, her voice wasn't much louder than a whisper. "Romeo wants the husband to hurt as much as he does. That's why he needs to see it."

"That's why he waits for them to come home. I'd bet the bank that he was inside the house watching Brant discover his wife's dead body."

Mack covered the phone again and said something to someone. She could hear digital noise over the line, the sound of footsteps and a car. Mack wouldn't be sleeping tonight but was heading into the desert.

"I've gotta go, Lena."

"Thanks for the heads-up," she said. "Maybe we can—"

The signal blurred into static. Lena stared at the handset, then switched it off. After a while she noticed the saxophone playing in the background. Her CD player had cycled through all five discs, ending with Art Pepper's *Winter Moon*. But as she listened to the music, she couldn't get the image out of her head. Romeo watching Brant discover his wife's body. It was beyond the pale.

She pulled a sweater over her shoulders, grabbed her glass, and stepped outside for some fresh air. The wind had changed, blowing from the east and pushing the marine layer out of the way to reveal a sky absent of stars. As she sat down by the pool and sipped her wine, she heard something in the darkness and looked into the yard at the edge of the hill. A coyote glanced at the water in the pool licking his chops, then gave her a long look before retreating into the brush with his tail down. His drink would have to wait until later when the coast was clear.

She turned back to the city, following the lights until her eyes stopped on Venice Beach fifteen miles away. Romeo's comfort zone. The place where he knew the escape routes and the quickest way back home.

She tightened her grip on the sweater and finished her drink.

Nothing about the view seemed especially comforting tonight. Only the stillness, the cool, breezy air, and the promise of another glass of wine so that she might be able to close her eyes at some point and settle into a dreamless sleep.

Her cell phone rang from its charger on the kitchen counter. When she caught the name flashing on the LCD screen, she yanked the wire out and snapped open the phone.

Novak—calling at 6:30 a.m. All she could think about was Avis Payton. She should have called SIS. She fucked up.

"You work late?" he asked.

She didn't answer the question, her mind going. Novak's voice sounded better than rough, as if maybe he'd just rolled out of bed. A car door slammed, then an engine fired up.

"We've got another one," she said.

"We'll see when we get there."

"You're heading for the marina."

"No," he said.

She felt a sudden rush, the relief tainted, but still there. At least it wasn't the young woman from Marina Del Rey with the electric maroon hair.

"This one's closer to you," he said. "Just on the other side of the freeway in the hills below Mulholland. Hollywood Division's already there. They went in for a look, then backed out. Barrera just called. He thinks it might have something to do with the press conference last night. Maybe Romeo heard it on the radio. Maybe we yanked his chain and he got pissed off. Or maybe we're in luck and it's not Romeo at all."

This one was closer to her in a lot of ways. She had worked out of Hollywood as both a cop and a detective until she was promoted to RHD. She still had a lot of friends there.

"Who's the victim?"

Novak didn't respond right away. She could hear the Crown Vic picking up speed and imagined he was hitting the 405. After his divorce, Novak had found an apartment two blocks from his ex-wife's home in Culver City. They remained friends, and he wanted to live close by so that he could see his daughters before he retired and left town.

"We've got two dead bodies," he said finally. "The house belongs to Sally and Joe Garcia. That's why I said we'll see."

He gave her the address, and she wrote it down: 4701 Vista Road.

"The freeway looks clean, Lena. I'm guessing I'm only twenty minutes behind you."

"What about Sanchez and Rhodes?"

"I'll make the calls, but hurry. If it's Romeo, I don't want Hollywood to fuck anything up."

He said it as if he thought they might, but she took it in stride. By the time he hung up, she had found the address in her *Thomas Guide* and was gunning it down the hill in her Prelude. Ten minutes later she passed beneath the Hollywood Freeway and made the climb back up the next hill, weaving in and around the tight curves along Mulholland Drive. The air was brisk and she drove with the windows open and the radio off, still revved up from her conversation with Teddy Mack and the gut feeling that she'd made real progress last night. As she thought it over, the idea that Romeo may have wandered beyond his comfort zone didn't undercut that progress. Nor did the possibility that he'd altered his schedule and picked up his pace. If Romeo's madness was truly burgeoning, then so was his confidence. It was only a matter of time before he left his neighborhood in order to protect it. Any way she looked at it, her theory remained intact.

Lena tightened her grip on the wheel, working a deep curve with her foot stamped to the floor and blowing out the other side. When she caught the street sign, she jammed on the brakes and made the turn onto Vista. The street dipped sharply down the hill, then flattened out as it twisted back and forth through the shadows beneath long-standing trees. Passing the first driveway, she started looking for street numbers. But the houses were spread out in increments of one per fifty yards. And they were set back from the road and hidden behind security gates and high walls.

She rounded the next bend, spotting two cruisers and a detective's car parked before a stone wall that had been whitewashed. Pulling onto the shoulder, she took a last sip of coffee and gazed through the windshield. Two cops were stretching crime scene tape from tree to tree along the road. In the distance she could see a detective standing in the middle of the street. She caught the buffed head and ebony skin. The good-natured grin as he watched her getting out of the car. Terry Banks had taken her spot with Pete Sweeney at the homicide table when she'd moved downtown.

"Hey, Gamble," Banks called out. "Is this a takeaway case or did you just stop by to say hello to your friends in *Hollywood*?"

She smiled, waiting for him by the car. "That depends. Where's your good half?"

"Ten steps behind, as usual."

Banks glanced over his shoulder. Although Lena couldn't make out the neighbor's house, she saw her old partner pop through a gate in the fence and start down the street. Pete Sweeney was the size of a grizzly bear. His shoulders were extrawide, his manner extra-easy and somehow reassuring right now. When the two detectives finally reached her, Sweeney gave her an awkward hug.

"My old partner," he said. "It'll never be the same without you. How you doin'?"

"I'm good, Pete. I miss you, too."

They started moving toward the Garcias' driveway.

"I read the bulletin yesterday," Sweeney said. "Banks heard the press conference last night on KFWB. It's pretty weird inside, Lena. I thought we'd better call it in before we got too far."

She glanced toward the neighbor's house blotted out by a grove of tall pine trees. "What's going on up the street?"

"He's an early-morning jogger. Gets started when everybody else is just about hitting the sheets. The driveway gate was open. Same with the front door. When he rang the bell, no one answered so he went inside for a look."

Banks flashed a nervous grin. "No way he ever does that again."

Sweeney nodded, lowering his voice. "The dead bodies are upstairs in the bedroom."

They reached the drive. Lena noticed a FOR SALE sign dangling from a post beside the Garcias' mailbox.

"They were moving," she said.

"Shit," Banks said. "They must have sold the place before they could get the sign changed. Everything inside is boxed up and ready to go. Too bad they didn't make the move a day sooner."

"What do we know about them?"

Sweeney grimaced, reaching for an imaginary pack of cigarettes in his pocket, then pulling his hand away. He'd quit smoking when they were partners but forgot sometimes when things slid toward the edge.

"The jogger thinks maybe they worked for the studios but isn't sure. What's up with that? They lived next door to each other for ten years and the guy isn't sure. Seems like there's not much neighborly interaction going on around here. Just walls with gates and plenty of passwords to go around."

The cobblestone driveway sloped down from the street. As Lena's eyes met the death house, she suddenly felt uneasy, even nervous. As much as she tried to purge the feeling, it wouldn't go away.

The house seemed harmless enough. It was built of stone and white-washed like the wall that was supposed to protect it. Lush waves of ivy crept up from the gardens, weaving through the shutters but trimmed before the vines could reach the terra-cotta roof. Twenty-five yards behind the house, a small stable faced what looked like half an acre of open field and a well-worn horse trail leading into the hills. Lena guessed that the house and stable predated the invention of the car. Had she seen the property in any other context, she would have been drawn to its age and beauty. Its serenity and warmth.

But not this morning. Not right now.

She slipped on a pair of gloves and followed Sweeney and Banks through the front door. Although the furniture remained in place, packing cartons stacked to the ceiling blocked much of the view.

Sweeney gave her a nudge. "Nice place, huh? The stairs are down here."

Lena noted the wood-plank floors and richly detailed moldings. Reaching the stairs, she glanced through the doorway into the kitchen and spotted a sandwich set beside an open bottle of beer. Someone had obviously made a snack last night before being interrupted. As she climbed the steps and reached the landing, she heard something and stopped.

"It's the TV," Banks said in a low voice. "We didn't go in."

Banks seemed more than a little anxious. Sweeney pointed to the bedroom door and they moved in for a closer look.

A moment passed. Then another until Sweeney cleared his throat.

"Like I said, Lena, it's seriously fucked up in here. You tell me if it's your guy and we'll back out. No hard feelings out of Hollywood. We've already got a full plate."

She nodded, grabbing hold of the doorjamb and trying to compose herself while the hosts from a TV morning news show spewed their meaningless banter into a room in which two people were better than dead. Lena gritted her teeth and stepped through the doorway.

Joe Garcia's body sat in the chair by the window, his left hand still clutching the revolver he'd used to blow his brains all over the ceiling and wall. Sally Garcia was sitting up in bed, her naked corpse posed to look something like a marionette dangling from the headboard. But her arms weren't bound with strings. Instead, her body was drawn upward by a sheer, black stocking pulled over her face and tied around a bedpost. Over the stocking a garish smile was painted in with red lipstick. Two holes had been cut through the nylon, revealing the woman's eyes, which remained open and were hard to look at.

Lena checked the floor before taking a step closer, then zeroed in on the knife wounds in search of the keys—Romeo's signature that would never be released to the public until they had a suspect in custody and went to trial. The wounds were an exact copy of the trauma Nikki Brant had endured. A through and through just below the collarbone, followed by a second cut in the young woman's belly. Although she couldn't see Sally Garcia's face, she knew that the woman was young. Her skin was gray but appeared supple, her breasts remained unusually perky, and her stomach and thighs appeared toned. Even more telling, her bikini line revealed that she was still able to wear a thong.

But there was a significant difference here. A significant lack of blood. Lena took another look at the woman's head, pointed toward the television, sensing that the angle was odd, even severe, and wondering if Romeo hadn't snapped her neck before using the knife.

Her eyes flicked back to the young woman's vagina, noting visible traces of seminal fluid. And then down to her feet until she spotted the missing toe.

The keys were here, neatly locked in a ring. Romeo had repeated his MO in almost every detail. An MO that remained his alone and seemed to be evolving.

"What do you think?" Banks asked from the doorway.

"It's him," she said. "It's Romeo."

Sweeney stepped into the room. "The other two were like this?"

"Variations on a theme," she said. "It looks like Sally Garcia went quicker though."

"Okay, so she was lucky," Sweeney said. "What about Joe over here?"

She turned to look at the husband's body and what appeared to be a single shot through the roof of his mouth. High-velocity-impact blood spatter stained the white wall behind his head.

She took another step closer. The gunshot residue dusting Garcia's left hand was visible to the eye, and Lena guessed that the .38 revolver was old and worn-out. She couldn't make out his face because the exit wound appeared to be just above the forehead. Considerable bleeding had followed the gunshot, cascading down the man's face and forming a thick crust that had blackened as it dried. His eyes remained open, but appeared dislodged and unnaturally bugged.

"The second body's a first," she said.

Sweeney shook his head, crouching down for a better view. "He found his wife like this and took himself out. Plenty of guys might do the same thing if the love was still good."

She nodded, but that feeling of impending doom was back. That feeling that they were missing something. She shook it off and turned toward the landing. Romeo could easily have watched Joe Garcia blow himself away from the stairs without being seen. She remembered her conversation with Teddy Mack last night. Experiencing the husband's grief and anguish was just as important to Romeo as the rape and murder. It might be the very reason he made the kill.

If Mack was right, then last night had been a grand slam. A command performance for someone lurking in the shadows who fed on heartbreak.

The noise from the TV was back and Lena could no longer filter it out. The hosts were laughing at something. When she glanced at the tube, the chatter appeared scripted. One more reason on the list of every other reason why she still subscribed to a newspaper.

She turned off the TV and scanned the room. Although it appeared in disarray, the Garcias hadn't started packing yet, and she found what she was looking for on the bedside table. The radio CD player was one of the best. A Bose Wave player. Stepping around the bed, she opened the lid and read the label on the CD without much surprise. Beethoven's Symphony No. 8. The Garcias hadn't moved. They were screwed in F Major.

Someone called out her name and she took a step back. It sounded like Novak, shouting from the entryway. As Sweeney and Banks left the room to direct him upstairs, her eyes drifted down to the telephone. A digital answering machine was attached, the message light blinking.

She glanced at the empty doorway, then turned back to the answering machine and hit PLAY.

"Tim, it's me," she heard the caller saying. *"Sorry I wasn't here when you called. I'm working on something right now, but maybe we can get together next week. I'll try calling you back tomorrow around lunchtime. If not, let's talk this weekend."*

Time appeared to stop. Her chest tightened, the dread seizing her by the back of the neck and snapping her spine as if it were a bullwhip.

She had been playing phone tag with her brother's best friend. She made the call at a time when she thought Tim Holt wouldn't be in. She remembered feeling guilty about it.

Her eyes darted over to the dead man slumped in the chair, her mind spitting out a quick reconstruction of the face hidden behind the mask of dried blood. The shape of his jawline and what was left of his nose. The color of his hair. She could feel the heat radiating through her body. Everything burning up from the inside out as the dots connected and the face evolved into someone she knew.

The Garcias had packed up their boxes and taken them away. The new owners were just settling in for what turned out to be only a short stay.

A shadow passed over the death house as she stared at what was left of her brother's best friend. Through the fallout she thought she could hear Novak entering the room ahead of Banks and Sweeney. They were shouting something at her. They were rushing toward her. She could feel her knees buckling. Her hands slipping away. The sound of the wind in her ears as her soul collapsed into the abyss.

32

She looked tired. Withdrawn. The circles beneath her eyes visible despite the makeup. But when she smiled at him from the other side of the lab, Fellows melted as he usually did, then caught himself and nodded at her from his desk.

It had been a private smile. A special smile that meant more than all the rest. The one she only used when No. 3 was out of the lab and they were alone.

He watched Harriet step around the other side of the table, still trying to hide that limp. He wondered if it hurt and knew that despite everything that had happened, despite his anger and rage, he still loved her. He still needed to protect her. After a few moments, he returned to his notebook and made a new entry beside the time and date.

Looks like shit today. Probable cause the same as always, though not yet confirmed. Another all-night fuck session with Burell.

Fellows kept two sets of lab books. One for his experiments, which always sat on the counter beside his microscope. And another devoted entirely to his observations regarding Harriet Wilson, kept safely locked away in his desk and carried home every night for careful review. Fellows liked to write things down to clarify his thoughts and feelings and ponder new ideas. Besides, he'd noticed over the past year or so that his mind liked to wander more than usual. If he didn't get his thoughts down on paper, sometimes they ran off and never returned.

He reread the last sentence, drew a line through Burell's name, and replaced it with the words *soon to be dead*. While the revision may have been more accurate, he noticed a disturbing shake in his penmanship, took a deep breath, and tried to relax some.

It was difficult. For the past twelve hours his mind had been rolling through different scenarios of how Charles Burell might spend his last few minutes on earth. And as he thought it over, not one of his fantasies required the help of his friend and spotter, Mick Finn.

There was the guillotine dream in which Fellows played the part of a henchman fulfilling the wishes of his king. Fellows liked this one because it always ended with a crowd cheering as Burell's head rolled down a long ramp into a basket. But there were other dreams. Some drawn from his favorite Bible stories. Others rooted in his past that remained less formed and less desirable because sometimes it wasn't Burell taking the abuse. More times than not, it was him. He could remember his grandmother telling him that little boys who touched themselves received black marks from the Virgin Mary. The marks were tallied up at the end of each month and sent by angels directly to God. If his score was high enough, the naughty boy might be fed to the lions or even that angry dog chained to the tree next door. Fellows spent years keeping an eye on that dog from his bedroom window and throwing treats over the fence. Countless hours estimating how high a score might need to become before he received a thumbs-down from the Almighty. In spite of the risk, he couldn't help himself and continued to masturbate once or twice a day. But over time the act became more of a need than a pleasure, mixed with fear and terror and the idea that he would one day tip the scales and be eaten alive. As his grandmother used to say while pointing a shaky finger, Martin Fellows was the only kid in the world who liked to jerk off.

The lab door opened, the memory collapsing as No. 3 returned from lunch and launched another of his stupid grins across the room.

Fellows checked the time, trying to ignore the smell of fish tacos in the air. He was meeting Finn at the Pink Canary in fifteen minutes. Hopefully, his friend had come up with a scenario of his own. Something with more realism that didn't require a crowd or historical detail. After locking his notebook in the drawer, he got up and stopped by Harriet's lab table.

"You want the usual?" he asked.

She winked at him and pulled a menu from the drawer. "Em," she said, "I'm in the mood for something different. What are you having, Martin?"

She slid the menu between them and moved closer. When she inadvertently moistened her lips with her tongue, Fellows turned to the menu and tried to regain his composure.

Deciding what to eat had become more difficult ever since mad cow disease was discovered in Washington State a few years ago. Although the brain-wasting disease had been found in only one cow, the animal was from a lot of more than eighty cattle that couldn't be located, were lost in the system, and by now, had probably been consumed. In five years, Fellows estimated that pets would begin dying. In about seven, young children. Two or three years after that the horror would strike adults. Fellows found it astounding that no one cared. When the government sided with the beef industry instead of public safety, when the Department of Agriculture suggested that only one-tenth of one percent of all cattle be tested, no one spoke up. Instead, people still lined up on Lincoln Boulevard to eat their burgers like cows hoofing their way to slaughter.

Fellows had always liked eating cows. Even though the Pink Canary only used organic ingredients, he still shied away from the meat. For a while he couldn't even eat chickens for fear of contracting bird flu and was forced to feed on lambs and pigs. The food supply was obviously in flux, a fact that made life for a bodybuilder particularly difficult. Since beginning training, he measured his consumption with scientific precision: 40 percent protein, 40 percent carbohydrates, and 20 percent fat, usually in the form of two tablespoons of flaxseed oil taken after each meal. Worrying about the tainted food supply only made his regimen more difficult.

He looked at Harriet, gazing at the menu with those gentle blue eyes. Her hair was pulled back the way he liked it.

"I'll probably just order chicken," he said in a quiet voice. "You haven't had rigatoni this week."

"I was thinking eggplant."

"Lasagna?"

She smiled through a yawn. "Eggplant lasagna with marinara sauce and an iced tea."

"I spoke with them about half orders the other day."

"That's okay. What I don't eat I'll take home. I was up late last night and want to go to sleep early."

He had it. Confirmation that she was with Burell last night. He could see it in her eyes. He turned back to his desk, wondering if he should make the entry in his notebook before he forgot.

"Is something wrong, Martin?"

He shook his head. "I'm fine."

He wouldn't forget, he decided. He couldn't.

"I'm fine," he repeated.

She handed him a $10 bill and he headed for the door. Until two months ago he had been convinced that Harriet was a good girl. Quiet, simple, the kind of woman he had always dreamed of. Until two months ago he thought she might even be the Virgin Mary, making a return visit to show him the way to his salvation. Now he realized that the situation was reversed and he needed to find a way to save her.

Ignoring the receptionist, he slipped on his sunglasses, pushed the front door open, and legged it across the parking lot. Although the diner was within walking distance, the sun was out so he would have to drive. Ten minutes later he stood in line, waiting on his order and watching Finn through the window. His friend had just arrived and was sitting at their table in the shade reading a newspaper. Fellows turned to the old woman behind the counter, straining to remain patient. She was short and round and telling another one of her crude jokes to the customer ahead of him. Fellows had stopped listening to her banter months ago. But everyone seated at the counter seemed to think she was funny and he could hear them laughing. When his order finally came up, he stepped over to the register, paying the woman with a forced smile as if he were in on the joke and adding his usual 10 percent to the tip jar. Then he grabbed a tray, two bottles of mineral water, and hurried outside to join Finn.

"I'm sorry, Martin. I can't stay long. Something's come up at work."

Fellows didn't say anything, trying to conceal his disappointment. Setting both orders of chicken cacciatore down, he wiped off his fork with a paper napkin and got started on his salad.

"You look tired," Finn said. "You should've gone straight home from the gym last night. Instead, you took that drive in the hills."

Fellows adjusted his sunglasses and gazed at his friend. "I'm not tired. It's the light. It's bright today."

"The sun's reflecting off that window. Want to switch places?"

Fellows looked at the apartment over the Pink Canary. The bright light bouncing off the glass seemed to be picking him out of the crowd.

"I'm okay," he said. "What about tonight?"

"Everything's set. We're on."

Fellows lowered his fork, his body shuddering with excitement. "Why didn't you just say so? Last night it sounded like you wanted to back out."

"No, Martin. There's no backing out. Tonight's the night. I'll be there to spot you."

Finn smiled. Fellows took another bite of salad, his hand trembling.

"How?"

"I'll tell you when we get there," Finn said. "And do me a favor. Stop talking with your mouth full. People are staring."

There were four tables by the diner's entrance. Fellows turned to have a look over his sunglasses. By the time he craned his head back, no one was looking their way. Still, he made a point of chewing his salad without speaking. There was something different about the dressing. A new ingredient that he found disturbing. He wondered if the olive oil hadn't turned. He hoped he wouldn't get sick and ruin his friend's plans for the evening.

"Does any of this concern you?" Finn asked, thumping his knuckles on the newspaper.

Fellows glanced at the article as he took a sip of water. The police had held a press conference yesterday and the story wound up on the front page. He remembered hearing excerpts on the radio last night after leaving the gym. James Brant was no longer a suspect in his wife's murder. Jose Lopez was due to be released from jail, but remained inside the building for some unknown reason. According to the police, DNA results linked both murders to someone else.

Fellows stopped reading and turned toward the beach to think it over. It was a difficult view, a view that didn't go well with lunch because an indigent on Rollerblades was pushing a stolen grocery cart filled with trash down the promenade. The man's shirt appeared tattered, his pants, heavily soiled. Although he lacked any sense of personal hygiene or self-esteem, he wore a smile on his face. A big smile that hinted at madness.

"You still with me?" Finn asked. "Or do you have something on your mind?"

Fellows watched the homeless man skate into the bright sunlight and vanish in the sheen.

"The DNA is irrelevant," he said finally.

Finn leaned closer and lowered his voice. "It's your DNA, Martin."

"It doesn't matter where it came from."

"It connects two murders. I guess your definition of irrelevant is different than mine."

"Without me, the DNA doesn't point to anything but itself," Fellows said. "It's a closed set. Besides, it couldn't be helped."

"I think you take too many risks. They're unnecessary. You should know better."

"What time?" Fellows asked.

"You're not listening to me."

"I heard everything you said. What time?"

Finn got up from the table. "Around ten."

33

She couldn't go there. Even though Novak insisted that she leave the crime scene, take the day off and get some rest, she couldn't go home. She had seen the tears in her partner's eyes, heard his voice cracking, thought he was making sense. Yet she couldn't do it.

That's where all the memories lived. Inside the home she once shared with her brother.

The light turned green at Franklin and Gower. The decision beckoned. When someone behind her started working their horn, she made a right and followed the hill down to Sunset.

Her body was still trembling, her mind, unable to lock in on the present. Somehow she didn't think that her memories qualified as memories anymore. She didn't have her back to the past. She was facing it again, staring at it. Her personal history was lurking in the gloom from somewhere in the future, waiting to be rewritten and reused.

Tim Holt had moved back to L.A., buying a home from Sally and Joe Garcia. Now he and his girlfriend were dead.

She crossed Sunset and pulled into the lot at Gower Gulch. Seconds ticked off as she bought a pack of smokes at the drugstore. Minutes streamed by in a direction of their own as she ordered a tall coffee-of-the-day at Starbucks.

It had been her choice. Get juiced at the Cat N' Fiddle until the world blurred or sharpen the edge with both eyes open and force herself to gaze at the infection. Before she knew it, she was back in the car, watching herself drive up Gower, make the left onto Hollywood Boulevard, and then the right of all rights onto Vista Del Mar.

Her brother, David, had been gunned down on Vista Del Mar. A single shot in the center of his chest.

She eased off the gas, rolling forward at a crawl. To her left was an empty parking lot. To the right, an auto body shop surrounded by a chain-link fence and barbed wire. The road petered out at the base of a short hill and an abandoned one-room chapel, the grounds blanketed with spent needles. The refuse left behind from cash-and-smack deals and trips to the moon via the Holy Grail.

She pulled over and cut the engine. Leaning back in the seat, she removed the lid from her coffee. The hot steam rose up into her face, warming her cheeks and mouth as she took a first sip and savored its strength. After several moments, she let her eyes wander past the cup and outside the car, crossing the street slowly, deliberately, until they reached the spot where she'd found her brother's body five years ago.

The stillness hit her in waves. One after another until she finally let the nightmare in.

She had been on duty that night, cruising the boulevard with her partner when their radio lit up. An anonymous call had been placed directly to the front desk at the Hollywood station over on Wilcox, bypassing the 911 system and the audio recorders that backed it up.

In spite of the darkness, Lena could remember homing in on the make and model of the car. The front tires had rolled up over the curb. The headlights were on, the engine running. Even though the driver's-side door stood open, the interior light remained off and she couldn't make out any detail. But she could recall that sharp feeling of terror gripping her as she switched her flashlight on and approached the car. The blow she took in the gut as the beam of light washed over the victim and ferreted out a face. An identity.

Her heart locked up and she couldn't breathe.

He was lying across the front seat in a fetal position and, at a glance, appeared to be sleeping until she noticed the hole in his chest and the pool of blood. But what Lena couldn't forget were his hands. His long, elegant fingers. They were clasped together between his thighs. The same way he'd held them when he was a little boy and had a stomachache or the flu. Her brother's death hadn't been peaceful and hadn't come quick. When David died, he knew what was happening to him and it obviously hurt.

Lena didn't remember much more than that—something Dr. Bernhardt called retro amnesia during their sessions. Everything remained in a haze, taking years to clarify and pin down. According to Dr. Bernhardt, retro amnesia could be caused by any traumatic event and wipe out three or four days. Even worse, no one was immune. Rescue workers and cops could be struck by the experience just as easily as the victim's friends and family. It was all about the shock. The depth of the bite. The sudden jolt of power shorting out the nervous system.

The irony was that it happened here, she thought. In the shadows of the Capitol Records building just on the other side of the empty parking lot.

She turned away from the building, sipping her coffee and opening the pack of cigarettes. Lena and David Gamble had been a team. Since childhood. Since the beginning.

Their mother had run off just after David's birth and missed out on meeting him and getting to know who her children might become. Their father raised them. On his own in Denver without the help of anyone.

Despite her mother abandoning them, most of Lena's childhood memories were good. Her father had been a welder, highly sought after for his ability to work at great heights in spite of the wind. Nearly every high-rise building in the Denver skyline erected between 1976 and 1990 bore its shape from the labor of his torch. She could remember her father laughing one night at a fireworks display over the city. He was holding her in his arms and the explosions overtop the buildings looked just like the sparks she saw spewing from his torch. When she mentioned it, he pulled her closer and kissed her on the forehead, calling the display his "magic torch."

They were more than happy. And money had never been an issue in their lives. At least not until the recession hit in the early nineties and no one seemed to need tall buildings anymore. Her father's hours changed after that and he began working a series of part-time jobs. Still, they managed. Lena was sixteen at the time, keeping an eye on her little brother most nights even though all he ever did was listen to music and play his guitar. Somehow it all worked out until one night the doorbell rang and everything went black.

Two men delivered the news. Two ugly men with white hair and puffy, red noses, wearing windbreakers marked with a company logo she had never seen before and smelling like a broken whiskey bottle.

It seemed her father had been in an accident, they told her. A bad accident and it didn't look good.

By the time they reached the hospital, it was already over and Lena was smart enough to know that the two men had lied to her. Their father had been working the night shift at a pipe-manufacturing plant. When his arm was sucked into a conveyor belt, he bled to death before a coworker found him and hit the kill switch. According to a third man, an attorney who met them at the hospital, the accident appeared to be the result of something called *operator error*. In the days that followed, Lena learned that there had been many other accidents just like this one. That the plant had been cited for numerous safety violations but had attributed each and every accident to operator error rather than fork up the money to comply. Because their father had been a part-time employee, financial restitution would be slim to none. Even worse, both Lena and David were minors. As wards of the state, they would be picked up by the Department of Human Services and institutionalized until they were adopted or reached the age of eighteen.

Lena laid her head back, thinking about that photograph of Nikki Brant standing outside the orphanage. Shaking it off, she looked through the windshield at the dilapidated chapel just up the hill. The steeple had toppled over. She could see a junkie inside the building, peeking through the window and staring at her. His face had withered. His eyes had that hollow look that could only mean that he was on his own and one or two steps away from the finish line.

Lena and David Gamble had been a team, signing a pact and shaking on it and fleeing their home before the Department of Human Services had a chance to ruin their lives.

Driving south, then west, they stayed away from the freeways until they got outside the city—everything they owned in the back of their father's Chevy Suburban. Within two days they were in L.A. Within a week, both of them found jobs. After another six months, they'd saved enough money to pay rent on a small efficiency apartment and finally move out of the car.

As she thought it over, it sounded more bleak than it really was.

For some bizarre reason, those six months living in the car usually brought on a smile. A deep feeling of satisfaction and warmth. David always liked to say that they made it because they had to. If there had been a safety net, someone feeding them money anytime they asked, they would have taken the bait and ended up losing who they were. That the trick was that they had each other and didn't spend a lot of time looking back.

She took another sip of coffee, grateful that the junkie had vanished from the window and was no longer staring at her.

She could remember watching her brother's development as a musician and a songwriter. The shock of pleasure and pride she felt when she realized his talent was genuine and that he really would succeed. By eighteen David was playing guitar behind real names in the studio. By twenty he had met Tim Holt and formed their band. Articles began to appear in newspapers and magazines, and months were spent on the road developing an audience. A few years later, David was three CDs in on a five-album deal with Blue Moon Records, while Lena had graduated from college and the police academy and earned enough air miles to begin thinking about the detective civil service exam.

She looked at the pack of cigarettes in her hand. Although her brother and Holt chained them in the studio, Lena had never been a user. She struck a match and drew the smoke into her lungs. Blowing it out the window, she realized that she was holding the cigarette between her thumb and first finger as if smoking a well-rolled joint.

There had been two theories about her brother's murder. And maybe that was why the case had never been solved.

David was playing at a club on the Strip that night. When they found his body, his wallet was missing, along with a collection of CDs he kept in a box behind the front seat of his car. Some believed that he drove to this spot to score and was shot before the deal went down. Others, including most of his fans, thought it had more to do with his girlfriend, Zelda Clemens. Zelda was a rock-and-roll rag doll, clinging to David and trying to hang on for the ride. When she insisted on moving into the house, he dumped her as quickly as he could.

Unfortunately, Zelda wouldn't go away.

Lena could remember the woman calling the house over and over, and realizing that Zelda had snapped. Over the week before the murder Lena counted 117 calls. If David answered, he hung up. If she answered, Zelda would call her a stupid bitch and order her to put her "lover-brother" on the phone. The night David died, Zelda showed up at the club, drinking herself into oblivion and causing a scene when she saw him slip away with another woman after the last set. The last call.

But in the end, the detectives working the case couldn't skin the cat. The murder weapon had never been found. And like many witnesses, the woman David left with that night never came forward. Once the various forensic labs finished their reports, the investigation slowed down to a creep and a crawl until it was finally shelved for lack of evidence. Either David was murdered in the midst of a drug deal, or Zelda followed him to Vista Del Mar, saw him in the car with another woman, and pulled the trigger.

The two theories confused Lena as much as they had the detectives. David experimented but wasn't a user of hard drugs. Still, he could have come here to buy anything. On the other hand, Zelda had reached an emotional froth. She had a motive and appeared irrational enough to do the crime. Lena spent years thinking about it and couldn't put her finger on which track made the most sense. Dealing with her brother's death seemed hard enough and was made all the worse by Zelda's sudden rise as a celebrity. For better or worse, David's murder finally gave Zelda Clemens the publicity she had been seeking her entire life. Within a few months she latched onto another musician. And now there was talk that she had become an actress, landing a part in a movie.

Lena shrugged. Maybe it was as bad as it sounded after all.

She took another drag on the cigarette, a deep pull, and started coughing. When she caught the foul taste entering the back of her mouth, she flicked the butt out the window and grabbed her coffee. It wasn't the smoke. It was the unmistakable flavor of death seeping down her sinuses and working through her tongue. The tastes and smells from the morgue, and a latent reminder of Nikki Brant's autopsy performed four days ago.

She finished off the cup, squelching the bad taste in her mouth and noticing that her body had finally stopped trembling.

Why did Tim Holt call?

As she thought it over, she understood that this was the real reason why she'd come here. Why was her brother's best friend trying to reach her?

She started the car, revving up the engine. She felt the push of anger rise up from her belly. She wanted to hit something. Smash it. Kill it. Instead, she turned the car around and drove off.

You look great," Okolski said. "How long's it been, Lena? Three years?"

Warren Okolski was president of Blue Moon Records, the label that had signed David Gamble and Tim Holt and launched their careers. Okolski produced all three albums, spending a lot of time at the house. And his memory appeared tack sharp. The last time Lena had seen Okolski had been three years ago—a chance meeting on the promenade in Santa Monica that led to dinner and drinks and a game of darts at some out-of-the-way pub.

His face blushed with color and he stood up from his desk. His assistant, a young blonde, seemed perplexed that her boss could be so pleased to see someone who had shown up without an appointment. Someone she didn't know.

"It's Lena," he said to her. "David Gamble's sister."

The girl appeared to get it, but something was eating at her. Lena figured that it might have something to do with the gun clipped to her belt, but ignored it and gave Okolski a hug. She liked him. She always had, and it felt good.

"You want anything?" he asked. "Coffee, water, anything at all. You name it and it's yours."

She knew from experience that when he said *anything*, he meant it. She shook her head. As his assistant left the room, eyeballing Lena's open blazer, he told her to hold his calls.

"Sit, stay, talk," he said.

Lena sat down on the couch, feeling uneasy because she knew that she was about to ruin the man's day. Okolski returned to his desk and grabbed a bottle of spring water. Glancing at his computer monitor, he flashed a wide grin.

"What's so funny?" she asked.

"My assistant just sent me an e-mail."

"What's it say?"

"You're armed and dangerous. You're carrying a big fucking gun."

They laughed. Lena tried to relax as Okolski slid into the leather armchair on the other side of the coffee table.

"When are you going to give it up, Lena? My offer still stands. You want a job, you've got it. Either way, I hope you're staying for lunch."

"I don't think I can."

Okolski gave her a look, then did a double take as if he just figured out that something was wrong. He was tall, lean, in his late thirties. His eyes were more gold than brown, his face, soft and easy and devoid of any lines. He wore his light brown hair tied behind his back, and Lena had never seen him in anything but a pair of jeans and a black T-shirt. But what made Warren Okolski so successful was his ear. Blue Moon Records was a renegade entertainment company because most of the musicians he developed refused to make music videos and didn't sound like derivations of somebody else. Unfortunately for music, the industry had declined to such an extent that Okolski's ideas were seen as unique, even odd. Okolski didn't care about what an artist looked like on camera. And he didn't work with pop vocalists or dancers one step away from the cheerleading squad. The only thing that mattered to Okolski was music and pushing the ball forward. Over the years his passion for exploring new sounds had paid off, and his client list quietly became the envy of every major label in town. Okolski had redefined the word *cool*, and listeners of jazz, blues, and alternative rock were eating it up. Lena remembered a conversation she had with him six or seven years ago, when David was still alive. They were working on their third or fourth beer at the kitchen counter, and Lena had just set out a bottle of tequila with two shot glasses. Okolski was saying that it came down to a matter of style. The more style an artist had, the less substance. He wasn't interested in working with people who could double as an act in Vegas.

He cracked open the bottle of spring water and took a long swig. When he finally spoke, his voice was so low she could barely hear it.

"You didn't come by just to say hello."

She shook her head. "No, Warren. I'm afraid I've got bad news."

"How bad?"

"Bad as it gets," she said. "Tim's dead."

Okolski took it quietly, lowering his head and wiping his eyes. As the stillness deepened within the room, Lena heard the muffled sound of a bus lumbering up the street through the window.

"How?" he managed.

"Looks like suicide."

An image flashed before her eyes. Tim Holt's crumbled body in the chair beside the window in his bedroom. She could see the wound above his forehead. The gun in his hand. His dead girlfriend on the bed.

"Things were so good," Okolski said. "Why would he do that?"

"He saw something he couldn't handle, Warren."

Okolski laughed at what she said through his grief. "Tim could handle anything. I was with him last night. We were working on a new album. What kind of fucked-up story is that?"

She started to say something, but Okolski waved her off. She reached in her pocket for her pad and pen.

"Give me a second," he said.

He got up and started pacing. When he finally returned to the chair, Lena filled him in on everything she thought he needed to know. There had been a series of murders, she told him. Tim had left a message on her machine and wanted to talk about something. At least for now, it looked as if Holt's girlfriend was the intended victim, and Holt couldn't deal with finding her body.

"It doesn't make sense," Okolski said.

"Tell me why."

"He never mentioned that he called you, but I can tell you this. It wasn't about reopening the studio. We went through all that more than a year ago. He knew where you were at. Both of us totally agreed that it was cool."

Hearing Okolski say it only confirmed something she had been feeling since she'd left Vista Del Mar. Holt was trying to reach her. He wanted to talk to her about something that didn't have anything to do with music or the studio.

"Where were you recording the album?"

"He'd formed a new band, and they were good. So good that he knew he needed to get clean. He checked himself into a clinic in Arizona. While he was away, construction began on a studio of his own. When he got back, they finished up and everything was ready to go. He was proud of it, Lena, just like David. Even better, he was pumped. He'd bought a new house. He was back in business and delivering the goods."

"You said you were together last night."

Okolski nodded. "They played a short set over at the Viper Room. I wanted to get a feel for things. See how some of the new stuff sounded live. Tim left sometime around eleven. After the set, I caught a late dinner with some friends over at Pinot and we talked about how it went."

She lowered her pen and looked at Okolski, slumped in the chair.

"Something else is bothering you," she said. "What is it?"

"That part about the girlfriend. You said he found her body and couldn't handle the load."

"That's the way it looks. What of it?"

"We were close, Lena. Tim and I talked just about every day."

"So what's the problem with his girlfriend?"

Okolski cleared his throat. Their eyes met.

"He never told me that he had one."

35

Lean spotted the gated drive and pulled over. Cutting the engine, she noticed the roadie-turned-security-guard staring at her through a pair of dark shades from the other side of the guard shack. He was sitting on a lawn chair with a magazine, shaking his head and scratching his long beard as if her presence just wrecked his day.

Lena ignored the attitude and looked past the gate. The drive wove through the trees, circling before a house with columns and porches and a slate roof that reminded her of a miniature version of the plantation in *Gone with the Wind*. But this wasn't a movie, and the location wasn't set in the deep South. Lena had made the short drive from Okolski's office to the hills overlooking the Strip on Sunset because she was curious and needed time to think before she drove home.

Something Okolski had said was troubling her. A loose end that wouldn't go away. If Tim Holt committed suicide as a result of his love for a woman, why hadn't he told Okolski about her?

Before she left his office, Okolski told her that he had been in contact with Holt and his doctors during his entire stay at the clinic. That his name and number were on record with the facility rather than Holt's own family in Austin. Okolski had even found the house off Mulholland and held it for Holt until he returned. They were more than business partners. They had become close friends. If Holt had a woman in his life, Lena felt certain that he would have mentioned it. Even worse, if the woman found in Holt's bed had been someone he'd picked up or just a friend he fooled around with, then Holt wouldn't have been brought to the emotional brink and committed suicide after finding her body.

She saw a flash of color and looked past the fountain before the house. She could see Zelda Clemens in the distance, cutting flowers from a garden on the far side of the yard. Her golden brown hair was frizzed out, and she wore a denim dress and leather flight jacket. Although her back was to the gate, she turned suddenly and met Lena's eyes as if she felt her presence and knew that she was there.

The security guard groaned like a walrus protecting his beachfront property. Tossing his magazine on the lawn, he stood up and sauntered toward the gate.

"This is private property," he said in a gruff voice. "You can't park there, lady. Snap your picture and scat."

The man looked more like an aging biker than anything else. Rough and ready and designed to scare. Lena knew the type and was immune. She also knew that the house belonged to a rocker who'd peaked in the late eighties. Because he'd hooked up with Zelda Clemens, the media returned and his music was no longer hard to find on the radio.

"I'm not fooling around," the guard said. "Now move out, lady. Time to go."

He opened the gate and jerked his thumb down the hill. When he stopped at the curb, she glanced beneath his jacket and caught the semiautomatic clipped to his belt. A shiny new 9 mm Glock, right out of the box.

"You got a permit to carry that?"

"Who the fuck is asking?"

She pulled her badge out. "I am."

His eyes lit up and then narrowed down some, still locked on the badge. "That thing's a phony. You're just trying to mess with my head."

"Let's see the permit."

His wallet was chained to his belt. As he unfastened the clip, he sighed and wallowed across the street. Sifting through his credit cards, he found the permit and handed it to her. Lena glanced at the name, Dennis Miller, then checked the date and passed it back.

"You don't look much like a comedian," she said.

"I'm way more funny once you get to know me."

"I'll bet you are, Dennis. Where you from?"

"Memphis. Lots of funny people get their start there. You want a head shot, call my agent. He's listed in the yellow pages under *bullshit*."

At least the goon had a sense of humor. Lena watched him slip his wallet into his pocket, then turned back to the open gate. Zelda was standing at the end of the drive staring at her as if a ghost. Although she hadn't lost her looks, she didn't appear to be aging well. Her legs were stick thin. Her eyes seemed lifeless, her face devoid of any emotion.

"Hello, Lena," she said in a low voice.

Lena nodded evenly. "It's been a long time, Zelda."

"Why are you here?"

Lena paused a moment. "Just taking a trip down memory lane."

"You got a lot of good memories, Lena?"

David's ex-girlfriend was a strung-out ice bitch. "Yeah, Zelda. I've got tons."

"Me, too," she said. "Wouldn't change a thing."

36

The pain was gone. She could thank Zelda Clemens for that. Seeing her. Listening to the woman's vicious bullshit. Somehow that trip down memory lane revived her.

Lena slid the chest drawer open, searching for the guitar pick amongst her brother's coins and rings. She was in the bedroom at the top of the stairs. Her bedroom when they first moved into the house. One year after David's murder, she left the furniture intact, but switched rooms with her brother to clear the air and chase the blues away. She had searched the house for the pick when she moved her brother's things upstairs. She even braved an entire day in the studio, scouring through all forty-three guitar cases without success.

Although it was possible that her brother hid the pick in a secret place that became lost with his death, she guessed that it had probably been ripped off a long time ago. At one level it was merely a guitar pick with a certain history no one could really document. At another, the heart-shaped disk had been forged out of fourteen-karat gold. Something small and rare enough that someone could easily have slipped it into their pocket if they had a mind to.

Lena remembered the first time she'd set eyes on it. She could still see David holding the pick in the palm of his hand. It had been a gift from an admirer in the business, a legend who showed up one night at a concert and liked what he heard. Over drinks the piece of gold changed hands. The edges were worn, the surface scratched. But what made the pick so exquisite was the work of the artist who had engraved it. Etched into the gold was an image of the moon, rising majestically from a bed of grapelike clouds. According to David, the moon's face had been inspired by Georges Méliès and a film made in 1902 entitled *Voyage dans la lune*. As in the film, the man in the moon was smoking a rocket ship the way one would smoke a cigar.

Lena closed the drawer and opened the next.

At first she thought that the housekeeper David had hired stole it when Lena told her she could no longer afford her salary and would have to let her go. It was also possible that Holt took the pick in memory of their partnership. But the more Lena thought it over, the more convinced she became that the thief was Zelda Clemens. Zelda had seen the pick. She would have understood that its value was derived from its past.

Some said that Jimi Hendrix designed the piece and gave it to Muddy Waters as a gift to his legacy. Others said Waters gave it to Hendrix, thanking him for introducing the blues to a middle-class audience so that he could finally make a decent wage playing music. But that was only the beginning. There were rumors that Buddy Guy used the pick for a time before passing it on to Eric Clapton. That B. B. King gave it to David Gilmour, who passed it to Mark Knopfler. That Keith Richards slipped it to Kurt Cobain and somehow the gold piece wound up in Neil Young's hands. None of the stories were documented. Lena had never heard any musician talk about it in public. Still, if the pick had been stolen, Zelda Clemens was probably the one.

A stray sound skipped off the ceiling and her mind surfaced. Someone was tapping their feet on the pavement outside. Lena moved to the window and saw a Crown Vic in the drive with the trunk open. Novak was sitting on the front steps. His tie was loosened, his dark gray suit crumpled like an empty pack of cigarettes.

She gave the window a knock. When he didn't move, she hurried downstairs, flipped the dead bolt, and opened the door.

"Why didn't you ring the bell?"

Novak turned and looked up at her. "I needed a break and the view from here seemed just about right. The cooler in the trunk's hot enough to boil dogs in. You got anything to drink?"

She nodded. His eyes were as shaky as his voice. His face so pale that she thought he might be ill. She watched as he rose to his feet and stretched his legs.

"Where's Rhodes?"

"Glendale," he said. "We pulled the slug out of the wall at Holt's place. Tomorrow's walk-in Wednesday and he wanted to get a head start."

SID was spread out all over the county. The firearms unit was housed in a building adjacent to the Northeast Division on San Fernando Road. Like every other unit, it was backlogged, at over two thousand cases. Ballistic results might not come for months, even years, and cases were prioritized based on trial dates. Any new case automatically went to the back of the line. In an attempt to cut through the red tape, the lab supervisor designated one day a week when any detective could bring evidence over and work with a ballistic analyst, no questions asked. Since the program had been instituted, the lab had scored more hits on the ATF's database than any other firearms unit in the country.

"What about Sanchez?" she asked.

"He's working with a sketch artist," Novak said. "We can't ID the fucking girl."

His eyes glazed over and he headed for the kitchen. Lena had kept a six-pack of diet Coke on hand ever since she'd learned that he didn't like coffee and no longer drank beer. She watched him pop the can open and take a long swig. He was unusually quiet and seemed extraordinarily troubled. When he noticed the map on the table, he walked over for a look. Moments passed as he studied her notations and thumbed through the case summaries she'd set aside. She could see him putting it together.

"The murder went down around midnight," he said without turning. "Same time you made that call over there and no one answered. The temps on both bodies are nearly identical. Gainer says the suicide had to happen within an hour after the girl was killed."

He was calling Holt's death a suicide. Lena remained silent, keeping her thoughts to herself as she moved to the couch and sat down.

"The knife used on the girl was found in the dishwasher," he said. "The autopsy's scheduled for the day after tomorrow. Barrera wants the same ME that cut open Nikki Brant, and Art Madina's at a conference in Vegas he can't get out of. But like I said, Lena, this one's a Jane Doe. We went through the boxes. No shoes and no clothing. She didn't live there."

"What about her purse?"

"We checked her driver's license. Her ID's phony."

"What about credit cards?"

"She didn't have any."

His voice trailed off. When he turned to look at her, he couldn't hold the glance. Instead, he set his diet Coke on the coffee table and found a chair. When he finally spoke, his voice was extremely gentle.

"What you're thinking, you can't think, Lena."

She kept her eyes on her partner as she mulled it over. Her gut instinct that Holt didn't commit suicide seemed to have been confirmed. Holt had never mentioned the woman to his friend, and none of her clothing could be found at the house. Whatever Holt's relationship might have been with a woman carrying fake ID, it didn't strike Lena that it could be very close. Odds were that Romeo didn't make this kill. That Jane Doe and Tim Holt were murdered by someone who knew Romeo's MO. Someone who was trying to bury his motive by writing a double homicide off to a serial killer. She took a deep breath as the possibilities surfaced. She tried to remain calm and control her anger. The list of people who knew Romeo's MO was short because the keys were never made public. She knew that Novak was smart enough to see this. She also knew that, beyond their friendship, this was the real reason why he'd stopped by. Yet he seemed to be keeping it buried. He was wrestling with it. Fighting it.

"You're thinking about your brother," he was saying. "The irony that both he and Holt are dead. If I were you, I'd be doing exactly the same thing. I'd be looking for the connection. And this gets back to why, at least for now, you shouldn't be thinking it. You're looking at Holt, Lena. But Romeo would have been following the girl."

It hung there. Something to be carefully weighed along with everything else. Romeo following the girl. The possibility that Holt was only a second-ary issue, and for Romeo, a surprise that most likely delighted him. The chance, however slight, that Holt's death wasn't a coincidence at all. Just bad timing mixed with a heavy dose of bad luck.

"Did you find a note?" she asked.

Their eyes met, but only briefly. Just long enough for Lena to know that she'd struck a nerve. Then Novak got out of the chair, crossing the room to the slider for a look outside.

"Holt was a writer," she said. "Did he leave a note?"

Novak shook his head. "No. If he did, we couldn't find it, and we tore the place apart."

A heavy silence filled the room. She could see her partner thinking it over. She could see the possibilities gnawing at him. He cracked the door open, the breeze striking his face.

"I'm standing here trying to convince you, Lena. And I can't even convince myself. I've got a problem calling this a suicide, too. Teresa Lopez and Nikki Brant were murdered in their homes. Jane Doe wasn't. Why?"

"That's one question," she said.

"I wanted to retire in peace. I wanted to turn my badge in and get rid of my gun. Trade it all in for a life where a guy like me didn't have to watch his back and might even sleep with both eyes closed. It was sort of a dream I had. Make a clean break. Walk away from all this with the feeling that in spite of my fuckups, I closed most of my cases and did a decent job no matter who the victim was."

She had been thinking the same thing. That if they opened the box, what they found inside would rattle its tail, hunt them down, and bite back.

Novak flashed a sad grin. "You said you were playing phone tag with Holt. Any idea what he wanted?"

She shook her head. "That's the other question."

He turned back and gave her a long look. "If what we're thinking is true, then someone's chalked up two murders on Romeo's account and made a move on our case. They're fucking with us. If we're wrong, then Romeo's picking up speed and we're chasing another phantom just like James Brant. Either way, we're in the weeds and the shit just got a whole lot deeper."

He had spent the last hour watching Burell do Harriet on a towel beneath the gas heaters by the pool. She didn't appear tired or cold. And it didn't look as if she had taken her eggplant lasagna home and hit the sheets early.

Instead, Harriet was here, servicing the motherfucker and cooing like a tweety bird.

In the beginning, Fellows couldn't watch. When he first realized that it was her, truly her, he turned away thinking he might puke. For a moment, maybe. For a second or two. But then he turned back, riveted to the spectacle, his eyeballs superglued.

The world could be a terrifying place, he thought. What people did to each other to get what they wanted. What they needed to chill.

Fellows knew full well that he had experienced these kinds of emotions before. And that over the years he had become an expert at regaining his composure. A master at tapping his enormous inner strength. Perched on the hill in the backyard, he found a place to hide that sported an uncensored view. And as he watched Burell remove Harriet's clothing, as he looked at her naked body in the light of the moon, as he witnessed the dirty old man kiss and fondle his beloved Harriet's young and voluptuous breasts, Fellows remained motionless. Not one muscle twitched. Not a single bone stirred.

Just that wretched feeling in his stomach. His juices churning like a storm trying to break through his rib cage but bridled by his oversize will.

He watched and listened, recording every detail in his head. The images had been so vivid that he knew he would never forget them and had no need to write anything down. Burell fucking Harriet. Harriet fucking Burell. It was a spectacle that cut through. And when Burell finally entered her from behind as if a dog, when Fellows heard Harriet moan with pleasure and thought the sky was falling and the world might end, he was grateful for one thing and one thing only. His friend and spotter didn't have to see this. Finn was keeping watch somewhere in the front yard.

He took a deep breath, replaying the images in his head as he watched Burell remove his stupid wig and serve Harriet a glass of red wine. Even from this distance he could make out the label and knew that it was from a cheap, $3 bottle on sale at Trader Joe's. When the show finally ended, Burell rose to his feet quickly and grabbed a robe while Harriet lingered on the towel. Fellows was replaying the image because he found it so disturbing. That look of disappointment on her face. He could tell that she hadn't wanted Burell to leave her so quickly and guessed that she wanted to be held.

He could feel his heart pounding as Burell ignored her. His blood reaching a rapid boil as she finally picked herself up and limped over to the chair. The wince of pain on her face as she reached for her clothes.

Fellows was thinking about that copy of her employment records he'd stolen from the office. Her medical history that was attached to page two. Although Harriet's legs were breathtaking, one was shorter than the other by more than an inch. The aberration wasn't a birth defect but the result of an operation after breaking her leg as a teenager. When Fellows had asked about her condition, she told him that she fell down a flight of stairs. Maybe it was the glint in her eye when she talked about the accident. Perhaps it was the way she always tried to change the subject that triggered his doubts. In either case, and after probing her as delicately as he could, Fellows came to believe that Harriet had been pushed. Even worse, the most likely suspect was her father, whom she never mentioned and no longer talked to. He knew that she grew up in a strict religious family. That the setting was rural Nebraska, and as a child, Harriet was rarely allowed to play with her friends from school. After learning about her double life on Burell's Web site, the picture seemed complete and he felt certain that she had been sexually abused.

He checked his watch. It was getting late. When he turned back to the house, he could see Harriet finishing her wine and heading for the stairs. Burell didn't offer her another. Nor did he follow her up the steps. Like most animals, once he had taken advantage of her weaknesses, once he'd used her body and played with her head, all he wanted to do was move on. It was the law of the jungle. He had marked his territory and returned to the mundane. He was rolling up cable and putting the camera away.

The light from Harriet's car brushed against the neighbor's house. As the sound of the engine evaporated into the night, he spotted a familiar face in the side yard. It was Finn, motioning with a wave that the coast was clear. When his friend and spotter jogged back into the front yard, Fellows rose from his hiding place at the top of the hill.

He glanced at his clothing folded neatly on the ground. He could feel his muscles percolating. The cool midnight breeze breaking against his shaved skin. He rocked his head back and forth, rebooting his brain and shaking the blood in his arms.

It would be a mercy killing, he decided. A moral calling. No different from taking down a horse with a broken leg. In his own small way, he would be saving the world.

And then he dug his toes into the soil, charging down the hill and bolting for that sliding door. As his legs chewed up ground, he caught a whiff of Harriet and filled his lungs with air. He could smell her body, the sweet fragrance of her sex lingering over the towel, and thought he was passing through heaven. Energy ripped through his body in a series of crisp waves. His skin flushed. By the time he reached the house and burst through the door, his arms had become wings and his entire body went red-hot.

Charles Burell was having another bad day, two in a row, and he wondered what he'd done to deserve this kind of shit. It had started yesterday when those two cops knocked on his door and pressured him into forking over his fucking client list. Now, as he tossed the cables onto the shelf and glanced into the mirror, he could see some weird geek hiding behind the stairs following his every move.

What next?

Although he didn't recognize the man's face, he guessed that he was from the neighborhood. His fuck session with Harriet had been a command performance. And let's face it, he knew what turned the bitch on. At this time of night, sound carried. The guy probably wandered into the yard, saw him getting a piece of ass, and got all worked up. Maybe if he ignored the idiot, he'd cool his jets and split.

Burell closed the cabinet, reached for his wineglass, and took another peek in the mirror. He was still there. Still fixated on him from behind the stairs.

He glanced at the phone as he considered his options. Calling the cops didn't seem like the way to go. He hated cops. Particularly the local-yokel variety. If they came to the house and got a look at his basement, they'd start snooping and want to know more about his business just as those detectives had. Only they wouldn't keep their big mouths shut because they wouldn't be working a murder case. It might cause a problem in the neighborhood, even damage his reputation and standing. Burell had taken great pains to keep his business secret. Every clodhopper in the neighborhood still thought he practiced law. That he was just lucky with women. Getting laid five or six times a week by different women went with his success like the Rolex he wore and the fleet of Mercedes he drove.

He would be much better off handling the situation on his own, he decided. Chase the rat bastard out and lock the door. He set the glass down, dusting off his courtroom demeanor. When he thought he'd found it, he breezed into the basement, looked straight at the guy, and spawned a healthy dose of this-was-bound-to-happen surprise.

"Show's over, buddy," he said. "Take a hike and get the hell out."

The man was hiding in the shadows. But as he rose to his feet and stepped into the light, Burell took the jolt and fought to regain his cool.

The intruder was completely naked. Built like a shit house and hung like a mean horse. Yet it was his face that shook Burell to the core. His eyes were beyond lifeless, smoldering in their sockets and reaching out to him from across the room. No doubt about it, this one was a bona fide loony tune. Time to bite the bullet and call 911.

"You're too late," he said, back-stepping his way toward the office. "She went home. You want a piece, get your own gig. This one's mine."

The man didn't say anything, but just stared at him with those eyes. When he suddenly charged forward, Burell yelped but was too frightened to make a move. The man seized him by the neck and rammed him into the wall. Something snapped and the air rushed out of his lungs. Before he could scream, the bodybuilder picked him up like a man toy and drove his face into the floor.

He blacked out after that. Everything went lazy until he finally came to.

Then he cracked his eyelids open, watching the hairless giant step away. He tried to catch his breath. Tried to think through the fucking haze. His courtroom routine was working about as well as it ever had, and he needed a new plan. He saw blood puddling on the floor, his Rolex beside his foot with the lens smashed. When he noticed that his mouth hurt, he ran a finger over his teeth, felt the pins in his gums, and realized that several caps were missing. Two in the upper front, and three on the bottom. His mind cleared as he calculated what the night had cost him. Twenty grand easy, plus $3.19 for that bottle of wine.

He needed a way out of this. Something that would be agreeable to both parties.

He knew from experience that the trick to any successful negotiation was figuring out what your adversary wanted. He looked the man over. His chiseled body and extrasmooth skin. He was perusing the studio, passing the office and bedroom sets. When he reached the bogus hospital room and stopped, Burell lifted his face off the floor and finally spoke.

"I could make you a star."

The man turned back and looked at him, remaining silent. Burell's heart fluttered in his chest, but somehow he dug deep down, found his voice, and kept going.

"I could make you a fucking star. The way you're built. You're a stud and I could do it."

He had the odd-looking man's attention. He was sure of it. In spite of his broken mouth and slurred speech, he had his attention. If he could just get him to bite. If he could somehow manage to get him out the door.

"I've got friends in the business. Lots of friends. All it would take is a phone call. You could get laid any day you want and make real money."

The man smiled at him like an idiot. Burell sat up, snatched his Rolex off the floor, and slipped it over his wrist. He had him. He was in the game.

"We'll make an audition tape. You pick the model. I'll pay for everything because I take care of my friends. Say, you're not much of a talker, are you?"

"No, I'm not."

"What's your name? A stud like you needs the right name."

The man didn't say anything. Instead, he grabbed a patient's gown off the hospital bed and threw it at him.

Burell giggled nervously. "Not tonight. Not with me. We'll pick a girl and shoot the tape tomorrow. Anytime you want. If you're into kinky, they charge extra, but I can afford it. I can afford anything."

The man kicked him. "Shut the fuck up and put it on."

It had been a hard kick. One that would leave a bruise. Even worse, it looked as if the guy wanted to do *him*. Burell suddenly became aware of his erection and tightened his robe. It hadn't come from the bodybuilder. It came from the double dose of Viagra he'd dropped an hour before Harriet arrived. His dick was still so hard it actually hurt more than his mouth. It would take another two or three hours to subside. But what worried Burell was what this man might think if he noticed. What really worried him was that the bodybuilder might think he turned him on.

His face heated up and he started sweating. He chewed it over in his head.

He didn't have those kinds of thoughts and considered himself the original *ungay blade*. While it was true that he'd sucked his best friend's dick when he was eleven, it had been the one and only time. Something that had ruined his confidence with girls as a teenager and he'd tried to keep buried ever since. He didn't want to get screwed by a guy tonight. Not by this creepy guy or any other guy.

The man gave him another kick. So hard he thought his leg might be broken. He moaned, then shook the pain off and climbed to his feet as best he could. His legs were shaky, his body quivering as he removed his robe and nearly died from embarrassment. He could feel the man looking at it, measuring it, not turning the fuck away.

He wondered if what was about to happen qualified as rape. He was certain that it did. If he could do it privately, he would prosecute the rotten son of a bitch to the full extent of the law. But as he pulled on the gown, well aware that the clothing remained open in the back and his ass hung out, a faint glimmer of hope rose to the surface. The man picked up his bottle of Viagra. He was reading the label. Thinking something over that Burell couldn't quite grasp.

"You want that bottle, take it," he said. "It's on me, pal. I've got a whole case in the office. I get it cheap over the Internet. Works like an insurance policy but it still takes time. At least one hour, sometimes two."

At least one hour, sometimes two. More than enough time to figure a way out of this.

The man's smile changed, almost as if he had come to some kind of decision. And then he pushed Burell over to the hospital set, tossed him on the bed, and started laughing.

Burell panicked, clawing at the sheets and weeping in a frenzy. "We'll do it tomorrow," he blurted out. "If you don't like girls, we'll find a guy. Another stud just like you. There's a market for that stuff. You could still make a lot of dough."

The man didn't seem to hear him. All he wanted to do was laugh. And it was a high-pitched laugh that lacked control. Giddy and hideous at the same time. The most horrifying sound Burell had ever heard.

And then the man made an unexpected move. Without warning, the bodybuilder shoved a pill down Burell's throat. He sputtered. When he finally realized through the mental confusion that it was Viagra, he tried to spit it out. He could see his face in the mirror by the bed. The massive hands clutching his throat. His broken teeth and the pins in his gums. His bright red cheeks shuddering. His entire body a bundle of raw nerves.

He'd swallowed it.

When he tried to turn away, he felt another pill being jabbed into his mouth and started gagging on the guy's finger. He swallowed this one, too.

He squirmed onto his back and looked up at the giant, pleading silently as their eyes met. Too many little blue pills and his heart might blow.

He lowered his eyes, noticing for the first time that the man was wearing a pair of vinyl gloves. It dawned on Burell that the naked giant hadn't come to the house because he was feeling horny or wanted to become a porno star.

The art of any negotiation was understanding what your opponent really wanted.

He'd miscalculated. He'd blown the deal. Sadness rushed through his body. A deep and spacious wave of gloom.

He needed a new plan, and nothing short of a magic genie would probably work. Something that included three wishes and a beautiful woman to
serve him like on that old TV show. Even better, he hoped the man might
come to his senses and grant him some degree of clemency.

Instead, the motherfucker drew a third pill from the bottle, jammed it
down his throat, and said, "Hope you're hungry, you piece of shit."

38

Lena glanced at the chopper on the pad as she walked from her car to the beige-colored building. Her early-morning drive over to the Records Retention Center at Piper Tech had been filled with apprehension. This was where the case files ended up when the trail went cold. This was where the files were stored when a case slipped through the cracks and no one had the time to care anymore.

This was the place where she would find her brother's murder book.

She'd never had the courage to look at it before. Never wanted that much detail. Never wanted to remember her brother by the files inside a three-ring binder. But Holt's death changed everything. That feeling in her gut that wouldn't go away.

She'd spent most of last night on the phone with Novak. Together they estimated that the list of people who knew Romeo's MO wasn't as short as they first thought. Everyone who attended the Teresa Lopez and Nikki Brant crime scenes would have to be included, along with two FBI profilers, anyone and everyone who processed evidence in the labs, the coroner's office, every detective in RHD, and most of the department's administrative staff. While the keys to the case had never been made public, they weren't exactly private either.

She swung the door open, collecting herself as she stepped up to the counter. An old black woman wearing a light blue smock and thick bifocals looked up from her cart halfway down the center aisle. The stacks were long and deep. And it was quiet here. As still as any other morgue.

After placing a manila folder in a box, the old woman turned back to her and flashed an odd smile as if maybe she were a mirage. Lena pulled her badge from her belt and found the case number in her notebook. The woman started forward.

"How can I help you, young lady?"

"I need to pull a case, ma'am."

"Why didn't you just call?"

"No time," Lena said. "And I was in the neighborhood."

The woman gave her another look, then climbed onto her stool before the computer. In spite of its short distance from Parker Center, not many investigators made the drive over to Piper Tech. Usually the case number was phoned in and the files were delivered by messenger right to your desk on the floor. Something Lena had discussed with Novak and knew she couldn't afford.

The woman picked up Lena's badge and examined it carefully, her face dusted with curiosity and suspicion. If she had antennae, they were up.

"You're a detective."

"That's right."

Lena slid her pad across the counter and watched the woman punch the case number into the computer. After a moment, the old woman turned from the screen as if she finally understood.

"You have the same last name," she said gently.

Lena thought she'd prepared herself for this moment. When she couldn't speak, she nodded.

"I know exactly where this is, Detective Gamble. I'll only be a moment."

"Thanks."

She watched the clerk vanish into the stacks, then turned away. She heard the rotors from that chopper squeal, then beat the air as they wound up. Listening to the bird take off seemed a whole lot better than what she'd heard on the radio just ten minutes ago.

The Holt murder-suicide had sprung to life, including the name the department was using to identify the serial killer. But her brother's murder also made the story. A brief recap, along with the irony that both musicians were dead and David Gamble's sister was one of four detectives working the case.

Unfortunately, the Romeo investigation was already taking needless criticism as well. A professor from the drama department at a local college had stepped forward, attacking them for debasing a character and a play by William Shakespeare. In a shrill voice filled with vibrato the man grabbed his moment at the mike, demanding that the new chief change the name or else.

Or else what?

It had become another circus—the kind only L.A. could stuff inside the tent—and she wondered how the brass would handle damage control.

She turned back to the counter and saw the woman clutching the murder book.

Without hesitating, Lena drew her pen from her pocket and reached for the checkout card. She found the first blank line, then stopped as her eyes drifted upward.

Stan Rhodes had checked out the murder book one week after she'd made the jump from Hollywood to RHD. According to the checkout card, he kept the files for a week before returning them. Her eyes rose up the list to the next name. It was Rhodes again. When she checked the date, she realized that it was only three days after the detectives assigned to the case had finally given up and sent the files off to storage.

His reasoning could have been harmless enough. She had to admit that Rhodes might have a credible explanation for why he wanted to look at her brother's murder book. His reasons could have been professional, she told herself, or even personal. After all, they once shared something together. If the timing had been better, they might have shared a lot more.

But what troubled her was his signature. It was on the card, which meant that he'd pulled the file on the q.t. just as she was doing. Not once, but twice.

She felt a twinge light up between her shoulder blades. Shaking it off, she signed the card and pushed it across the counter. When the old woman passed over the three-ring binder, she pulled it into her chest and walked out. Before the door slammed shut, she heard the words "God bless you" follow her into the lot and burn up in the sunlight.

Lena entered the Blackbird, ordered an extralarge cup of the house blend, and looked about the dimly lit café. In spite of the crowd, she spotted an empty table by the far window and cut across the room.

It was quiet here. Somehow comforting. Although the building had once been an auto repair garage, the place now had the look and feel of a community reading room. The corrugated-aluminum ceiling was pitched and remained unfinished, the only architectural detail to survive the renovation. The brick walls were lined with books and art donated by patrons. The only music she ever heard in the café was classical, which seemed to distinguish it from every other commercial space in the city.

She took a sip of coffee and pulled the murder book out of her briefcase, her eyes flicking over her brother's name on the label. She spent a few minutes staring at the binder, measuring its size and weight in her hands. When she noticed her fingers trembling, she took a deep breath and opened the book.

It had been a takeaway case from the very beginning. Once David was identified as both a musician and the brother of an LAPD officer, the investigation bounced from Hollywood Division to RHD. Two detectives were assigned to the case, Barry Martin and Joe Drabyak. Lena looked at their names listed on the preprinted table of contents. She could remember their faces, the way they treated her during their numerous interviews, the kindness they bestowed. Both retired before her transfer. Both left town once the case went to Piper Tech and hit the black hole.

The murder book was divided into twenty-six sections, offering a complete picture of the investigation in chronological order. Lena found the Death Investigation Report and started reading. A description of her brother was listed, along with the location of the crime on Vista Del Mar and their home address in Hollywood Hills. Lena's name had been filled in as NEAREST RELATIVE. Above her name three boxes were checked, indicating that she'd discovered the victim, reported the death, and identified the body. Confirmation that she had been notified of her brother's death as next of kin was checked in a fourth box off to the side.

She shrugged at the bureaucratic redundancy. As she combed through the Chronological Record, it seemed clear that both Martin and Drabyak were approaching the investigation as a robbery gone bad. That David had driven from the club to Vista Del Mar to buy drugs, even though Lena had told them that he no longer used anything but alcohol.

A slug had been cut out of the passenger seat. Gunshot residue was found on the driver's side mirror, the upper left section of the steering wheel, and the palm of David's left hand. Based on the bullet's trajectory and GSR evidence, the shooter had to be standing within one foot of the car. Both Martin and Drabyak seemed to agree that the victim was aware of the threat. Both detectives believed that David was backpedaling his way into the passenger seat when the single shot was fired at point-blank range.

Lena played the scene out in her head. Her brother trapped in the space of a front seat, making a futile attempt to block the shot with his hand. She looked out the window for a moment, wondering if she could really handle this. Pushing her coffee aside, she straightened the book on her lap and dug in.

From the number of entries in the Chronological Record, she could tell that Martin and Drabyak had worked the case hard. Even though their first impressions seemed to be pushing them toward a street killing, they pushed back and managed to keep an open mind. And then two days after the murder, they interviewed Zelda Clemens. Lena noticed that one of the detectives had drawn a circle around her name and underlined it twice. When the results from the autopsy came in, the investigation shifted into another gear.

Lena found Section 19, the Coroner's Report, carefully avoiding the plastic covers beneath the medical examiner's findings because she knew they contained photos from the autopsy. It had been the ME who confirmed the investigators' suspicions that another theory was more than possible. It was his examination of her brother's corpse that transformed everyone's first impression of the crime scene and turned it into something else.

While no illegal drugs were found in David's system, his blood-alcohol level was so high that the ME openly wondered how he managed to operate the car. At five times the legal limit, David Gamble would have had no need and would most likely have been incapable of buying or ingesting anything more. And there was evidence that he had sex shortly before his death. Swabs taken from her brother's body indicated that he had both vaginal and anal sex with a woman before he was murdered.

An image surfaced. The theory both Martin and Drabyak wrestled with until the end. Zelda Clemens following the man who'd dumped her to that dead-end street in Hollywood. Seeing him with another woman in the front seat of his car. Drunken sex flowing into the aberrant before her very eyes. Waiting for it to end. Knocking on the window. Waving the gun. Watching her lover fucker squirm. Then pulling the trigger and fleeing into the night. David Gamble dies in Hollywood. Shot by a jealous bitch on the run.

Lena flipped to Section 12 and read Zelda's statement. She remained angry even as Martin and Drabyak put the pressure on. But she didn't break. "I got drunk that night," she was quoted as saying. "I saw David leaving with that cunt. I went crazy and made a fool out of myself. I'm pretty good at that, but listen up, you losers—all I fucking did is go home." When asked to describe the woman Gamble left the club with that night, she said, "All I caught was her ass. It was totally hot."

SID couldn't place Zelda Clemens at the crime scene. The detectives scoured the streets for two weeks but couldn't turn up a single witness. When her apartment was searched, no weapon was found. Analysis of the dress she wore that night yielded nothing as well.

Lena skimmed through the Field Interview cards. Only a few people had seen David leave the club that night, and no one was able to describe the woman he left with. The investigation slowed down after that. When Lena checked the Follow-up Reports, she could tell from the tone of the entries that the case had slipped into a deep freeze. Even worse, if there was any connection to Tim Holt's death, the link remained hidden.

She turned back to the Coroner's Report for a look at the medical examiner's final summary. She knew that her brother's CAUSE OF DEATH was listed as excessive bleeding due to a gunshot wound. But as she read the report, she learned more than she wanted. The bullet broke up as it entered her brother's chest, a fragment glancing off the aorta before exiting below the shoulder blade. Because David was young, the artery remained elastic. There was evidence of clotting. The wound had begun to heal, and at least one hour had passed before he finally died.

Lena tried to get a grip on herself. The injury in and of itself had not been fatal.

It is the opinion of this medical examiner that if the victim remained still and received medical attention in a timely manner, he would have survived.

She read that sentence three times. She closed her eyes and took the jolt in the dark.

No one had told her that he could have survived.

She turned to Section 17, her eyes zeroing in on the first photo taken at the crime scene. Her view as she held a flashlight over his body and prayed that he was only sleeping. She could see him lying there in a fetal position with his hands clasped between his thighs. The pool of blood on the passenger seat.

No one told her.

She tried to concentrate on her breathing. The pressure in her head as her eyes slid onto the ground. The rain drizzling down her cheeks.

The sadness was eternal. So deep, so oppressive, she thought it might ruin her.

"What are you doing here, Lena?"

She heard the voice, snapped out of it, and looked up. A man in a dark suit was standing before her, but it took a moment to place him.

"Your cell phone's off, for Christ's sake. The lieutenant wants to see you."

It was Tito Sanchez, snapping his fingers at her.

"Not later," he said quickly. "Now."

She glanced at her coffee. She hadn't touched it. When she slipped the murder book into her briefcase, she caught Sanchez staring at her brother's name on the label. The recognition in his eyes.

"Hurry," he said. "It's important."

She gave him a look as she got up. He seemed angry.

Entering the squad room at Parker Center felt something like a death march. Sanchez leading her down the aisle between the desks. Twenty detectives looking up from their work, nodding at her, then turning away a beat too quickly. The usual banter clipped short as if someone had hit the MUTE button.

"He's in the captain's office," Sanchez said.

Sanchez stopped at his desk. Continuing down the aisle, Lena opened the glass door. Lieutenant Barrera was sitting on the far side of the conference table, flanked by Novak and Rhodes. Like the detectives on the floor, they were talking about something but stopped short when they saw her approach. She glanced at Novak. When their eyes met, she felt a ping and knew that she had at least one ally in the room.

"Have a seat," Barrera said quietly.

"I'm okay standing," she said.

His eyes moved to the murder book stuffed in her briefcase, then back to her face.

"That's an order, Gamble. Take a seat."

She pulled a chair out. There were no papers on the table. No files. Just three cups of coffee and a plastic bag containing a .38 revolver.

"I have news," Barrera said. "Good news and bad news. Any way you look at it, I'm afraid it's gonna be hard to take."

She nodded, keeping her hands beneath the table because she knew that she was trembling. Barrera slid the gun across the table. She saw Holt's name written on the label but had already figured out where it came from. Rhodes had brought it back from Glendale.

"The firearms unit let us step to the head of the line," Barrera said. "Rhodes spent the night working with an analyst. They test-fired the gun for verification. Then they went through the database comparing slugs. Two hours ago the results came in."

Barrera paused a moment before continuing in a lower voice.

"They got a match, Lena. The gun Holt used to commit suicide with is the same gun used in your brother's homicide. It looks like Holt shot your brother. It looks like there was a motive and he's the one."

She didn't move. Something deep inside her told her to keep her mouth shut. Just take the bullshit. Wait until it's over and get the hell out of the room.

"We found journals," Rhodes said. "Holt wrote a lot of things down. I haven't read everything yet, and at the time he didn't come out and say he pulled the trigger. But he was extremely jealous and sounded confused. He was doing a lot of drugs. He loved your brother but he hated him, too. He bought the gun at a show in the Valley. We've got the receipt. Tim Holt owned that gun and murdered your brother. Five years later it caught up with him. He found Jane Doe's body in his bed and couldn't take it. That's why he committed suicide."

A moment passed. Lots of silence billowing into the room. Enough to choke on. She couldn't look at Rhodes. His face had hardened up and she found it revolting. She could smell tobacco on his breath and caught the pack of cigarettes in his pocket. When she glanced at Novak, his skin was pale but he managed to shoot her another look.

"Not many people can live with themselves after committing a murder," Barrera said. "Particularly when the victim's someone, at least at one level, he called a friend. It was probably only a matter of time. Either he'd confess, and that's why he called you. Or he was ready to jump off the cliff and take his secret with him."

Rhodes cleared his throat. "Holt saw what Romeo did to the girl and it brought it all back."

The silence returned, heavier this time.

Barrera reached across the table. "You've got your brother's murder book. Better turn it over so we can get to work. We'll close the case out once the lab verifies that Romeo killed the girl. In the meantime, there's paperwork to do."

Her briefcase was on her lap. She pulled the binder out and pushed it across the table, then watched Barrera pass it over to Rhodes.

"What if it's not Romeo?" she said.

Barrera's eyes flared up. "The keys are all there. Confirmation that the DNA belongs to Romeo is only a matter of time. You need to keep your head above water on this one, Gamble. You need to concentrate on identifying Jane Doe and finding Romeo. I realize it's a heavy load. If you can't handle it, everyone in this room would understand. If you can't handle it, speak now so you can be replaced."

At least he knew how to motivate people, she thought. Get underneath their skin and—

Someone gave the glass door a double tap and opened up. It was Sanchez.

"Sorry, Lieutenant," he said. "North Hollywood just called. A Jeff Brown from Homicide. He's looking for Lena."

She turned in the chair. She'd never heard of the man. "What's he want?"

"Charles Burell was murdered last night. He's dead."

40

The case was radioactive now. Incinerating the atmosphere. Leaving nothing in its wake but shadows on the walls from the people burned in the hot-white flash.

Lena was so amped up her mouth had gone dry.

She ran across the street and followed Novak into the LAPD garage, a three-story structure that had the look and feel of an erector set that might fall down with the wave of a child's hand. The Crown Vic was by the guard shack on the first floor, ass backward and ready to roll.

"I'll drive," he shouted.

They pulled through the entrance onto San Pedro and Novak gunned the engine.

"Any chance Holt could have done what they just said he did?"

Lena gave him a look.

"I didn't think so," he said. "I knew it was bullshit, but I had to ask."

She rolled her window down and let the cool air beat against her face as she watched Parker Center fade into the background. Sanchez and Rhodes had stayed behind to do the unthinkable. Close a murder case out by pinning circumstantial evidence on an innocent man. A dead man who couldn't speak out or fight back. As she chewed it over, the implications seemed better than clear. A key ingredient had turned and everything about it was rotten.

They hit the freeway at high speed. Novak switched on the running lights, found the left lane, and brought the car up to a ragged ninety. Then he reached into the backseat, grabbed his briefcase, and dumped it on her lap.

"Open it," he said. "I want you to see something."

She flipped the latch and looked inside.

"The papers on top," he said. "They're not in a file."

She pulled them out and quickly realized that it was a case summary from the sexual-assault database they'd divvied up two nights ago.

"Keep it," he said. "And add it to your map. I think it's number two on that list you've started."

She checked the date. The rape had been reported last November.

"After we talked last night, I went through my share and finished up. This one popped out and floated to the top."

The car was vibrating. Lena found it difficult to read but skimmed through the summary as best she could. The rape occurred in Santa Monica, well within Romeo's comfort zone. And it hadn't been an attempt. This time Romeo succeeded. The woman woke up in the middle of the night, thinking the man in her bed was her husband. By the time she remembered that he was out of town on a business trip, the doer was already on top of her. The shock and terror was enough to awaken her survival instincts. Instead of screaming, she went along with it and kept her eyes closed. She pretended to be groggy and waited until the intruder finished. When she heard him slip out the window, she called 911. Because she kept her eyes closed, because it happened in the dark, her only description of the assailant was that his chest seemed well-developed, she thought he might be bald, and his skin seemed extraordinarily smooth.

"What about DNA?" she said.

"He didn't wear a condom. They're trying to locate it."

The case fit like a glove. Except for the aftermath, it was an exact copy of their theory on how Nikki Brant was killed. If the sexual assaults began last October and were occurring once a month, then they could account for every month except February. After February, something happened and the assaults escalated to murder.

Novak glanced at her from behind the wheel, raising his voice above the wind.

"You're a good cop, Lena. Don't let this bullshit knock you too far down. You've had some tough breaks. Getting the call on your brother's murder five years ago was just about as bad as it gets. If I could change that night for you, I would. But you've gotta tough it out. You've got real talent. Your instincts are all there. You saw the pattern when no one else did. Thanks to you we have a feel for what the motherfucker looks like and where he lives."

She looked over at him and knew what he was trying to say. She felt the same way about him. When he turned back to the road, she followed his eyes to a low-riding Honda Civic doing eighty-five through the Cahuenga Pass in spite of their presence. The driver looked about twenty and had a shaved head. As they passed the car, the kid flipped them the bird. Ten minutes later, they cut through the press line, pulled past Burell's house, and legged it down the street toward the front door.

The coroner's van was parked in the driveway. Crime scene techs were milling about as if on hold. As they signed in at the bottom of a long list, a detective stepped out of the house, met them on the steps, and introduced himself as Jeff Brown.

"Thanks for coming out," he said, turning to Lena. "We were going through Burell's office when I found your card. With all this stuff in the news about your boy Romeo, I thought I'd better shut things down and give you a call."

"How long have you been here?" Novak asked.

"Long enough to get past go and figure out what this guy was into."

Brown smiled and grimaced at the same time, and Lena knew instantly that she liked him. He was the size of a fullback, about forty-five, with skin the color of cocoa and close-cropped hair. His face was flat and wide and heavily creased by laugh lines, and he wore a light brown suit and a crisp white shirt with a patterned tie.

She glanced at the houses on the street. "What about the neighbors?"

Brown shook his head. "Nada. Burell thought he was keeping his lifestyle in the vault, but everybody in the hood knows this place is a fuck pad. The two people living next door got a telescope in that window aimed at the guy's hot tub, but they're over eighty and only good for matinées. Last night they went to sleep early. Everybody else around here has kids. They keep their blinds closed."

She saw Novak fight off a grin, Brown glancing at the TV cameras perched on a hill at the end of the block.

"Let's get downstairs," the detective said. "I wouldn't let them touch the body until you guys got here. This one's kind of different and takes some getting used to."

They entered the house. Lena glanced at the photo on the windowsill of Burell with his ex-wife and kids as they hit the kitchen and hustled downstairs. When she spotted Burell's corpse on the hospital bed, she didn't need a set of keys to know that Romeo had been here.

The mattress had been raised, Burell's head propped up with pillows. He was dressed in a patient's gown, and a fake IV had been taped to his arm. Cuts and bruises scarred his chin and much of his face. But what gave the crime scene its punch were the man's eyes. Romeo had shut the right eye after Burell's death and kept the left eye open. As Lena gazed at his face, it looked as if Burell were winking at her from a very still and lonely place on the other side.

She felt a chill roll down her back but took a step closer. Something was oozing out of the man's mouth and nose, even his ears. A powdery blue foam. When she noticed the pool of blood below Burell's waist, she saw the same powdery blue foam oozing out from beneath his buttocks.

Novak gave her a nudge and pointed to the shelf behind the bed. Twelve empty bottles of Viagra were lined up in a neat row. She looked back at Burell's corpse, his face and that dead eye of his, playing out the murder in her head.

"Viagra," Brown said. "Burell bought the shit by the case and had it shipped in from Mexico. But that's only the half of it. You're probably gonna want a look underneath that gown."

His face lit up, his eyes pinned to Burell's crotch. The coroner's investigator, a small Asian woman whom Lena had met once or twice, had the same look on her face as she lifted the gown. Lena followed her eyes to the wound. Burell had been castrated. Nothing remained between his legs but the wound.

Brown shook his head. "This guy didn't die easy. This one went out like a champion. Gives new meaning to the phrase *dickless wonder*, huh?"

He smacked his lips and stepped away, his body shivering. Pockets of nervous laughter rose and died throughout the room.

"You search the house?" Novak asked.

"Inside and out," Brown said. "All we found were his capped teeth over here on the floor."

Lena spotted the bloodstain beside the detective's foot, then turned back for another look at Burell's corpse laid out on the bed. The wink and the stare and the Viagra oozing out of every orifice of the man's body. She guessed that Romeo force-fed Burell until he could no longer swallow, then stuffed the rest of the pills anywhere they would go. Judging from the amount of blood, his penis and testicles were removed while his heart was beating, and probably while he remained lucid enough to know that it was happening.

Brown had been right. The way Burell ended up took some getting used to.

Her eyes drifted over to the Rolex on Burell's wrist. Burell had everything in the world that money could buy, yet he didn't possess anything worth living for. From the way he'd stared at his watch the other day, she figured that somewhere deep inside he knew it as well as she did. It was almost as if he needed the Rolex to convince himself that the lie he was living might be true.

But now the lens was smashed, just like his body. She thought about that picture of his family he kept in the kitchen. It told her everything she needed to know. What was worth living for in this man's life had moved to Phoenix a long time ago.

Martin Fellows selected a knife from the drawer and drew the blade down the center of an apple, then flinched as the two halves split open. He looked around the lab to see if anyone had been watching. No. 3 was on the other side of the room. Harriet was doing paperwork at her desk.

His eyes slid back to the piece of fruit. He stared at it, felt a jittery lift as his blood curdled and took off for the moon.

The flesh inside the apple was black. Bright yellow crystals clung to the seeds. When he caught a whiff of sulfur in the air, he quickly sealed the apple in a plastic bag, dumped it in the wastebasket, and ripped open the greenhouse door.

Hellfire and lightning. His experiment had been a complete failure.

Why?

He ran down the aisle and examined the tree he had picked it from. The specimen was part of a lot grafted three years ago. One of six trees that were the foundation for his experiments now. His mind was buzzing. His ears ringing. All six plants were brimming with ripened fruit and looked healthy.

"Dead fruit," he heard himself whispering. "Devil's candy."

He reached down to check the soil and gasped. It was bone-dry. The entire goal of the project was to mimic a tropical environment. To produce apples where they had never grown before. He yanked the irrigation tubes out of the soil and noticed that the nozzles were clogged again. Cheap fixtures maintained by an outside firm he considered totally incompetent. The last time they screwed up, he told the company rep that they were in way over their heads. When she called him cute, he stopped barking at her but couldn't put the fire out. His plants needed water, and that stupid bitch with her pipe wrenches was a fucking moron.

Bristling with anger, he picked one apple from each tree and scurried back into the lab. He cut them open and smelled the fumes. The flesh inside all six apples was black.

He opened his notebook, trembling as he thought through his computations. Every formula. Every step. None of it added up to black.

And then his eyes crossed the room to Harriet's desk. She was whispering to someone on her cell phone. Wiping her eyes and trying to hide her face beneath her shiny blond hair. He knew that she was getting the news and hearing it for the first time. It was official. They'd found the piece of shit. Charles Burell was en route to the morgue.

He kept his eyes on her, grabbed a piece of graph paper, and started writing everything down. The time and place. What he heard and what he only thought he heard. She was on the phone with a friend, that much was clear. A girlfriend who didn't have her number at work and called her cell phone. Probably someone from her double life. Another victim of the late and nasty Charles Burell.

It suddenly occurred to Fellows that he needed to prepare himself for consoling Harriet after she got off the phone. It seemed obvious that she would need a shoulder to cry on. Someone to listen to her sorrow, perhaps even hold her. With Burell on ice and No. 3 smelling like fish tacos, she would undoubtedly turn to him.

He looked at the six black apples on his lab table, wondering if he should postpone his lunch with Finn at the Pink Canary. Harriet might want to go out and talk.

He bagged the apples and threw them away. Then he straightened the papers on his table and sauntered over to his desk. He timed his move perfectly. Harriet had just switched off her phone and was placing it in her purse. He gave her a look. Gentle. Even. The kind that said *I'm ready when you are* mixed with *Even though I cut off your boyfriend's dick, I'm a true friend.* When she turned toward him, he could see her wheels turning.

"I'm not feeling well," she said.

He waited for her to make the next move. Coffee for two at the Ivy. Fellows didn't drink coffee because it dehydrated his body. Given the circumstances, he decided to make an exception and sip at least half of one cup before switching to mineral water.

"I'm going home," she said. "See you in the morning, Martin."

He tried to speak but couldn't find the words. He watched her gather her things. Watched her get up and rush out of the room. When the door swung closed, he caught No. 3 staring at him.

"What happened?" the little heathen asked. "Is she okay?"

Fellows shrugged off the questions and tried to get a grip on his emotions. Tried to ignore the smell of fish tacos and sulfur wafting about the room. That feeling deep inside that he was a loser. The world's biggest fool.

She hadn't come to him. She ran away.

42

They were still going through Burell's basement office. Keith Upshaw from the Computer Crime Section was giving them a tour of the Web site.

As Lena watched with Novak, she couldn't help but think of a pyramid. The top was the front door. Once you gained access with a password, you had a choice of viewing the movie-of-the-day or watching a rerun from the archives. Reruns were listed by date and categorized by the model's popularity. Candy Bellringer, the woman with black hair and blue eyes Lena remembered seeing on the couch, was listed first with fifteen hundred more hits than anyone else.

But more to the point was Romeo's history with the Web site.

Logging on as Avis Payton, Romeo visited the site only three times. Once to establish a membership with Payton's credit card. Then three days later on the afternoon before Teresa Lopez was murdered. His third visit, lasting an hour and forty-five minutes, came on the night Nikki Brant was killed. When Upshaw went into the archives and found the movie-of-the-day that played that night, Burell had been with a young blonde calling herself Barbie Beckons.

Lena thought it over. The timing was important. And Burell knew that they were working a homicide case. He could have shown them the statistics he kept when they were here the other day but chose to keep everything hidden. Instead of offering assistance, it looked as if all he did was close the account under Avis Payton's name once he figured out the credit card was no good.

Lena followed Novak over to Burell's desk, taking another look at the file they'd found in the bottom right drawer. Burell kept records on the twenty-three women he was paying to have sex with. Eight-by-ten head shots were included, along with their contact information and up-to-date records of their HIV status. Each of the twenty-three women drew paychecks every three or four weeks, some more often than others. Each was listed as a *consultant*. The fee for spending an hour with Burell on camera came down to an even grand. Although the addresses seemed righteous, each woman was listed by her stage name. After searching the entire office and combing through his checkbook, it was clear that Burell didn't keep or use anyone's legal name. Each woman received a check from Charles Burell Enterprises made out to cash.

Lena gazed through the doorway into the basement. Burell's corpse had been removed two hours ago, still winking at them as they zipped him up in the body bag. SID techs were packing up, the whereabouts of Burell's sex organs still a mystery. Like every other crime scene in this case, they were able to document what happened, but they couldn't come up with a single piece of evidence that pointed to the doer. No fingerprints. No hair or fiber. Just the murder weapons. Twelve bottles of Viagra and a foot-long carving knife that Novak found when he checked the dishwasher.

It was like hitting the void. Until now, she thought. Until Romeo murdered Burell and a picture began to form. Not just a sketch of *what* happened, but their first glimpse at *why*.

"We're not chasing a serial killer, are we, Hank. Romeo's angry. He's insane. But there's a decent chance none of this is random."

His eyes shimmered in the dim light. "I think we've finally caught a break. The blonde lives in Santa Monica. Let's start with her."

43

Barbie Beckons's legal name turned out to be Esther Ludina, a twenty-four-year-old female who emigrated from Moscow to Tijuana and now lived in a two-bedroom condo at Eleventh and Ocean Park in Santa Monica. She weighed in at about ninety pounds, stood five and a half feet off the ground in a pair of spiked heels, and wore skintight jeans with her stage name embroidered on a low-cut, semitransparent blouse.

She had been willing to speak with them, off the record and with a frankness Lena didn't expect. Although both detectives agreed that the description of Romeo they'd worked up on the drive over had enough meat to make the trip worthwhile, Ludina couldn't provide much more than an offer to shed her doll-like top and show them her boob job.

She knew plenty of men who worked out and had what she called "girlie skin." It went with the job, she said. Half of them even had English names and were tall. But not one was bald, and that went with the job, too. A buffed head might be sexy in real life, but reflected too much glare, she told them. It looked bad when they switched on the camera lights. It was something she'd noticed as both an actress and director of her first triple-X film, *Barbie Meets the Three Kens*. Something that took the viewer's eye away from the girl. No good, she said with Russian verve. The only reason guys buy this crap is to look at the girl.

Lena crossed her name off the list and they got back in the car. As they pulled into traffic, she paged through Burell's file, found another model, and gave Novak the address. Of the twenty-three women on the Web site, all but a handful lived in or near Romeo's comfort zone.

They worked the list hard and by the end of the day had cut it down by half. Five women had been home, and six answered their cell phone and agreed to meet them so quickly that Lena thought they might have been waiting for the call. Every one of them had been willing to talk. By the time they reached the twelfth model, a TV was on and Lena understood why.

It was sweeps week. The local news stations were beating the terror drum and speculating on the blind that Burell's death had something to do with what they were now calling the Romeo Love Murders.

No one could deny that the body count was piling up. Three women were dead, a rock musician with a brand name, and now a sleazy porno operator. But Romeo was no longer just a story. He had become a franchise, consuming the first fifteen minutes of the six-o'clock broadcast, with updates promised throughout the night and more *team coverage* at eleven. When the newsreader offered his own theory that just maybe Romeo got started five years ago by murdering David Gamble, and the reporter in the field shook her empty head and said, "Only time will tell," Lena stopped listening.

Novak's cell phone rang. After glancing at the LCD, he mouthed the words *My ex-wife* and pulled to a stop before a run-down apartment house one block east of Main in Venice. It was 11:30 p.m. Lena could hear the rain tapping against the roof. The rush of wind pushing against the car, then letting go. In spite of the weather, Novak gave her a nod and climbed out of the car with his cell phone.

Lena settled back in the passenger seat, watching her partner find cover beneath the building's open-air garage and letting her mind drift.

Ever since James Brant had been cleared in his wife's murder, everyone had been looking at Romeo as if he were a boilerplate serial killer choosing his victims at random. Although she thought the sexual assaults might still be random, and that until last month Romeo was a serial rapist working off the grid, the murders had an entirely different feel about them. Something that hadn't revealed itself until Burell was tortured and killed.

As she gazed out the window, she mulled it over. Burell's death read like punishment. Romeo might be angry and psychotic, but when he murdered Burell, he had a motive. A reason Lena could see and touch and understand.

She heard the door open and watched Novak climb in behind the wheel, his face dusted with rain. When he looked at her, she could see sadness in his eyes. Worry.

"What did she want?"

He flipped on the wipers and pulled away from the curb. "It's Kristin. I think she's using again."

It hung there. Novak's favorite daughter falling off the wagon. When Lena saw her the other night, she thought she was doing better than that. Novak made a left on Lincoln, heading for the freeway a half mile up the road.

"They had a fight," he said. "When Kristin ran off, she searched her room."

"What did she find?"

He paused a moment, his mind going. "Sounds like coke. But I need to make sure. Okay if we call it a night?"

She nodded. It was too late to work Burell's list anymore.

"Who's got the keys to Holt's house?" she asked.

He turned, trying to get a read on her.

"I'm not tired, Hank. And we've got the autopsy in the morning. I left Holt's place early, remember."

"Rhodes has 'em. If you want, we can stop by his place on the way downtown. I'll go in and you won't have to deal with him."

She thought about how Rhodes had spent his day, tagging her brother's murder on Tim Holt's dead body. Whether it had been a perfect fit, or if changes needed to be cooked up behind the great blue curtain to make it all fly.

"That's okay," she said.

He shrugged and turned back to the road. As the light from a passing car struck his face, she could see him wrestling with his thoughts just as she was.

"It's been a long day," he said.

She nodded at him.

"The kind that used to end with a drink," he said.

She caught the slight grin.

"Fuck it," he said. "I'm not tired either. If you get the keys, I'll check out my daughter's stash and meet you at Holt's in an hour. Sound good?"

"I'll buy you a Diet Coke."

Rhodes slid the keys across his desk. "Take them, Lena. Do whatever the hell you want. I lost a night's sleep working that gun and I'm too tired to argue."

He lit a cigarette and leaned back in his chair. They were sitting in his home office, a converted sunporch that hung over a steep hill halfway up Beachwood Canyon on Glen Alder. But as Lena studied his face, his dark eyes, she didn't think he was looking at the close-up view of the Hollywood sign, or even the lights strung across the basin leading to downtown. Rhodes had shut her off and was as cold and distant as he was when she'd made the move to RHD.

He tapped the head of his smoke into an ashtray brimming with dead butts. Although Lena had noticed the pack in his pocket this morning, she had never seen him smoke before and couldn't remember ever smelling it on his breath or clothes. He looked pale and strung out and stiff as a machine. In spite of the leather jacket he wore over his T-shirt, his body now appeared more skinny than lean. Even the scar from the earring he used to wear was more pronounced than just a day or two ago. Not from the dim lighting or even losing a night's sleep, she figured, but from a case of nerves and what she estimated was a sudden loss of five to ten pounds.

Her eyes moved to the papers on his desk. Her brother's murder book removed from the binder and piled up in sections. Three spiral notebooks were set beside the telephone, which she guessed were Tim Holt's journals. When she first arrived, the notebook on top had been open. Rhodes had marked his place and quickly set it aside.

"Why are you doing this?" she whispered in a hoarse voice.

"It's over, Lena. Holt shot your brother. Case closed."

She felt the fire in her belly—a pain that hadn't been there before—and wondered if she was getting an ulcer. Tito Sanchez might be green enough to go with the flow, but not Rhodes. He was an experienced detective. Cool, thoughtful, inventive, with a wicked sense of humor that used to make her laugh.

Had their meeting so many years ago been a matter of bad timing? Or was it really her good fortune that nothing happened? As she looked at his sullen face smoking that cigarette, she couldn't be sure.

"I don't understand why," she repeated.

He kept his eyes on the window. "In the end I guess you're no different than anybody else."

"What's that supposed to mean?"

"Everybody's got an opinion, Lena. Especially these days. Everybody wants to tell you what they think. That's okay with me as long as no one crosses the line. As long as nobody thinks they have a right to the facts. Facts have nothing to do with opinion. Facts are facts, and with your brother's murder, there's no turning back."

"You think Romeo picked Holt's house out of a hat. You think he stepped off his home turf and just happened to kill Jane Doe."

He wouldn't look at her and didn't respond.

Lena pressed forward. "With all the years you've put in at the homicide table, you don't see even the possibility that something's wrong?"

"Facts are facts. I won't color them, and I can't change them. When the DNA comes in, maybe even you will see the light."

"Who's pushing this through? Barrera? The new chief? Or is everything coming from you?"

He actually smiled. Leaning across the desk, he raised the window an inch. When he spoke, his words came slowly, deliberately.

"The firearms unit confirmed that the gun Holt took his life with was the same weapon used to murder your brother. It wasn't a throw-down gun. Holt bought it and we have the receipt."

"I heard that before. If you can plant a gun, I guess you can plant a receipt."

"Yeah, sure, Lena. Just like OJ's glove. I buried the fucking thing when no one was looking."

"Facts are facts," she said. "And it seems like you're the keeper of the facts."

"I don't care if you hate me. I don't give a shit. I spent the afternoon talking to Holt's doctor. His shrink at the clinic. He told me that your brother's death had become an obsession for Holt. That he was so fixated on the murder that it slowed down his recovery. Meeting after meeting, all he wanted to talk about was the murder. His shrink said Holt had a lot on his mind. A lot to get off his chest."

She kept her eyes on him. "Guilty people usually do, right?"

"I didn't put the words in the shrink's mouth and I didn't lead him on. When I called and told him Holt was dead, it was the first thing out of his fucking mouth."

"What about Jane Doe's identity?"

He fell back into his chair, looked at her a moment, then shook his head.

He was angry. Visibly attempting to reel his emotions in. Her mind clicked back fourteen hours to the moment she'd seen his signature on the checkout card at the Records Retention Center. The old woman handing her the murder book and blessing her on the way out. As she tossed it over, she heard Rhodes's girlfriend bang a pot in the kitchen. She looked through the French doors and saw the woman staring at them as she did the dishes. Lena had seen her before. A green-eyed blonde with a gentle face and a figure drawn in curves. Tonight she seemed particularly moody. When their eyes met, the woman turned away.

"It's been a long day," Lena said. "I'd forgotten what you said with Barrera this morning. Holt was jealous. I guess that's as good a reason as any to take a shot at your best friend."

Rhodes picked up Holt's journal and found a page he'd marked. "Read it. You tell me what was going on in the guy's head."

He pushed the notebook her way, then pointed to an entry. As Lena glanced at the page, she realized that it was more of a sketchbook than a notebook. Holt made journal entries but also drew in the book and even

Scotch-taped mementos beside what he wrote down. As she started reading, it occurred to her that the entry was made on the day her brother played that ballad for Holt. The story of Lena and David Gamble, two bank robbers on the run. Holt was describing what he felt after hearing the music. He wrote the lyrics down, understanding immediately that the crimes were only a metaphor for the life Lena and David had been dealt and shared. That in its way it was a love song, something Holt found so beautiful he became overcome with self-doubt. He wrote about his wrath after hearing the song. Feeling inept and depressed and fighting the urge to kill the pain with another hot load in the arm. The spike of anger he had for his writing partner because it all seemed to come so easy for David Gamble, while he himself always had to work so hard.

She looked up from the journal and caught Rhodes staring at her. His eyes were gentle at first but quickly iced over. As he turned away, the scar on his left earlobe became more vivid. Rather than a puncture wound, it looked more like an *X*.

"This doesn't mean what you think it does," she said.

He crossed his legs and worked on the cigarette in silence.

"My brother used to say the same thing about Holt," she said. "That it came too easy, and he had to work to keep up. They were pushing each other."

The phone rang. Rhodes picked it up, said hello, but not much else. It was a one-sided conversation that began with a no, meaning that he wasn't alone, followed by a yes, indicating he couldn't talk because someone was in the room. Lena turned back to the journal, leafing through the pages until she found the first entry after her brother's death. Three weeks had passed. As she started reading, she realized that the entry hadn't been written in Holt's own words. It was pulled from *The Maltese Falcon* by Dashiell Hammett. Sam Spade talking about the meaning of a partnership as he grilled Brigid O'Shaughnessy, a woman he could have loved but now knew murdered his partner.

When your partner's killed, you're supposed to do something about it.

The words had a certain weight about them. When she heard Rhodes hang up, she closed the book and returned it to his desk.

"I've gotta go to the market," he said.

She met his eyes and knew that he was leaving the house to meet some-one. That he hadn't listened to her and, at the very best or even least, had no interest in what she said. Rhodes was using the journal to define the context for the murder and clarify the motive. Anything that interrupted that vision was being ignored.

Rhodes checked his watch, then slipped the pack of cigarettes into his pocket. "Holt writes about a gold pick," he said. "Someone gave it to your brother as a gift. Someone famous."

Lena shrugged. "You're saying Holt hated him for that, too?"

"Doesn't sound much like love. Your brother got the pick. Holt didn't. He wrote about it."

The green-eyed blonde started banging pots again. Rhodes looked through the French doors for a moment before turning back.

"She knows about us," he said.

"Knows about what? Nothing happened."

He gave her a look as he grabbed his keys. "Right, Lena. Nothing hap-pened. Whatever you say."

She'd had enough. She grabbed the keys to Holt's house and stood up.

"I'll find my way out."

She pushed the glass doors open, watched the blonde turn her back in the kitchen, and passed through the foyer without a good-bye. Her car was parked at the bottom of the hill before an A-frame cottage. On the way down she counted the steps. There were seventy-two between the street and Rhodes's front door. Reaching the bottom, she paused a moment and looked up at Rhodes's house hanging over the precipice. The rain had stopped, the wet ground cover glistening from the light venting out the win-dows of the A-frame.

What Rhodes was calling context and motive were irrelevant. History was littered with one artist pushing another forward. Lennon and McCart-ney came to mind first. But even van Gogh and Gauguin challenged each other and would easily have made the list. If anything could have been drawn from Holt's journal, it was that Holt wrote everything down. That his entries were made regularly. If he committed suicide, if he was involved in her brother's murder and wanted to get it off his chest, he would have left a note. Without the note, his suicide wouldn't have any meaning. If the murder had been preying on his soul, the note would have been his one and only chance to offer an explanation and have some say in the way he would be remembered.

The question was, why didn't Rhodes see that?

Something was going on with the man. Something she didn't want to guess at, imagine, or make up. But it was there.

You're a nobody. You don't count. In America everybody counts, just not *you.* . . .

The words rippled through Fellows's entire being. It was almost as if he could hear them through the dash over the car radio. The same words playing over and over.

You're a nobody.

You don't count in Harriet's life.

Everybody and anybody counts in her life. Just not *you.*

Fellows made a left and tooled down Fairfax heading north in his '98 Ford Taurus. He wished he could snuff the words out of his head, but knew that he wasn't hearing his own voice or even Harriet's. It was Mick Finn, glaring at him from across the table at lunch this afternoon. Fellows thought it sounded a lot like an argument. Finn said that it was time to wake up and called it a reality check.

A real worldview.

He had murdered Burell hoping to save Harriet. He thought she would be drawn to him, but she ran off. The dream was over. Even worse, according to Finn, LAPD detectives connected the Burell murder to the Teresa Lopez and Nikki Brant killings. And where and how did Jane Doe and Tim Holt fit in? Fellows had lost control of himself and taken unnecessary risks. He was letting all the press coverage go to his head. And for what? A whore living a double life who couldn't be saved, didn't love him, and never would.

Fellows switched the radio on, found KFWB, and turned the volume up, hoping the late-night news might help prevent a meltdown. Then he checked the rearview mirror.

That Mercedes was back. The same silver coupe that had followed him off the 10 when he abandoned the freeway in favor of surface streets. His eyes flicked back through the windshield and he tried to concentrate. The rain had stopped. In spite of the hour, it looked as if all 7.9 million cars registered with the DMV last year were on the road tonight. Chances were that the driver was headed for Hollywood just as he was and knew the shortcut.

He made a right on Willoughby, a narrow, tree-lined street with an east-west cut through a series of residential neighborhoods. When he checked the mirror, he saw the Mercedes make the turn and speed up, then back off just before hitting him.

Fellows shook his fist in the air, then took a deep breath as he considered the possibility that he was being followed. That Finn had been right and a trip to the crime scene at Tim Holt's house wasn't worth the risk tonight. He glanced at his digital camera on the passenger seat and, for a moment, dreamed about the shots he might get inside the house. The darkness and ultrasilence that seemed to inhabit a home after a death occurred. What it would feel like to breeze through the rooms. He needed a place to think. A chance to get a grip on himself. Finn's obvious skills in security wouldn't be required because the owners were already dead.

The front end of the Taurus suddenly lifted upward. Fellows's stomach dropped as the car began to hydroplane, his eyes riveted on the pool of water flooding the right lane. He wrenched the steering wheel to the left. Checking the mirror, he slammed on the brakes and felt a bump. Then the Mercedes veered off, skidding into a tree.

A moment passed. Fellows stared at his camera on the floor, wondering if it was broken. He jammed the gearshift into PARK and ripped the door open, bristling with anger as he noticed the damage to his car. His bumper was intact, but the left taillight was gone. His eyes danced across the wet pavement, picking out the pieces of broken plastic. When he heard the other driver begin shouting at him, he looked up slowly.

The man was in his early twenties. He was kneeling before his Mercedes, examining the damage.

Fellows caught the buzz cut. The basketball jersey and baggy pants. He knew who he was in a single instant. An unhirable undesirable, driving what looked like a brand-new Mercedes CL65 AMG Coupe with a twin-turbocharged V-12 under its crinkled hood. List price $178,220.

He wondered whether the car was stolen, but guessed that the money to buy or lease the car was how they played the game. His hands were trembling. He knew that he could snap at any moment. That he was on the verge of losing it, if he wanted to lose it.

"You were driving too close," he said in a low voice.

The little heathen flashed his eyes at him, then stood up and spit. "Too close, motherfucker? This is your fault. Look what you did to my fucking car."

The man was only ten feet away. The muscles on his arms lacked definition, and Fellows estimated that he was fifty pounds overweight. He knew what he could do to him in as little as fifteen seconds. That it would be painless, soundless, over. His vision began to take in the lit windows along the street, his eyes frozen in their sockets. Someone was watching them. He could feel it. He could see their shadow in a window on the second floor.

"You were driving too close," he repeated. "Are you all right?"

"Fuck you."

The man jumped in behind the wheel and sped off. Once he got halfway down the block, the little giant worked the horn and shot Fellows the finger.

But at least it was over. And Fellows had demonstrated that his ability to control himself, his unique strength, wasn't exactly lost. As he returned to the Taurus and examined his camera, he wished that Finn had been here tonight to witness the way he'd handled himself.

He switched the camera on and pressed the button. The flash bounced off the windshield, filling the car with white light that poked at his eyes and hurt more than sunlight. When the flash subsided, he studied the shot. No harm done at all. His camera was in perfect working order.

He pulled around the flooded section of the road, continuing east on Willoughby. Five minutes later, he made a left on Vine and could see Hollywood Hills less than a mile up the road. The radio was still on, the story switching from storm coverage and a mud slide in Malibu to Romeo, who was now the talk of the town. It was a sound bite from the chief of police. They were making progress, he said. But investigations like these take time.

Romeo. That was the name they had given him.

Romeo.

He liked the way it sounded and the meaning it conveyed. He even liked the heart-shaped graphics the TV stations were using to frame pictures of his victims on the news.

He pulled to a stop at the light, gazing through the windshield at the homes nestled into the hills. The lit windows. Tim Holt's house couldn't be seen because the lights were off. No one lived there anymore.

He smiled as the light turned green. Everyone in the City of Angels was looking for him. Everybody wanted to know who he was. He reached for his water bottle and took a long swig. Martin Fellows might not count, but Romeo did.

46

Lena glanced at the house behind the wall as she rummaged through the trunk for her flashlight. It was dark, quiet, fifteen minutes past midnight. The only sound seemed to be coming from a dry breeze shuffling the leaves overhead and stirring the branches until they let go of the rain.

Her meeting with Rhodes had a troubling aftertaste, something she was having difficulty shaking. An internal dialogue that turned into something of a war. She had always taken pride in her ability to size people up. As a police officer she relied on her instincts to read a situation quickly and act with confidence. It was a survival skill. Something that came with growing up hungry and living in a car. Something she needed to be able to count on. While it would be jumping the gun to suspect Rhodes of anything, his behavior was more than unusual. Yet just as she wanted Tim Holt to be found as nothing more than an innocent victim, she needed Rhodes to come out clean as well. She couldn't be wrong twice. Not that wrong about two men she cared about and thought she knew. It came down to her internal compass. The main wheel. And whether she could trust it.

She remembered buying that pack of cigarettes yesterday and found them on the dash. With Rhodes still in mind, she lit one and wondered if self-destruction was contagious. She had followed him down to Franklin, then lost his car in traffic when he made a right on Gower. She had been keeping her distance, twenty car lengths' worth of insurance so that she wouldn't be seen. Had she anticipated the volume of cars on the road to-night, she would have played it tighter. Still, she confirmed that he'd lied to her. The market was two blocks up Franklin in the other direction. Rhodes was on his way to meet someone.

She checked her watch as she drew smoke into her lungs. Novak was at least a half hour off, maybe more. Switching the flashlight on, she pushed the crime scene tape out of her way and started down the driveway on her own.

She wanted a look at the house first. All the way around. Novak had told her over the phone that the point of entry hadn't been an unlocked front door. Instead, the intruder broke a window around back and entered from the basement. She found a gravel path at the end of the drive, following it down a series of steps until she reached the backyard. Panning the light across the perimeter, she spotted the stable and horse trails leading into the hills. One trail caught her interest, and she moved deeper into the yard for a better view. As she took another drag on the cigarette, she panned her flash-light up the hill and watched the beam crisscross in the sky with the head-lights from a passing car. It struck her that this wasn't a horse trail, but a footpath leading to Mulholland Drive. If the intruder hadn't parked out front, this was a viable entrance to the property, something she would never have noticed if not for the darkness and a passing car.

She dropped her cigarette in the wet grass and gave it a tap with her boot. The breeze was steadier now and she could hear it wisping through the tall grass behind her.

She thought about the owner, her brother's best friend, and took in the breadth of what was supposed to be his new home. The windows were larger in the back, the ivy covering the whitewashed walls more carefully trimmed, no doubt because of the view. To the left at the top of the steps was a stone terrace with French doors opening to the living room. To the right, an enclosed porch that ran the length of the house. Tilting the beam of light beneath the deck, she located the basement door.

This was the point of entry. The weak link. She stepped beneath the porch, noting the gardening supplies and wood stacked beside a shed. Mov-ing closer, she panned the light over the door and examined the damage. Three panes of glass remained intact, while the fourth was crudely broken away with what Novak believed had been a log from the woodpile.

She gazed through the broken window. Dim light could be seen cascading down the basement steps, and she guessed that one of the crime scene techs had left a lamp on somewhere upstairs. She glanced at the moving cartons littering the floor by the furnace, then turned back to the door and zeroed in on the outdated lock. When she rattled the doorknob, she felt the loose fit and raised the flashlight. Above the doorframe was a foot-long crack. And the damage wasn't limited to the mortar. Several stones were split in two. It looked as if the jamb had shifted more than a half inch away from the door. Lena knew that she was looking at damage from the Northridge earthquake. Even more, she'd found another loose end in the logic of the case.

She grabbed the doorknob and gave it a hard push. Then tried again, thrusting with her hip. As the lock gave way and the door popped open, she considered the possibilities.

The intruder's first instinct would have been to try the door. Just as obvious, anyone with any strength could have forced the door open as easily as she had. From what they knew about Romeo, he was both cunning and strong. And there was a risk to breaking the glass. The sound it would make and the possible injury it might cause.

As she mulled it over, she realized that her revelation cut both ways. Romeo probably wouldn't have entered the house this way. But no one carrying a badge would have punched out the window either.

Filing it away for later, she stepped around the moving cartons and headed upstairs. When she reached the kitchen, she saw a small lamp burning on a table by the front door and switched on the overhead lights. It took a few moments for the crime scene to register in her mind. Novak and Rhodes must have unpacked every moving carton. When they were through, they repacked Holt's things, but the result was chaos. A house that was difficult to move around in and looked as if it had been turned.

The ice maker in the freezer clicked, then dumped a fresh set of cubes into the tray. Something about the sound made her feel uneasy. Almost as if a presence remained in the house. Pushing a stack of boxes aside, she cut a path toward the stairs and aimed her flashlight up to the second floor. The steps creaked under her weight. Cool air swept across her face as she reached the landing. She paused a moment, struck by that feeling again. That presence. Only this time it had more definition, and it felt as if she were being watched. She panned the flashlight down the hallway and gazed at the dark rooms at the very end. Lena had spent considerable time at crime scenes, on her own and at all hours of the night. As a homicide detective, experiencing a location and replaying the crime was part of the job. So why this feeling? Why now?

She turned away, the door to the murder room directly before her. Gutting it out, she entered the room, found the light switch on the wall, and flipped it. When nothing happened, she spotted a lamp by the bed and moved deeper into the room. The smell of rotting blood caught up with her, then lessened slightly as she finally got a light on and felt that draft of cool air again.

A window had been left open, perhaps because of the blood. She gazed at the roof outside, then closed the window and secured the lock.

She could feel it now. She could see it. Jane Doe's body strung to the bedpost with the stocking. What was left of Tim Holt, slouched in the chair holding the gun.

She heard something downstairs and flinched. Moving to the door, she listened to the peppered silence for a moment, then took a deep breath and tried to relax. She had a job to do. Why this feeling now?

She turned away, her eyes drifting back to the chair. Something about it bothered her. Not the bloodstains on the fabric. It was the position of the chair. The idea that it faced the bed.

The doorbell rang and the thought slipped away. She heard Novak calling her name. Hurrying downstairs, she pushed her way past the cartons and opened the door.

"Find anything?" he asked.

"Thoughts," she said. "Ideas."

She led her partner up the steps into the murder room and pointed at the chair.

"I'm just thinking out loud, Hank. But the chair's facing the bed."

"So what?"

"If I was gonna blow myself away because I couldn't deal with the guilt of being a murderer, I'm not sure I'd want Jane Doe's corpse to be the last thing I ever saw. I would've turned the chair toward this window and looked at the view."

"If Holt shot your brother and flamed out when he found Jane Doe, then I guess it's possible he would've turned away before he jumped. You know I've had trouble calling this a suicide from day one, Lena."

"Rhodes said he couldn't let go of my brother's murder. What if Holt was onto something? What if he got too close?"

"Anything's possible," Novak said.

The main wheel in her gut rotated slightly, then clicked so hard she could almost hear it. With every bone in her body, she knew why Holt had been trying to reach her. In an instant, she knew why he was dead. It came down to her internal compass. The main wheel. And whether she could trust it.

Holt found something, or walked into something. Either way, that was why he was trying to reach her. That was why he wanted to talk.

She turned back to Novak. The wear and tear on his face was more visible now.

"What's wrong, Hank?"

"The semen sample we pulled off Jane Doe. Even if Romeo's not good for it, I've got a feeling the science will be. I'm betting the DNA will match. Whoever did this put real time into it."

His words hung there. In the murder room with the scent of ripened blood wafting in the air. She was thinking about her brother. About Jane Doe and Tim Holt. She looked out the window at the hills tumbling into the basin. The lights to the City of Angels feeding into a not-so-distant ocean. Someone had the keys to the Romeo murders and was using them.

Fellows wriggled with excitement as he watched two sets of headlights roll by his car. After a beat, and then another, he started the Taurus and followed the last car up the hill.

He knew her name. Lena Gamble. He had read about her in the newspaper and even caught a glimpse of her on TV. But when she entered the murder house on Vista Road and he saw her in the flesh, it was like an epiphany.

He was standing in the dining room when she first stepped into the kitchen. Hiding in the shadows and angry at the intrusion until he laid eyes on her. He followed her through the house. Watching her. Smelling her. Mesmerized by the total package. The vision of it all.

He guessed that she had probably been a blonde as a child and liked the way her tangled light brown hair fell off her shoulders as an adult. Her sleepy eyes were as blue as a waterfall set against an early-morning sky. But it was her body that shook his being to the core. The way she took care of herself and the curves hidden behind her clothing that he could only see with his eyes closed.

She was driving a beat-up Honda Prelude. When she made a right on Mulholland, he slowed down some, taking extra care because the Crown Vic had turned left and they were the only two cars on the road now. Within a few minutes, he saw her make another right, heading down the hill to Franklin.

He thought about touching her. It had taken all his strength and willpower *not* to touch her. He could still see her standing outside the bedroom door as he hid in the empty linen closet directly behind her. He could hear her breathing as he consumed the different scents of her body. He wanted to take her right there. On the floor of a murder house. In the darkness and ultrasilence where he could think and be himself. He could hear her moaning. He could hear her whispering in his ear.

Romeo. Romeo.

The best part was that she knew he was there. He was sure of it. She kept pointing her flashlight down the hall. Staring into the gloom with a certain reach in her eyes. He could see her mind going. She knew he was there but couldn't find him in the shadows. Couldn't see him gliding from room to room. All she had was an impression of him. A feeling that they were alone together, and for the first time, very close.

Fellows suddenly became aware of his erection pressing against the seat belt. A chill curdling between his shoulder blades just before his entire body flushed with heat. He smiled at the warm feeling, his eyes locked on that car.

The Prelude crossed beneath the 101 Freeway and was making a left on Gower, heading back up into the hills.

"Heading home," he whispered. "The night's not over yet."

The climb steepened as they passed a stop sign. When her car vanished around the first bend, he switched his headlights off and rolled out a hundred yards before turning them back on. It was a technique he used when following someone in the hills. Something he'd learned from Mick Finn, who told him one night that it was all about perception. Not his perception, but what was going on in the mind of the person he was following. Every time he switched his headlights off, he vanished and was perceived as a car that had turned off the road. Every time he switched them on again, he was seen as a different car rounding the bend. A new car. Someone harmlessly using the same road.

Fellows knew that it worked when Lena Gamble pulled into her driveway and, before he passed the house, climbed out of her Prelude and headed for the front door.

He felt the adrenaline coursing through his veins and tightened his grip on the wheel. Continuing up the road to the next house, he found a place to park and doubled back on foot. Something was in the air tonight, a certain brand of electricity he couldn't quite define. All he knew was that the wind beating against his chest seemed unable to cool him down.

At the very least he needed another visual fix. More time to look at her, study her, think about what it would be like when they were together. Contemplate a world in which Harriet Wilson didn't reject him, but instead, he left Harriet for another woman. This woman. The one with the tangled hair.

He legged it around the bluff and started down the drive. As he picked out a window, he thought he might be in heaven. It was a bedroom window. A bedroom on the first floor that opened to the living room. He could see her pouring a glass of wine and crossing the room to her CD player. He watched as she sat down on the couch and peeled off her boots. In spite of the wind, he could hear the music passing through the house. It was a saxophone.

He listened for a moment, devouring the image before him as the saxophone wobbled and swayed. And then he suddenly realized that the woman he was watching, the vision he'd followed home, was in some kind of pain. He could see it in her smoky eyes. The way her lips were parted. The frequent sips of wine. She was listening to the music, and something about something hurt. When the song ended, the hurt didn't go away but seemed to get worse.

He stepped away from the window, quickly eyeing the house and searching for a weakness. He needed to get inside. He needed to get closer. The night wasn't over yet.

48

Lena turned from Novak and gazed at Tim Holt's X-rays on the light box as the medical examiner pointed to the exit wound.

"It was a clean shot," he said. "Straight up from the roof of his mouth through the skull."

Art Madina was slim with short black hair and green eyes that remained bright and alive despite his calling. Although he was young and fairly new to the coroner's office, Madina had already earned a reputation for being extremely thorough and had become the DA's new first choice when presenting evidence to a jury at trial. Lieutenant Barrera had delayed the autopsies until the pathologist could return from his conference in Vegas. When Lena called in this morning to verify the time, she learned that he had been the keynote speaker.

"The injury was obviously catastrophic," Madina said. "The force was so great that most of the frontal lobe followed the path of the bullet exiting here. Death would have been instantaneous. But with Jane Doe it's another story."

Madina took a step to his right, the film on Jane Doe clipped to the light box beside Holt's. The autopsies had been scheduled for 11:00 a.m. In spite of their importance, Lena and Novak had been more than forty-five minutes late. They'd spent the first three hours of the day working Burell's list of sex partners from his Web site. Working through the remaining ten women as quickly as they could. Although they knocked three more names off the list, four of the ten had become frightened and left town, and the last three weren't home and didn't pick up when Lena tried their cell phones. The morning had been a bust. None of the women they interviewed knew or remembered seeing or even meeting a virile man with a buffed head and smooth skin. By the time they arrived at the coroner's office and got suited up in their scrubs, the only thing they missed were the X-rays.

Madina adjusted his glasses as he examined the film. "The knife wounds on the girl follow the same path as the wounds we found last Friday on Nikki Brant. They're almost a perfect match. The big difference is the cause of death. I'm betting we'll find it here." His hand moved away from Jane Doe's torso and rose to her neck. "We've got severe trauma. A definite break. We'll see which came first when we open her up."

"Let's start with the male victim," Lena said. "He's our primary focus right now."

She didn't use Holt's name because she needed distance. Autopsies were hard enough. Watching a pathologist cut open someone she knew skidded into a parallel universe. As she sniffed the Vicks VapoRub behind her surgical mask, she wondered how long she would last and wished she'd caught a better night's sleep. In spite of the wine, she spent most of the night tossing and turning. Listening to the house creak in the wind and fighting off nightmares from an eighteen-hour day spent at two crime scenes. Charles Burell winked at her from the other side. But so did Romeo. She could remember seeing his hazy figure standing over her bed last night. And he was a giant of a man, completely hairless. When she looked at his face, she couldn't find it in the gloom. All she could see were his eyes, glowing back at her in the dark. She woke up after that, her heart racing, and kept her eyes open until the sun rose over the city and the shadows went away.

Madina grabbed his clipboard, skimming through his notes. "You're thinking Tim Holt isn't a suicide? That's not in my preliminary report from the field. Gainer called it an obvious suicide."

"That's why we're here," Novak said. "All we want to know is what's possible."

"You mean that what we're looking at could be a homicide."

Lena cleared her throat. "We have reason to believe that it's worth keeping an open mind."

She glanced at Novak, then followed Madina across the operating room to the two bodies already laid out on a pair of stainless-steel gurneys. Five autopsies were under way in the same room. As her eyes drifted over Jane Doe's corpse, she realized that she had never seen her face and was surprised by how young she looked. How innocent and pretty she must have been, and why Holt would have wanted her in his bed. When she turned to face Holt's naked corpse, she tried to ignore the sound of a technician working his skull saw on a gangbanger directly behind them.

"Was there any sign of a struggle at the house?" Madina asked. "Anything specific I should be looking for?"

Novak shook his head. "Not that we know of. But it was a tough crime scene, hard to walk around in. He'd just moved into the place and never got the chance to unpack."

Madina nodded and seemed to relish the challenge. "Then let's have a look."

He began his examination by carefully studying Holt's hands. Lena remembered seeing the gunshot residue at the crime scene. Because GSR samples were so delicate, Ed Gainer would have performed the lift in the field, and she wondered if that hadn't been what Madina was looking for just a few minutes ago when he checked his notes.

"His fingertips are heavily callused," the ME said, glancing at Lena. "He was a lefty, right? He played keyboards but also a little guitar."

She met his eyes, surprised by his knowledge of what Holt did for a living. "Yeah," she said. "He was a lefty."

Madina turned back to the corpse, examining Holt's wrists and ankles and lingering over a slight bruise just above the stomach. "I was sorry I couldn't get back sooner," he said. "They had a new album coming out, and I listened to the sample tracks on the band's Web site just last week." He glanced at Lena, his voice quieter now. "I was a fan."

She nodded and understood, then took a step back with her partner. For the next two hours, she watched as Madina and two technicians dissected her friend's body. It was about surviving the spectacle. Not flinching when the ME made the Y-cut down the center of Holt's chest with his scalpel. Ignoring the sound that the zap lights made every few minutes when another insect drawn to the dead bodies made a wrong turn and went down hungry.

But it was also about flooding her mind with thoughts about the case. Hoping that the three women from Burell's Web site they hadn't been able to reach would return her call and that one of them actually knew who Romeo was. Weighing the differences between Romeo and the cop who murdered her brother with the understanding that while one couldn't help himself, the other could, yet both were lethal. She glanced at her partner, admiring his strength and resolve. She had been upset last night and forgot to ask Novak about his daughter. When she apologized this morning, he told her that he'd found crack cocaine hidden in her bedroom but couldn't do anything about it until she returned home. In the past her binges lasted for a day or two. Sometimes as long as a week. Yet here he was, by her side working the case.

And then it was over. What remained of Holt's body was hosed down, his empty chest cavity laced up with a thick, black twine by a technician as Madina stepped forward and wanted to talk.

"I don't see it," he said. "Nothing about this victim looks like a homicide. There isn't even a hint that something's wrong."

Lena moved closer, trying to block out the din of the room and those zap lights. Madina glanced at his notes.

"The fingernail clippings taken by Gainer at the crime scene revealed no human skin. Nothing that would indicate that he scratched someone or fought back. There are no abrasions on his knuckles. No ligature marks on his wrists or ankles, and his neck is clean. No signs of hemorrhaging around his eyes or beneath his eyelids, and when we opened him up, his hyoid bone was intact. He wasn't held against his will and he wasn't strangled. I'm sorry if the results don't fit with what you had in mind. But there are no defensive wounds on this body."

"But what about that bruise on his stomach?" Novak asked. "It looks fresh."

"I agree," Madina said. "It probably happened within an hour or two of his death. But it could have been caused by anything. You said that he hadn't unpacked. That the house was hard to move around in. He could have easily walked into something."

Lena traded a hard look with her partner.

Madina moved closer to the body. "That's what we didn't find," he said. "Now let's talk about what we did. The gunshot residue. Enough GSR was lifted away from his skin and already verified by the lab to prove that his left hand fired the gun. When we removed the blood from his face, we found his left cheek tattooed from the muzzle flash. Burns on his chin, his lips and tongue. I'm guessing he held the muzzle an inch or two away from his mouth when he fired the weapon. But there's no guessing at all when it comes down to how the man died."

Novak's cell phone rang. Digging into his scrubs, he glanced at the LCD and mouthed the words *Lieutenant Barrera* as he flipped it open. The call didn't last more than thirty seconds. When it was over, he said, "We've gotta get back to Parker."

"What about Jane Doe?" Madina asked.

"You'll have to fly solo. We can talk about the results when you're done."

It was difficult to get a read on Novak because he was wearing a surgical mask. But Lena could see it in his eyes. And when he told her that the DNA results were in from Jane Doe, she had to think twice because of the way he said it. The way he shot her the look and heavy nod. The DNA results were in, but it sounded more like he was saying, *It's done, Lena. The fix is in.*

They left Madina in the operating room. Scrambling out of their scrubs, they raced up the back steps and out of the building.

"Give me the keys," Novak said. "I'll drive."

"What did Barrera say?"

"What we thought he would."

She tossed Novak the keys, then climbed into the car and took a deep breath of fresh, L.A.-flavored air. As Novak sped past the guard shack and pointed the Crown Vic toward the city, her eyes drifted out the window to what looked like an endless parade of homeless people trudging up and down the sidewalks in rags. The American Dream had a back door, she thought. Once it hit your backside, you were out.

"It's not like we didn't know this was gonna happen, Lena. We guessed as much last night."

She turned and gazed at Novak. "Then why do you look scared?"

"Because we don't know who it is. We don't know who we can trust.

We're dealing with a motherfucker in our own house and he's pushing a lot of buttons right now."

That summed it up, she thought. But the implications ran deeper than that. The way the record would be written. Romeo killed Jane Doe. Holt murdered her brother, then shot himself. Forget about the rag sheets at the grocery store. That's the story that would be produced for television. Those were the words that would skip the California Section and make the front page of *The Times*.

She could feel her stomach turning as they approached the Glass House and pulled into the garage. Her pulse fading as they rode the elevator up to the third floor. The desire to vomit when Lieutenant Barrera waved them into the captain's office and she saw Stan Rhodes already sitting at the conference table with his eyes down.

"Have a seat," Barrera said, closing the door. "We've got work to do."

Lena pulled a chair away from the table and sat beside her partner, then watched Barrera cross the room and take a seat beside Rhodes. A line had been drawn, she figured. Us versus them.

"The DNA results are in," Barrera said. "The semen samples taken from Jane Doe at the Holt crime scene match the samples we got from Teresa Lopez and Nikki Brant. Romeo's good for the kill. He did Jane Doe, then waited for Holt to get home so he could watch."

She glanced at Rhodes. He hadn't acknowledged their presence since they entered the room. He looked strung out, and it seemed obvious that he'd missed a second night's sleep. Her eyes moved to the scar on his left earlobe, the *X* even more pronounced than last night.

"You with us, Gamble?" Barrera asked.

She turned to the man and nodded without saying anything. He slid the lab report across the table as if that might help them see the light.

"Romeo's good for the kill," he repeated. "And Holt's good for your brother's murder. We've got verification now. It's over, Detective. It's time to close the case out."

Barrera's eyes were on her. He was sizing her up as he spoke. She could tell that there was more, so she kept her thoughts to herself and remained silent. The question was how much more.

"Your brother's murder was a high-profile case," he said. "It's a feather in our cap that the department was able to solve it. The new chief is extremely pleased, but he's also worried about leaks. He's holding a press conference in an hour instead of waiting until later in the day. I know it's short notice, Gamble, but he wants you to make a statement. He wants you standing on the podium right beside him."

She could feel the weight of the moment pulling her under the surface, then turned when she realized that Novak had knocked over his chair and jumped to his feet.

"This is total bullshit," Novak shouted.

"Sit down, Detective," Barrera said.

"It's bullshit and you know it."

"Sit down or get the fuck out."

Berrera's words bounced off the windows and echoed about the glass room. After a moment, Lena finally spoke.

"I'd like to see Holt's journals."

"Why?" Barrera snapped back at her. "It's over. It's done."

"I want to see them. All of them. Everything up to the day he died."

Rhodes's eyes slowly rose from the table. He was staring at her now. She had followed their outrageous request with one of her own. A request that seemed righteous. It occurred to her last night when she returned home that if Holt was investigating her brother's murder, there was a good chance he wrote things down.

"His journals aren't here," Rhodes said in a low voice. "But I've read them. They're irrelevant to what you might be thinking."

"How would you know what I'm thinking?"

Barrera broke in. "Forget about the lousy journals. You've got one hour to memorize your statement and get downstairs. And it's not a request, Detective. It's an order. A direct order."

He slid a sheet of paper across the table. Her statement had been written by the brass on the sixth floor. It was short, only two paragraphs long, thanking the department for finally solving the crime and giving her closure on her brother's murder. While the outcome would be difficult to endure, it would deepen her resolve and make her a better police officer. . . .

She looked up and saw Novak's eyes locked on the statement that had been prepared for her. She caught the burn, the grimace—her mind rolling at a hundred miles an hour. She thought about what he'd said just fifteen minutes ago in the car.

Someone in their own house was pushing a lot of buttons.

And they wanted her to feel the pain. They wanted her in the wind.

She kept quiet, weighing the danger. She didn't say anything. Instead, she slipped the paper into her briefcase, met Barrera's eyes, and walked out.

49

She hit the 101 with her foot on the floor, bulldozing cars out of her way into the center lane. When she checked the speedometer and realized she was doing a hot ninety, she backed off the gas some and lowered her windows. She could feel the wind pulling her hair and chopping against her face. The sound of Eddie Vedder on the radio with those haunting guitars raging behind him.

Nothing is as it seems. *Nothing is as it seems.*

She hit the brakes, lost in the music and almost missing her exit. Gliding off the freeway, she made a left on Franklin and another left at the light. Ten minutes later, she was walking out of the Starbucks across the street from Gower Studios with a cup of coffee in her hand. She got back in the car, made a left on Hollywood, and tooled down the street until she hit Vista Del Mar. Easing around the corner, she rolled past the auto body shop and switched the radio back on. She would listen to the press conference here, she decided. At the spot where she'd found her brother's body. The place where he was murdered.

She found KFWB on the radio, then took a first sip of coffee and lit a cigarette. When her cell phone rang, she glanced at the LCD screen but didn't take the call. It was Lieutenant Barrera, probably wondering where the fuck she was.

She thought about the statement they wanted her to recite to the press.

The work of fiction written by some drone taking up space on the sixth floor. Her decision had been instantaneous, but difficult just the same. She was out on a limb and she knew it—not a single piece of physical evidence to back her up. They had the DNA results and the gun. When Barrera got his copy of Madina's autopsy report, he would probably think her reasoning was certifiable and recommend her transfer out of the unit. Or even worse, he might tag her with an involuntary stress leave and boot her down to the "Fifty-One-Fifty" building in Chinatown so the department shrinks could take another six-week look under the hood.

Nothing much would be left after that, she figured. Just the brand on her forehead that told everyone she was crazy and couldn't hack it.

She shook it off with another sip of hot coffee, listening to the headlines over the radio, the live press conference due to begin at any moment from Parker Center. According to the news broadcaster, a wind advisory remained in effect for the next three days. The Santa Anas were back, diminishing this afternoon, then increasing again tonight. Local gusts could exceed 65 mph. A fire had already broken out just north of the city in La Crescenta. Two teenagers had been spotted running from the scene. Although twenty-five homes were endangered, firefighters believed they had the blaze 75 percent contained.

And then it began. She could hear the new chief talking about her brother's murder, his pride in the detectives who solved the case, and a department that remained underpaid and understaffed but worked tirelessly and never gave up. When she heard Rhodes begin talking about Holt's gun and the match they'd made at the lab, her gaze lost its focus, wandering across the sidewalk, taking in the empty parking lot, the Capitol Records building, and the abandoned one-room chapel set behind a fence with all those spent needles littering the ground.

She flipped the radio off, took a last drag on the cigarette, and stubbed it out in the ashtray. Then she tightened her grip on the wheel and made the short drive home. As she pulled up to the house and got out, she checked the northeast sky and spotted the plume of smoke in the distance. The fire looked bigger than what was reported on the radio. And as she grabbed her briefcase and unlocked the front door, she wondered if they would get it out before the winds returned.

She stepped inside and turned the dead bolt, suddenly aware that someone was leaving a message on her answering machine. She listened to the voice, trying to place it. It was a male voice frothing with anger. "I'm watching this thing on TV," the caller was saying. "And there's no way Holt killed David. No fucking way Holt even owned a gun or would know how to use one. I knew them, Lena. These guys were my friends. Why are the cops doing this? How much shit do they expect me to take?"

It was Warren Okolski, Holt's producer. Even though she agreed with what he was saying, she didn't want to take the call right now. By the time she crossed the living room, he'd hung up and the message light started blinking.

Her eyes moved to the phone. The wireless handset wasn't in the cradle, which struck her as odd. After making a call, she usually returned the handset to the charger. She checked the counter, thinking about this morning. When she made that call to the coroner's office, she was sitting here with the *Thomas Guide,* mapping their morning route so she and Novak could get their interviews in before the autopsies. The handset wasn't here or in the kitchen.

The phone started ringing. Listening for the handset, she followed the sound into her bedroom and spotted it on the bed by her pillow.

Maybe the brand really fit. Maybe Barrera would be right sending her back to Chinatown.

She let the thought go, then picked up the handset, saw Novak's name on the LCD, and switched on the phone.

"Rhodes is trying to get you thrown off the case," he said.

A moment passed before the words registered. Rhodes was trying to get rid of her. She walked into the living room and sat down at the table by the window. The plume of smoke was moving south, hovering over the city on its way to Long Beach.

"You there, Lena? I'm on my cell and it's breaking up."

"I'm here," she said. "What happened?"

"I'm still at Parker. Everybody's pissed off that you were a no-show except me, I guess. Rhodes wants you off the case."

"What about Barrera?"

"His tail's up. He keeps talking about following orders. But given what just went down with your brother's case, I think he knows how firing you would play on TV. For what it's worth, I would've done what you did. I would've done it twice. These guys are assholes. It was all about getting your face on TV."

"You went to the press conference," she said.

"Yeah. And it looks like I'm stuck down here for the rest of the day. The chief wants a briefing on Romeo."

"I've got the murder book," she said.

"I don't need it. What about callbacks from Burell's list?"

"We didn't get any. I'm gonna try again."

"If you connect, give me a call, but don't wait on me. Do the interviews on your own."

She glanced at her watch: 4:15 p.m. "I'll call you back either way."

"And I'll let you know what's up," he said.

She switched the phone off, her mind going. The map she'd made of Romeo's comfort zone was still on the table. As her eyes flicked from one victim to the next, she pulled the murder book out of her briefcase, along with her case files. February remained blank. And two of the three women from Burell's list lived within Romeo's comfort zone.

She found the phone numbers in her file, using her cell to make the calls so her number would be recorded on their phones. She hit three blank walls and left three more messages, keeping her eyes off the map and trying not to think about the month of February and what it might imply. She pursed her lips, deciding to give them another try around six. Then she opened the murder book and started reading from page one.

In spite of the circumstances, she was grateful to be out of Parker Center. Grateful for the peace and quiet of home. Ever since Holt was murdered, ever since Rhodes turned on her, she had the feeling that things were moving too fast. That the case had a track of its own and they were missing something. Too many loose ends were turning up, and none of them had been written down.

As she read through the Chronological Record and checked it against the SID reports, she grabbed a pad and began to make a list. Jane Doe looked like the kind of woman someone would miss. Why was it so difficult to ID her? And why was the break-in at Holt's house so needlessly crude? She drew a line beneath the last question because it still troubled her. And what about Rhodes? He was keeping Holt's journals at his house. Was he altering them? Was he cleaning them up for some horrible, though unverified, purpose? And why did he ask her about the gold pick her brother received? He tried to make it sound like a throwaway question, but as she mulled it over, she could see through it now. Rhodes asked her about the guitar pick because he thought it was important. He was trying to deceive her.

She glanced at her watch. Two hours had flown by and it was dark outside. As she got up and made a fresh pot of coffee, she considered ways, both legal and otherwise, of getting her hands on those journals. Although Rhodes's girlfriend had been there the other night, Lena knew she didn't live in Hollywood and kept her own place somewhere down near the marina.

She let the thought of committing a burglary go—at least for the night. After trying to reach the three remaining women again and leaving a second set of messages, she turned back to the murder book. The questions were eating at her, fed by her growing concern for the three models, and she grabbed her pen. If something or someone on Charles Burell's Web site set off Romeo, how did he pick his actual victims? And why, if he defined a comfort zone, was his first homicide outside that zone? As she thought it over, it didn't make sense that Teresa Lopez wasn't close to Romeo in some fundamental way. And what about Burell's genitals? Why had Romeo removed them? Was it really a double dose of jealousy and rage, or was it something else? Even more grisly, why couldn't Burell's genitals be found when they tore the plumbing apart? What had Romeo done with them?

Her mind surfaced and she flinched. The house was shaking, the windows rattling as if a freight train were rumbling by. Her eyes shot through the room. When nothing moved yet the house wouldn't settle, she knew it wasn't an earthquake. It was the wind.

She opened the slider and stepped outside, the violent gusts swirling around her. She saw the debris floating in the pool and could smell the scent of something burning in the blast of bone-dry air. The shutters were beating against the house. She could hear the palm trees flapping in the wind and mimicking the sound of a hundred kites flying in the darkness. It was 10:00 p.m. and the Santa Anas had arrived—the Devil Winds—and she could taste the grit in her mouth.

She checked the yard, then cast her eyes over the hill to the lights below. A dust cloud was rolling west, consuming buildings a block at a time and shrouding the city in gray. As she watched a car slide down Hollywood

Boulevard and vanish in the haze, she thought about the list she'd made and was struck by an uncomfortable feeling.

Nikki Brant had been murdered one week ago on this very night. And the train she and Novak had been waiting for had most likely hit the station and passed them by.

50

"Where are you taking me?" Harriet asked.

He turned and looked at her in the passenger seat. "A friend's house," he said. "A special friend. He's out tonight. His place has a view."

She nodded, smiled a little, seemed to accept his explanation at face value. Fellows took it as another sign that the script was prewritten and all things happened for a reason.

Twenty minutes ago he had been parked outside her apartment in a rage because he knew this was his final move. When she walked out the front gate and spotted him in the Taurus, he capped his anger and told her that he'd just pulled up and was about to knock on her door. He was worried about her, he said. Worried when she didn't show up for work. It's a dangerous world.

"You think your friend has any vodka?" she asked. "I could use a drink tonight."

He nodded, trying to contain himself. He was still stunned that she hadn't run away from him. Still couldn't believe that she agreed to get in the car. After all, he was Romeo, and Romeo had another woman now.

He took in the scent of her body. Between streetlights he peeked at her legs and short dress.

"You like my legs, don't you, Martin. You like looking at them."

A moment passed. His eyes flicked back through the windshield and he hoped he wouldn't crash the car. He had never heard her use that tone of voice before. It was low, husky, just above a whisper, and the words themselves had a certain reach.

"In the lab we play our games," she said. "I like playing them. It makes the day go by faster. But I see the way you look at me. I know what you really want."

He turned to her and caught what looked like a lazy smile. After a moment, she spread her legs open as if relaxing in a pair of jeans.

The situation had become more complex than he anticipated. He thought he might need a time-out.

Although his friend and spotter couldn't be with him tonight, he had followed Finn's instructions and put together a plan. He made his mental calculations at each step and tried to stick to the plan. He even came up with a list of if-then scenarios, just in case the plan fell apart and he lost his way in the moment.

He made a left on Beachwood, trying to sort through the conflict. After passing the market a mile up the canyon, he made another left and followed the narrow road up a steep hill. Harriet was quiet, gazing at the homes, and it gave him a chance to think. She was finished, he kept telling himself. She was done. Like Finn said, he had gone the extra mile for a whore living a double life who couldn't be saved, didn't love him and never would. Now it was time to cut his losses and move on. Stow her away and get rid of her for good. Still, her birthday began at midnight and they shared a history he couldn't ignore. He even had a present for her. He could feel it poking him through his jacket pocket—still frozen and wrapped in aluminum foil. He wanted to surprise her with his gift. See the look on her face when she figured out what it really was.

He pulled the Taurus into the carport and watched her get out. She was standing at the foot of the steps beneath the streetlight. The wind was blowing her hair and she looked good. Real good. Like somebody's lucky night now that Burell was dead.

"Up the steps," he said. "You okay in the wind?"

She nodded and her eyes sparkled. "I like it."

She grabbed the rail and started up the steps. As he followed her, it occurred to him that she had an agenda of her own. That his imagination wasn't playing tricks on him. That even though she was a whore and he was a fool, she was a gorgeous whore while he remained a low-life fool. The thought lingered. And by the time they reached the front door, he played it out to its radiological end. For Harriet he was merely serving as a stand-in for Burell. He was a nobody in her eyes who rose by luck and circumstance to second best. He wasn't in control. She was. No doubt she likened her plans for the night to something along the order of a mercy fuck.

An image surfaced. Lena Gamble resting in her bed. Detective Lena Gamble of the Los Angeles Police Department. A woman who could bring him more than physical pleasure. A woman who had the power to elevate his place in history and give him the headlines no one in the past ever achieved. She was a cop working the Romeo murder case. She was tracking Romeo while Romeo tracked her. Poetry.

He checked his watch, wondering if Lena noticed the telephone he left on her bed. A reminder however faint that he was close and had spent some time there. When he glanced back at Harriet and she smiled, he felt cheap and dirty and wondered just who was second best.

Finn had been right all along. He could see it now. He was immune.

He spotted the old boot in the garden and dug inside it for the key. Opening the front door, he found the light switch and watched his next victim enter the house still trying to hide that stupid limp.

"Your friend's got a nice place," she said. "Is he away on business?"

Fellows nodded. "He won't be back until morning."

"Where's he keep the booze?"

He pointed to the kitchen. Finn told him that it would be in the pantry beside the basement door. But as he picked out a bottle, Harriet reached for his hand and stopped him.

"You don't drink much, do you?" she said, choosing a different bottle. "I'll make the drinks, Martin. Why don't you put some music on."

"What would you like to listen to?"

She smiled. "Something soft. Something slow. You pick it out."

He stepped into the living room and found the CD player already loaded with a dozen albums by artists he had never heard of. Deciding to live dangerously, he selected disc 1 and hit PLAY. When the music started, he felt a chill ramble up his spine and spread its wings across his neck.

He knew the song. He never listened to anything but classical music, yet here was a piece of jazz he was familiar with. He had listened to it with

Lena. Heard it through her bedroom window as he stood outside her house. The same saxophone. The same song.

"Perfect," Harriet said.

He turned and looked at her. She was crossing the room and seemed almost giddy as she passed him his drink and sipped her own. When she turned away to look out the window, he eyed his glass carefully, thinking about the alcohol content and weighing the damage it might do to his body. At least it didn't have the chemical vulgarity of gin.

"It's beautiful, Martin. You were right about the view."

He sipped the drink, playing along. Sipped his poison slowly, fighting the urge to take a swing at her. He felt the heat slip down his throat, the fire in his belly. As he looked at Harriet, the war going on in his head lessened slightly and he realized that the only thing left to do was find the moment. She might think she was running things tonight, but his plan remained intact. He wasn't a fill-in or a stand-in or even a stunt cock for a pimp like Burell. He was Romeo and she was done.

She sipped her drink, then reached out and smoothed her hand over his shoulder. She was standing close, her gaze dropping down to his mouth, then bobbing up again. He took another sip of vodka and looked at her standing before him. It was a shame that it had to be this way. Perhaps even tragic.

"Have you ever wanted something?" he said.

She giggled. "Who hasn't?"

"I mean have you ever wanted something really badly? Thought about it, dreamed about it, wished upon a star?"

She seemed surprised and moved closer. "You've never talked like this before."

Maybe it was the alcohol, but he thought he owed her something. Maybe not an explanation for what he had in mind, but at least something for her to go on.

"Have you ever wanted something so much you thought you might die if you didn't get it?"

She paused, considering his question. "Maybe. But I don't think I'd wish that hard for a house or a car or anything in the material world. A person maybe. Or even a job or a way out."

"A way out?"

"When I was younger I needed a way out."

"From your daddy," he said.

She nodded and looked more sad than giddy, perhaps remembering the sexual abuse she endured, or the broken leg she received when her old man pushed her down the stairs. Something came over him and he kissed her— on the neck, her cheek, and finally moving to her open mouth. Closing his eyes, another image of Lena appeared and he grabbed it. The hunted kissing the hunter, or was it the other way around? Either way, he found the idea exciting, and Harriet Wilson, the ex–Virgin Mary, the woman who got off fucking Charles Burell on all fours in front of the entire World Wide Web, didn't seem to notice.

He opened his eyes. He could feel her hand rubbing him. Squeezing him. It was an experienced hand, stroking him like a pro.

"Have you ever wanted something?" he whispered. "Wanted it and gotten it and then realized that the timing was off and you were too late? You didn't really want it anymore. When you finally got it, you felt like you were stuck with it. You found it disgusting. Even the thought of it made you sick."

She dropped her hand and giggled again. A little nervous this time. A bit unsure as she checked her glass.

"You want another drink?" she asked. "Then maybe we could sit over here on the couch."

His eyes narrowed and he nodded. The moment was coming. The script had been written and all things happened for a reason.

She took his glass and he followed her into the kitchen. As she poured the drinks, he opened the basement door but decided it would be easier if he didn't turn the light on. A moment passed—thoughts streaming by in an anxious blur. When she finally joined him, he took his drink and clicked glasses.

"What's down there?" she asked.

Her eyes got big and she smiled. He watched her lap up the alcohol with that mouth of hers.

"Your birthday party," he said.

And then the moment arrived. Everything steady as he reached for her neck and gave her the big push. He listened to her tumble down the stairs. Watched her vanish in the darkness. Heard the thud and groan followed by complete silence. Although he felt some degree of regret, it wasn't much more than a ping because he knew that she had been through this before.

He switched the light on. Just long enough to see her sprawled out on the concrete floor. She was still breathing. He checked his watch. It was after midnight, and Harriet Wilson was twenty-nine years old.

Her present could wait until later, he decided.

As his mind quieted, he dumped his drink in the sink and poured a glass of mineral water. The liquid was clean and refreshing, and he spent several moments savoring its crisp, pure taste as he stared out the window and admired the view.

She could hear voices. Fast and slow and cutting through the haze. She tried to root them out. Tried to focus, but she couldn't understand what they were saying. Two or three men—everyone speaking Spanish. And they were close. So close that she thought they might be standing over the bed watching her sleep.

Lena's eyes snapped open. Looking out the window, she knew that something was wrong. Three men were standing beside her car at the end of the driveway. She had seen them before, mowing her neighbor's lawn. Now they were staring at her house and looked concerned.

She ripped the covers off and pulled on a pair of jeans. Rushing out the door in her bare feet, she unlocked the slider and stepped outside into the wind. Something was burning. She could smell it in the air. When she checked the sky and looked to the east, she saw the plume of smoke over the city. Yesterday it had been a grass fire. Today, with the Santa Ana winds still blowing, people in La Crescenta were losing their homes.

She hurried down the steps. Two sheets of plywood were floating in the pool. Her lawn was littered with roof shingles and debris. As she legged it around the house, she gazed up and saw the rafters. At least one-third of the roof was missing. Papers were swirling about in the attic and jetting out the opening. Things belonging to her brother that she'd packed away for safekeeping.

"Devil winds," one of the men said in broken English. "*Diablo. No bueno.* No good."

He looked at her bare feet and flashed a timid smile, then pointed at the pool. He seemed shy and she guessed that he was asking permission to enter her backyard. She nodded, leading them down the path. When they reached the pool, the man eyed the water carefully, then spotted something.

"*Sí,*" he said. "We get it out of pool."

Lena looked beneath the plywood, realizing why the gardeners were here. Her neighbor's umbrella had broken loose from its stand and sailed over the trees. As she watched the men remove the sheets of plywood and hook the umbrella with the skimmer, she wondered how she could have slept through the storm. When the roof pulled away from the house, it would have made considerable noise, yet she hadn't heard it. It had been a dead sleep. A sleep without dreams that hit the moment she laid her head down.

Her phone started ringing. She could hear it through the open slider. Her cell.

Thanking the men for their help, she ran up the steps and hurried over to the counter. When she checked the LCD, she read the words OUT OF AREA and hoped that it was one of Burell's models finally calling back. But as she ripped the phone away from its charger, she caught the male voice at the other end. It was Art Madina, the pathologist who'd performed the autopsy on Tim Holt yesterday.

"I thought rock and rollers lived the life we mortals only dreamed about," he said. "I thought they got their pick of women. All they ever had to do was snap their fingers and say you're the one."

The tone of his voice seemed strange. Up and down, light and dark—all at the same time. She didn't know him well enough to get a read on where he was going.

"Slow down, Art," she said. "What are you talking about?"

"Tim Holt. I've read the stories. I was a fan, remember. I always thought he got more women in a week than I'd ever see in a lifetime."

She glanced at the time. Madina called her at 7:00 a.m. to talk about what?

"You're losing me," she said. "What's this got to do with the autopsy?"

"It's not Tim Holt. It's the work I did on Molly McKenna."

"Who's McKenna?"

"Jane Doe. The body I examined after you and Novak left."

A beat skidded by, and Lena glanced out the window. The gardeners were carrying the umbrella toward the driveway. When they vanished around the corner, her view turned inward. She was out of the loop. Jane Doe had been identified and no one called.

"When did they make the ID, Art?" Her voice had been steady. Rock steady.

"I don't know. But they called me last night."

"Who?"

"Stan Rhodes."

That pain in her stomach was back. A searing pain that lasted for about ten seconds before easing up.

Rhodes. She should have expected it.

"So what's this stuff about dreams and rock and roll?" she said.

Madina cleared his throat. "Molly McKenna was a virgin, Lena."

It hung there. Another loose end that didn't make any sense. Another black hole in a case shot through with black holes.

"I thought she was found in Holt's bed," Madina went on. "That she was supposed to be waiting for him to come home. That he found her and loved her and blew himself away when he saw what Romeo did. Wasn't that your working theory? Romeo likes to wait and likes to watch, and when he saw Holt blow himself away, he got everything he ever wanted?"

"That's what Novak and I believe happened to Nikki Brant and Teresa Lopez," she said in an even voice. "Romeo likes to watch the husband's response."

"But not with Holt and not with McKenna. I see where you and Novak are going with this. And I heard that press conference yesterday on the radio. It's pretty clear the department's headed in another direction. But this is bullshit, Lena. Molly McKenna was a virgin. She was seventeen years old and still lived at home with her parents. What the department's saying doesn't make any sense if McKenna had never been fucked. It sounds like spin. Like bullshit."

Lena didn't know Madina well, but she could tell by now that he was wrestling with the same bag of loose ends she was. There was no way that

Holt would commit suicide over a woman he wasn't involved with. No one would.

"Who have you talked to?" she asked.

"About McKenna? Nobody. It's your case. I'm calling to give you my report. I know it's early, but I wanted the night to think things over."

"What else did you find?"

"The knife wounds follow the same path we laid out with Nikki Brant. Almost a carbon copy. But here's the difference, and it makes about as much sense as everything else. The knife had nothing to do with the cause of death. McKenna was stabbed *after* she died, not before. I thought Romeo liked a bloody crime scene."

"He does. If he's going for the husband's response, he needs blood to get the effect. Yesterday you showed us the X-ray and said her neck was broken."

"Her neck was snapped, but I was wrong. It was a brain injury from a skull fracture that killed her. I found blood in her ears. When we folded her scalp back, her skull looked like a cracked eggshell. The brain contusion is textbook."

"So it was fast."

"So fast her blood didn't have time to clot. The doer grabbed her by the forehead and smashed the back of her skull in. The force was so explosive, he broke her neck along the way."

"Would he have known she was dead before he stabbed her?"

"That's the key question, isn't it?" he said. "If he's a copycat and didn't want to deal with a lot of blood. If he's not Romeo and didn't want to get his hands dirty. He'd kill her to stop her heart, then use the knife to make it look right."

"What do you think, Art?"

"Unless he was blind, he knew she was dead. Her neck would no longer be able to support the weight of her head. It would have been hanging off to the side. Maybe that's why he tied it to the bedpost with the stocking."

Lena paused a moment, thinking about the DNA match. The hard science that was in the way. "What about the semen?"

"A lot of these guys jerk off on their victims, Lena. Sometimes they can't even get it together to do that."

"But that's not Romeo. He's more than able."

"And that's why I'm having so much trouble signing off on these reports. I can't explain why the semen's there or why it matches Romeo. All I know is that McKenna died a virgin. At least on paper she was a virgin."

"What do you mean, on paper?"

"I don't know, what do kids call it? Friends with benefits? It's irrelevant to the case. McKenna wasn't raped, that's all that matters. No penetration occurred. And I've been thinking about that bruise on Holt's chest."

"What about it?"

"I think it could have been left by a Taser. It's possible, Lena. That would explain why he didn't fight back."

"When are you sending over the report?"

"Rhodes said you wanted it first thing this morning."

She grimaced. "What are you gonna do?"

"I don't know. I've been tossing it back and forth all night."

"Any chance you could slow things down and spend the day thinking it over?"

He didn't say anything right away. She knew that if her request got back to Barrera, what was already boiling might spill over the top.

"Tomorrow's Saturday," he said. "I'm not sure this can wait until Monday."

"It probably can't, but this case has strings attached. A lot of issues. Do what you've gotta do, Art. Do what you think's right. That's all I can ask."

"I appreciate that. You need anything more from me right now?"

"Just McKenna's address."

"It's here in the file."

She moved to the table by the window. After jotting the address down, she thanked Madina and hung up. It was 7:15 a.m., and Madina would have to make the decision on his own. She knew that it wouldn't be easy. While the physical evidence pointed one way, their interpretation of that evidence and common sense pointed in another. She turned to the window as she thought it over. The light raking the pool seemed unusually orange. She stepped outside and looked toward the horizon. The sun had risen over the city but lost its way in the plume of smoke. The entire basin was cast in a vivid red light that flickered and glowed all the way to the ocean.

She checked the yard, taking in the debris and damaged roof. She knew whom to call but would wait until she got in the car. Her eyes wandered back to the pool and up the porch steps. When she glanced at the chaise longue, her heart skipped a beat and everything skidded to a stop.

The cushion was wrinkled. Several towels were rolled up in a ball and tossed behind a planter on the deck. She took a step closer—the chill of her discovery prickling between her shoulder blades and working through her scalp.

Someone had been here. Slept here. Spent the night on her porch.

She made the turn off Fourteenth Street in Santa Monica, spotted McKenna's house on the right, and pulled over. The driveway was empty. When she checked the front door, she looked behind the screen and saw that it was open.

Someone was home.

She unfastened her seat belt and took a quick look around. It was a modest, two-story house, probably built in the 1960s. A nondescript house with wooden siding that had been bleached out from the sun and appeared run-down. A house people would be pointing at and staring at when the identity of Jane Doe was released to the press.

It was eight-thirty and her cell phone began ringing.

She had made good time and hadn't become fixated or overly distracted by her discovery that someone had spent the night on her porch. Instead, she made her call and arranged to have her roof tarped until the winds died down and repairs could begin. She went over her list of loose ends, hoping that most of her questions about the Holt crime scene would be answered in the next hour.

She checked the LCD, saw Novak's name, and opened the phone.

"They ID'd Jane Doe," he said.

Getting a read on her partner was easy. Novak was pissed off.

"The fuckers made the ID and didn't say anything," he shouted. "It's our case."

"I know," she said, glancing at the house. "But I can't talk right now."

"How'd you find out? Where are you?"

"Madina called me about an hour ago and said he got the word last night. I'm parked outside the McKennas' house."

"Why didn't you call?"

"Because I want to verify something first. I'll be in by ten. We'll talk then."

"Rhodes hasn't shown up yet, but I'm waiting for the guy."

"It might be better to let it go, Hank. Let me talk to these people first."

She closed her phone, clipping it to her belt as she got out of the car and walked to the front door. A radio was on, and she could hear music filtering down the hallway from the kitchen. When she knocked on the door, the music stopped.

"Who's there?"

It had been a male voice. A boy's voice. Someone startled by the knock on the door. Lena peered through the screen but didn't see anyone. Just a piece of the living room and the foyer leading to the kitchen.

"I'm a detective. I'd like to talk to you."

She heard the sound of a chair moving and watched as a fifteen-year-old boy appeared from the other side of the kitchen counter. He stared back at her and seemed hesitant to approach the door. His hair was dark brown and almost shoulder-length. He looked pale and thin and wore a black T-shirt and black jeans without socks or shoes.

"What do you want?" he asked.

"Are your parents around?"

"No. They're at the funeral home."

"I know it's hard, but would you mind if I came in?"

He didn't answer. In spite of the distance, she could see his eyes rocking back and forth. She knew that he had a reason to be upset. Even devastated. But why did he look so nervous?

He turned away from her, glancing at his bare feet as he thought something over. Then he made a sudden move for the back door and bolted outside.

Lena ripped the screen door open, legging it through the house and getting a quick read of the kitchen on her way out. Nothing was on the table except for a bowl of cereal. Nothing visible seemed worth hiding.

She spotted the kid running through a hedgerow, lowered her head, and burst through the bushes to the other side. It was a small park with no one around. Sprinting forward, she could hear the boy's labored breathing. As she closed in on him and made a grab for his T-shirt, she heard him yelp and squeal and realized that he was crying.

She tackled him to the ground, rolling him on his back and holding him down with her body. The boy's eyes widened, reeling off her face. She sensed recognition in his eyes but didn't understand it.

"Please go away," he said, trying to catch his breath. "Leave me alone."

"What is it? Why did you run away?"

"Please don't hurt me. I didn't do anything. I didn't say anything. Just leave me alone."

Lena sat up, watching the boy avert his eyes and roll back over on his stomach. He was shaking. Trembling. Unable to stop.

"What's your name?"

He paused a moment, but said it. "John McKenna."

"Okay, John. I need to know why you looked at me and ran away."

He shook his head, burying it in the grass.

"I need to know why you're so frightened."

The boy closed his eyes. "He said you'd come."

"Who?"

He shook his head again. "I don't know."

"Okay, so a man said I'd come. I'm investigating your sister's case. I'm supposed to come. I'm here to help you and your family. Why is that so frightening?"

The boy raised his head, then glanced at her and turned away.

"He was a cop, too."

She paused a moment. The words had a certain weight about them. A certain reach.

"You mean a cop told you not to talk to me?"

He didn't move and didn't say anything, his hands still trembling.

Lena decided to let the thought ride for a while and looked at the reddish sunlight glistening in his dark hair. He was thin but strong. She had seen several skateboards leaning against the back of the house on her way out. It would probably have been a better race if he had a pair of shoes on.

"I can't say that I know how you're feeling because I don't," she said quietly. "But I lost my brother, John. It was a long time ago. I loved him a lot and never really got over it. I never stopped missing him. When it happened, I kept asking myself why it had to happen. Why him? Why me?"

His shaking lessened some and he raised his head enough that she could tell he was listening.

"Your brother was murdered?" he whispered.

"Five years ago."

He was thinking it over. She could see it on his face.

"Did they get the guy?"

"Not yet," she said. "They haven't figured it out."

He turned toward her and sat up. "But it's been five years."

"It's been a long time."

She let the thought sit there, giving him a chance to chew it over.

"Let's go back to the house," she said.

He shot her a look but rose to his feet. Crossing the lawn, they passed through the gap in the hedgerow and stepped into the house.

"I need to know some things about your sister, John. It's important."

"Like what?"

"Let's take a look at her bedroom."

She followed the boy upstairs and down the hall to a room just past the bathroom. When they entered, Lena took a quick look around and then stopped.

"Is something wrong?" the boy asked.

She was staring at a poster tacked to the wall. It wasn't Tim Holt's new band. It was a photograph of the old one. She looked at her brother's face. The sweat streaming down his cheeks. His hands on the guitar. The people rushing the stage.

She turned away, taking a moment to scan the rest of the room. She noted the stacks of CDs, the fashion magazines, a stuffed animal. Molly McKenna may have looked like a woman. But when she died, she had been a girl.

"Your sister didn't know Tim Holt, did she?" she said.

He pulled the chair away from his sister's desk and sat down, eyeing her bed.

"No," he said quietly. "She was just a fan."

"Did she tell you what she was up to?"

"It was crazy. If I'd known about it, I would've stopped her. I heard about it from one of her friends."

"What did her friend say?"

"Molly thought that if Holt came home and found her in his bed, he'd do her. That's what she wanted. She was living a fantasy life. All she could think about was him."

"How'd she find out where he lived?"

"I don't know. My mom works in real estate. I heard on the news that Holt just moved in."

His voice trailed off. And Lena had confirmation now. Holt didn't even know the victim. She played the scene back in her head. The break-in at the house had been crude because it was performed by a seventeen-year-old girl, not the killer. Lena could see McKenna removing her clothing, getting into Holt's bed, and waiting for him to come home. It was supposed to be her big night. No matter how irrational, it was supposed to be the night she lost her virginity. When the killer entered the bedroom instead of Holt, she would have been terror-stricken. On the plus side, it would have been quick, just as Art Madina said. Just a few seconds of horror before the killer smashed her head open and everything went black.

The boy cleared his throat. "Can I ask you a question?"

Lena's mind surfaced and she looked at him.

"What if it takes you five years to find out who murdered my sister? What if takes even longer?"

She sat down on the bed. "I need to know about that cop, John. The one who told you not to talk to me."

His gaze fell away from her face. His hands were trembling again.

"I don't know his name."

"What did he say?"

The boy took a deep breath but didn't shut down. "Would this help you find out who killed Molly?"

"It could. Of course it could."

He thought it over, then spoke. "He told me that if I talked to you, I could end up like Molly."

"He threatened you."

The boy nodded. "He said lots of people would die and it would be my fault."

"What did he look like?"

"He wasn't wearing a uniform, if that's what you mean."

She leaned closer. She could barely hear him. "Then how did you know he was a cop?"

"He showed me his badge. He made me look at the gun inside his jacket."

"But you didn't see a name when you looked at the badge?"

"He was covering it up with his thumb. He was wearing a leather jacket. And he had a scar. It was on his ear. It was shaped like an *X*."

She could feel the rush of anger flooding her body, a hot load of wrath cut with overwhelming sadness. She wasn't sure she could stand up right away. Wasn't sure that she could maintain her footing. She had gone the extra mile for Rhodes, rationalizing his actions and reserving judgment until later. But now her doubts had been transformed into certainty. Rhodes had slipped into the dark. He was the ticket. He was the one.

53

Lena walked around the corner, entering the bureau floor and slamming into a wall of silence so dense that she could feel it in her ears. There were ten, maybe twelve RHD detectives in the room. No one looked up, but she could tell that every one of them knew she was there.

She spotted a single pair of eyes. Novak, at his desk staring back at her with empathy and concern. As she moved down the aisle, she glanced at Rhodes, but only briefly. Just long enough to measure the distance between them, not in feet, she decided, but miles.

And then someone began shouting.

"Gamble. Here. Now."

It was Lieutenant Barrera, standing in the alcove and waving her into the captain's office.

She dropped her briefcase on her desk, glanced at Rhodes before giving Novak a long look.

"Don't say anything to him," she whispered. "We need to talk."

"I'm waiting on you, Gamble," Barrera shouted.

She entered the alcove and stepped into the captain's office. She heard the glass door slam behind her.

"Have a seat, Detective."

Barrera hustled around the conference table, too upset to sit down. His face was more purple than red as he stewed over what he wanted to say.

When he leaned over the table to face her dead on, she could see the vein in his neck ticking like a snare drum.

"I don't give a shit how smart you are," he said. "I gave you an order yesterday, and you acknowledged that I gave you that order. Now tell me what it was."

She met his gaze. She knew that she had to take whatever Barrera wanted to give. That she had to eat it and remain silent about what she knew. Barrera would never believe her. But even worse, if Rhodes found out, he'd react. And if he was willing to murder two innocent people to cover up her brother's murder five years back, then it followed that he would be willing to kill again to protect his growing list of secrets.

"What was the order, Gamble?"

"You wanted me to attend the press conference and recite a statement that had been written for me by someone on the sixth floor, Lieutenant."

He gave her a hard look. He was angry, but he was true. She could tell that for a split second, he knew the order was just as bogus as she did.

"Listen, Gamble. I know things have been tough. If someone I called a friend murdered someone in my family, I'd be at my wit's end."

Her eyes flickered. Barrera was talking about Holt, but Rhodes had been a friend, too.

"So maybe these are special circumstances," Barrera said. "That doesn't change who you are or what your job is. This is an elite unit. We follow orders, right?"

She nodded but couldn't help wondering if something else was going on. Something more than her ducking the press conference yesterday.

"When I say jump, you jump or you're out, Gamble. All the way out. I sponsored your promotion out of Hollywood, so I'm taking this personally. You're making me look bad. And if I give you the boot, I'll make it my personal calling to fuck you up. We follow orders, is that understood? Every order. And we follow the evidence. When the science comes in, it's as good as an order. It's like it's coming from God. We've got a problem, Gamble. Not two problems. Just one problem. And his fucking name is Romeo. Is that clear?"

Someone knocked on the door and opened it. Barrera's head jerked up. When Lena turned, she saw Novak standing beside Upshaw, the analyst from the Computer Crime Section.

"Sorry, Lieutenant," Novak said. "But I need Lena and I need her now."

"What is it?" Barrera said, trying to regain his composure.

"It could be Romeo's motive for killing Charles Burell."

"Show me," he said.

Upshaw entered ahead of Novak, placing a nude photograph of a model on the conference table.

"Romeo visited two porn sites the night he murdered Nikki Brant," Upshaw said. "There's no way to know what he did when he got there, but this model is the only one that appears on both sites."

Candy Bellringer. Lena recognized her face instantly. Bellringer was the woman with black hair doing Burell on the couch when she'd first visited the Web site. Even more troubling, Bellringer was one of the models who lived within Romeo's comfort zone and hadn't called her back.

"Did you talk to her?" Barrera asked.

Lena shook her head. "We haven't been able to reach her."

"She's the most popular model on Burell's Web site," Upshaw said. "Fifteen hundred more hits than anyone else. She caught my interest because most of her hits are coming from L.A. With every other model, the hits are spread out. And then I noticed her left foot."

Lena's eyes went back to the photo and she spotted the toe ring.

"It's the toe Romeo severs from his victims," Novak said. "The second toe on the left foot."

54

Novak wheeled the Crown Vic down the freeway with the Christmas lights running. By the time they reached the north end of Santa Monica, Lena had brought her partner up to speed on what she'd learned from Art Madina and Molly McKenna's brother. Novak didn't say anything for a long time. She could see his eyes going as he chewed it over. The fear and pain that wouldn't let go when she told him that McKenna had been an innocent teenager, a young girl who broke into the house ahead of the killer and had no relationship with Holt at all. It didn't take much to know that he was thinking about the horror as both a detective and a father. That in the end, he was thinking about his daughter Kristin.

"Maybe he's using again," Novak said.

"I didn't know he ever did."

"Rhodes got sent down to Chinatown. It was about five years ago, but I can't remember whether it was before or after your brother's death."

Her mind clicked back to the time she'd spent with Rhodes. Although she remembered thinking he seemed intense, she never saw any indication that he had a drug problem. But then, she knew so little about the man and what he was capable of.

"What was he using?"

Novak shook his head. "I don't know. He looked like he does now. He was strung out and went on leave. Not for a couple of weeks, but for two or three months. Lots of sessions with Dr. Andy. When he came back, he was different."

"How?"

"I never really thought about it. He was just different. I didn't hold it against him because I work homicide, not dope, and I knew what my daughter was going through. Rhodes was a good detective and I trusted him and that's all that mattered. Whatever problems he had seemed like they were over when he came back. Now I'm seeing it in another way."

"Things were quiet today on the floor. You didn't say anything, did you?"

Novak shrugged, then turned up the fan and adjusted a vent on the dash.

"What did you do, Hank?"

"I told him that if he ever made an ID in one of my cases again and waited a day to tell me about it, I'd throw him out the fucking window."

She gave Novak a look. "You said it in front of everyone?"

"No. I had a one-on-one with the piece of shit in the hall. I don't think I blew it. I did what anybody would do. Things were dead up there for a lot of reasons, Lena. Madina called Barrera and said he wouldn't sign off on Holt or McKenna until he had a chance to think things over. He's hedging on the suicide and Barrera's having a shit fit. Lots of pressure from the sixth floor. They're out on a limb because of that press conference yesterday. They think it's a suicide, but with Madina stalling, the possibility that it isn't just got real."

"Barrera didn't mention it."

"Of course he didn't. It's a major-league fuckup. The kind that knocks people down the totem pole. The kind that sends us back to the good old days when we were the problem and juries decided to set all the assholes free. And if it's like you say and Rhodes did your brother, then he's gotta be feeling the heat, too. Like just maybe the motherfucker committed two more murders and screwed it all up. Without the suicide, the DNA looks bogus and Romeo's not good for the kills."

She gazed out the window as she mulled it over. A single question buried deep inside her. A question she would have to come to terms with before she could confront anyone and resolve the problem for good.

Why did Rhodes do it? What possible motive could he have had to gun down her brother on a dark street in Hollywood?

The question was buried because she found the answer so disturbing. She couldn't help thinking that the murder had something to do with her. Something to do with Rhodes and their attraction for each other. A relationship that had plenty of juice but never got off the ground. What she had always called *bad timing*.

Her mind surfaced as they rolled past Candy Bellringer's condominium. Unable to find a parking space in the endless line of cars, Novak made a U-turn and doubled back.

"And what about the DNA?" he said. "How did Rhodes plant Romeo's semen on McKenna's body?"

She had been thinking about it all morning. "It had to come from Nikki Brant."

"But we were all there. All in the same room."

"Rhodes laid out the crime scene tape. He was alone in the house for at least ten minutes."

"More like fifteen," Novak said, thinking it through as if for the first time. "He went in before you got there. When we pulled the covers, Romeo's semen had been wiped off the sheets."

Lena nodded. "We thought it was her husband, trying to clean things up. Instead, Rhodes saw an opportunity and took it."

They looked at each other—Novak visibly shaken. When he turned back to the road, he spotted a fire hydrant and pulled over.

Like most condominiums in Los Angeles, this one was surrounded by a security fence and a "feel good" gate that stood about seven feet high. Novak approached the residents' directory and grabbed the phone.

"I'm gonna guess she isn't using the name Candy Bellringer," he said. "What's her unit number?"

"Six."

"I count twenty-five. Everybody else is listed, but not six. All of sudden I've got a bad feeling about this. Why didn't she call us back?"

Novak pressed the button and waited for an answer. Lena noted the blank tag on the console and looked through the gate. It was a modern building with slanted roofs that appeared well maintained. White stucco and glass with lots of ivy and palm trees. Each unit included a second floor.

"Nada," Novak said. "Now I've got a real bad feeling about this."

"What about a manager?"

He went back to the directory and found the manager assigned to unit 1. As he made the call, Lena turned back. Although the building appeared luxurious, an oppressive stillness was in the air. That feeling that went with a crime scene. When Novak hung up, she grabbed the top of the gate, swung her leg over, and dropped down on the other side to let her partner in. Then they hurried down the walkway, checking condo numbers. As they passed a fountain, she spotted unit 6 by the pool. Novak knocked on the door. When no one answered, Lena glanced back at the pool and noticed that the vacuum was out. The door to a utility room stood open with the light on.

"Maybe it's the manager," she said.

They stepped over to the utility room, but no one was there. Lena noted the pool supplies and strong smell of chlorine in the air. Turning back to the condo, she scanned the windows. There was a balcony on the second floor, probably opening to a master bedroom, but the slider was closed.

They hustled back to the door. Novak examined the lock.

"She's a possible victim," he said. "Our link to Romeo."

"We've gotta go in," she said.

He nodded with determination. Taking three steps back, he lowered his shoulder. Then he plowed forward and threw all his weight into the weakest point of the door. Lena heard the wood let out a sharp crack and watched the door burst open and smash against the wall. As they entered, she surveyed the damage. The lock had been a dead bolt. Novak hit the door with such force that the jamb ripped away from the frame and cut the molding in two.

Lena took a quick whiff of air. Nothing was rotting. No decomposing bodies were here.

She moved into the kitchen, taking the room in quickly. She checked the fridge, the trash and garbage, and watched Novak examine what was left in the coffeepot for mold. When she moved to the sink, she found the basin dry.

"She hasn't been away for very long," she said. "But I don't think her day started here. She left the house sometime yesterday and didn't come home last night."

"She's a porn star and probably hooks on the side. For all we know, she spent the night working. Let's check upstairs."

They hurried up the steps and split up. Lena swept through the master bedroom, checking the bathroom and closets. In less than a minute, Novak was back.

"There's a spare bedroom with a full bath," he said. "She's not here."

Lena took another look around, this time searching for a magazine or piece of mail that might have the model's real name on it. But everything has its place, and inside this condo, everything was in its place. It seemed so odd. She noticed a pile of books by the bed, a cane, and a knitting bag overflowing with yarn. There wasn't a TV in the room. Since Burell's murder they had interviewed most of his models and visited more than half in their homes. In each case, the places had a tacky, quick-and-dirty feel about them. But not here.

"You think we fucked up?" Novak asked. "Are we in the right condo?"

Lena turned to the closet, eyeballing the woman's clothing and counting ten conservative business suits.

"Something's fucked up, Lena. And we didn't just walk in here. I broke the door down."

"This is the right place," she said.

He didn't seem convinced and moved to the chest, yanking open the top drawer. Scarves, jewelry, and an old wallet that was empty. He pulled open the second drawer and found T-shirts and tops. When he slid open the bottom drawer, he paused over the woman's lingerie.

"Unfold it," Lena said. "Let's see it."

Novak pulled out a nightgown. The fabric was cotton, the piece of clothing designed for comfort, not foreplay.

"Everything here is rated PG," Novak said.

He tossed the nightgown back and slammed the drawer closed. Glancing underneath the bed, he pulled a gym bag out and fumbled with the zipper. When he finally got it open, his eyes lit up.

"She's got a stash," he said.

He turned the bag upside down, dumping its contents on the bed. Lena moved in for a closer look. There were several negligées with maybe a dozen G-strings and bras. Rifling through the clothing, she noted the garter belt and stockings. When she fished out a black wig, she turned to Novak.

"We're in the right house," she said.

She grabbed the gym bag and opened the side pocket. Inside, she found Candy Bellringer's makeup, along with a vibrator and an ample supply of K-Y jelly. She spread the woman's makeup out on the bed and studied the colors. They were severe. Racy. It didn't take much to realize that the woman didn't use this makeup when she wore a business suit and went to her day job.

"What is it?" Novak asked.

"She's living a double life, and this is her mask and costume. She's not a pro. She's an amateur, trying to hide her identity. Maybe that's why she never called us back. She doesn't want anyone to know."

"You mean like maybe everything's copacetic. She spent the night banging some guy, then got out of bed and went to work. That's bullshit."

"I didn't say that. All I'm saying is that she's living two lives that don't mix."

Lena took the room in again, her eyes coming to rest on the antique table and chair by the window. There was a drawer underneath the lip of the tabletop.

She pulled the chair away and ripped open the drawer. She saw the checkbook and stamps, a pen and several bills held together with paper clips. But what really caught her interest was the envelope on top: a paycheck.

Novak leaned in over her shoulder. As she tore the envelope open, she felt a sudden rush of adrenaline hit her body and shake it. When she pulled the check out, she heard her partner gasp and thought her heart might not be able to handle the load.

The check was made out to Harriet Wilson. She worked for the Dreggco Corporation. The same company that employed Nikki Brant's husband, James.

55

Lena glanced at the sign by the door and winced as she entered the building with Novak.

THE DREGGCO CORPORATION

FOOD TASTES BETTER IF DREGGCO EATS IT FIRST

They stepped into the lobby and found Milo Plashett, the biologist who owned the company, engaged in light, even giddy conversation with five men dressed in expensive suits. As they approached, the banter slowed down and the laughter died off. Lena knew with a single glance that the five men were attorneys. Even better, she could tell that the five attorneys read them as cops the moment she and Novak entered the room.

Plashett broke away from the pack. "What is it? What's wrong?"

"We need a minute," Novak said.

Plashett lowered his voice. "I don't have a minute. The deal went through. We did the numbers yesterday, so if you're looking for James, he's not here and won't be back until Monday. He's up north burying his wife. The funeral's today."

"We're not looking for Brant," Novak said. "We'd like to speak with Harriet Wilson."

A wave of concern rippled across Plashett's face. "She's sick."

"She's not here?"

He shook his head, then turned his short, robust body toward the five attorneys. "Why don't you guys go up to the conference room and grab a cup of coffee."

One of the suits took a step forward. "Is everything okay, Milo?"

"Everything's fine. I'll meet you upstairs in a few minutes."

The attorneys crossed the lobby, eyeing them carefully with their tails raised. When they started up the steps, Plashett turned back.

"She told her supervisor that she wasn't feeling well on Wednesday afternoon and left early. Yesterday, she called in sick. When she didn't check in this morning, my assistant tried to call her but got a machine. We're worried about her."

Lena traded a quick look with Novak. All of a sudden nothing was copacetic.

"Let's go back to the lab and talk to Marty," Plashett said.

"Who's Marty?" Novak asked.

"Martin Fellows runs the lab. Maybe she said something to him. It's Friday. Actually, it's her birthday. There's a chance she took a long weekend."

Lena watched her partner manage a tentative nod as she thought about Harriet Wilson's long weekend. Her birthday.

She followed Plashett and Novak through a set of double doors. As they walked toward the rear of the building, she looked through the glass walls and counted three labs. Three sets of people in lab coats. She studied their faces, keeping Romeo's physical description in mind. Nikki Brant had been murdered last Thursday night. Now Harriet Wilson had gone missing. Romeo worked here. She was certain that he did. When Plashett pushed the door open at the end of the hall and she entered yet another lab, the vibe was unmistakable.

Only one employee was in the vast room. A biologist munching on a fish taco at his desk. In spite of the full head of black hair, the aura had resilience and sprang back at her. She could feel its weight and density. She could almost touch it.

"Where's Marty?" Plashett asked.

"At lunch," the man said, awkwardly trying to swallow his food. "He just left. He'll be back in an hour."

Lena took in the room. The concrete walls were lined with equipment and workstations. While the glass ceiling rose to the roof and provided a rich ambient light, tungsten fixtures hung from the steel beams over three lab tables set in the middle of the room. To the right, three desks stood side-by-side with plenty of space in between. Behind the desks a set of glass doors opened to the greenhouse. Two technicians dressed in blue overalls were in the greenhouse working on what she guessed was the irrigation system.

"This is Tommy Tomoca," Plashett said. "Tommy, these detectives are trying to find Harry."

Lena picked up on the informality of the work setting as she watched Tomoca push his fish taco aside. When she tried to get a read on Novak, he had his game face on.

"Is she okay?" Tomoca blurted out.

"Probably," Novak said. "But we're not sure."

Lena cleared her throat. "Her name came up in an unrelated matter. We think she might be able to help us. Did she say anything about taking her birthday off?"

Tomoca's head rocked back and forth. "I thought she was sick."

"Any chance you could show us around?"

Before Tomoca could answer, Plashett broke in. "Do whatever they say, Tommy. Give them whatever they want." Plashett turned to Lena and Novak. "I wish I could stay, but we're signing papers today. If you need me, just call. I can be down in two minutes."

They thanked Plashett and watched him exit the lab. When Lena turned back to Tomoca, he was staring at the center desk.

"Is this where Harriet sits?"

He nodded, then started pointing around the room. "Her workstation is that one against the far wall. Mine's the one you passed on the way in. Martin works at this one by the greenhouse door. A lab table goes with each workstation."

"What about her name?" Lena asked. "Do all her friends call her Harry?"

"Everybody except Martin."

"Why doesn't Martin?"

"I'm not sure. He's the boss. He goes by the book."

"What's he call you?"

Tomoca turned to her. "Number Three," he whispered.

"Why Number Three?"

"We don't get along very well."

"What about Martin and Harry?"

"I'm the third wheel," Tomoca said.

Novak coughed. Lena glanced at him, catching the look as he pulled out his notebook and pen. While she spoke with Tomoca, her partner would listen and take notes as he looked around. She turned back to the biologist.

"Have they got something going?" she asked.

Tomoca laughed. "They like each other. Martin has a crush on her, but I'm not sure it goes both ways."

"Why do you say that?"

Tomoca shrugged. Lena thought about the cane Harriet Wilson kept by her bed.

"Does it have something to do with her disability?" she asked.

"Harry's got a limp, but I wouldn't call that a disability. She's a knock-out."

"Would you mind if I had a look inside her desk?"

"Go ahead. We keep company secrets locked up in the filing cabinets over there."

Lena looked around the lab for Novak. She had seen him make a quick sweep of the room. Now he was standing by the glass doors, gazing into the greenhouse. She moved around the desk and began sifting through the drawers. Everything seemed innocuous enough. When she found the woman's day planner, she opened it on the desk.

"Who runs the greenhouse?" Novak asked.

Tomoca swiveled his chair around. "We do."

"Do you keep maintenance records?"

Lena looked up from the day planner. It wasn't Novak's question. It was the way he asked it. The precision in his voice.

"Maintenance is handled by a variety of outside firms," Tomoca said. "We keep records of their hours so accounting can check them against their invoices."

"What about Global?" Novak said. "Did you have any trouble with the plumbing last month?"

"We've had a lot of problems with the irrigation nozzles. It would be on my computer. Let me check."

Lena turned sharply, her view of the greenhouse obscured by Novak's back. But as one of the men wearing blue overalls knelt down, she got a look at the company logo embroidered on his shirt. Teresa Lopez worked for Global Kitchen & Bath, a plumbing supply house located in Whittier. When they'd gone through the company files and pieced together her last week of life, there was no record of Lopez ever working for the Dreggco Corporation.

"I found it," Tomoca said. "March third. It was a freebie, so it never went to accounting. We had a problem and Martin told me to call Global. I guess they were afraid of losing the contract. Someone stopped by to help us out."

Novak finally turned away from the greenhouse and shot Lena a look, his eyes sparkling. Teresa Lopez had been murdered on March 3.

"Would you remember who?" Novak asked.

"Not really. That's the problem. Global always sends somebody different out."

Lena turned back to Tomoca, measuring her breathing. The lab had gone electric. The air, thin as on a mountaintop.

"How about printing us a copy of that," she said.

The biologist nodded. When the printer fired up, he shut the program down and another window popped up. Tomoca was logged on to the Internet. He had been eating lunch and going through e-mails when they came in.

"Do you spend a lot of time on the Web?" she asked.

"No more than I have to."

"Do you know a woman named Candy Bellringer?"

Her question had a certain punch to it. Tomoca blushed, fighting off a smile and averting his eyes.

"Why are you embarrassed?" she asked.

"Because you're talking about Harry," he said quietly. "You're asking about her secret."

"Then you know about the Web site."

He nodded. "Harry thinks it's still a big secret. She wears that wig and makeup and thinks nobody can tell who she really is."

"Who else knows?"

"Everybody."

It hung there. Now she knew why Bellringer's hits on the Web site were coming out of L.A. Everybody in the company was watching her. Everybody knew.

She turned back to Tomoca. "What about your supervisor? It sounds like he's wrapped a little tight."

"Martin was the last to find out."

"How did he take it?"

"Not very well," Tomoca said. "He got angry and everybody laughed."

Lena thought it over for a moment, then leaned forward. "So Martin had a crush on Harry. Who gave him the news that she was living a double life?"

"The same guy who found the Web site. The guy who spread the news."

"And who's that?"

Tomoca grimaced. "James Brant."

A long moment passed as Brant's name settled into the room. A stillness. A motive for murder finally revealed. She met Novak's eyes. They had found the nexus. The core. The white heat burning at the end of the road.

She turned back to Tomoca, her voice easy and dead calm. "You told us Martin's at lunch. Any idea where he went? He might be able to help us find Harry. We'd like to speak with her as soon as we can."

Tomoca didn't say anything. Instead, he got up from his desk, walked over to Harry's lab table, and yanked open the top drawer. When he returned, he tossed a menu on the desk.

"Martin eats at the same place every day. The Pink Canary. It's that Italian place at the beach."

"He goes with Harry," Lena said.

"No. I think he meets a friend."

"Who?"

Tomoca shrugged. "I don't know his name, but I'm pretty sure it's a guy."

"How will we know it's Martin?" she asked. "What's he look like?"

Tomoca thought it over, then returned to his computer and clicked through a number of windows until he reached the company's Web site. Glancing at the home page, he highlighted the words WHO WE ARE. A moment later, a photograph rendered on the monitor. A team shot of every employee standing in front of the building. Lena consumed the image in a single bite as the molecular biologist pointed at the screen.

"He's that tall guy on the end," Tomoca said. "The one with the shaved head."

56

He was sitting at a table set for two beneath a palm tree.

He was alone.

In spite of the dark glasses, Lena could feel his eyes on her as they moved down the sidewalk toward the diner. Not on Novak. He was craning his neck and staring at her, almost as if he couldn't control himself. Almost as if they were the only two people in a world that had stopped spinning and flamed out.

The feeling was incredibly uncomfortable. Something that gained momentum with each step she took, digging beneath her skin and infecting her soul.

Romeo. Ten feet away. Staring at her as if she was prey.

They entered the Pink Canary and grabbed a pair of seats at the counter. When Lena gazed into the mirror and found Martin Fellows, she realized that he hadn't turned away. He was still eyeing her through the window.

"You catching this?" she whispered.

"I'm catching it," Novak said. "I wonder where his friend is."

She glanced about the diner, checking faces and trying to pick out the one that might fit. It was a loud place, filled with regulars from the neighborhood. A man was standing against the wall, waiting to use the restroom. Another was by the cash register.

She turned back to the mirror, zeroing in on Martin Fellows. There was a rawness about the odd-looking man. A visible edge. Even though he was seated and fully dressed, she could tell that he was in extraordinarily good shape. She measured the width of his shoulders, his biceps, the muscles in his neck. His strength was too well defined to come from sports. It had to come from a gym.

"How do you want to handle this?" she said.

"I want to see who he eats lunch with."

"I mean after that?"

"I don't know. The clock's ticking. Harriet Wilson could still be alive, but we don't have enough to make the arrest."

The words hung there. Out in the open and clear enough to see. Their identification of Romeo was pieced together by circumstance. A mutated gene, delta 32, had kicked off the process. Someone in Romeo's family tree had survived the Black Plague, so they knew they were looking for a Caucasian. The rest came from bits and pieces of statements from rape victims, but no hard evidence linked the sexual assaults to the murders that had begun last month. Now they had the Dreggco Corporation and its connection to Charles Burell's Web site. If James Brant had told them what he'd done to Fellows the night they interviewed him, she and Novak would probably have been sitting here a day or two sooner. But that wouldn't have changed anything. They would still be facing the same problem. They had their man. And now they needed his DNA.

Someone tapped a pen against the counter. It was the waitress, an old, round woman sizing Lena up and stealing peeks at her badge and gun.

"You two working or are you gonna eat lunch?" the old woman asked.

Novak ordered a diet Coke and said he hadn't looked at the menu yet. Lena thought about coffee, but was too revved up and ordered a glass of water instead.

"The water's no good here," the waitress said. "You can still wash clothes with it, but you can't drink it. Bottled water's the only thing we've got. That okay with you?"

Lena nodded. When the waitress left, she looked back at the mirror. Fellows had begun eating his lunch. And it wasn't a sandwich, but something that required a fork. If he left it behind, they could rush it down to the lab.

"There's something going on with his sunglasses," she said.

"They're not the kind you'd find at a drugstore, are they."

"More like a doctor's office after an eye exam."

"But he didn't come from a doctor's office," Novak said.

The door to the restroom finally swung open and a man stepped out. He appeared to be about thirty with a lean figure and long, dark hair. As he stood in the middle of the floor and looked out the window, Lena followed his gaze—not to Fellows, but to a young woman skating down the sidewalk on Rollerblades. Once she vanished, the man returned to his seat at the counter.

Novak shook his head and gave her a look. Then the waitress returned with their drinks.

"Can I ask you a question?" he said to the woman.

"Take me, I'm yours," she fired back.

Novak winced, then pointed at Fellows's reflection in the mirror. "Somebody told us that guy eats lunch with a friend."

The old woman gazed into the mirror. "Who are you pointing at?"

"The guy with the shaved head."

She found his image, then crinkled her nose. "Two Lunch?"

"That's what we heard," Novak said.

"Well, you heard it wrong. Two Lunch doesn't have any friends. At least no one I've ever seen."

"Why do you call him Two Lunch?" Lena asked.

"Because he's got a big appetite and he likes my food. We might laugh at him more than we should, but he's not bothering nobody and we leave him alone."

The old woman walked off. Lena glanced at Novak, then swiveled her stool around and looked directly out the window. Fellows had shaken a pill onto his palm and was studying it. After a few moments, he decided he didn't want or need the med and returned it to the bottle.

"If I don't take my medication," she whispered, "then I'm not sick."

"What are we dealing with, Lena?"

"Someone with issues."

Novak's eyes narrowed and his jaw stiffened. "He's on the move."

She jerked her head around and saw the empty table. Fellows had packed his lunch and was hurrying up the sidewalk. Novak threw a $5 bill on the counter and they rushed for the door.

"We may not have enough to arrest him," Lena said, "but we've got enough for a search warrant."

Fellows ripped open the leather briefcase and fished out a plastic bag. He needed to prepare a needle, and he needed to do it quickly. He was parked across the street and he could see Lena walking up the alley with that horrible man.

"He's a detective," his friend and spotter said. "He's her partner."

Fellows looked at Finn sitting in the passenger seat. "I don't give a shit who he is. Shut up. I'm in a hurry."

"They've found you. They know who you are."

"I thought I told you to stop."

Finn quieted down and shrugged. Then Fellows tore into the plastic bag, selected a brown vial, and opened a clean syringe. He had been using ana-bolic steroids for more than five years. Ganabol, a form of boldenone, stacked with a dose of Sustanon 250, was his clear favorite. While Ganabol couldn't be counterfeited, Sustanon 250 came in redijects, so he didn't have to buy so many needles.

He drew two milliliters of Ganabol into the syringe, the equivalent of a hundred-milligram dose. Then he pulled his trousers down, searching for an injection site in his upper thigh.

"You spend so much time talking about purity," Finn said. "You won't even eat the things you cook up in the lab. Clean food makes a clean body. So why do you do this to yourself?"

"You wouldn't be here if I didn't," he said through clenched teeth.

"How can you be so sure?"

Fellows jabbed the needle through his skin and hit the plunger, watching the synthetic form of testosterone enter his body. When the syringe was empty, he yanked it out and reached for the Sustanon 250 package.

"You're getting an abscess," Finn said. "Better shoot this one in your other leg."

"I see it. Why are you acting like such a loser?"

"I don't know, Martin. Maybe you should take a look in your rearview mirror."

Fellows checked the mirror as he ripped the packet open with this teeth. Lena and her bullshit partner were sitting in a Crown Vic two cars back. He shrugged, snapping the needle onto the rediject and stabbing himself in the thigh. A moment later, he felt the anger drift away, his body flooding with a tranquillity that only the stack could provide. It wasn't as if he were high. He was just good. Good and stacked and ready to roll.

He zipped up his pants, started the car, and pulled away from the curb. Slowly. Easily. The office was just down the road.

"Where do you think you're going?" Finn asked.

"Back to work."

"Are you insane?"

Fellows didn't say anything.

Finn shook his head. "They're following us, Martin. They've got your license plate and the make and model of your car. They know your name, and one of them is on the phone. Once they get a blood sample, they'll match the DNA and you're dead. If you're dead, then I'm dead, too. Why don't you get it? What's wrong with you?"

Fellows's eyes rocked back to the mirror and he saw Lena's partner barking into a cell. He could feel the anger coming back, the rage that shouldn't be here for another half hour but was. For a moment he thought about jamming on the brakes, dragging them onto the street, and squeezing the life out of them with his bare hands.

"But they're armed," Finn said. "They've got guns."

Fellows curled his lip and looked at his friend and spotter in the passenger seat. A regular mind reader.

"Then tell me what to do," he screamed.

"Let me take the wheel, Martin. I can fix this."

He checked the mirror, thinking it over. Oddly enough, the Crown Vic was slowing down. As the car reached the corner, it made a U-turn and headed back, vanishing in the distance.

"They're not interested in you right now," Finn said. "Only your DNA and finding Harriet. They're on their way to your house."

Fellows shuddered, his world evaporating before his eyes. They'd found him. They knew. He checked the mirror again. Two men he didn't recognize were following him in another Crown Vic.

"You can't handle what's ahead on your own," Finn said.

"You want to drive the car?"

Finn nodded. "There's no real need to pull over. Just let go of the wheel, Martin. I'll take care of the rest."

Lena spotted the van in the driveway and pulled before the house. The front door was open and she could see painters working inside.

"You sure about the address?" Novak asked.

"This is it."

"Then if he's keeping Harriet Wilson here, she's dead."

Lena tried not to think about it and got out of the car. The house wasn't what she expected. It sat too close to the neighbors and had too much glass. She turned and gazed at the ocean half a mile off, then looked back at the deck on the second floor. If Fellows's life required privacy, and she was certain that it did, he probably didn't spend too much time here.

They hustled up the steps. As they reached the door, a Japanese man in white overalls climbed off a ladder in the foyer and shouted, "He no here."

His voice bordered on shrill. Lena didn't like the man's face and flashed her badge as he approached them. He looked about fifty, his arms and hair dusted with flecks of paint, his eyes and mouth devoid of any laugh lines.

"He no here," he repeated. "He pack bag and stay with friend."

"Who's the friend?" she asked.

The man shrugged. "We start yesterday. He stay with friend. He no like fumes."

"We don't either," Novak said. "You're gonna have to split."

The man looked at them as if he didn't understand or didn't want to.

Novak took a step forward. "Pack up and go. Police business."

Lena pulled a generic business card out of her pocket. After writing her name and number down, she handed the card to the painter. Once his crew started packing, she and Novak entered the house. Because they were still waiting on the warrant, their initial search would be limited to Harriet Wilson, dead or alive.

She glanced at the first floor. The painters were pulling their tarps away, revealing a living room and dining room that were starkly furnished. Except for a blender, the kitchen counters were bare. They checked the closets and found a door leading downstairs to a basement. The windows had been covered with black paint. A poster of Arnold Schwarzenegger training at Gold's Gym in the 1970s hung on the wall beside the furnace and a full-length mirror. In the middle of the floor was a rack of hand weights, a bench, and a barbell. Lena examined the barbell, calculating the weight.

"How much?" Novak asked.

"Three hundred pounds."

"What about the hand weights?"

"Another hundred each."

She saw the glint in Novak's eye as they hurried upstairs. The worry. At some point they would have to confront the madman. At no point would they be able to overpower him.

The thought lingered, following her into the foyer. The front door remained open, the painters driving off. Lena honed in on the stillness but couldn't stop moving. They climbed the steps to the second floor, drawn by the light to the master bedroom at the front of the house. She gazed at the twin beds and spotted a Bible on the table, but didn't stop to think about it. Instead, she ripped open the closet door. When Novak switched on the bathroom light, she eyed the sink and counter.

"Guess he doesn't have much use for a brush or comb," Novak said. "But there's enough here for the lab."

More than enough, she thought. There were two razors. Two tubes of toothpaste. Two toothbrushes and two empty vials of something called Ganabol set beside two spent needles. There was two of everything for a man without a friend a waitress had called Two Lunch.

They doubled back, passing the stairway and turning the corner. The door at the end of the hall was sealed with a hasp and padlock. Lena searched the wall for a light switch and flipped it on. As she moved closer, she could hear Novak's rapid breathing and was aware of her own. They were in Martin Fellows's house, Romeo's house—juiced up and staring at a locked door.

And then someone called out their names. Loud. Nervous. Lieutenant Barrera. It had taken a moment to cut through.

"You got the warrant?" Novak shouted.

"I've got it," Barrera said. "Where are you?"

"Up here."

Novak gritted his teeth, breaking the door down with a hard kick. They took a step forward and stopped. As Lena's eyes adjusted to the dim light, it occurred to her that Fellows hadn't locked the door to keep people out. Instead, he'd sealed the room to keep something inside.

Barrera gasped from behind them. "Jesus Christ."

A half inch of dust blanketed everything in the room. The grime on the windows was so dense that it mimicked a coat of paint, blocking the sunlight and casting the room into a permanent state of gloom. Lena noted the furniture. It didn't match the rest of the house and appeared dated. And it didn't go with the wallpaper, which was obviously a child's. As she thought it over, she guessed that Fellows had probably grown up in this room but switched the furniture out.

"What are those two boxes?" Barrera said.

Lena turned back to the bed. Two packages about the size of shoe boxes were resting on the pillows. They were wrapped in brown paper and she could tell that they had come through the mail but never been opened.

She slipped on a pair of gloves and moved toward the bed, the dust on the floor so thick she left tracks as if walking on the moon. As she picked up the first package and wiped it off, the air about her face seemed to vanish. She read the postmark, then the label and return address. She felt her pulse rising and grabbed the second box. Both packages were addressed to Martin Fellows and had been sent from the Hollywood Crematorium.

"What is it?" Barrera said. "What are they?"

Lena read the names on the labels, noticed the dates, and did the math. "His grandparents."

"His what?"

"His grandparents. Their ashes were sent to this address twenty-one years ago."

She felt the chill. The flash. The monster taking on more definition now. She looked at Novak standing beside Barrera by the door. She heard the footsteps on the stairs. SID was here.

"He was raised by his grandparents," Novak said. "This is his childhood home."

"What are you saying?" Barrera asked.

She met her partner's eyes. They were bright and alive and everything was in perfect sync.

"Two of everything," Novak said. "He's got a second house."

Within an hour the contents of the bathroom had been logged into evidence and were speeding down the 10 Freeway in a black-and-white cruiser to the lab.

Barrera stayed behind but was spending most of his time on the phone. Lena could hear him as she combed through Fellows's desk in the living room. Barrera was standing outside the front door talking to his new best friend, Stan Rhodes. And it sounded as if Rhodes was doing the background work on Fellows but hadn't come up with anything. Tito Sanchez, his trusted partner, was coordinating surveillance with the Special Investigation Section. Fellows would be monitored for the twenty-four to forty-eight hours the lab needed to deliver a preliminary result. SIS had been on the job since Novak had made the initial call. After leaving the Pink Canary, Fellows drove to the mall in West Hollywood. From what Lena could tell, both Barrera and Rhodes took this as a sign that Fellows didn't know he was being followed. But as she mulled it over, she felt uneasy about it. If she wanted to shake a tail, the first thing she would have done was find a parking garage with multiple exits in a congested neighborhood. The mall at Beverly and La Cienega fit the bill.

Lena stopped listening, yanked the last drawer open, and spotted Fellows's checkbook and bills. She started with the bills, but couldn't find a single statement that wasn't related to the house in Venice. As she opened the check register and skimmed through the entries, every check Fellows wrote matched the utility companies that serviced this address. There was no evidence of a second residence.

Her eyes drifted across the room. A painting was over the mantel. Something familiar that she couldn't place.

She got up from the desk. The painting wasn't an original, but a print matted behind glass. A young woman with blond hair stood on a corner at night waiting on a red light as men in suits openly stared at her naked body. The buildings in the background were littered with graffiti. Moving closer, she realized that the graffiti hadn't been painted with a brush. Instead, it was inked in by hand and the buildings had the look and feel of a tattoo artist working on skin.

It was difficult to see with the entire room reflecting off the glass. And the quality of the print was so poor that she wondered if it wasn't a counterfeit. Still, the mood of the piece broke through and emoted a certain violence. The longer she stared at it, the more certain she became that the artist had been working with real human skin.

She turned away, wishing she had time to smoke a cigarette. She walked back to the desk and sat down, her eyes focusing on the checkbook. Curiously, Fellows had selected a design that looked like graph paper. Returning to the drawer, she found a stack of canceled checks and studied the man's handwriting. The machinelike precision that seemed so familiar now. Fellows wasn't writing across the check the way most people would. He was filling in the boxes as if working a crossword puzzle.

She pulled her notebook out, paging back to Sunday and their meeting with Irving Sample from the Questioned Documents Unit. Sample had found an anomaly in the way Romeo formed the letter *P*. She remembered him calling the deviation as good as a fingerprint, but she couldn't recall the details. After reviewing her notes, she sifted through the checks until she found the letter *P*. She wasn't a document analyst, but the anomaly was so obvious, she didn't need to be. Martin Fellows began at the bottom of the loop and finished the letter off in a single stroke. It was enough for an arrest warrant. In the Ennis Cosby murder case it had been enough to win a conviction. There was no need to wait forty-eight hours on the lab.

"Lena," Novak shouted. "Hurry."

His voice had come from the master bedroom. She ran through the hall, saw Barrera rushing inside, and sprinted up the steps. Novak was on the floor between the twin beds. A rug had been pulled away and several floorboards removed. Two SID techs were standing by as Lamar Newton fired off three quick pics with his motor drive and strobe.

Novak shot her a look as she entered. Jazzed.

"The boards were loose," he said. "There's a file folder down there. Looks like it's a couple inches thick."

Lamar finally backed out with his camera. Then Novak reached inside for the folder and opened it on his lap.

"What is it?" Barrera said. "What's he hiding?"

The first sheet of paper looked like a document. It was a photocopy of Harriet Wilson's employment records and included her medical history. When Novak turned the page, Lena could see his fingers trembling with excitement.

The file contained a stack of pictures. Eight-by-ten photographs of women in their bedrooms. But the shots weren't posed. And the women in the pictures had no idea that Fellows was even there. He had used a night lens, snapping off shots in the dark as they slept.

The horror settled in as Novak flipped from one picture to the next. The sheer number of faces without names. Sleeping. Dreaming. Alone in their beds.

When several pictures of Harriet Wilson turned up, Lena sat down beside her partner for a closer look. It was an entire series of shots, and Wilson was dressed in more than one nightgown. Fellows was infatuated with the woman and risked multiple visits. More than one break-in. As Novak came to the last photo of Wilson and tossed it on the pile, Lena turned to the next face and reached for the picture.

"You know her?" he asked.

"She was in the paper last week. She's pregnant but claims she hasn't had sex for two years."

"The Jesus lady," Lamar said. "It was in the paper last Friday morning."

Lena nodded. She had started to read the article but stopped when the woman claimed it was an immaculate conception. At the time it seemed like just another L.A. story. Another American version of a religious fanatic no one wanted to admit was a problem.

A moment passed. Novak finally turned the page over to someone new.

Someone both of them recognized. It was Avis Payton, the young woman with the electric maroon hair.

Lena looked at Novak. His eyes were glassy and he was trying not to show any emotion.

Fellows had used Payton's credit card to access Burell's Web site. The day they'd interviewed Payton, she was sick with something that resembled a stomach flu and claimed her purse was stolen. But now they knew what the young woman was trying to hide from them. What she didn't want her cop father in Salt Lake City to find out. Lena could still see the new security bar the girl had installed on the sliding door. Martin Fellows had given Avis Payton the gift that keeps on giving. A wound that would never heal. He'd raped her. And now she was pregnant, carrying the monster's child.

Novak flipped to the next picture without saying anything, but Lena could see him struggling with the revelation as he wiped something away from his eye. After reviewing the next ten photos, the shock was enough to bring them both back.

The women weren't sleeping anymore. They were dead.

And the pictures looked more like Lamar's work, rather than Martin Fellows's. Crime scene photos of Teresa Lopez stretched out on a cross painted on the sheets with her own blood. Nikki Brant's nude body lying on the bed with her face and hands packed up in grocery bags.

Novak stopped before reaching the end of the pile and turned to Barrera, his voice low and raspy.

"What do you want to do, Lieutenant? There's no reason to wait for the lab."

Barrera took a step back with his hands in his pockets. He seemed to be having a tough time making the decision. Lena understood his dilemma and filled them in on the handwriting samples she'd found downstairs. Then Barrera turned away, considering his options. A bead of sweat hit the floor.

"The girl could still be alive," he said finally. "He could lead us to her."

Novak shook his head. "He's a motherfucker from another planet. Harriet Wilson's probably dead. We need to get him off the streets."

"But we don't know she's dead."

Lena remained quiet, thinking that this might be the first time she agreed with Barrera in the past two days. Every other woman had been victimized in her own home. For reasons that remained unclear, Fellows had taken Harriet Wilson away with him. Lena thought about Brant showing Fellows that Web site. Brant was essentially calling the woman a whore and probably laughing about it and teasing the man. But Fellows had feelings for her. So much feeling that he murdered Brant's wife and waited around to watch Brant find the mutilated body. Harriet Wilson wouldn't be like the rest. Killing her wouldn't be as quick or easy. It was more than possible that she was still alive and that Fellows would return to her.

Barrera wiped his forehead. "As long as SIS is following him, he can't hurt anyone."

"Sounds good on paper," Novak said. "But how can you take the chance?"

"I think we should keep things as they are, Hank. Give SIS a couple of hours and see where he goes. If Fellows doesn't lead us to the girl, then we'll bring him in and hope we can get him to talk."

Novak grimaced, slamming a fist at the remaining photos in his hand. When they scattered across the floor, he looked at them and let out a yelp. Lena followed his shaky gaze to the pictures. Everybody did. She tried to focus, but it took a beat before the images rendered in her brain. Then her chest tightened and the room began to spin.

There were three photographs of another woman sleeping in her bed. Another series of snapshots taken by a madman in the dark.

Lena eyeballed the pictures, spotting the gun on the table. The ID and badge. As her eyes finally came to rest on her own face, she saw Novak take her hand but couldn't feel it.

60

Martin Fellows, aka Mick Finn, aka Romeo, a true lover of women, and for the moment star of both print and screen, turned from his workbench in a small room off the basement and looked at Harriet Wilson's wild eyes staring back at him. She was stretched out on a cot, her wrists and ankles handcuffed. Her blouse had been ripped open, her dress, torn.

"Why are you doing this, Martin?"

"Stop calling me Martin. That's not my name anymore."

"Then what do people call you?"

He didn't say anything because he wasn't sure. All he knew was that something significant had happened in his life. For the first time in a long time he was one person, one voice, a single entity on a historic mission. The epiphany had occurred after lunch as he drove to the mall. A clarity he'd never experienced before. He could see the cops following him, almost as if they were wearing neon signs. As he headed toward West Hollywood, he could predict their every move. And when he entered the parking garage, found a dark spot to park, made a quick purchase at Williams-Sonoma, and doubled back on foot, what had become a nuisance was finally gone. Two dead cops were resting easy in the front seat of their parked car.

He hoped the vision would last. He thought just maybe he'd reached what a Zen monk spends a lifetime yearning for. A Christian version of nirvana. The view from the cross and nothing less.

"Why are you doing this?"

Her voice wasn't much more than whisper.

"Because they know," he said. "Everybody knows."

"Everybody knows what?"

"Who you really are, Harriet. What you do when you're not at work."

Something flared up in her eyes. He could see her chewing it over. The door opening on her secret and letting the panic in.

"They've known for months," he said. "You're not the cute little blue-eyed girl from Nebraska you pretend to be. How many guys at work jerk off every night watching you get laid by that old man wearing the wig? How 'bout everybody?"

She turned her head away. He could hear her weeping. She was doing it quietly, but he could hear it.

"We work together every day," she said. "We're friends. Why didn't you tell me?"

"I was the last to find out. Everybody knows I dug you."

She turned back to him. "I knew it, too. I knew it from the beginning."

He didn't say anything. Instead, he played back the memories in his head. There was Harriet, but there was his sister, Tilly, as well. He could see her tangled blond hair strewn through the clean sand at the beach. He could hear her giggling. See her face splashed with warm light as the sun slipped into the ocean. They were planning to run away. Talking it over at their secret hiding place on the beach. It had been a long time ago. An image from his childhood that had somehow become lost until he reached this view from the cross.

"Who told you?" Harriet asked.

The memory vanished, and he looked at the woman chained to the bed.

"James Brant," he said. "Now do you know who I am?"

He could see her connecting the dots, and he was surprised when the tears stopped flowing and she pulled herself together. Moments passed before she finally spoke again.

"We're a lot alike," she said.

"What's that?"

"I haven't hurt anyone, but I know what it's like to have a secret life. An imaginary life."

"I guess you do," he said.

"I've lived two lives for a long time. One runs this way, the other runs back."

"I did my best for you, but that's all over now."

"Why does it have to be over?"

He didn't say anything. He looked at the bruises on her body from the fall down the stairs. The push. He couldn't protect her anymore, not even from himself. He couldn't change her into something she wasn't. This was the only way.

"Why does it have to end?" she repeated. "We share so many things together. Our jobs. Our interests. If everyone knows about my double life, then no one would believe what you've done to me. All you'd have to say is that she wanted it. She's a bitch and she wanted it."

He thought about Burell and her birthday present he was trying to keep fresh in the freezer. The timing seemed right.

"Is that the kind of talk that turned Burell on?"

She didn't answer. Instead, she rattled the handcuffs against the bed, twisting her wrists and ankles.

"Is there any way you could loosen these?"

"I'm afraid not."

"Then could you at least do me a favor?"

"That depends on what it is."

"I've got an itch and it's driving me crazy."

"Where?"

"My cheek."

He moved to the cot and sat down beside her. Until Lena Gamble, Harriet Wilson had been the most beautiful woman he had ever seen. As his eyes drifted over her gorgeous body, he could smell her skin. Her essence wafting in the air from between her open legs. And there was something about her face. A glow that beckoned.

"Where's the itch?"

She turned her head into the light. "Just below my left eye."

He leaned closer and saw the tearstains. Wiping the residue away, he stroked her skin with his thumb. Gently. Evenly. Acknowledging her sigh and the relief in her eyes.

"Keep going," she said. "Don't stop."

61

If Lena was certain about one thing, it was that she hadn't been raped. Martin Fellows could take all the pictures he wanted, but when he touched a victim, she knew. Every one of them woke up and knew.

How they handled the terror was a different matter. Some victims would play along to survive. Others might fight back in a futile attempt to beat a monster hyped up on steroids. When the ordeal was finally over, it went down like every other sexual assault. Some victims would report it, while others would keep it buried. And if the victims were anything like the woman claiming an immaculate conception, then they were lost in denial and couldn't even admit that the crime occurred to themselves.

It was 8:30 p.m. Novak sat beside her at his desk, sifting through three of the six evidence boxes they'd carted out of Martin Fellows's house in Venice. Five years' worth of tax returns, bank statements, and utility bills. Anything, no matter how small or difficult to see, that might give them a lead on that second house. Sanchez and Rhodes were on the other side of the floor, rummaging through the three remaining cartons in silence, but with plenty of attitude. Lieutenant Barrera had sent everybody else home and locked himself in the captain's office with Dr. Bernhardt from the Behavioral Science Section. They had been in the glass room for a couple of hours. Ever since they'd returned from the crime scene at the mall where two SIS detectives were found with their throats slashed.

Two cops were dead, and Martin Fellows had vanished. TV cameras littered the entrance to Parker Center while reporters stood in the Santa Ana winds, braving the smoke from the fires still burning in the hills north of the city. When Lena glanced at the TV on Barrera's desk, she noticed Tito Sanchez exiting the room with his cell phone and guessed that he was making another call to his wife. When she glanced at Rhodes, she caught him staring at her and turned away. He still had that faraway look in his eyes that gave her the creeps.

She shook it off because she knew she had to. She felt uneasy about their background check on Fellows. Rhodes had uncovered pieces of superficial information—an argument with a restaurant manager, a road-rage incident from two years ago—but nothing that steered them any closer to the whole of the man. Nothing that even hinted at his essence. Yet it had to be there. And it had to be in the system. Martin Fellows didn't evolve overnight.

She reached for the phone. Because Fellows lived in Venice, Pacific Division was already assisting them with the case. On the drive back from West Hollywood, she had called Matt Kline, a detective she went through the academy with. But that was more than two hours ago and she hadn't heard from him. Kline picked up on the second ring.

"Sorry, Lena. I was just about to give you a call."

"Then you've got something on Fellows."

"No," he said. "On his sister, but I think it'll help."

The investigation of Martin Fellows was less than nine hours old. No one involved knew or talked about Fellows having a sister.

"What did she do?"

"She got killed, Lena. Her name's on a murder book. Tilly Fellows. It took me a while to hunt down, but I'm looking at it right now."

Lena turned to Novak and hit the speaker button.

"You're on speaker," she said to Kline. "Who murdered Fellows's sister?"

Novak's eyes lit up. Kline cleared his throat.

"The case is still open, but it's ice-cold. She was only fourteen years old when it happened. She was two years younger than her brother, so I guess that makes it twenty-three years ago. I thought the murder book would be at Piper Tech collecting dust. When they couldn't locate it, I tore the office apart and found the binder in the lieutenant's desk."

"We need to see it," Lena said.

"You'll have everything in less than an hour."

"What do we need to know before it gets here?"

"Tilly Fellows was raped and bludgeoned to death. There was evidence of longtime sexual abuse. Their father was killed in Vietnam. Their mother ran off after that. Both kids were raised by their grandparents, Maurice and Alma Fellows. From what I can tell, Maurice was more than a person of interest. He was the only suspect. But DNA evidence was only a wet dream back then and nothing could be proved."

"What about now?" Novak whispered.

Lena repeated the question, adding, "Was anything saved that we can get to the lab?"

"I haven't had time to check," Kline said. "Maurice died two years after his granddaughter, so I'm not sure it makes much difference. But here's where it gets interesting. Maurice and Alma died on the same day. The autopsy report is in the murder book because the circumstances were suspicious and probably related."

"What was the COD?" Lena said.

"Food poisoning. Both of them went down from food poisoning."

"Anything significant about the date?"

"That's what took it over the top," Kline said. "They died on Martin's eighteenth birthday."

The words hung there. Bright and hot as napalm burning a village down.

She met Novak's eyes. Caught the glint. The smoke. And for the next forty-five minutes, paced up and down the floor trying to bridle her nerves. When the courier finally arrived, a retired cop, she thanked him for his help and raced to her desk with the three-ring binder.

They had Martin Fellows's essence. The spring that made the man tick.

Novak rolled his chair closer as she tore the book open and began reading. Tilly Fellows had been raped and murdered in an abandoned house at the end of the street. Martin found his sister's body. He was sixteen at the time and, according to the detective who took his statement, so distressed that he required medical attention. It had been Martin who made the frantic call to the police. And it had been Martin who pointed the finger at his grandfather.

Lena quickly paged forward to Section 12 for a look at Fellows's actual statement. It was difficult to read for a variety of reasons. First and foremost was that he was only sixteen, caught in a situation he couldn't handle and crying out for help. He told detectives what he saw, then ripped through a list of darker things his sister had told him in confidence. According to Fellows, his grandfather liked to put Tilly to bed at night with the door closed. He had been doing it every night for five years. And now with her murder, the sixteen-year-old blamed himself.

A picture was attached of a skinny boy with long hair and a crooked smile. Lena stared at it for a long time, then flipped the page to a picture of an unshaven man with gray hair and dark circles under his eyes. Maurice Fellows sitting on the couch with his weather-beaten wife, Alma, in a cheap housedress. The photograph of the couple was so bizarre, so telling, that Lena instantly thought of Diane Arbus, a photographer working in the 1960s she admired.

"Let's take a look at the crime scene photos," Novak said.

She turned back to the previous section. The first picture said it all. Tilly Fellows was on the floor. She looked more like a broken doll than a fourteen-year-old girl. Her eyes remained open, blue and toylike and staring just off camera as if they were made of plastic. Her clothing had been ripped away from her small body, and a baseball bat was leaning against the wall. But it was the girl's face that gave Lena pause.

Her face hadn't been touched. And Tilly Fellows was almost an exact replica of Harriet Wilson. The color of her hair. The shape of her cheeks and chin. The gentle slope and grace of her nose and forehead.

Lena glanced at the dividers in the notebook and found the Related Crime Reports. Martin Fellows spent the next two years living in isolation with his grandparents. And the help the boy needed never came.

He told the police everything that happened, yet nothing tied his grandfather to the murder. Even worse, Alma was standing by her man with an alibi. The detectives working the case didn't buy it. From what Lena could tell, they interviewed Maurice without an attorney. The sessions were extensive and included sleep deprivation, but the man wouldn't turn. No evidence could be found linking Maurice to the sexual abuse of his granddaughter or the murder. Just the word of Martin Fellows, who one week after the murder didn't want to talk anymore and had a black eye.

Two years later Maurice and Alma Fellows were dead. And from the way the reports were written, it seemed as if Martin Fellows had pulled it off.

The source of the food poisoning turned out to be a salad bar at a restaurant on Sunset. Although Martin admitted to detectives that he was there with his grandparents celebrating his eighteenth birthday, he pointed out that he became mildly sick as well, along with three other patrons. SID confirmed that bits of rat poison were found on the floor, with heavier concentrations around the buffet tables. While the manager denied any knowledge of the poison, the restaurant had been cited for several violations and was the primary subject of a health-watch series broadcast on TV. Detectives believed that Fellows watched the news program, knew about the violations, and picked the place out. But given the circumstances, nothing could be proven.

Lena sat back in her chair, thinking about Maurice's and Alma's ashes collecting dust for twenty-one years. She could still see the sealed boxes from the crematorium lying on the bed. Fellows waited until he was eighteen, so the need for a guardian was pointless. He could live his life on his own, turning his skinny body into a machine while pursuing his interests in biology and chemistry.

She glanced at the TV. The eleven-o'clock news was just getting started. Novak found the remote and turned on the sound. The hotline number was up. For the first fifteen minutes, the coverage ignored the fires threatening the Valley and concentrated on what they were still calling the Romeo Love Murders, with live feeds bouncing all over town.

There was a chance, Lena thought. A chance they could catch a break. When the program ended, she heard a phone ring in the captain's office and hoped the call was coming from the sixth floor. Five minutes later, Barrera walked out of the glass room. But from the look on his waxen face, there was no real need to listen. She could see the decimation. The blowback from his decision not to grab Fellows when they could.

"Nothing," he said. "The hotline didn't receive a single legit call."

No one said anything. Barrera's hands were trembling and he slipped them into his pockets.

"It's late," he said. "Tomorrow's gonna be a long day. I want everybody to pack up and go home."

"What about Harriet Wilson?" Novak said.

Barrera met his eyes, remaining quiet for several moments before speaking again.

"You said it yourself more than six hours ago, Hank. The girl's dead. There's nothing we can do for her now."

Novak shook his head, aghast. "But I could be wrong. I want to be wrong."

"You're not wrong. I was, and two cops are dead. Let's leave it at that. Now go home, and that's an order from the top. They've lost control of the fires, and there's a chance the freeways will be shut down. If you don't leave now, you might get stranded." Barrera took a step forward, then paused as if remembering something. "Lena, Dr. Bernhardt wants to see you before you go."

Barrera pulled his keys out of his pocket and walked out. Lena listened to his footsteps shuffling down the hall. The sound of the elevator as the bell rang and the doors closed.

"Lena, can I see you for a minute?"

She turned and saw Dr. Bernhardt standing behind them. Glancing at Novak, she followed the psychiatrist into the glass room.

"Have a seat," Bernhardt said. "We won't be long."

She gave him a look, dumbfounded. She couldn't comprehend what Bernhardt wanted or why Barrera and the sixth floor were pulling the plug. She noted the cartons of Chinese food on the conference table and watched the burly man take a seat. Was he here because of his work as a psychiatrist for the Behavioral Science Section? Or was it his connection to the Professional Standards Bureau, the new name for Internal Affairs?

She sat down, her back straight.

"Relax," he said. "I just wanted to ask you if you needed medical attention."

She shook her head. The question was insane.

"Why would I need medical attention?"

He shrugged and seemed embarrassed. "I saw those pictures Fellows took."

It was late. They were in the hunt. She didn't have time for this.

"I'm fine."

He nodded, thinking it over. "There's nothing you want to talk about? Nothing you want to get off your chest?"

"This is the wrong time and place for this."

"I'm wondering if you're not suffering from denial, Lena, like that woman in the papers. We talked about denial when you had trouble dealing with your brother's death."

She felt something burst inside her. Anger igniting into rage. She got up and closed the door. She pushed the chair away and leaned over the table.

"I've got a question," she said in a low voice. "Something only you can help me with."

"What is it?"

"When Rhodes went on stress leave, was it before or after my brother's murder?"

"What's this got to do with anything?"

"Answer the question, Doctor."

"After," he said, placating her.

"How much time did you spend talking about the murder?"

Bernhardt hesitated. He shouldn't have hesitated, but he did. "You know everything that's said in my office is confidential. I can't answer that."

"You already did. I can see it on your face. If Rhodes talked about the murder, then you're withholding evidence in a homicide investigation. And you couldn't possibly be familiar enough with the case to know what's relevant and what's not."

Bernhardt narrowed his eyes. "You need to change your tone of voice, Detective. You're headed in the wrong direction. What you're insinuating is ludicrous."

"I'm not hinting at anything. And this isn't a game anymore or some theoretical puzzle. Martin Fellows didn't know Molly McKenna. No matter what the lab says, he couldn't have killed her. And Holt didn't know her either, so the suicide's bogus. He didn't murder my brother. Everything about that crime scene is bogus."

He yawned, looking at her as if she were a child. When he turned away, she followed his gaze up the table to a carton of rice and three fortune cookies.

"Maybe this will help," he said, scratching his beard. "I don't think I'm breaking a trust because it would be a matter of record. Rhodes was with your brother that night. He blames himself for the murder because he left early."

As the words settled in, she tried not to show anything on her face. Tried to cushion the blow.

Now she knew why Rhodes had checked out the murder book.

She had read it from cover to cover. If the files were complete, there would have been a statement from Rhodes, along with field interview cards from witnesses who saw him at the club. Rhodes removed them. Because the detectives working the case were retired, no one noticed.

Rhodes had been with David that night, but left early.

She looked at Bernhardt reaching for a fortune cookie, but didn't say anything. Instead, she walked out.

She splashed her face with cold water, then returned to the floor. The lights had been dimmed, the TV shut down. Novak was still at his desk, talking to someone on the phone. Although Sanchez had left, she could see Rhodes in the glass room talking to Bernhardt. Even worse, the door was closed and Rhodes had seen her enter.

His hollow eyes were on her. He *knew*.

She walked down the aisle to her desk thinking about how badly things had gone. She could have worked Bernhardt in a different way. She could have pulled the information out of the irritating man without revealing her point of view. Maybe it was burnout. She should have seen the warning signs. She should have kept her mouth shut.

She slung her briefcase over her shoulder. Then she picked up one of the evidence boxes, deciding to take it home.

Novak gave her a look and cupped the phone. "I'm right behind you," he said. "I'll take the other one. You good to call?"

"All night," she said.

He nodded and returned to his phone call.

Then Lena headed out, keeping her eyes off the glass room. She rode the elevator to the basement, the dread following her around the corner and down the hall.

Rhodes *knew*.

She could hear people talking but couldn't see anyone. The sound of a distant television was bouncing off the walls. Someone dropping coins into a vending machine and laughing. When she finally reached the door, she gave it a push with her hip and stepped outside.

Barrera said they might close the freeways. And it took a moment for Lena to compute exactly where she was. The parking garage was just across the street, yet lost in a blur of dust and smoke that burned her eyes. Ash was falling from the sky as if snow, the smell of fire, extremely close. Even more eerie, this was downtown Los Angeles and there wasn't a single car on the road.

She looked up at the sky, searching for the Library Tower. After a beat, the ring of lights at the top cut a fleeting path through the clouds, throbbing like a beacon, then vanishing again.

Lena tightened her grip on the evidence carton and hurried across the street. As she entered the dilapidated garage, she could hear the Santa Ana winds whistling, the steel beams squeezing the river of air and blowing it out the other side. She could hear the music cut to the beat of her own shoe leather.

The Devil Winds.

She spotted her car in the gloom and rushed toward it. Tossing the box in the trunk, she got rid of her briefcase and slammed the lid. That's when she saw Rhodes running across the street.

She ducked behind the car, instinctually moving away from it. When she reached an SUV five spaces down, she peered over the hood. Rhodes was standing in front of her car, searching for her in the darkness.

"We need to talk, Lena."

She could taste the sand in her mouth. The ash and fire. She tried to swallow, but her mouth was too dry.

"Why are you hiding?" he shouted. "This is crazy."

He was moving down the aisle now, quickly checking between the cars. Lena lowered herself to the pavement and rolled beneath the SUV, her eyes glued to his feet. Although she couldn't see the guard shack on the other side of the wall, she guessed that on a night like this the door would be closed. If she called out, no one would hear her.

"Come on, Lena. Let's talk this out. The Blackbird's still open. I'll buy you a cup of coffee."

He was less than three feet away. When his boots disappeared behind the next car, she listened to his footsteps. She counted them and waited, then rolled out the other side and peered through the window. Rhodes was ten cars away, moving toward the ramp to the second floor. He looked nervous. Jumpy. She squeezed the keys in her fist, doubling back to her car. After taking several deep breaths she couldn't quite catch, she gritted her teeth and made a run for it.

She heard him shouting at her. His voice raw and overloaded with panic.

She inserted the key in the lock, ripped the door open, and jumped in. She saw Rhodes running toward her as she jammed the key into the ignition and lit up the engine. He was sprinting toward her. Closing fast. She grabbed the shift and hit the door locks. As Rhodes slammed against the window, she snapped the clutch and saw him leap out of the way.

She took the corner hard, tires screeching and her eyes on the rearview mirror. Rhodes was chasing her on foot. She blew past the guard shack, pulled out onto the street, and barreled through the red light. When she checked the mirror again, Rhodes was gone. Everything was gone. All she could see was smoke.

No music. Just the hum of the engine underneath the wind. Something to hold on to as the car sliced through endless billows of white clouds and her jumbled nerves filled the seats around her. She couldn't see the road. Only a pair of taillights floating beyond the hood. Every half mile or so the truck she was following would appear before her eyes, then vanish again—a ghostlike object crawling through the smoke toward Hollywood with a heavy load. As she finally reached the Beachwood exit and made the slow climb into the hills, she stopped checking the rearview mirror. Five minutes later, she pulled into her driveway and cut the engine. But she couldn't relax. Couldn't let go.

Someone had turned her outdoor lights on. The windows were dark, but the outside lights were on.

A chill rolled up her spine as she stared at her house shrouded in the gloom. She could see a tarp stretched over the roof, but wondered if it would last the night. Her bedroom shutters had broken loose from their clasps and were beating against the window frame. When she noticed the crime scene tape wrapped around the entire first floor, she got out of the car.

For several moments she watched and listened without moving.

She had buried the thought of coming home ever since seeing Martin Fellows's collection of photographs. She had made every effort to keep busy working the case with the assurance that he'd never touched her. But as she stared at her broken house, she realized exactly what she had been hiding from herself.

Fellows had found a way to get inside. What she thought had only been a vivid nightmare was a reality. She had seen Fellows standing in her bedroom. Seen the madman through her sleep.

She turned to the street and listened for Rhodes's car. She tried to get a grip on herself. Tried to chill.

Someone had jammed a business card into the front door. Moving out of the shadows, she grabbed the card and held it to the light. The card had been left by her old partner, Pete Sweeney, out of Hollywood. A note was written across the top. Two simple words. *Call me.*

She slipped the card into her pocket, brushing her hand over her gun because she needed to know that it was there. Easing her way into the backyard, her eyes swept across the pool and up the steps to the chaise longue. It was empty—the towels still hidden behind the planter. Martin Fellows was not here. She didn't expect to find him here, yet she needed to be sure.

She walked around the house, checking the windows and doors. Everything appeared secure. Returning to the front steps, she slashed the crime scene tape with her key and opened the door.

A fly was knocking against the ceiling. For a split second she thought about that hole in her bedroom window screen that needed to be replaced.

She turned on the lights in the kitchen. When she looked at the trash, she saw a roll of discarded paper towels soiled with fingerprint powder. Sweeney had obviously been inside, along with SID, and they took the unusual step of cleaning up. She entered her bedroom, checked the closets and bath, then moved upstairs for a quick look at the second bedroom. No one was here. Just that fly following her through the house.

She took a deep breath, her nerves slowing down as she returned to the kitchen. She understood why her home was a crime scene. Martin Fellows had been here. What she didn't get was why no one had said anything. She grabbed the phone and punched in Sweeney's cell. He must have been waiting for the call because it was after midnight and he picked up on the first ring.

"You okay, Lena?"

"I'm good."

"You don't sound so good."

She shook it off. "Who gave you the order?"

"Your boss, Barrera. He called us after the SIS guys were found in West Hollywood. He said he needed a favor. Me and Banks volunteered."

"Why didn't you call me?"

"He told us not to. You already had enough on your plate."

"Why did you tape around the house?"

"Barrera ordered us not to call, but I thought it sounded like bullshit. I wanted you to know we were there. I wanted everybody to know we were there. Who's gonna break into a crime scene?"

His voice trailed off. Sweeney was worried about her. She could hear it.

"You sure you're good?" he repeated.

She realized that she was pacing. Grabbing a stool, she forced herself to sit down.

"Did you find anything, Pete?"

"A lot of smudged prints that are probably yours. But I think I know how he got in. A window lock on the second floor was broken. We didn't have time to hit Home Depot, so I nailed it to the frame. I'd be happy to stop by and fix it anytime you say."

She heard the sound of road noise in the background. Sweeney was in his car.

"You headed home?"

"Only in my dreams, Lena. We're working tonight. Someone spotted a body in Griffith Park and we can't find it. We can't even find the fuckin' road. Guess we'll keep looking till we do."

His easy manner felt something like reaching an oasis. She thanked him and switched off the phone. Glancing at the clock on the microwave, she hoped Novak got home all right and wondered if she should call. But her briefcase and the evidence box were still in her car. And that sound of the shutters banging against the house had become unnerving. She set the phone down and walked into the bedroom.

The shutters were authentic. She had never used them because they were on the other side of the window screens. Getting to them wasn't easy and she had never had any interest in blocking the view. As she stepped around the bed, she could see the wind drawing the heavy wooden panels open, then slamming them shut again. She switched on the table lamp, released the lock, and raised the window. Glancing at the hole in the screen, she pried the frame out, awkwardly fished it through the window, and leaned it against the wall. Then she reached outside into the darkness, digging her fingers into the slats as the shutters rushed toward her.

For a split second, she knew something was wrong but couldn't place it. Something flashed in the darkness. Something shiny in the wood.

She pulled the shutter against the window frame, holding it in place as she reached for the table lamp. When her eyes drilled through the hole and locked on the metallic object burrowed inside the wood, she lost her grip and watched the shutter sway into the darkness, then swing back through time.

Her body shut down, her ticket on the night train punched.

The hole in the screen matched the location of the hole in the wooden shutter. She had looked at that screen for five years and never replaced it. Now she could hear something in the wind. Something that sounded a lot like her brother's voice, and he was weeping.

She managed to get to her feet, noting the wobble in her knees. After grabbing a steak knife from the kitchen, she pulled the shutters in and watched them rattle as she threw the latch. Smoke was venting through the slats and tumbling into the room. The smell of fire eating away at her broken house that really was a crime scene now.

She started cutting. Slicing. Shaving the wood away from the hole and ignoring the voices in the wind. The only thing that mattered right now was the knife in her hand digging deeper. And then she wedged the tip of the blade inside the hole and gave the handle a nudge. When the small piece of metal popped out, she palmed it and held it under the light.

It was a slug. A slug from a .38. And from the weathered look of the wood shavings on the floor, she guessed the slug was about five years old.

64

She couldn't risk making the call. Couldn't trust anyone with a piece of evidence that might force the department to admit it had made another major mistake. The slug in her pocket was too small. Too easy to get rid of. And the headlines would be too big. The department was on the right track now and couldn't afford to be embarrassed. Their claim that a rock musician had murdered his partner, then years later turned the same gun on himself, had been made public. No one on the sixth floor would want to admit that the real murderer had been working at RHD and was one of their own. Instead, the evidence would turn up missing. And for exactly the same reasons every piece of evidence in the Black Dahlia case went missing some sixty years ago. Not just the physical evidence. Every interview. Every wire recording.

The department was an institution. Its reputation was more important than a single life.

Lena needed a break. A fistful of luck that wouldn't require another white-knuckle trip down the freeway to the lab. And she found it when she pulled into the lot behind the Hollywood station and spotted an SID truck idling by the back door.

She skidded to a stop and jumped out. No one was inside the cab, but a discarded cigarette was burning on the pavement. In spite of the smoke from the fires, someone needed even more. The kind with nicotine in it.

Her eyes slid across the lot, then stopped on two cars parked beside the line of cruisers. She had seen the black Mercedes SUV and yellow Corvette before and knew they belonged to a pair of experienced detectives. From the amount of ash on the hoods, she guessed that they had been here for a while.

Something was going on. Something important enough to keep everyone busy at 1:00 a.m.

She moved to the rear of the SID truck, rolling the door up and climbing onto the bed. Then she rushed down the aisle and ripped open the first locker. Her eyes burned and it was difficult to see in the dim light. But she skimmed through the contents quickly, closing the door and moving on to the second locker.

Lena wasn't anxious anymore. She was two or three miles down the road, rifling through the tools of the trade with machinelike precision. She had reached a new place. Ground zero fifteen minutes after her life went radioactive. Nothing mattered anymore, yet everything mattered. Everything she saw or touched seemed to glow.

"That you, Lena?"

She recognized the voice and froze. When she turned, she saw Lamar Newton standing on the pavement with a camera slung over his shoulder. She caught the suspicion in his eyes, the look of disappointment. She didn't care.

"What are you guys doing here?" she said.

"They've closed the freeways down. Something's going on at Griffith Park, a possible dead body, so we're gonna hang here for a while."

His eyes moved to the open locker behind her, then bounced back.

"They can't find it in the smoke," she said.

He nodded slowly, acknowledging the ash falling from the sky. "The flames jumped over the one-oh-one about an hour ago. The north side of the city's burning from Malibu all the way east to Rim of the World road. Probably take a week or two to put out. In the meantime we've all gotta find a way to breathe. Why don't you come inside? It's no good out here."

She shook her head. "Can't do it, Lamar. I'm in a hurry."

"Then why don't you tell me what you're looking for?"

"Luminol," she said. "Mixed."

His eyes widened a little as he chewed it over. Luminol was a chemical used to detect faint traces of blood evidence.

"You're working a crime scene on your own?"

"I'm in a hurry, Lamar."

He sized her up from head to toe, then lowered his voice. "What you're doing is wrong. You look like a fucking zombie and I won't help you. But if I was looking for luminol, I'd probably try that one over there."

He pointed at the locker in the corner. She turned and ripped the door open. When she saw the spray bottle wrapped in a rag, she grabbed it.

"It doesn't last long," he said. "You'll need a camera."

"I'm all set," she said, leaping off the truck and racing to her car.

She was alone, her hands trembling. She wondered if she could take it. Whether or not she could deal with a new truth shimmering above the surface.

Lena powered up her digital video camera, flipped through the menu until she reached the LOW LIGHT settings and toggled the GAIN all the way up. Moving the tripod to the center of the room, she framed the shot to include the shutter, carpet, bed, and side table. Although she'd replaced the art on the walls and moved the chest, everything else in the shot remained exactly the way it had been when her brother was alive.

She watched her finger press RECORD and waited until the icon on the screen stopped blinking. Then she watched herself grab the bottle of luminol and step around her bed. She knew that she had to be careful. Knew that luminol could detect trace blood evidence but was used as a last resort.

She pointed the nozzle at the hole in the shutter and gave it a pump. Taking a step back, she covered the lower wall and carpet. She could feel her heart fluttering as she sprayed down the table and headboard.

Nothing mattered anymore, yet everything did. When she caught a glimpse of herself in the mirror, she didn't recognize the woman staring back at her and turned away.

She gave the bottle a shake, eyeballing every surface. Squeezing the handle one last time, she watched the mist drift through the smoky air and cling to the foot of her bed. Then she closed the bedroom door and switched off the lights.

It took a moment for her eyes to adjust to the darkness. She could hear the Devil Winds pushing against the house. The shutters rattling as if someone were trying to break in. A ringing in her ears that seemed in tune with the howl of the wind.

And then time swung back again. The view of views smacking her in the face. Her eyes were locked on the luminol and it was working. Splotches of bluish green light were beginning to rise out of the black. She heard herself sigh as she moved closer and stared at it—a prickling sensation eating up her skin.

It hadn't been a stray bullet accidently fired through the screen into the shutter. David had been shot here.

She could see the murder going down as if she had been in the room. She could see remnants of her brother's blood splashed on the floor and against the wall below the window. When the blood spatter began to glow on the headboard, the image poked at her soul and she struggled to catch her breath.

He had been murdered in bed. In the same bed she'd slept in for the past five years.

The thought had a certain corrosive feel about it. An aftertaste that burned the throat and would never go away.

She leaned against the chest, wiping her eyes and lowering herself to the floor. She could see herself finding his body that night. Running toward the car and searching out his face. The jolt she took as she made the ID and the horror punched through her gut.

Her brother's body had been dumped there. Thrown out on a Hollywood street like a bag of trash. Rhodes had shown no remorse. No respect. He picked Vista Del Mar because that's where the junkies hung out. Beside that abandoned chapel with all those spent needles on the ground.

Moments passed, memories rushing at her with a clarity that appeared surreal. Her father's face. David telling a joke one night as they tried to get to sleep in the car. When the thought stream suddenly dried up, she bolted to her feet.

The glow from the luminol had brightened, the definition more vivid now. She could see the blood spatter on the headboard and floor. But bluish green spots were beginning to appear on her comforter. A comforter that was less than one season old. Her body shivered as she watched the spots sharpen and grow. She reached out with her right hand. When she ran her finger through the spatter, she realized that it was semen. And it was still wet.

Her heart skipped a beat, her mind racing. Then she heard the bedroom door opening behind her back.

She froze, her mind flooding with adrenaline. Someone had turned the lights out in the living room and kitchen. The house was dark. But she knew that he was here. She could hear him breathing. She could feel the electricity skimming across her scalp and shooting through her hair.

She turned and saw the outline of his nude body in the gloom. His buffed head and ultrawide shoulders.

Martin Fellows was running toward her. In a full sprint and leaping through the air.

She reached for her gun as he crashed into her, but felt his hand already drawing it from the holster. She felt his overwhelming strength seize her body and toss her across the room. When he knocked over the camera, she made a run for it but couldn't get past the door. His hands were wrapped around her jacket—pulling her toward him, then pushing so hard, she flew into the living room and bounced off the floor.

Lena scrambled onto her back. He was on top of her now, ripping her blouse open and pulling away her bra. She could feel his hands squeezing her breasts. See the red-hot coals smoldering in his eyes.

She tried to scream but he covered her mouth. She could smell cocoa butter wafting from his sweaty skin.

She dug her teeth into his finger as if chewing through steak. She could taste the lump of human meat in her mouth, his blood streaming down her chin. He pulled his hand away but didn't make any sound. Instead, he watched her spit it out, then grabbed her hair and knocked her head against the floor.

Her strength slipped away after that, almost as if her will were carried out to sea. Then a wave of panic washed back in as her entire body went lazy. She looked through the sliding door and saw someone standing by the pool. When the figure turned, she shuddered. It was Rhodes.

She turned back to Fellows. He had followed her gaze and seen Rhodes. She caught the grin on his face and connected the dots.

Fellows wanted Rhodes to be here. He needed a witness to find the body just as he had found his sister's body. That's why he wanted to watch. He needed to examine the reaction. Calculate the witness's moves for comparative study.

What he couldn't possibly know was that Rhodes was here for the same reason and would probably thank him for the kill.

Fellows cupped his bloody hand over her mouth, his eyes staring right through her.

"Do you know what's happening?" he whispered. "Have you figured it out?"

She nodded.

"Then let it happen, Lena. Let go and no one will ever forget you."

He pulled her belt away and opened her jeans. She heard the sound of plastic rustling in the darkness, then a grocery bag went over her head. His hand clamped down on her mouth again as she tried to scream. She reached up and caught his ear, twisting it and digging her nails into his flesh. But then she let go, her body writhing as it ran out of air. Her head began to spin. Round and round until the ride went black and came to an end.

Her mind buoyed to the surface. She gagged on the air, heaving until she took in a breath. The bag was gone. Her cheek still stung from what felt like a hard slap.

Rhodes was kneeling over her with that faraway look in his eyes.

She flinched, then caught herself. She didn't say anything. Instead, she watched him switch the lights on and walk outside. Glass crunched beneath his boots, and she noticed that the sliding door was gone. His gun was drawn. He looked toward the driveway, then stepped back inside and slipped on a pair of gloves.

"He's gone," he said. "I got here just in time."

He was trying to justify his presence, but it wasn't working. Her eyes flicked across the shards of glass on the carpet. Her gun was by the bedroom door. Too far away to reach on a night that had the look and feel of a doubleheader. What Fellows didn't accomplish, Rhodes would.

"Why the gloves?"

"I don't want to leave fingerprints," he said. "This is a crime scene now."

She shook it off, watching him light a cigarette. He still appeared nervous. All wound up like he was when he chased her through the parking garage. As she sat up, Rhodes snatched her gun off the floor and whispered something.

"What's that?" she managed.

"Your blouse is open."

She lowered her eyes, still groggy. Her breasts were exposed, her jeans pulled down to her knees. Although her underwear was ripped, it was still in place. She replayed the attack in her head and tried to calculate how long she had been unconscious. Seconds, she thought. Not minutes or hours. No real damage done except for the terrifying memory.

"Do you need an ambulance?"

She shook her head, fastening her bra and buttoning her blouse. As she zipped up her jeans, she wondered if he had seen the luminol in her bedroom. Her mind was beginning to clear. She needed an escape plan. Some way of reaching the broken slider. And if all else failed, some way of connecting Rhodes to the crime scene. Something that would stick when it hit the system, even if she wasn't here anymore.

The phone rang. Rhode's eyes flickered. After the third ring, he said, "Answer it, Lena. But use the speaker. I want to listen."

She took a deep breath and rose to her feet. Moving to the counter, she clicked the phone on as Rhodes got rid of his cigarette in the planter outside and grabbed the stool beside her. When she heard Novak's voice, her body flooded with relief.

"I'm here with Rhodes," she said.

Rhodes didn't react when she mentioned his name. Something was going on she couldn't see. The relief vanished.

Novak groaned. "What's he doing there? Put me on speaker."

"You're already on," Rhodes said.

Maybe it was the way Rhodes had his hands wrapped around her gun. Maybe it was the tone of his voice or that he let Novak know that he was here. Either way, it looked as if Rhodes had reached the finish line. He had a plan of his own and didn't care.

"I've found him," Novak shouted. "I've found the second house. It's up by the reservoir."

"How?" Lena said.

"Phone records. I figured a guy like Fellows didn't have too many friends. But he probably kept an answering machine he checked every once in a while. He made regular calls to someone listed in the phone book as M. Finn. It was a toll call because it crossed town. I drove out and woke up his next-door neighbor. When I showed him a six-pack, he pointed at Fellows's picture and said that's him."

Novak gave them the address and said that he was already there and would call Barrera after he hung up. Lena gave him a three-sentence summary of the attack and warned him that Fellows was probably on his way home. She knew the street. And from the look on Rhodes's face, he knew it as well. The service road to the Hollywood reservoir was open to the public. Anyone who lived in the hills and rode a bicycle or liked to walk or run in a safe place had to drive right by Fellows's second house.

She turned the speakerphone off. When she glanced back at Rhodes, he was staring at her.

"Let's go," he said.

66

The carport was empty. Novak gazed through the smoke at the house looming on top of the hill as he thought it over.

It was a question of balance, he decided. Like all things good or bad, in the end it always came down to balance. Karma. Doing what was right to make up for what went wrong.

From what Lena had told him over the phone, Fellows was on his way home. Novak figured that he had at least three minutes to get inside the house, find the girl, and, if she was still alive, pull her out. Three minutes that could possibly save her life. With road visibility hovering near zero, he might be able to stretch his time inside the house to five.

He checked his watch. The second hand appeared stuck on the number ten. When it started moving, he realized that there was nothing wrong with his watch. It wasn't a bad omen. Just a case of deep-fried nerves.

His eyes rocked back to the empty carport. Because Fellows wasn't home, he could search the house without worry. Rip through the rooms from top to bottom as fast as his legs could carry him.

He started up the steps, his heart pumping quick but steady. Reaching the house, he moved around back until he found a window that looked about the right height beneath a tall tree.

Novak drew his gun, punching the muzzle through the glass and breaking it away from the frame. Then he climbed into the living room and headed for the stairs.

Quick and dirty, he kept telling himself. Don't waste time looking for anything but the girl. And if everything goes to shit, start shooting and keep shooting. Take the alien out.

He cruised through the bedroom, checking the closets and bath. Then a second room that was furnished exactly like the first in every detail. He turned his brain off and kept moving as the oddity cut through. He kept searching. No one was on the second floor. As he hustled downstairs, he checked his watch. Two and a half minutes had blown by.

He needed more octane. More speed. He followed the hallway around the stairs and found a den and powder room but not Harriet Wilson. Doubling back to the kitchen, he glanced in the pantry and found the basement door. When he flipped the light on and saw dried blood staining the concrete floor, he knew the girl was down there.

He spent ten long seconds listening to the silence. He could feel time running out. Instead of pulling back, he checked his gun and raced downstairs.

Martin Fellows needed a quick glass of mineral water. Something clean and fresh to slow the anger and cool his jets down. His dick was still hard. Nothing had gone according to plan. He wanted to hit something. Smash it open and gut what was inside.

He locked the front door and headed for the kitchen. Halfway through the living room he stopped dead in his tracks. The window was broken. Shards of glass littered the floor.

Someone was here.

He tried to get a grip on himself and sniffed the air. He could smell their odor. Faint traces of perspiration. The intruder was male.

He pricked up his ears, breaking the silence down into multiple components. There was the sound of his heart beating like a champion. The sound of fire engines spilling through the broken window, up-front and personal as they rolled toward the reservoir. And then there was the stillness. A heavy stillness that no longer included Harriet Wilson. After he'd given the woman her birthday present, the bitch had become so ungrateful that he taped her mouth shut. It wasn't Harriet in the stillness. It was someone else, poking their fucking nose around.

He gazed at the carpet and saw the blood still dripping from his hand. The shape of Lena Gamble's wide mouth permanently sculpted into his finger. He craned his neck around and peered into the kitchen. Someone had left the basement door open.

He felt the power rack through his shoulders. The heat percolating on his cheeks and forehead and igniting his hands and legs. Moving silently into the kitchen, he prepared a needle and found an injection site on his arm. Then he drew a ten-inch carving knife from the block and started downstairs.

Slowly. Evenly. Without making any sound.

He reached the last step and peeked around the corner. A man was standing in the tunnel just outside Harriet's room. Fellows lowered his body, hiding in the shadows.

It was Lena's partner. The cop he'd seen at the Pink Canary and read about in *The Times*. From every appearance, the detective one reporter called "experienced" was alone.

He could see the man's face. The beads of sweat raining down his forehead and bleeding through his suit. The gun he held in his right hand.

The man must have just arrived. He looked eager and worried and kept glancing at his watch. He probably came in alone thinking he could save the girl. And now he was staring at Harriet chained to the cot, checking the tunnel in the gloom, and hoping for silence so he could listen and make sure everything was good.

Fellows couldn't help feeling sorry for the stupid man. He could hear the springs from the cot jiggling up and down and guessed that Harriet was hysterical and wouldn't play along. When the detective couldn't take it anymore and rushed into the room, Fellows slid behind the furnace for a better view.

He could see Harriet's big blue eyes wild like a cat as she tried to scream through the tape. The cop with his back turned, all revved up and ripping through the pile of handcuffs on the workbench searching for the keys.

Fellows inched toward the door. His opponent was middle-aged and right-handed. Although he carried excess body fat and obviously no longer worked out, he looked as if he could still throw a punch. As Fellows thought it over, he realized that his success depended on surprise. Neutralize the right hand, and the big man would panic and wilt.

Novak fished through the handcuffs, snatching the keys and rushing over to the cot. He could feel time streaming by. Fear cutting a hole in his stomach and gusting through his chest.

Harriet Wilson had obviously been tortured and needed medical attention in a hurry. Stretched out on a soiled mattress, she was completely naked and sweating profusely. Her inner thighs were smeared with blood and her eyes were glued to her vagina. Even worse, she was riddled with body tremors and appeared to be slipping into shock. Novak couldn't be sure, but he didn't think she even knew that he was in the room.

He leaned closer, fumbling with the keys as he held on to the gun. When she started thrashing her arms and legs, the keys slipped out of his fingers and dropped onto the floor. He scooped them up and holstered his gun. Reaching over her head, he held her hands down and inserted the key.

And that was when the handcuff slapped over his wrist and there was no need to check his watch anymore.

He tried not to panic, but couldn't help it. He wrenched his body around and saw Martin Fellows yanking the other end of the cuffs and locking them around the steel tubing at the foot of the cot. His heart started pounding as he heard the telltale click. When he reached around his waist for his gun, he couldn't make it. Just his sweaty fingertips stabbing at the handle and slipping away. He tried to focus. Tried to stretch and extend his reach. Then everything he ever stood for burned up as Fellows lifted the gun out of his holster and stepped back.

He looked at the madman standing in the corner. His lifeless eyes were locked on him, and his mouth was clamped shut. When Novak lifted the bed up and lunged at him with his left fist, the piece of shit didn't even move.

Fellows tossed the gun on the workbench.

It was over, he thought. And the intruder knew that it was over, every inch of his body shaking now. He could see the man twisting his wrist in the cuff and heaving the bed up and down. His wheels turning as a hot load of panic rushed his senses and everything went numb.

Neutralize the right hand and the big man would fall.

Fellows reached inside his pocket for the camera and snapped three quick pictures. As he gazed at the digital images, something about them smacked of genius. The terror in the man's eyes. The sweat dripping down his forehead. That ghostlike expression on his face as he looked down the line and stared at the end.

Fellows picked up the carving knife, grasping the contoured handle firmly with his bloody hand and using the pain to give him the ultimate strength. The high-carbon-steel blade flashed and glistened and lit up the small room. He could see Harriet bouncing on the springs again and making grunting noises through the tape. Destiny turning its black thumb down and giving him the final okay.

The frightened man backed into the wall, flinching as he ran out of space and time. When Fellows raised the knife and moved in, the man took another wild swing but missed. All he hit was air.

Her heart sank as she looked out the window and didn't see Novak in his car. Rhodes jammed on the brakes, blocking the Taurus in the carport. But Novak wasn't around. He wasn't waiting in the shadows to join them. He wasn't hiding somewhere in the smoke until backup arrived. She ripped the door open, searching through the darkness for her partner.

Then three shots rang out, one after the next, shattering the windshield. She spotted her gun on the front seat and ducked behind the door, her eyes leaping up the steps to the house on top of the hill. The lights were out, but she had seen the muzzle flash from the last round coming from a window on the first floor. She grabbed her .45 and raised it, sending five rounds back. When she didn't hear Rhodes returning fire, she swung her body around and saw him slumped over the steering wheel. Blood was spewing out of his left shoulder. His eyes were glassy.

She lunged across the seat, pulling him toward her and dragging him to the back of the car.

"Are you still here, Rhodes?" she whispered in a shaky voice. "You still with me?"

He nodded but couldn't seem to move.

Lena opened his jacket and pulled his T-shirt away, eyeballing the wound. It was high, but the spread looked wide and nasty. Rhodes could have a punctured lung. Tearing his shirt away, she eased it over the wound, then transferred her hand with his.

"How's your breathing?"

"Okay," he managed. "I didn't see it coming. No signs he ever used a gun."

She heard the sirens in the distance, but knew that it was rough driving and response times were up. Help would be here, but it would take a while. She looked at Novak's Crown Vic buried in the clouds, then back at the house.

"What have you got in the trunk?"

Rhodes gave her a look. "You can't go in."

"My partner's inside. What's in the trunk?"

"A Winchester. The keys are in my . . ."

She dug her hand into his jacket and fished out the keys. Then she cracked the trunk open and peered inside, locating the twelve-gauge pump gun and an ammo bag. When she spotted an assault light, she clipped it onto the barrel. Then she unzipped the ammo bag and tore open a box of shells, feeling a sense of comfort that they were high-brass magnums. Fellows had his needles. She had the magnums. One pull would break the motherfucker in half.

She glanced at Rhodes leaning against the bumper loosely holding his hand over the wound. His eyes were on her as she jammed five shells into the magazine, pumped the slide and added a sixth. That faraway look was gone, but she couldn't get a read on him.

"You gonna be okay?" she said.

He nodded again, tried to say something, but stopped. No matter what she thought of him, he didn't deserve this. From a jury maybe, or even from her. But not from Martin Fellows.

She dug into the bag for more shells and dumped an extra fistful into her pocket. After giving Rhodes a last look, she bolted up the steps to the front door. Then she lowered the pump gun and pulled the trigger, watching the three-and-a-half-inch magnum rip the locks out and blow a six-inch hole through the wood. The sound was deafening. The smell of burning gunpowder, somehow reassuring.

She kicked the door open, reaching along the wall until she found the light switch. As she gave the living room a hard look, she realized that there was no need to search the house. Fellows had left a trail of blood on the white carpet. And for a split second, she remembered biting that chunk of meat out of his finger and spitting it on the floor.

But the memory vanished as she followed the blood drops with her eyes and spotted the broken glass on the other side of the room. Novak had entered from the window, she figured, and Fellows stopped when he found it. He must have spent some time there because a puddle had formed. Then the blood drops crossed the room to the kitchen.

That was the first set. But a second blood trail started from the kitchen and moved through the living room to the window by the front door. The same window the muzzle flash had come from. Lena checked the far wall and ceiling, noting the holes in the plaster from the five rounds she'd sent back. After a moment, her eyes flicked down to the white carpet and the blood trail leading back to the kitchen.

Martin Fellows was alive and well and somewhere on the other side of that wall.

She crossed the room. Everything quiet and hypersteady. As she reached the corner, she took a peek, following the blood on the tiles to the open basement door. The lights were on and she could see a vial and needle on the counter beside the sink. She tried to concentrate on slowing her mind down, her eyes rocking back to the basement door. Then she took a deep breath and started down the steps. One at a time until she reached the corner and found the basement clear.

She heard something. A jiggling sound. Close.

As her eyes cut a shaky path down the corridor, she could feel her heart pounding. Her nerves breaking through her skin. The corridor had been cast in concrete tubing and looked like a tunnel that extended well beyond the footprint of the house. A bend in the tube twenty-five yards off masked the tunnel's direction and hid its end. Lights sealed within glass jars were strung along the right side, and she could see the roots from trees penetrating the walls and reaching out through the concrete as if they were fingers attached to hands. When she spotted the steel door on her left, she looked back at the roots swaying up and down in the breeze.

The room on the left was a bomb shelter. A remnant of the 1960s when a nuclear attack seemed imminent and bomb shelters were a status symbol that outclassed a Mercedes for the lowlifes who kept score. As she eyed the tunnel, she guessed that there was a second entrance somewhere on the property away from the house. A backup exit just in case the house blew down. Even worse, there was a good chance Fellows had used it to escape.

She checked the concrete floor, but the blood drops overlapped and she couldn't find a pattern. As she stepped into the tunnel, that jiggling sound became louder and she realized that it was coming from the bomb shelter. She locked her eyes on the doorway, tickling the trigger with her finger. Then she peered around the corner and felt her stomach back up into her throat.

She didn't want to look at it. She couldn't, even though she knew that she had to. It was a vision from hell. A sign left behind by someone whose humanity had been ravaged and cut down.

Novak's body was here.

He had been stripped and thrown on top of Harriet Wilson. His head was turned toward the door. His eyes remained open, but were lost in a lazy, thousand-yard stare. As she moved closer and touched his face, as she searched his skin for warmth but couldn't find it, something deep inside her rattled and rolled. She looked at his outstretched hand. His wrist locked to the cot with a pair of handcuffs. When she realized that she was weeping, she tightened her grip on the pump gun and pushed back.

The mattress was vibrating. She stepped around a large pool of blood and looked down at Harriet Wilson. The woman was still alive, trembling beneath the weight of Novak's dead body.

Lena took a deep breath and exhaled. She needed to keep cool. Find a way through the horror and punch out the other side.

She gave her partner's body a push, rolling him off the girl toward the wall. From the amount of blood, she sensed that he had been gutted, but kept her eyes pinned on Wilson. She ripped the tape away from her mouth. Spotting a set of keys on the floor, she unlocked the woman's wrists and ankles. But it didn't seem to make much difference. Harriet Wilson was frozen in terror. When the woman opened her mouth, nothing audible came out. She was in another place, two or three stations beyond words.

"Help is coming," Lena said, stroking Wilson's hair. "You need to hold on."

Her voice broke and she forced herself out of the room. Raising the

Winchester, she started down the tunnel. Shoot first, she told herself. Shoot fast.

The lights strung along the wall stopped as she reached the bend. Switching the assault light on, she plowed through the darkness. The roots eating through the concrete were thicker here. More horrific and harder to see through. As the tunnel straightened out, her eyes leaped forward to the steel ladder bolted into the concrete.

There was a hatch and it was open. Waves of smoke were streaming by, the wind howling above.

She wiped her sweaty hands on her jeans. Tightening her grip on the rifle, she climbed up for a look at the madman's escape route. But as her head popped through the ground, she wasn't sure she could believe her eyes. It was a wooded landscape with a view of the Hollywood reservoir. And the hills were burning, the flames reflecting off the water and reaching two hundred feet into the sky. A vision of hell from another angle. L.A. was on fire.

She looked around but didn't see any sign of Fellows. Just bands of fire-fighters on the other side of the water, backing away from a burning house.

Then something skimmed across her leg and she flinched. Before she could look down or even jump out, someone grabbed her ankles and pulled. In a split second she lost her grip on the rifle and was falling through the air. Hitting the floor ten feet below with a devastating smack and covering her head. As her eyes cut through the gloom, she saw Martin Fellows walking toward her brandishing a long knife.

His massive chest was bare, his skin oiled. He was wearing a pair of skintight workout pants and high-top athletic shoes. And something was tied around his neck. As he moved closer, she got a better look. He was wearing a necklace. Two toes were attached, one old and one new. Lena's first thought was Nikki Brant. The second toe had to belong to Harriet Wilson.

He swung the blade at her, grunting under the strain. When she managed to get to her feet, the giant burst forward and knocked her down. She wanted to scream, but didn't. She kept her eyes on the blade swinging through the darkness. And as the tip smashed against the floor an inch from her face, she spotted the rifle behind her.

Fellows wheeled the knife through the air, missing her body and bouncing it off the concrete again. She could hear voices shouting now. Footsteps pounding down the basement steps at the other end of the tunnel. When they caught the view from the door to the bomb shelter, they would stop just as she had. Just like Novak. Help wouldn't reach her in time.

She grabbed the rifle, pulling it into her body. As Fellows raised the knife, she slapped the balls of her feet against his stomach and pushed her legs out with all her strength. Then she swung the gun around, blinding the madman with xenon light.

He squinted at the brightness, arching back on his knees as if he had been hit with a punch. Scrambling to her feet, she stepped away and lowered the barrel. He got up and froze, shielding his light-sensitive eyes with his hands and glancing at the ladder. His escape route and a list of options that added up to zero. When he dug his toes into the floor and charged her, she wasn't thinking about Fellows or even her own survival anymore. She was thinking about her partner. Her mentor. The man who had shown her the way. A cop who wanted to retire and spend the rest of his life fishing but was murdered when everything went to shit.

She pointed the muzzle at Fellows's chest and pulled the trigger. Then she pumped the slide and pulled it again.

What was left of his body slammed against the wall and flopped onto the floor. As the noise radiated through the tunnel, Lena kicked his head with her boot. His eyes were open and it looked as if he was smiling at her. Pumping the slide, she felt the weight of the weapon in her hands and took another shot.

68

Lena entered the bureau floor and noticed the small package on her desk. It had been five days since she'd lost her partner. And five days wasn't long enough to forget. Every time she glanced at Novak's empty chair, she lost her way and had to pick herself up again. The weight of the silence in the room, the absence of the usual banter in the unit, only deepened her loss and made everything worse.

She sat down and opened the package, revealing a box. When she figured out what it was, she pushed it away. The printer had finally delivered her business cards. She would never have to jot her name and number down on a generic card again.

More bad timing. The kind that played with the soul and cost $25.31.

She left the room without a word, rode the elevator down to the ground floor, and walked over to the Blackbird. Ignoring the recognition on the server's face, she paid for her coffee and found an empty table on the other side of the room.

Lena Gamble had caught Romeo and gunned the madman down.

It was the kind of story the sixth floor liked. A story the new chief could offer the media and watch them eat it like candy. When she saw a video clip of herself on TV over the weekend, a shot of her face splashed with blood outside Fellows's house and still holding the Winchester, she poured a stiff drink and spent the rest of the afternoon out by the pool.

The memory faded. Removing the lid from her coffee, she let the steam warm her face. After a first sip, she turned and gazed out the window. The view seemed more like the planet Venus than downtown L.A. The wildfires were still spewing tons of smoke into the air, shrouding the city in perpetual darkness. Although the sun was visible, it burned a dark red and appeared so powerless that she could look straight at it without squinting.

She took another sip of coffee, still groggy from the ordeal. Still unable to shake that amped-up feeling in her stomach. Still plagued with nightmares and unable to sleep.

She'd completed her paperwork over the weekend. Martin Fellows's body parts were examined by Art Madina and deemed officially dead. Burell's missing body part was located and examined and appeared even more dead. Although Harriet Wilson remained in critical condition, her doctors had become hopeful, citing her strength of will. And Rhodes had been lucky, too. The bullet missed his lung. He was released from the hospital and convalescing at home. When the coroner's office delivered Novak's autopsy report to RHD, the papers were quietly slipped into a three-ring binder, along with the horrific photos SID downloaded from Martin Fellows's camera.

Her partner's last moments had been recorded for posterity, but no one other than Barrera had the courage to look.

She checked her watch. Novak's funeral was scheduled for tomorrow morning. The sixth floor had written another speech for her, ordering her to commit the words to memory. The new chief would introduce her, then follow her speech with one of his own. But Novak's ex-wife was holding an unofficial service this afternoon. A tribute to the father of her children. It was due to begin in an hour at a funeral home on the Westside. Everyone in the unit would be there, but she wondered about Rhodes. Over the weekend she went out to retrieve his cigarette butt from the planter. Brushing the leaves away, she found more than twenty butts stubbed into the soil and didn't know what to make of it. She wanted to talk to him. Confront him in a place with lots of people around. She hoped he was well enough to show.

She dumped her coffee in the trash—it wasn't working anymore—and walked over to the parking garage. As she drove to Santa Monica, she was thinking about her bag of loose ends and the evidence she'd collected. The slug she'd dug out of her bedroom shutter and the videotape revealing the blood spatter from her brother's murder at home. It was all about timing, she decided. Finding the right time to confront Rhodes and present the evidence to someone she could trust. The question was who?

By the time she reached the funeral home, the memorial service was already under way. But as she hurried down the hallway and opened the door, she didn't see anyone and became confused.

It wasn't a sitting room. Instead, it looked more like a movie set designed to mimic a basketball court. She closed the door, continuing down the hall. When she opened the next door, she found another set designed to look like a golf course. A man dressed in a black suit was wheeling a bronze casket onto the putting green beside a bag of clubs.

"You look lost," the man said. "And I'll bet you've never been here before."

"I'm looking for the Novak family."

"One door down," he said with a smile. "He's in the captain's room."

The captain's room.

She cringed at the thought, but managed a nod and walked down to the end of the hall. She spotted Novak's name printed on a card and set on an easel. Then she swung the door open, saw the room filled with people, and found a seat in the back row.

It was another bizarre movie set. One that included a rowboat and a fake pond. Novak was lying in his open casket dressed in his fishing clothes and wearing an old Dodger cap. His tackle box was inside the casket, along with his rod and reel. Instead of music, sound effects were playing and she could hear ducks quacking and flies buzzing through the air. A pastor was standing behind the podium, talking about the ultimate fishing trip. It was somewhere in the sky, he said, and the fish were biting.

Lena looked at Novak's ex-wife sitting in the front row and wondered if she was out of her mind, then back at her partner's wooden figure posed like a doll in the casket. It was an image she wished she hadn't seen. Another glimpse at hell she didn't want to remember but wouldn't forget.

She turned away, noticing an open bar and a table filled with taco chips and salsa, burritos and refried beans. As her eyes darted through the crowd, she found Lieutenant Barrera in the second row. Two seats over, her eyes locked on Rhodes.

She took a deep breath. His left arm was in a sling, but he was here. She kept her eyes on him until the service ended and everyone headed for the bar. But before she could get out of her seat, she caught Novak's daughter staring at her from the front row. She was wearing a black dress and a thin gold chain around her neck. Even from a distance, Lena could tell that she was stoned.

She didn't want to talk to the girl and turned away, looking for Rhodes in the crowd. But as she walked down the aisle, she could feel Kristin approaching like a magnet, reaching out and clutching her arm.

Lena turned and gave her a long look with Novak's corpse directly behind them. She caught the nervous smile, Kristin's right hand fiddling with the gold chain.

"I wanted to talk to you," the girl said.

Lena tried to get rid of her anger but couldn't. And she needed to talk to Rhodes before he took off, not Kristin Novak clinging to her on a trip through yesterday.

"I'm sorry for your loss," Lena said.

"Me, too."

"And you're higher than a kite."

The girl frowned. "Why are you being so mean?"

Lena turned away, spotting Rhodes on the other side of the room. He had stepped away from Barrera and was watching her. When someone tried to approach him, he shook him off.

"I'm not mean," she said to the girl. "You're stoned."

"Maybe I needed something to get through this."

Kristin was nervous, still playing with that gold chain. And something was attached. A disk in the shape of a heart. When the disk flopped out of the girl's dress, Lena's eyes zeroed in on the object.

It wasn't a heart. The girl was wearing her brother's guitar pick. She could see the one-of-a-kind image etched into the piece of fourteen-karat gold. The moon climbing out of a bed of grapelike clouds and smoking a rocket ship.

It took her breath away. What it implied cut to the bone.

Her eyes rose to the girl's face. Her dilated pupils and idiotic smile.

"Where did you get this?"

The smile burgeoned. "From a friend."

"What friend?"

"Someone I fucked a long time ago. Someone who liked to fuck me up the ass. I took it as a keepsake."

The room began to spin. Time doing its back-and-forth and dragging her worn-out being away for one last ride into the black. Novak's daughter would have been sixteen at the time. She had a drug problem and Novak was deeply worried about her. She was a fan of her brother's music.

The dots connected in a single instant. All the dots. Her bag of loose ends was finally empty. So empty she couldn't bring herself to believe it.

She thought about the blood she'd found in her bedroom. Her brother's blood splashed all over the headboard and walls. David had left the club that night with a woman who never came forward. He hadn't died making a drug deal in Hollywood. He was gunned down in bed.

Past conversations with her partner began to stream by. One after another. Hints that something was wrong. Hints that she never picked up because they had no foundation and were beyond the pale. She could recall the way Novak had tried to convince her early on that Romeo was responsible for the girl's murder at Tim Holt's place, cut against his back step when even he realized that it didn't make any sense. The look on his face, the fear and pain that wouldn't let go when she told him that Molly McKenna had been an innocent teenager, a young girl who'd broken into Holt's house ahead of the killer and had no relationship with Holt at all. Novak said he wanted to retire in peace. Trade his gun in for a life where he didn't have to watch his back anymore and could sleep with both eyes closed. She could see it now. All of it. Novak wanting to get rid of the David Gamble murder case so no one would follow him to Seattle.

It felt like a knockout. A blow so devastating she wasn't sure she could trust it or get up off the floor.

"Are you okay?" the girl asked.

"What do you remember about that night? The night my brother fucked you up the ass."

The girl blushed and flashed another idiotic grin. Lena no longer felt any sympathy for her. She hated her.

"Nothing," the girl said. "I was really high. I must've passed out."

She said it as if she was proud. As if she had achieved something signif-icant in her life. As if she knew things nobody else did. Lena could have told her that it was retro amnesia, but she didn't give a shit.

Her eyes were pinned on that necklace. She grabbed it and snapped the chain away from the girl's neck. Ignoring the stunned look on Kristin's face, the silence in the room and the people staring at her, Lena gazed at the man in the moon etched into the gold. He was laughing at her. Winking at her. Smoking that rocket ship like a cigar. When the girl's mother approached her, she told her to fuck off. Loud. So even Novak might hear it on his fish-ing trip. Then she closed her fingers around the moon's face and hustled out of the room.

69

She didn't want it to be true. Didn't want to play any part in the big lie. Didn't want to admit that she might have shared something with the man who'd deceived her and murdered her brother.

By the time she climbed the stairs to Novak's apartment, she was so tuned up she broke the door down with a single kick.

Not Rhodes. Novak.

Working beside her. Showing her the way. The thought rippled through her brain with edges sharp as glass.

She looked around the living room, ignoring the fragrance of her partner's body and the pictures of his ex-wife and daughters. The apartment was sparsely furnished but appeared comfortable. When she checked the kitchen and snapped open the fridge, she found a half gallon bottle of cheap vodka and realized that Novak was drinking again.

She slammed the door closed and walked out. When she hit the bedroom, she spotted a pile of receipts on the table and sat down on the bed. Most of them were for gas. But two or three were from a diner over on Lincoln she knew he went to for the meat loaf.

She was feeling nauseous. She shook it off, her eyes ripping through the room until they landed on the wastebasket. She dumped the contents on the bed, sifting through the candy wrappers and junk mail. When she found a wad of paper beneath the refuse, she scooped it up and carefully unwrapped it. The small piece of discarded paper was another receipt. But it wasn't for food or gas. This one was from a music store over on Sunset.

She looked at it. Read it. Novak had bought a copy of Beethoven's Eighth Symphony the day before Holt was murdered.

It felt like a chunk of her heart just died. Reaching into her pocket for her cigarettes, she lit one and turned on the lamp. She checked the date and looked at the title again. She knew that Novak didn't like classical music. All he ever listened to was country.

She walked back into the living room and opened the armoire. His CD collection was neatly laid out in the bottom two drawers. Skimming through the titles, she flipped the CD player on and opened the tray. Nothing but country.

She took another pull on the cigarette, her hands trembling. She could hear someone climbing the stairs outside. Someone wearing boots. It was Rhodes.

He stopped in the doorway, and she looked him over.

"You knew."

"It was a guess," he said in a low voice. "Something I didn't want to come true."

It settled into the room. Deep and heavy and dark as night.

"When?" she asked.

"I knew that Tim Holt didn't commit suicide, Lena. The minute we got there I knew something was wrong."

"Then why did you push it through?"

He shrugged. "I didn't know who made the kill. All I knew was that it had to be someone close. Someone over the edge. I wanted him to think he got away with it. I didn't want to give him a reason to hurt you."

A moment passed, Lena thinking about what Rhodes just said. She saw a plate on the table and stubbed her cigarette out. Then she passed over the receipt for the CD.

"Novak murdered Holt and the girl," she said.

Rhodes remained silent, taking it in. She saw the glint and sparkle in his eyes mixed with equal cuts of disappointment and pain. She liked looking at his face, she decided. More now than before.

"We've already got the CD in evidence," he said. "Matching the bar code won't be very hard. You got the pick?"

She nodded, pulling it out of her pocket and handing it to him.

"For what it's worth," he said, "I don't think Novak meant to kill your brother. The more time you spent working together, the more it tore him up."

"We don't work together anymore," she said. "And that doesn't account for Holt's murder or Molly McKenna."

"No, it doesn't."

He turned the pick in his hand, examining the image in the window light.

"I knew this was important," he said. "But I couldn't figure out how it played. Not until about twenty minutes ago when I saw you rip it away from the kid's neck." Rhodes passed it back, along with the receipt. "Novak was crazy about his daughter, Lena. Especially back then when he only thought she was fucking up. He used to follow her around at night and pull her out of bars."

"She was a fan. She probably heard that Holt was back in town. That he had a new band."

Rhodes nodded. "She went to see him playing somewhere and wore the necklace. I'll bet she did it on purpose."

Lena thought it over. When Holt saw the necklace, he would have been stunned. He'd found the girl when no one else could—the girl David Gamble had left with on the night he was murdered. He called Lena to tell her about it. He must have pursued Kristin and confronted her in some way. Somehow Novak found out and realized he needed to do something. Time was running out.

When Nikki Brant was murdered, Novak read the crime scene as a serial case and took a chance. He stole a sample of Martin Fellows's semen, tossed it in the cooler with his Diet Cokes, and waited. When James Brant was cleared, he started planning his trip to that place where he could sleep with both eyes closed. He bought the CD Lena would find in Holt's bedroom.

But he was drinking again. Beside himself.

He drove out to Holt's place. He found Molly McKenna waiting in bed and assumed she went with the furniture. He knew what he had to do and he did it as quickly as he could. He committed a brutal double homicide thinking he'd found a way out. When he took a deep breath and realized it didn't add up, when Lena began to suspect Rhodes, Novak rolled with it. Improvising on the bottle she found in the fridge and grabbing at straws.

She looked at Rhodes, sitting on the couch adjusting his sling. The thought occurred to her that Novak's next move would have been to take Rhodes out. Make it look like another suicide. As if Rhodes were involved just as Lena said and couldn't handle it.

A memory surfaced. Her conversation with Molly McKenna's brother that pointed directly to Rhodes.

"Why did you threaten McKenna's brother?"

"The kid talked?"

She nodded. "Yeah. He told me everything."

Rhodes flashed a grin. "Once Jane Doe was ID'd, I read it the same way you did. It was confirmation that the crime scene was a hoax. Holt wouldn't take himself out over someone he didn't know. I saw it, you saw it, the doer had to see it, too. Romeo couldn't have been good for that crime scene. I was trying to buy a little time before you found out. I needed to keep you out of the mix. I even tried getting you thrown off the case. I knew it was impossible because of your brother. I knew you wouldn't stop, but I had to try."

"What about my brother's murder book? Your statement's missing."

"What statement?"

"Bernhardt told me you were there."

"Early. I met your brother for a beer and left before the place opened. I always felt guilty about it. I told Martin and Drabyak that I was there, but guess it wasn't worth writing down. That's what I wanted to tell you the night you ran away from me in the garage. Bernhardt told me what you said, and I couldn't live with that. I wanted to tell you what I'm telling you now."

She was thinking about the cigarette butts she'd found in her planter. She was gazing at Rhodes's face and witnessing the birth of yet another truth. Her mind clicked back to the night Martin Fellows attacked her. The look on his face when he saw Rhodes out by the pool. Fellows had been watching her house and knew something she didn't. It hadn't been Fellows sleeping on the chaise longue. Instead, it was Rhodes, working a twenty-four-hour day until his body wore out. Fellows knew he had his witness because Rhodes was trying to protect her.

A moment passed. The afterglow settling in.

Rhodes got up and crossed the room to the door. Lena followed him down the steps to the street. The sun had darkened, the neighborhood concealed in a blanket of clouds. In the distance she could hear the C-130s flying in slow and dirty, just above stall speed, dumping their loads of fire retardant in the hills and pulling out. When she turned, she found Rhodes staring at her. A lot like he had the other night. She knew in an instant that he wanted her, but the timing was off again. Whatever might happen wouldn't happen today.

He got in his car and rolled the window down. He flashed a melancholy smile and gave her another look.

"Nobody's gonna like the news," he said. "The department's about to give one of their own an official send-off. An RHD detective who died in the line of duty."

"You think we can trust them with the evidence?"

"It's not just you anymore," he said. "It's you and me."

"I'll make copies just in case, then head over to the lab."

"And I'll find Barrera and give him a heads-up. I'll call you on your cell."

He waved at her and drove off. She followed the car until it evaporated in the haze.

You and me.

She didn't want to dwell on it because she knew that it would cost them something. Lena would be the messenger. Rhodes would pay the same price for pushing Holt's suicide through the system and making the new chief look like a fool at his press conference.

As she turned and looked back at Novak's apartment, her brother's murder began playing in her head. She could see Novak following his sixteen-year-old daughter to the house. Snapping as he watched David have his way with her in bed. Firing his gun in an emotional frenzy, then cleaning the place up and ditching the body like a piece of trash.

She could see her brother trying to hold on until the very end. Novak firing a second shot into the empty car and dressing the crime scene with gunshot residue.

She was thinking about blowback and partnerships and what the truth could do to a soul. She was staring into the abyss and realizing that at some level she made it. She closed the case and survived.